D0010096

ALSO BY BILL LOEHFELM

FRESH KILLS

BLOODROOT

THE DEVIL SHE KNOWS

DISCARDED
Valparaiso-Porter County
Library System

THE
DEVIL
SHE
KNOWS

BILL LOEHFELM

PORTER COUNTY LIBRARY

Valparaiso Public Library
103 Jefferson Street
Valparaiso, IN 46383

SARAH CRICHTON BOOKS

FARRAR, STRAUS AND GIROUX   NEW YORK

FIC   LOE   VAL
Loehfelm, Bill.
The devil she knows /
33410012113256
                    MAY 2 3 2011

Sarah Crichton Books
Farrar, Straus and Giroux
18 West 18th Street, New York 10011

Copyright © 2011 by Beats Working, LLC
All rights reserved
Distributed in Canada by D&M Publishers, Inc.
Printed in the United States of America
First edition, 2011

Library of Congress Cataloging-in-Publication Data
Loehfelm, Bill.
    The devil she knows / Bill Loehfelm. — 1st ed.
        p.   cm.
    "Sarah Crichton Books."
    ISBN 978-0-374-13652-9 (alk. paper)
    1. Bartenders—Fiction.   2. Political corruption—United States—Fiction.
    3. Staten Island (New York, N.Y.)—Fiction.   I. Title.

PS3612.O36D48 2011
813'.6—dc22

                                                    2010033099

Designed by Abby Kagan

www.fsgbooks.com

10   9   8   7   6   5   4   3   2   1

For AC

THE DEVIL SHE KNOWS

1

Blood. Maureen sniffed again at the dark smears on her fingertips. Pungent sweetness and a hint of iron. Definitely blood. Not the answer she'd hoped for, but the fresh stains couldn't be anything else. She studied the spray pattern of red dots peppering the outside of her windowsill. That's the effect of sharp teeth, she thought, punching holes through skin. She hadn't seen or heard anything, a surprise since she'd left the kitchen only for a few moments to answer the phone. Nothing left of the body but what looked like sticky feathers. The culprit sat in plain sight. These attacks had to stop.

"You're killing me!" she shouted out the window, down at the fire escape landing a floor below her kitchen. Narrow yellow eyes stared back at her, fearless and devoid of mercy or empathy. "You're absolutely killing me, you fuzzy little prick." Maureen put the phone back to her ear, turning away from the window. "And you are too," she said to her caller. "You know that, don't you, Dennis? You're gonna be the death of me."

"You better not call me *fuzzy*," Dennis said.

"I wouldn't know about that." Maureen headed to the kitchen counter. "And I don't wanna know." She grabbed a half-full beer bottle and carried it back to the window. "All I know is I worked the past five nights."

Reaching out the window, she emptied the beer bottle over the skinny calico on the fire escape landing. With one twitch of its tail, the cat launched onto the railing and away from the beer shower. The cat looked down at the beer, up at Maureen, and then sailed without a sound from the railing to the leafless bough of a nearby tree. A dozen sparrows hit the air, chirping in panic and warning. "Sorry."

"C'mon, Maureen," Dennis said, teetering on the edge of whining. "I'm really stuck here. Help me out."

Maureen sat at the kitchen table, jamming the phone between her ear and shoulder, crossing her ankles. "You're totally murdering me. One more night might do me in, for real."

She pulled a cigarette from the pack on the table and lit it, listening to the bar manager, her boss, apologize and then beg some more.

"I'll tell you what's wrong with Tanya," Maureen said, "in three words: O. Pee. Ates. She's either too high or too sick from getting high to work. Don't believe that bullshit about her sinuses, please . . . Yeah, she told me she was done with it, too, but you know better. We both do." Maureen leaned forward, pressing her forehead into her free hand. "Okay, I'll come in, but not as a favor to you. I need the money. This is for me. Not for Tanya, not for you."

She disconnected and tossed the phone on the table. Well, so much for the gym. Good thing she had maxed out her credit card renewing the membership yesterday.

Maureen got up from the table and went back to the window. Leaning out from the waist up, she grabbed the bird feeder and pulled inside. She'd have to move it again. Taking the feeder down meant letting the cat win, and Maureen hated that, but it wasn't fair to make the neighborhood birds pay the tab for her pride. Eliminating the cat, which Maureen knew damn well she couldn't stomach, was the only other option. Besides, punishing the cat for doing what it was built to do wasn't fair, either. I'm the person, she thought. It's my job to be smarter, to find the high road. She was sure a situation existed where cats could be cats and birds could be birds and everyone could go about their business in peace. She just had to find it. She set the feeder on the counter, silently promising to get it back outside in a cat-proof location as soon as possible. She couldn't let the situation linger; the birds needed her. Winter was coming.

On her way to the bedroom, she paused at the calendar hanging on the kitchen wall. For a full five seconds she let her eyes rest on the picture above the black and white grid of dates. The Outer Banks, at sunset. A vast pink and orange sky floated over the sea like a clean sheet floating over a bed. Silhouettes of seagulls hovered over purple water flecked with gold. What island was in that photo? Not this island, she thought, that's for sure. It's not cold, gray, late-November Staten Island. Well then, boohoo for you.

Her eyes dropped from the picture and she found the date. Who was playing the bar tonight? Full House. Okay. At least there's a decent band, a great band, really, on the schedule. Old-school R & B. Large crowd, older crowd. Liquor drinkers, top shelf. That meant good money, possibly great. All she had to do was get there to make it. She walked into the bedroom where, arms crossed, she surveyed the contents of her closet. Two days ago she'd organized it. Work clothes, hanger after hanger of black, on the left. Real life clothes on the right, a few skirts, tops, dresses. Twice as much black as color, a depressingly accurate portrait of her life.

She slid her hands in among the blacks and examined her options, listing her selection criteria in her head. One week before rent. Her maxed-out Visa. And the electric bill was due yesterday. She pulled out a thin sweater and held it up. Tight and nearly see-through. Long sleeves but cut low at the neck and high at the midriff. With her free hand, she pinched the collar of her T-shirt and peered down. Already wearing the black bra. Sweater's a go; she put it on. Now where was I?

Business, she thought, this is business. I need to make three hundred tonight. She tossed a brushed leather skirt, very short, extremely short, onto the bed. Let them think she looked like a slut. Probably did already anyway. She made four hundred dollars in that outfit last time she wore it. Can't hurt to leave some room for error. Service would be surly to-night; she could tell already.

Maureen stuffed the skirt, plus black leather flats, black stockings, and her apron into her knapsack. She slipped out of her running shorts and into a pair of jeans. She paused for a quick look in the mirror. Her nose glowed red and raw around the false emerald stud she'd had punched through it a week ago. It was cute, it really was. A good birthday present, no matter what her mother said. "A nose ring? I gave you money for some-thing nice. For chrissakes, Maureen, you're freakin' twenty-*nine* years old. Be an adult. You're almost thirty."

Yeah, I'm an adult, Maureen thought, leaning closer to the mirror, and I bought jewelry for my birthday. And it looks good. So leave me alone about it. If only it would heal up already. Really oughta put some powder over that red. Then again, why bother? The dim lights of the bar hid a multitude of sins, red noses being the least of them. Hopefully, the black circles under her eyes would disappear as well. Christ, she was exhausted. Her nose twitched. Something smelled stale, like an old book left in the back corner of the attic. Was it the sweater? Her? She yanked open her bureau drawer and dug through the socks and bras. One thing the bar wouldn't do was make her smell better.

She pulled out a fistful of glass vials, her collection of scented oils, tossing them on top of the bureau. Lavender, patchouli, some junk she'd borrowed from Tanya called Wind Spirit that turned Tanya into a Turk-ish princess but had left Maureen smelling like a lamb kebab. Real per-fume was out of her price range, but the oils came cheap from the Rasta shop over by work. Some of the vials had lost their labels so she twisted off the caps, smell-testing them. Nothing caught her fancy until she un-capped a bottle a quarter full of white powder. God, how long had that been in there? She couldn't even remember who had sold it to her. She recapped the bottle but didn't screw it shut, pausing instead to stare again at her boxer's eyes. Fuck it.

Maureen made a fist and tapped out a dash, not even a dash, really, of coke onto her knuckle. To get her to work with a bounce in her step, so she didn't show up snapping and snarling at everyone, ruining her night before it even got started. She lowered her nose to her knuckle and sucked in the coke, coming up blinking at the mirror. Ouch. Bit of a kick to it. Bitter fluid gathered at the back of her throat and she swallowed it down, rubbing her knuckle over her upper gums. All right then. Time to get moving. She swept the bottles back into the drawer.

She dug the gym membership card from her discarded running shorts and tucked it tight behind her maxed-out Visa in a pocket of her wallet. No sense losing it. Replacements cost thirty-five bucks, and during the late nights and early mornings when Maureen figured she'd most often be going, the membership card was the only way into the 24-hour gym. And she would go. She'd promised herself that, too. She would go.

She dropped her arms in front of her, made fists, and then turned her arms until clean-cut triceps surfaced and pushed up against her hard shoulders. Her arms felt strong and looked it. The clinging sweater made that obvious. She knew her legs were in good shape too, even if they did wake her up three nights a week with their complaining. She peeked down her shirt again; now, if only push-ups, running the floor, and humping drink trays did something for those. And her belly, flat enough for the short sweater but getting soft. Maybe she'd stop going to the diner with Tanya after closing. Start keeping real food in the house. What good could waffles and ice cream be doing her anyway, at four in the morning? Wouldn't it be better, she thought, sniffling, the coke making her nose run, to wind down on the treadmill or the elliptical? Who in their right mind *enjoyed* trading a crowded, noisy, smelly bar full of demanding drunks for a packed and stinky diner full of the same jerk-offs? Not relaxing, even if you're not working. But the empty gym? Soundless except for the hum of the air conditioner and the thump of her sneakers on the treadmill? That could be heaven. That could put a girl in the right mind to sleep well. But *that* was all for another time. Tonight, she had to work.

Maureen tightened her ponytail, slung her bag over her shoulder, and grabbed her purse off the kitchen table. Makeup could wait till she got to work. By the door, she pulled on her battered wool peacoat and stuffed her purse into her knapsack. She double-locked her apartment and barreled down the stairs.

Outside, a frigid gust slammed the storm door against the side of the building. The door bounced off the wall and hit her, knocking the keys from her hand. She bent to pick them up, heard a pop in one knee. Not already. Come on. Happy hour hasn't even started yet. The wind kicked up again and a chill shook her. Really oughta call a cab. No, what you really should do, she thought, is hang on to that ten bucks and hustle your ass to the bus stop. She bounded down the steps, across the sidewalk, and into the street.

She ducked her head and quickened her pace when Paul called her name, stepping out from behind the propped-up hood of his long-dormant Chevy Nova. It was so irritating, the way Paul drew out the *e*'s at the end of Maureen, following that up with a bad Curly the Stooge impression. *Hey, Mo, ny-uck, ny-uck.* Nobody ever called her Mo, ever. Not twice, anyway. How thick could a guy be? What's it tell you when you call a girl's name every day and she never once stops and answers? Give it up, that's the message. But Paul wasn't hearing it. That's what I get, Maureen thought, for asking the guy for one favor. Should've put the ceiling fan in myself. She should've known it'd be like this when he wouldn't take the twenty she offered and asked for a date instead. When he said *call me* after she shot him down. She thought leaving a six-pack on his porch—no note, no phone number, nothing to give him the wrong idea—made it clear that she wasn't into owing favors. But Paul got the wrong ideas all on his own, no help needed. Because he was her landlord's kid, Paul thought that got him some leverage, some play. He called her name again. Maureen ignored him.

Turning the corner onto Richmond Terrace, Paul safely two blocks behind, Maureen slowed her pace. She pulled her purse from her knapsack, searched for her cigarettes. Not in there. She stopped in the street, digging through her knapsack, though she knew they weren't in there either. She knew where they were. She could picture them in her mind, sitting on her kitchen table, the nearly full pack of American Spirits. She started walking again, once more digging in her purse. I *must've* grabbed them when I grabbed my keys. No dice. Now she'd have to bum at work, be one of *those* people. Like Tanya, who was always bumming from her, telling Maureen she'd quit. "Yeah, you quit," Maureen had finally said one night. "You quit buying your own cigarettes."

No bumming, Maureen thought. Not me. I'll stop at the deli on the way to the bar. She opened her wallet. After bus fare, she'd have three dollars left over. Okay, after her first couple of tables, she'd run over. Won't take ten minutes. Or she could borrow a couple bucks when she got there. Or not. Maybe this is a sign, she thought. A sign she should quit. Yeah, because right before a shift is a great time to quit smoking.

When the bus came, Maureen paid her fare and plopped down into the seat behind the driver. She shivered, crossed her legs, and folded her arms over her bag, clutching it to her chest. No heat. A frail old lady wrapped in a tattered overcoat that had shed its buttons, groceries spilling from the plastic shopping bags at her feet, smiled when they made eye contact. Maureen closed her eyes and leaned her head back against the cold glass. Jimmy would probably be there tonight; he almost always came out for Full House. Maybe she could catch him before he left this time, invite him back for a drink at last call, when there'd be time and quiet for a decent conversation. As long as he didn't have that banshee Rose on his arm.

God, Jimmy hardly looked old enough to be out of high school, never mind teaching it. But he *was* cute. She could imagine the teenage girls primping in the bathroom mirror before his class, mooning over him while he lectured. She'd have had a crush on him if he'd been her teacher. She'd almost been dumb enough to tell him that, last time they'd talked. Yeah, she'd make sure he came back to see her. Maybe the skirt would help. She wasn't sure what she'd say exactly; she didn't want to look too eager. Hadn't he said parent-teacher conferences were coming up? She could ask about that. He'd have some hilarious stories. Good. She was looking forward to really laughing after a long night of pretending. Unless he asked about her classes at Richmond College. God, could she tell him she'd dropped out? Admitting she was, at twenty-nine, still working on her undergrad had been embarrassing enough.

And what if she was so exhausted after the shift she couldn't keep her eyes open, never mind talk to anyone? Should've brought the coke. Yeah, like there wouldn't be any at the bar. When the bus hit a pothole, banging her head on the glass, Maureen sat up, startled. The old woman giggled at her. Yeah, cocaine, Maureen thought, the magic elixir for intelligent conversation at 4 a.m.

Maureen watched the approaching road over the bus driver's shoulder. The streetlights flickered, the day nearly over. The last thing I need is less daylight, she thought. Where had the autumn gone? Not where she had hoped, that was for sure. No long afternoons on campus at Richmond, paperback open on her knee instead of closed and collecting dust on her coffee table. This early sunset wouldn't be so depressing, she thought, if I were on campus trying to read one more chapter of Conrad before the light faded. Long afternoons on campus filled with reading and deep conversation. Ideas. That had been the plan.

Instead she'd struggled through eight weeks of bleary, headachy mornings spent rushing to early a.m. pre-req classes wearing her work clothes. She thought of her fresh-scrubbed, fashion-labeled classmates staring at her as she stumbled to her seat fifteen minutes late, pen in her teeth and used textbooks tumbling from her arms, breaking the pained silence of the interrupted lecture. She knew her classmates saw her as a warning, a symbol of what awaited them should they not study hard and come to class.

She'd dropped those two morning classes, Psych II and History of the American Revolution, by the end of September. Shame about American history, Mr. Curran was cute and a great teacher. She'd hung on to

Shakespeare's Tragedies until the end of October. That met at two in the afternoon, though she always attended that one in her work clothes too, leaving early every third class to get to work on time. She felt more comfortable in an upper-level English class, pretending that wearing black every day marked her as arty and not overworked.

Dr. Travis wore black most of the time too. It was the first thing he'd pointed out they had in common. More things in common came up over rainy afternoon coffee on campus, even more over late-night drinks across the island.

At his Jersey Shore beach house, he recited poetry to her in bed, dense and ornate verse he claimed as his own life's work, a tragic retelling of "the fall of men and the dawn of time" that Maureen recognized almost immediately as John Milton's *Paradise Lost*. I actually finished that semester, she wanted to tell Travis, having stuck with that class mostly because of that poem, charmed as she was by Milton's portrayal of a defiant and driven Lucifer. But she suppressed the urge to call out Travis as a phony and instead tried to enjoy his busy hands at work under the sheets.

It's someone reading you poetry in bed, she told herself, and almost making you come as he does it. A man who can multitask. Be happy.

Maureen hadn't harbored any unrealistic hopes for either a future or a genuine gut-busting orgasm with Travis, but she figured they'd wear a hole in the carpet in front of the beach house fireplace pretending there was reason to believe in both. But Mrs. Dr. Travis, mother of their three sons, matron of the home the Travises shared on Todt Hill, had other plans. Mrs. Dr. Travis of the short black hair had found long reddish hairs in that carpet by the fireplace, and that was that.

In his office, after getting busted by his wife, weeping and moaning like a poor version of a character from the tragedies he taught, Travis offered Maureen an A and the rest of the semester off if she promised not to bring sexual harassment charges over getting dumped. She laughed at him. Like the last time this happened? she'd wanted to ask him. Then she laughed at herself. She hadn't considered herself his Juliet, and Travis was no fucking Romeo, but she had imagined herself an exception, a powerful if not intoxicating temptation. Instead, she felt revealed as only this semester's diversion, not significant enough to be tragic or comic.

When Travis had stood and reached out to embrace her across the desk, the glint of *once for old times' sake* in his eyes, Maureen walked out of the office. That afternoon she dropped the Shakespeare class, though she lost half the tuition she'd paid for it. She set her sights on a fresh start in the spring and that night posted a sign in the waitress station at work, offering to pick up extra shifts.

On the bus now, on the way to one of those extra shifts, she sat slumped, rocking her molars together and thinking of Jimmy's Rose and Mrs. Dr. Travis. Maybe Jimmy wasn't such a hot idea. Seen that movie already. It always ends the same. If she stayed out of trouble with Jimmy, maybe the money she lost on the Shakespeare class would end up being worth something after all.

Maureen rubbed her eyes with her fingertips and unzipped her bag. She picked through her purse, searching for her compact, needing some powder for the outside of her nose. She found the compact and popped it open. Oh, shit, she thought, staring down at her empty pack of birth control pills. When did this happen? When had she taken the last one, yesterday? The day before? She clicked the pack closed and dropped it back in her bag. No problem. Monday I'll go to Planned Parenthood and get more. Did this mean she'd have to go off and go on again? Start all over? There wasn't much point. Considering her total lack of prospects, she certainly wasn't in any danger.

But still, you hate to break the cycle.

She repacked her things and stood, grabbing tight to the cold metal pole beside the bus driver. The bus settled to the curb at her Bay Street stop with a groan like it was dying, like its own legs were all but worn out.

2

By nine, Maureen, dressed in her four-hundred-dollar outfit, was perched on a bar stool, waiting for the crowd, a second shot of Bushmills and thirty-nine American Spirits next to her elbow on the bar. Good thing I rushed to be here, she thought.

Upon Maureen's arrival, grateful she'd picked up the shift, Dennis had put up the money for her two packs of smokes — right after he'd told Maureen that her floor partner wasn't coming in either. Vic, the owner, had picked her to work a party for some local politico at the reception hall he ran upstairs. Maureen feigned upset over the situation and complained again about Vic never throwing her a catering gig, causing Dennis to plead powerlessness, exactly the reaction Maureen had expected. She bitched to Dennis, something all the girls did, only because he took it so well. He got the shit so the bartenders and the customers didn't. In reality, flying solo on the floor was a lucky break. She'd run like a dog but she'd double her money.

She'd already had a few easy early tables. Happy hour had been steady. A little bleed had trickled down from upstairs, early-arriving party guests—high rollers, it looked like—and that had helped. She thumbed through the roll of cash in her apron, guessing she'd already neared the hundred-dollar mark. A good start to the evening. People wouldn't start showing up in real numbers for another hour. The floor would fill by eleven. The band was set up, sound-checked, and huddled over a table in front of the stage, working out the set list. They'd spend the next hour adjusting the levels of their body chemistry before the first set at ten.

Most of the regulars, friends of Vic's, were already in place, as if the bar were a stage and each man had his unchanging mark. Big fans of Maureen's they were, and a steady stream of cash. They stood at the bar, leaning their arms across the backs of vacant stools, sleeves rolled up over hairy forearms, bellies pouting over their Italian leather belts, their pricey bourbons and top-shelf vodkas clutched in fat hands adorned with rings. Throughout the night they'd grab her elbow, maybe let a hand slide to her hip, while yelling simple requests over the band and into her ear: Got matches? Bring that lady over there a drink on me? She wearing a wedding ring? Excuses, really, these questions, to slip her some cash, the money a warm-up to whatever offers came later in the night: next weekend in the Hamptons, a limo and dinner, a Soho party full of heroin-chic models and D-list actors.

But holding court over the goodfella parade tonight was a tall wide-shouldered man Maureen didn't know. His gray suit jacket strained at its buttons, his silver tie bunched at his collar as he opened his arms wide, telling some tale that enraptured his audience. Maureen didn't know the man, couldn't hear his story, but she recognized the collective look on the faces of his admirers: greed. Bastards may as well have had drool running down their chins. Mr. Silver had something, or the keys to something, that they wanted. That was obvious.

Silver finished his story and someone else took the floor, adding on, Maureen was sure, his own complements to the previous tale. Mr. Silver settled half his weight onto his bar stool. Clutching a cocktail tight in his left hand, he stroked the short hairs of his silver goatee with the fingers of his right as he listened. His mouth strained to hold a grin. Misery, Maureen thought. Pained boredom. That's what that grin is hiding. Mr. Silver needed something in return and was at that very moment putting a down payment on whatever it was. Maureen felt a pang of empathy. I know the feeling, she thought. Whatever it was that had Mr. Silver faking it that hard, Maureen hoped it was worth it. And then it clicked in her head. Silver had to be the VIP upstairs.

As if he'd heard her good wishes, Silver turned his head ever so slightly her way, his fixed grin never moving. It was hard to tell in the dim light of the bar, but Maureen thought she saw him wink at her after a moment of eye contact. With the wink, the empathy in her died. Like a blush her professional armor rose to the surface of her skin. But of course. We all want something. Isn't that why we're here? Maureen raised her glass and polished off her whiskey, turning on her stool and letting her hair fall in a curtain between her profile and Mr. Silver. An authoritative kiss-off, she thought, without being gruesomely rude. After all, she might end up waiting on him later. She couldn't name the designer, but she knew an expensive suit when she saw one. No sense totally blowing a potential big tip.

Tapping her foot on the rung of the bar stool, she considered getting one more shot. Better not. Two was the limit before a shift, coke buzz or not. Enough to get her legs through the night and no more. She stared into her empty glass. She jumped when a deep voice rumbled above her.

"Thought I might see you at the gym today."

Maureen swiveled in her seat, craning her neck to look up into the face of Clarence, the Narrows's muscle-bound, six-eight, black-as-oil bouncer. "Gimme a break, C. I joined yesterday."

"I know, I signed you up," Clarence said. "You told me you wanted to get right to it. I'm just sayin'. You could've hit it yesterday, too."

With one enormous hand, Clarence smoothed his pink silk tie against his clamshell shirt. Her neck already aching from her head's steep angle, Maureen wondered as she often did what life was like from that height. Clarence was so large he had to have his shirts tailor-made. Maureen could wear one of those shirts as a dress, and the hem would drag on the floor.

"Like I told you," Maureen said, "I would have worked out, but I had to come here."

"That's two opportunities lost to poor planning." Clarence smiled. "Two days of pain that could be behind you already." He set one hand on the bar and leaned down to Maureen, his brown eyes the size of coffee saucers. "Seriously, you need to come in. I told you I'll train you myself."

Maureen tilted her head from side to side, working the kink from her neck. "Weights aren't for me. I wanna hit the treadmill and run, you know? Maybe hang from the chin-up bar and get taller."

"Nah, running ain't enough." Clarence rose to his full height, rested his chin in his palm. Sensing the appraisal in his eyes, Maureen fluffed her hair and lit up her best fake smile. Clarence grinned. "We're gonna take care of you, little girl. Buff you right up. You got good bones, a good frame for hanging muscle on. And I can teach you some things for your back and your legs, get rid of that slouch." He raised his forefinger from his chin, tipped it toward her. "And you're not afraid of hard work, I know that. But I can't get you in there; you gotta make the effort."

"Don't I know it," Maureen said, laughing.

Clarence tilted his head, directing Maureen's attention back to Mr. Silver. "Like that dude over there? Every single morning he's in there solo, banging it out. Every. Morning. Crack of dawn."

"That's a little psycho," Maureen said. "Don'tcha think?"

"That's commitment."

"I'm not up for all that," Maureen said. "I don't have that kind of stamina."

"Don't talk like that," Clarence said. "You're a powerhouse. We both know it." He made a fist, held it up. "You're just compact. Like dynamite."

Maureen smiled, lowering her eyes. She liked the way Clarence talked to her, and his training offer flattered her. Half the island's bodybuilders wanted to train with him, and here he was carving out time for little ol' her. She knew there was nothing untoward about his offer; Clarence worshipped his wife, a caramel-colored fireplug not much bigger than Maureen. Maybe Clarence was right, she thought. Running wasn't enough anymore. Might feel good, Maureen thought, to work toward something other than the rent.

"Hey, I'm all about the gym," she said. "It's where I was headed tonight when Dennis called. Blame him."

"Blame me for what?" Dennis asked, stepping up beside them.

Clarence raised his arm, curling his fist toward his shoulder. A bowling ball twitched in his sleeve. "Pain." He chuckled and walked away, heading back to his post beside the door.

"That dude," Dennis said, shaking his head. "He on you about the gym?"

"I joined yesterday."

"Good for you." Dennis slid a cigarette out of Maureen's pack on the bar. He held the cigarette in front of his nose. "Be careful, he'll be on you about these next." Dennis tucked his stolen smoke behind his ear, where Maureen watched it disappear into his thick black curls. "If we all listened to Clarence," Dennis said, "we'd have the healthiest staff on Bay Street."

Maureen touched her thin bangs. Dennis wasn't much to look at, a plain face with tiny eyes and no chin, and his shirts hung on him like he had a cheap hanger for shoulders, but the girls at the Narrows loved his dark, shimmering, curly hair. Tanya touched it every chance she got. That Dennis never did anything to it but wash it only heightened the communal envy.

"You best be careful," Maureen said. "The staff gets in shape, we might feel good about ourselves and want to make something out of our lives instead of working here. Then where would you be?"

"Here with the lifers like you. I'm not worried. Clarence can bench-press a Cadillac, and he's here five nights a week. Cash in hand is hard to give up."

Maureen picked up her cigarette pack, closed the top, and tossed it back on the bar. Lifer, my ass, she thought. This spring everything is gonna change: school, the gym. Hell, I may get crazy and find a decent, sane, single boyfriend. I might go out and get a life. Stop living for this goddamn bar.

Dennis cracked his knuckles. Maureen hoped he wouldn't do his neck, which was usually what came next. The *pop-pop-pop* of his bones always made her queasy. This time Dennis rolled his wrists and thankfully stopped there. He looked around the bar. "Decent start tonight."

"I've seen worse," Maureen said. She nodded toward the band. "These guys bring a good crowd."

"They always bring *him* in, too," Dennis said. "The teacher." He leaned into her. "Or is it you he comes to see?"

"Jimmy and his wife come for the band. I work plenty of other nights. He never comes in for those." She shrugged. "He's taken, anyway."

"Like that's stopped you before."

"I don't do that shit anymore."

Dennis tapped the tip of his nose. "Careful, other shit you don't do anymore manages to linger."

Maureen touched her new nose ring, though she knew Dennis referred to the coke. She considered reminding him that he'd called her in to work over Tanya's pill habit. Ol' reliable Maureen. Like a faithful dog or a strong horse. Like death and bills and taxes and middle-aged men who hated waiting for another round. Speaking of, she thought.

"Who's the suit?" she asked. "The white-haired guy. He seems pretty popular."

"That's it," Dennis said, "change the subject. Had your fill of skinny academics? Going more for the beefcake? He *is* your type; he's married."

"Christ, one mistake and I never live it down. You better hope I never find any skeletons in your closet."

"No one, ever," Dennis said, "has made just one mistake."

"Okay, Confucius." Maureen tilted her chin at Mr. Silver. "Every goombah in the room is kissing his ring. I'm just asking." She frowned. "I feel like I know the face, but I can't place it."

"You read the papers?"

"Almost never," Maureen said. "No time."

"Watch TV?"

"Same as above."

"That's Frank Sebastian," Dennis said.

"Never heard of him."

"He's the guest of honor upstairs. Fund-raiser. He's a friend of Vic's. He's running for state senator. South Shore district."

Maureen laughed. "Wow. State Senate. I had no idea that the road to political fame and fortune ran through the Narrows. When did Vic get so hooked up?"

"He and Vic go back," Dennis said. "They've known each other since before Vic took over the bar, ten, twelve years ago. Sebastian, he does the security up and down Bay Street. He's got every parking lot, from end to end."

"He's a rent-a-cop? He doesn't look it."

"He owns the company," Dennis said, "that provides rent-a-cops to most everywhere on the island that uses them."

Maureen narrowed her eyes, trying to get a read on Sebastian. Something about him wasn't right or, more to the point, not enough about him was wrong. The cut of his gray suit, his sharp jawline and high cheekbones: he was too cleanly drawn, too intentional, like a CGI special effect stepped down from a film screen. She thought, if she stared at him long enough, his whole body would ripple like a glitch in a hologram.

"He's getting a hell of a head start," she said. "Campaign-wise. Or he's really late. It's the end of November."

"Special election," Dennis said, "in April. He's running for Valario's seat. The guy who got caught with the suicidal stripper out in Flushing? Twenty-years-married Mr. Family Values? Heard of him?"

"Nope," Maureen said. She ran her eyes over the room. "But I can spit on a dozen just like him from here." She glanced over at Sebastian. "How's he doing? He gonna win?"

"Most likely," Dennis said. "He's way ahead. Running away with it, practically."

"He's such a big shot, then what's he doing down here schmoozing the league of ordinary gentlemen? The fat wallets are upstairs."

"I know these things?" Dennis asked with a shrug. "The money down here spends the same as everyone else's, far as I know. Maybe he's waiting to make an entrance upstairs. 'Pomp and Circumstance' and that shit. Though he probably knows a few of these guys from up on the Hill."

"He lives on the Hill?"

"I don't know where he lives," Dennis said. "But remember that rash of robberies on Todt Hill a couple of years ago? All those rich people getting knocked off? It was big news."

"If you say so."

"You need to get out more."

"I get out almost every night," Maureen said. "But it's always to come here."

"Anyway," Dennis said, "half these meatheads, their houses were robbed. Got so bad they eventually hired a private patrol. Heavily armed. Soon as that happened, the robberies stopped."

"Let me guess," Maureen said. "Sebastian's security firm."

"For a while, rumors went around that had him contracting the robberies to create the security work. But nobody could prove it. I don't know how hard people tried."

"Savvy," Maureen said.

"So you're okay with criminality as a business strategy?"

"Only in my politicians." She waited for Dennis to laugh. He didn't. "Listen, I'm just saying, if he's slick enough to pull it off, good for him. Maybe I'll vote for him. You should, too. Think about it. The guy gets shit done."

Dennis gave her a long, humorless stare. It lasted almost a full minute before a grin curled the corners of his mouth. "All I know is Vic's comping the upstairs for him. I'm putting up a full sit-down with an open bar, on the arm." He shook his head. "And then Vic cries at me that we're bleeding cash. And I got one girl on the floor for a Friday night with our best-drawing band."

"Woe is you," Maureen said, looking over at Sebastian. How much money would he make upstairs? Thousands, probably. Two times, five, six times what she made in a year. I need me a fucking fund-raiser, she thought. "I get it. This is you telling me I got the better deal tonight, sticking down here instead of being sent upstairs."

"You said it, not me. You can thank me later. Vic and I both know you're the only girl I got that can run this floor on her own. So you and me, we gotta hustle enough drinks to offset the big money-suck upstairs." Dennis patted Maureen's shoulder, tilting his chin in Sebastian's direction. "Think of it this way: you and me, we're making our own valuable contribution to the future of Staten Island. Behind the scenes, as it were."

Maureen snorted. "Whatever for that bullshit. The truth is, I'm the only one dumb enough to come running when you come calling." She pulled a smoke from her pack, held it up between their faces. "How about you let me have a few minutes' peace?" she said. "They're the last I'm gonna get for a while."

3

Maureen awoke into pitch black. The old leather of the couch creaked beneath her as she straightened her sore legs. Where the hell was she? What time was it? She sat up, a rush of nausea doubling her over. A fog of stale whiskey and sour body odor floated around her. Christ, her head was killing her. Dennis's office, that's where she was.

She did a quick body check. Fully clothed, thank you, Jesus. After a few deep breaths, Maureen felt she could move without hurling. Best to be careful, though, so she lay back down on the couch. She listened for noise from the bar. Everything was quiet. Must be after closing time. Was she the only one around? Had Dennis left her, locked her in the office? No, he wouldn't abandon her like that. He never even let any of the girls hit the parking lot alone after hours, and that was right across the street. Poor Dennis was probably sitting at the bar, nursing a cocktail and waiting for her to resurface.

Maureen squeezed her eyes shut, forcing the last of the night to replay across her lids. The fuzzy scenes materialized out of time and sequence.

She watched Dennis half-carry her to the office, saying something about her being too drunk to go anywhere. She saw herself ducking into a stall in the ladies' room for another bump of coke. More than once. Three, four times? Everyone had come down from the party upstairs, seventy-five, maybe a hundred people, *bam*, all at once. God, the bar had been slammed all night, like Vic was giving away the store. That was the logic behind the coke. And the coke, like always, had betrayed her in the end, sending her to the bar for shots of Bushmills. Still zinging when the band wrapped up and the crowd cleared out, she had doubled up on the booze. To make sure she could sleep that night. Well, it had worked. Trying to walk that tightrope again, Maureen: the coke to keep running, the booze to shave the frantic edge off the high. Keep it steady, manageable. She'd made it to the end of the night, at least.

So this didn't count as falling off the wire, right?

She put her hands to her waist, looking for her apron. Not there. Not good. On the floor? She bent, tipping bile to the back of her throat. She swallowed it down. She searched the floor around the couch. Her money. Where was her money? Hers *and* the bar's. She sat back up, dizzy. Calm down. Dennis had to have it. If he had walked her to the office, he'd taken care of the cash, too. How embarrassing, the manager doing your checkout like you're a rookie. She was gonna owe him for this, big-time.

Maureen leaned her clammy forehead into her palm. Tell me, please, where did I get the blow? She tried to settle her mind on a specific face. The band. I got it from the band. That's right, the drummer. The drummer with the shoulders and the cheekbones and the huge . . . wait, no. That last part she'd imagined, right before she passed out—oh, God—with her hand up her skirt. Another miserable effort to take the edge off. She felt dangerously sick again. What if Dennis had walked in right in the middle? Didn't happen. That I'd remember, no matter how twisted

I was. Did I even get off? Even give it a decent try? That, she couldn't remember. Fucking cocaine.

With an effort, she stood, kicking around in the dark for her shoes. What is wrong with you, Maureen? How many other girls have you watched run down this rat hole? That's why you ditched that stupid powder to begin with. She found her shoes and managed to squeeze her feet into them without having to bend over. She took a deep breath and strained again to hear any sound from the bar. She thought she heard voices. At least she wasn't alone. Time to face the music, lady. You gotta get home somehow, so you can clean up and come back here tonight. Nice life. When you get home, that coke goes down the toilet. God, I sound like my mother.

Arms held out in front of her like a B-movie zombie, Maureen shuffled across the dark office. She found the door and shoulder-leaned it open, her own brutal headache urging gentleness and caution.

The barroom glimmered in the flames of a few tea candles set out along the bar. No lights. The chairs rested upside down on the tables, the ceiling fans hung motionless. What's with the candles? At the end of the night, the candles went out and the lights went on. Maureen spotted a figure in the shadows, couldn't make out a face. There was definitely someone at the bar. Why not leave a light on? She was about to announce her resurrection but the words died as her eyes adjusted to the candlelight and she realized who it was, and what she saw happening.

Frank Sebastian was looking right at her, or at least in her direction. Kneeling in front of Sebastian was Dennis, his back to Maureen, his head bobbing up and down, piston-fast, at Sebastian's crotch. With one hand, Sebastian steadied himself on the bar. The other hovered over Dennis's head, just brushing the curly hair, as if Sebastian both wanted to grab hold of what was happening to him and feared ruining it.

Sebastian growled and his body shook; Dennis double-timed it. Maureen's knees went weak, almost out from under her. She turned to the wall, propping herself up with one hand. Sebastian roared. Maureen threw up on her shoes.

In the ladies' room, her stockings in the trash, Maureen stood barefoot on the dirty tile, holding her shoes under the hand dryer for a fourth consecutive cycle. The shoes only had to get her home, not even into the house; she'd leave them on the porch. Whatever she'd made that night, thirty of it was going to Payless. Tears welled in her eyes and she hadn't yet fully caught her breath. Her hands shook, and not because she was barefoot on the cold floor.

Maureen had worked late nights in bars for eleven years, ever since she was eighteen. The Narrows was her third on Bay Street alone. She'd witnessed more public sex, in cars, in alleyways, in bathrooms and broom closets, than, at the rate she was going, she might ever have over the rest of her life. Straight sex, gay sex, you name it. Masturbation, group sex. Shit that, had she gotten it on film, would make her a fortune on the Internet.

As a younger woman, she'd had sex in public places, had for a while gotten pretty into it. Though she'd been as careful about privacy as the opportunities permitted, she knew she'd been seen. Such was life in the big city, even her Staten Island corner of it. Hell, she heard John, her upstairs neighbor and former boss at Cargo Café, the last place she'd worked, and his girl, Molly, going at it like gangbusters all the time. So what had her so upset now? That *she'd* been caught spying? Had she been watching? Not really, she decided, more like she was just there at the time. Everything had happened so fast, at least once she realized what was going on, that she'd had no time to decide whether to keep looking or to turn away. She had turned away, even if it was to throw up and not out of any sense of decency.

Dennis had rushed over to her, steadying her with firm hands on her shoulders. Passing her bar napkins from the stack in his hand, he'd offered ice water and wet towels. Maureen refused everything in her desperation to run away and hide in the ladies' room. Of the three people involved, she was by far the most unnerved. In fact, Dennis was as calm as an uncle tending a niece overloaded on cotton candy, acting not at all like a bar manager moments ago caught blowing a local politician.

Sebastian had ignored Maureen, turning his back and sauntering away down the bar, so casual that Maureen felt like the one caught with her pants down. She even heard a quiet laugh from him as he moved out of the candlelight and into the darkness at the end of the bar, where he became a large dark shape among the other shadows.

Maureen punched the big silver button on the dryer to start another cycle, holding her shoes under the hot air in one hand. She held her free hand out in front of her. Still shaking. And not the sick shakes, or the hungry shakes, or the exhausted shakes. She knew the varied kinds and how to distinguish them. Her years on the floor had taught her the differences. What mattered was where the shaking started: your belly, your head, your muscles. These particular tremors had started deep in her chest, vibrations rising from under her heart. She had the fear shakes, the worst kind. Because whatever the amount bursting from the coffers upstairs, what she had witnessed between Sebastian and Dennis was worth a lot more. She could kill Sebastian's political career with a phone call, an anonymous e-mail or two. How many of those big checks would get canceled if word of this late-night hookup got out?

How big a check could *I* get, Maureen wondered, for making sure the secret doesn't get out?

Blackmail was an interesting thought, in an abstract kind of way, but Maureen didn't give it much credence. Sebastian was no kind of enemy to her. She had no reason to do him dirt like that, to mess with the guy's whole life. He could have good plans for his political career. At the very least he could have kids out there in the world. Maybe even grandkids. And what about Dennis? He'd be ruined too if word got out. Kissing ass was a bar manager's job, but sucking cock was a whole 'nother story. Dennis would be done in the bar business, not just at the Narrows, and up and down Bay Street, but all over the island. God, what would Tanya think? She and Dennis had extracurriculars of their own happening.

Not much hope for me, either, Maureen thought, at the end of the day. Nobody wants a waitress who can't keep a secret. Fuck it. Forget it.

When the hand dryer died, Maureen set her shoes on the counter. She leaned on her palms, her fingers splayed, and looked down at her hands, her knuckles white from the pressure of her weight. She was a realist; she knew damn well she'd never tell a soul what she'd seen. Blackmail? What was that? Moral quandaries aside, plans like that didn't even work in the movies, never mind real life. She knew a hell of a secret, but in real life the secret was worthless; she'd never use it. No great loss. Really, all she wanted was home and bed, to forget everything about tonight except the money.

Before she left the bar, she'd have to make sure both men understood she had no plans for what she'd seen. Because the fact remained that she was stuck, trapped, in an empty bar with them. She didn't need them getting nervous.

Man, she thought, I never should have quit Cargo.

After a couple of gentle knocks, Dennis leaned in through the door. "Everything okay in here?"

Glancing at Dennis in the mirror, wincing and nodding as she did it, Maureen slipped into her shoes. They smelled funky, but at least they were dry. Turning, she swept her hair from her face, smoothed the front of her skirt. "Listen, about tonight. As far as I'm concerned, it never happened. We counted our money and went home. Forget it."

Dennis came into the bathroom, easing the door closed behind him. He leaned against it. "It may not be such a bad thing, that you saw what you did. Between us, at least."

"Of course not," Maureen said. "I don't care what you do and who you do it with. It's not my business. It's not gonna change anything around here."

When Dennis took a step closer, Maureen backed up against the sinks. He noticed and stopped, raising his hand. Silent for a long moment, he seemed to be thinking something over. "I'm glad to hear that, though it's not really what I meant." He glanced over his shoulder. "You've had a long night and I'm sure you wanna get going. Let's continue this conversation another time."

"I'd rather not. Can't we leave it here?"

"I wish we could," Dennis said. "But believe me, once you hear me out, you'll see how important it is that we talk. And let's not mention anything about present or future conversations to Sebastian." He stepped back to the door, pulling it open and stepping aside for Maureen to walk through. "You and me. Next shift maybe?"

"We'll see." Maureen realized her backside remained pressed up against the counter. "Gimme another minute to get myself together." She tried to smile. "You know how girls are."

"I'll meet you out front," Dennis said, walking out the door.

As the bathroom door creaked closed, Maureen turned and hit the cold-water tap. So Dennis didn't want to let it go quite yet. That's outstanding. Things were getting complicated already. Maureen held her cupped hands under the rushing water until it flowed over her thumbs. Watching the water, she recalled a picture from her kitchen calendar, one of the summer months long gone. A waterfall someplace warm. A snowy curtain of water blurred by mist and framed by black stone and bright green ferns and vines. Long-legged birds waded in the rippling pool at the bottom of the falls. Central America, Africa, maybe the Caribbean; she couldn't remember. Wherever that waterfall was, that was where she wanted to be.

When the water ran so cold her knuckles ached, she moved her hands out from under the stream. She let the cold water leak through her hands and drip into the water rushing down the drain. When her hands were empty, she turned off the tap. She stood there, eyes averted from the mirror, staring at her white fingers splayed on the black tile counter and listening to her own labored breathing. Calm, cool, and smooth. That's what the men wanted to see, so that's what she'd give them. After a few more breaths, her game face back in place, she wiped up the puddles on the counter with a paper towel and tossed the towel in the trash on her way out of the bathroom.

Dennis waited alone for her at the front door, his hand on the key in the lock. Sebastian was nowhere in sight. He'd probably slipped away, Maureen thought, while she was cleaning up. Dennis wasn't wearing his coat, didn't look like he was leaving yet. Maybe Sebastian waited in the office or the men's room and they were gonna get back to it after she left. Well, good for them. Have at it. At least somebody was getting some.

When Maureen reached him, Dennis unlocked the door but didn't open it.

"Sebastian's gonna want to talk to you about this, too," Dennis said. "Probably soon."

"Like I said, you got nothing to worry about. And neither does he. I'm looking to let it go."

"When he asks you about it," Dennis said, "tell him you didn't see anything. Tell him nothing about what I said in the bathroom. Tell him you walked out of the office, puked, and that was it. It's better for all of us that way."

"That's what I've been trying to tell you."

"I know, but I'm different. Promise me you'll tell him you saw nothing."

"Dennis, you're scaring me."

"It's important. Promise me."

"Okay, I promise," Maureen said. "Geez. See you tomorrow. Or tonight, or whatever. Now let me outta here, please. I wanna get home before dawn."

Dennis didn't reply, but he opened the door. Cold air rushed into the bar. Maureen stepped outside into it. After a moment's hesitation on the sidewalk, her cheeks already starting to ache, she turned to tell Dennis one more time not to worry, that lying to Sebastian wouldn't exactly be hard. But he had already locked the door behind her and disappeared.

Maureen turned left and headed for the corner, realizing she had no idea of the time. Even the slight incline up Dock to Bay Street taxed her tired legs. After a few steps she stopped, leaning a shoulder against the rough brick wall, hunting through her purse for her cell. She'd get a car quicker if she called than if she waited on the corner, shivering like a wet dog and, with the condition she was in, looking like a low-rent Bay Street prostitute. A cramp seized the arch of her right foot, the pain regular as the North Star. She lifted her leg, rotating her foot, trying to work out the cramp. The smell of dead cigarettes rose from the gutter. The butts, mingled with the scent of the piss puddles drifting over from the parking lot, had Dock Street smelling like a filthy urinal. Why did men do that? Why piss in the parking lot *before* walking into a bar with a functioning bathroom? She wrinkled her nose. This, she thought, this is what your Friday night smells like. Nice.

Before she made the corner or found her phone, headlights snapped on in the parking lot across the street. Her nerves hit high alert. She hadn't even noticed the car sitting over there. Hadn't even looked. Stupid. The chemicals and the drama hadn't just made her sick, they'd made her slow and stupid. She knew better. She should've called a cab from inside the Narrows. Should've waited inside until it came. The car moved, rolling in her direction. Maureen doubled back for the bar, searching her bag now for both her phone and her switchblade knife. Two things, she thought, that should've been at the ready. Two things that would've been in her pockets and not her bag before she ever left the Narrows had she not been so muddle-headed.

She found her phone first. She flipped it open, scrolled in search of the bar number. She prayed Dennis was in a position, literally, to let her back inside. If Sebastian was around, it might be handy having him there, the size of him. Speaking of Sebastian, where were the rent-a-cops? One of their gray jeeps usually sat parked within sight of the Narrows while they locked up. Maureen checked the clock on her phone; it was after five in the morning, long after closing. Except for Maureen and that dark car, the streets were deserted in every direction.

The car dipped out of the parking lot exit, throwing its headlights on Maureen, blinding her. She blinked at the phone, trying to read the screen. She was at the door. She pounded on it.

"Maureen."

She refused to turn, kept beating on the door, shouting Dennis's name.

"Maureen," the voice said again, firm, calm. "It's just me."

She turned, shielding her eyes from the headlights' glare. A figure, a large one, too big to be Dennis but not big enough to be Clarence, stood in the street a few paces down the block. Who was left around who knew her name? The politician? Dennis had said the guy wanted to talk to her, though she'd figured he'd wait. Maybe not. The figure held out his hand. "It's Frank Sebastian, from inside. You remember. I saw you talking about me earlier, with Dennis. C'mere for a second. You got nothing to worry about."

The car turned out of the lot and onto the street, throwing its lights toward the corner. Maureen blinked, trying to focus, waiting for the spots before her eyes to fade. As her vision adjusted to the muted glow of the streetlights, she recognized him.

"I gotta get back inside," Maureen said. "I forgot my money." She realized it was true as she spoke.

"Dennis's a good guy," Sebastian said. "Me and him, we go back. He'll lock your tips in the safe for the night. You pick them up next shift." He set his open hand over his chest. "I need your attention for a few minutes." He reached into his front pocket. "You need some cash overnight? I can tide you over. Get it back to me when you can, no questions asked. I understand the need to have cash on hand."

"No, thanks," Maureen said.

She glanced at the car, idling now in the middle of the street. She couldn't see inside through the tinted windows. Who did Sebastian have with him, just a driver? Bodyguards? Maureen wasn't sure she wanted to know.

"Don't worry about the car," Sebastian said. "You don't think I drive myself home after drinking, do you? I'm a responsible man. I'm running for office." He smiled. "You might've heard." He raised his hands. "Hey, listen. Come over here and talk to me a minute, and I'll give you a ride home. Save yourself the wait and the cab fare. You work hard; keep your dough."

"I appreciate the offer," Maureen said, "but I know what you wanna discuss and I've got nothing to say. I didn't see a thing."

Sebastian took a step closer to her. "You may have nothing to say, but I do. You should expect that I have concerns. So come over here. Three minutes. Tops." He grinned. "And then we all go home happy."

"I'm working tomorrow night," Maureen said. "Come back then. My shift starts at five. Meet me here before five and we can talk."

Sebastian raised his hands at his sides, looking over the empty street. "I got plans for tomorrow night. Commitments. I'm busy. Let's do this now. Now is better."

Maureen stared over Sebastian's shoulder. He stood only a few yards from where the street dead-ended at the chain-link fence and the train tracks. Why were men so ignorant? She understood why Sebastian didn't want to talk in front of his driver, but did he really expect Maureen to follow him down a dark dead-end street in the latest hours of the night? Of course he did, she thought. Because he thinks like a six-foot-three two-hundred-pound man who gets his way, not like a vulnerable hundred-pound woman. Maureen realized she still held her phone open in her hand.

"I'm calling a cab," she said. "If we have to, we can talk on the corner while I wait. Or we can have this conversation another time. Or not at all. I don't know what there is to talk about. But if you wanna stand on the corner with me, it's a free country."

She turned her back on Sebastian and headed for the corner with the phone at her ear. She gave her location to the taxi dispatcher. Her stomach seized when she heard Sebastian trotting up beside her but she kept walking, suppressing the urge to run. Sebastian caught up to her but he walked in the street, leaving a couple of feet between them. The car crawled up the street beside them.

These boys, she thought. It's just sex. Let it go.

Maureen closed her phone, slipped it into her coat pocket. Guilt tickled the inside of her throat like a finger. She didn't want to be a bitch and didn't want Vic hearing she'd pissed off someone important. On the other hand, if the choice was between aggravating Vic and getting in this guy's car, everyone was gonna have to live with her attitude. When your girl-on-a-dark-street alarm goes off, Maureen thought, you listen. *Every* damn time. And when those headlights appeared, that alarm rang like it was three o'clock on the last day of school. If Vic couldn't understand that, Maureen decided she'd have to rethink working for the man.

Maureen dug her smokes from her bag and lit up. She offered one to Sebastian. He refused. They reached the corner. Sebastian stayed in the gutter. Maureen watched the muscles twitch along the edge of his jaw.

"So this is how it is," he said. "You'd rather pay hard-earned money for a ride with some towel-headed Taliban than let me, a respectable citizen, drive you home."

"Towel-headed Taliban. Your speechwriter invent that gem or did you write it yourself?"

Sebastian straightened his tie, rolled his shoulders. "Forgive me, Miss Bleeding Heart. When I think about what they've done to this country, I get upset."

"By *they*," Maureen said, "you mean *men*?" When no response came from Sebastian, she pulled hard on her smoke and turned her attention back to the empty street. "For your information, I get the same cabdriver almost every weekend night. We work the same shifts. He's a perfectly nice guy."

"That's what everyone says about terrorists and serial killers right before they start counting the bodies." He loosened his tie, popped open the top button on his shirt. "I can see I won't be getting your vote. Anyway, I'm not out here campaigning." He plucked the SEBASTIAN FOR SEN-

ATE pin off his overcoat lapel and slipped it into his coat pocket. "I don't hafta tell you what we need to talk about."

"I haven't the slightest idea. All I know is I'm tired and I want to go home and go to bed."

Sebastian stepped closer, setting one foot on the curb, grinding his foot as though he'd trapped a roach beneath it. The leather sole scratching on the concrete was the only sound on the block. Even standing in the gutter, he towered over her. That soft laugh came again, the one she'd heard inside. Goose bumps ran up the backs of Maureen's arms. Whatever the politician side of him said, she thought, that laugh, that laugh is the real him, inside. She hated it.

"We're both tired," Sebastian said. "It's hard work, peddling your ass for money all night, am I right?" When Maureen glared at him, Sebastian smiled. "What? Don't act all offended, I'm talking about you and me both. We're both playing the same game, right? Throw me a couple of bucks and I'll get you what you want. We're birds of a feather, Maureen."

"Birds of a feather? I don't think so. I get the feeling you're leaving here with a little more money tonight than I am."

"I'm also delivering a lot more than a round of whiskey sours."

"That's supposed to make me feel better?" Maureen said. "Do me a favor, Mr. Senator. You're twice my age, more than twice my weight, and you'll be helping run the state of New York. Don't try to relate to me. It embarrasses the both of us."

"Then I'll come to the point. What you saw inside, maybe it gave you some ideas, ideas about gaining certain opportunities, certain advantages. It wouldn't be unreasonable. I'm in politics; I would understand it. Because of who I am, you might think information of a private nature about me is valuable. But acting on those ideas would be unacceptable."

"I've been trying to forget what I saw inside since the moment I saw it."

"Right, good," Sebastian said. "I figured that about you. But continuing with the train of thought, maybe Dennis has similar ideas. Maybe he comes to you in the near future with these ideas, with a plan." He paused, waiting, Maureen figured, for her to give away whether or not he was right. "You see where I'm going with this?"

In her head, Maureen heard Dennis's voice: *You and me. Next shift maybe?* Goose bumps on her arms again. This guy was quick. He was already a step ahead of Dennis. Sorry, D, Maureen thought. Whatever dirty business you're into with Sebastian or anyone else, no way I'm getting mixed up in it. Not now, not later.

"I have plans, Maureen, for the future," Sebastian said. "I have commitments to other people and their plans, to their futures."

"You've got nothing to worry about," Maureen said. "And neither do your people. Nothing happened tonight, for any of us. I never saw you again after you went upstairs for the fund-raiser."

"That's what I wanted to hear," Sebastian said. "Was that so hard?" He let loose a long, false sigh. "I'm just looking out for you."

"You're a real man of the people." She could see her cab coming up Bay Street. The enormity of her relief at the sight of it surprised her.

"I don't think I like you very much," Sebastian said.

"I'm too honest for you," Maureen said.

The cab rolled up to the curb. Before she could even move toward the car, Sebastian had the passenger door open. Smiling, he stood behind the door, his hands across the top of the frame. Maureen slipped by Sebastian and slid across the seat, behind the driver and as far away from Sebastian as she could get.

Sebastian leaned into the car, bending over the front seat. "You the regular guy?" The cabdriver, confused, half turned to Maureen, then looked back at the big man twisted halfway into his cab. "Are you or are you not the regular guy on this shift?"

The driver stammered.

"English, motherfucker. Do you speak it?"

"Can I just go home?" Maureen asked.

"No, I'm not him," the cabbie said. "I picked up the shift. One of his kids got sick or something. Do I know you? I think I seen you on TV."

"Bullshit," Sebastian said. He stuffed something in the cabbie's shirt. "Anywhere she wants to go."

Maureen leaned forward and watched the stunned cabbie pull a fifty from between the buttons of his shirt. "Give that back," she said. "I got my own money."

"Keep the money, Abdul, or I break your fucking arm." He grabbed the small flag hanging from the rearview mirror, tore it down, and waved it in the cabbie's face. "What the fuck is this?"

Maureen could see the red and green bars at the top and bottom, a crowned lion seated in the white band across the middle. What country was that? Iran? Iraq? "This tough-guy bullshit supposed to impress me, Sebastian?"

He ignored her again. "You can keep the change, Abdul. Get yourself a goddamn American flag with it."

Sebastian wound his way out of the car like a fat serpent, leaning over the door to look at Maureen. "See you around, sweetheart." He slammed the door.

Muttering, the cabbie pulled the car from the curb. Maureen recited her address, slumped, closed her eyes, and settled her head against the seat. At the first red light, the cabbie said, "So what your boyfriend has money? That doesn't mean he can be mean to everyone. You're lucky I don't tell dispatch to ban your number."

"Put that money in your pocket," Maureen said, not opening her eyes, not moving. She was so tired that just speaking was a strain. "I'm paying my own fare, and the tip, too. He's not paying my way and he is not my fucking boyfriend."

The cold wind stung Maureen's hot face and her bare, thin legs as she stood on the sidewalk outside her apartment, watching the cab cruise away. Out on the bay, she heard the ghost-groan horn of a ferry pulling off the pier. She wished she were riding that boat. If so, it would mean she'd had a very different night, that she was living a very different life.

But she wasn't. When the last echo of the horn had faded, she turned her back to the boat, to the water, and hurried inside.

After a long hot shower, lying in bed, the rising sun bleeding into her room around the edges of the curtains, Maureen felt herself slide from fear into anger. What was this Sebastian guy's problem? Did he really think he needed to threaten her so she would keep his secret? Like she gave a shit who sucked whose dick. She worked in a bar: somebody was doing something nasty to someone else, or themselves, pretty much all the damn time. She rolled over, away from the window, pulling the blankets to her shoulder. But what was Dennis into, she wondered, that he *wanted* to discuss getting caught giving blow jobs? And one of them had lied to her. Dennis had said they were strangers; Sebastian told her they weren't. Why? Eyes open, staring into the dark, Maureen decided she didn't care about the answer. She had her own life to worry about.

She sat up and dragged her legs over the edge of the bed, her bare toes touching the cold wood floor. She rubbed her fingertips into her temples. Her eyes, even closed, ached and burned. She was so exhausted that just breathing required conscious effort, but she was too tired and too wired to sleep. Yawning hurt. This, she thought, this scratchy limbo, this is the worst feeling in the world. Can't sleep, my body's too tired to move, and my brain won't stop running like a psycho hamster in a squeaky wheel. This state of agonizing suspended animation snared her more and more often these days. Was this what happened, she wondered, when you finally wore out? Good Christ, I'm not even thirty and I'm dead in the water.

She hauled herself upright and trudged into the kitchen.

Hanging on the open door, she stared into the fridge, trying to decide between the OJ and the wine, her whole body one big, throbbing ache. She chose the wine. She filled a coffee mug with cold chardonnay and downed it. Just something to grease the hamster wheel, to make it turn more quietly.

4

Straight out of bed Saturday afternoon, Maureen tried purging the previous night's indulgences with push-ups. The shooting pains in her right wrist forced her to stop after ten. One too many heavy trays last night. Lying on her back and rubbing her wrist, the hardwood floor cool against her bare skin, she studied the fine cracks in the low plaster ceiling and considered the gym. The cheap travel alarm clock on her nightstand counted off the seconds. A long run on the treadmill would sweat out the chemicals lingering in her blood. Her body hurt—her head from the booze and drugs, her arms and back and legs from the busy night at work—and she wanted to fight back; the pain let everything from the night before bully its way into the new day. Maureen needed to slam that door closed, to put something solid between her and the Narrows and Sebastian and Dennis. But work was calling.

She'd slept away the time she had for the gym. Running the neighborhood streets meant dodging potholes while sucking down clouds of car exhaust. Coffee and a hot shower would have to do. She remembered the coke in her dresser. She certainly needed it more for the night ahead than she had for last night. Probably wasn't enough left for more than one more night anyway. Not enough to sell at work, that was for sure. See that? That right there? That's the kind of thinking that gets you in trouble, that gets you discussing things you shouldn't see in conversations you should never have.

Maureen did her crunches, then sat up, pulling her knees to her chest, her arms tight across her shins. The apartment was chilly. The heat had conked out overnight. Either that or in her stupor she'd forgotten to turn it on before bed. Music played in the apartment upstairs. Something mournful and bluesy, the words unintelligible. Two soft voices, a man's and a woman's, mixed in with the music. One of them laughed and then both went silent. The music kept on.

Maureen pulled the comforter off the bed and wrapped it around her bare shoulders. The heat from her sleeping body long gone, the blanket, already cool, smelled like smoke and vanilla, her cigarettes and her soap. Calling in sick, she thought, even if she could afford it, would worry Dennis. And what if Sebastian asked about her or came around looking for her? She had never called in sick. She couldn't risk giving anyone cause for concern. Things had to stay normal. Or appear normal, anyway. Rhythmic moans now from upstairs. Things were normal up there, at least.

Maureen struggled to her feet. She kicked the thermostat up to seventy. She pulled on sweats and thick socks. Moving felt good, even if it wasn't the exercise that she needed or the sex she was being forced to listen to. Again. Maureen snapped the comforter over the bed, watched it float down and settle. Still going upstairs. Had to give John props, the boy had some self-control. No wonder Molly was forever knocking at John's door, always smiling when Maureen passed her on the stairs. Actually, thinking about it, Molly was kind of stuck up. Like she knew how good she had it while Maureen wasn't getting any. Like not only did Molly not mind Maureen hearing it, but like she was proud of it, too.

Sliding open her closet, Maureen started planning her work outfit.

Saturday night or not, the goal tonight was comfort, not sex appeal. What was the big deal about sex, anyway? It wasn't something important, like rent money or tuition. The high didn't last. Giving yourself up guaranteed you nothing. Money mattered. It was a lot harder to get and it did a lot more for you, although, Maureen had to admit, sex and money did have one thing in common. Getting enough of either without degrading yourself was hard goddamn work.

Maureen raised her eyes to the ceiling, half expecting chips of plaster to start raining down on her face. Those two upstairs: they seemed to get enough of both with their pride intact. Teamwork. Mutual satisfaction. Respect. She'd heard rumors about such things. And you know what else, Maureen? she thought. Molly is not stuck up, and she's not weird—you're just bitter. Bitter like an old woman, thinking bitter old-woman thoughts.

Go down to the animal shelter right now, get your seven cats, and get it over with.

I would, Maureen told herself, but I have to go to work.

She ticked through her clothes: skintight leather pants, low-cut tank tops, sweaters two sizes too small. Black, black, and more black. She realized she'd memorized what each and every sweater did and didn't do for her nipples. Probably not what Aristotle had in mind when he'd instructed, "Know thyself." Or was that Plato? Or Emily Dickinson? Einstein, maybe? Closing her eyes, Maureen pinched the bridge of her nose. Christ. This is what happens, she thought, when you spend more time reading coffee mugs than books. She crossed her arms, shaking her head at the fabric of her life.

It really didn't matter what outfit she wore. It would be black, it would look better on her in the dark of the bar than it did in the light of day, and at the end of the night it would stink like liquor, sweat, and smoke. Same as it ever was.

Grabbing two towels for her shower, Maureen realized all was quiet upstairs. She'd missed the big finale. She went to her dresser and found the vial of coke.

Wearing loose black jeans and a black silk blouse under her coat, Maureen turned the corner off Bay Street and headed downhill along Dock Street toward the Narrows. She had a cigarette in her lips and clutched a can of Red Bull in one hand. Legal stimulants would have to do. Before her shower, she'd flushed the last of the coke, all of it, down the toilet. Watching the powder swirl away, she'd decided she had to get serious and talk to John about going back to Cargo. The whole time she'd worked there, she'd never touched cocaine.

Back when she'd taken the gig at the Narrows, she'd really considered the move a step up. As she'd hoped, the money was better, even if the shifts were longer. With its semiprivate side-street entrance down by the train tracks and its unwritten but enforced-by-Clarence rules of entry, the Narrows had the aura of a 1920s speakeasy, seedy and sexy at the same time, a combination Maureen liked. To find the place, you had to seek it out, the only outward sign a beveled-glass and black-metal door. While the front door was sidewalk level, the Narrows itself was underground, built into the brick-walled vault of an old bank-turned-catering-hall that faced Bay Street.

Her first couple of months there had been a relief. Drunken college boys never stumbled in, nor was it a yuppie meat market. The Narrows didn't run on dance music, ugly neon, and underage clientele, like so many other Bay Street joints, but on soft lights, live bands, and a killer jukebox way in the back for set breaks. Cocktailing there, Maureen served mixed drinks and imports, not well shots and dollar drafts. She'd been told there were opportunities: bartending, catering, maybe management down the road. But things hadn't worked out that way. For over a year, Maureen had done nothing but run the floor, night after night after night.

She crushed her empty Red Bull can and tossed it in the gutter.

Flicking away her cigarette, she reached for the Narrows's front door. It was locked. That didn't make any sense. She banged on the door.

Maybe the rest of the wait staff was running late; that certainly wouldn't be new. But it was after four. Had to be; she'd caught the 3:45 bus. The bar staff, tenders and backs alike, always came in by four. When you moved with the speed of a spoiled prince at court, which was the bartenders to a T, getting your long, narrow kingdom in order took three hours, even with your vassal of a bar back at your beck and call. And even if everyone else ran late, Dennis never did. Ever. He had endured a long night himself, though. Maybe he'd passed out on that couch at God only knows what time. There was a first time for everything.

Maureen hit the door again and called his name. A few moments later she heard someone headed up the stairs.

Relieved, Maureen stepped back from the door and studied her fingernails. They'd need repainting before the shift. She'd have to bum some paint from Tanya, her usual Friday- and Saturday-night partner, if and when she showed up. God, how did that girl keep her job? By being drop-dead gorgeous, duh. C'mon, Maureen. Well, bump in tips or not, she was not in the mood to work alone for another night. And if Tanya doesn't show, Maureen thought, Dennis is getting an earful, all night long. And Tanya, too, when Maureen got off work, no matter the hour.

A dark form filled the glass in the door. It opened, but it wasn't Dennis on the other side. "Clarence," Maureen said, surprised.

Why was he in early? Bouncers never came in before seven. And what gives with the sweatshirt? Clarence always worked in a shirt and tie. Maureen craned her neck way back to see his face. Clarence kept his eyes away from hers.

"What's up?" Maureen asked. "You know the door was locked?" Clarence stepped out of the doorway to let her into the bar. Standing up close to him on the landing, Maureen felt Tinker Bell tiny. "Everything all right?"

"Nobody called you?" Clarence said.

"No." Well, not that she knew of. She hadn't checked her messages before leaving for work. No big deal. Whatever information she lacked she was about to get now. Maureen glanced from the landing into the bar. The chairs sat upside down on the tables. Only the dim sconces on the walls were lit. Nothing had been done to get ready for the night. She turned back to Clarence. "Another pipe break?"

Clarence raised his chin in the direction of the bar. Vic sat at the near end on the only righted stool, a cigarette between his knuckles, a glass of something at his elbow. From the back of the floor, Maureen heard a sob. Tanya sat at a small table, hard to see through the thicket of chair legs. Her head lay on her crossed arms, her black hair spread across the table, her shoulders shook. Maureen looked at Clarence, then Vic, who seemed to have only now noticed her arrival. He waved Maureen over to the bar. She didn't have the nerve to ask out loud but the question roared in her head. Dennis. Where was Dennis? What had he done?

5

Vic brought a stool down off the bar for Maureen and set it close to his. She sat, hooking her feet over the bottom rung. Her right foot bounced like mad.

"Sorry you had to come down here," Vic said. He nudged his ashtray at her. "Smoke 'em if you got 'em."

Maureen fished her pack from her purse, drew out a smoke, and tossed the pack on the bar. Vic picked it up and stared at the label for a long while, as if it held some code he needed to break. Then he dropped the pack and took several long swallows of his drink: vodka neat; Maureen could smell it. Vic settled his glass on the bar. Dipping his head, he reached for the short black and silver ponytail at his neck, playing his fingers through it, stroking it. Maureen thought she might burst if he didn't speak.

"Boss?" Maureen whispered. "Vic? What's going on?"

"You want a drink." It wasn't a question.

"I'm fine."

Vic looked over her shoulder at Clarence sitting on the steps. "C, get Maureen a drink. Please." Vic looked at her. "Whiskey, right? The Irish? Catholic or Protestant, I can never remember."

The thought of whiskey turned her stomach. "God, no. Forget it, Vic. I'm fine."

But she got down off the bar stool. She held up a hand to Clarence. The big man returned to the stairs and his seat there, folding up his long, powerful arms and legs.

Behind the bar, Maureen made a weak Stoli and grapefruit. She replaced the bottle on the rack and leaned her elbows on the bar. She felt more comfortable with the bar between her and Vic, as if the long plank of wood could buffer what she was about to hear. The news has to be bad, she thought, like jail or hospital bad. She leaned down on her elbows, getting closer to Vic. "Boss?"

Vic sat motionless, transfixed by the burning tip of his cigarette. "Maureen, I hate to have to tell you this, but Dennis is dead."

Maureen stepped back from the bar, all the air kicked out of her chest. She held her hands in the air as if Vic had pulled a pistol on her. She'd known something was wrong the moment she'd seen Clarence at the door, but Dennis dead?

"What. The. Fuck."

What had that boy been into? How had she missed it before last night? Black stains oozed across the back of Maureen's mind. Shame. Guilt. Fear. What had happened here after she'd gotten in the cab? Had she made a terrible mistake leaving him alone?

Was she about to be accused of something awful?

Clarence appeared at the end of the bar, arms at his sides, palms turned in her direction. Offering an embrace. Or cutting off her escape. Seeing Clarence blocking her path to the door, Maureen wanted to run. But she needed to know what, if anything, these people knew about what she had seen. She eased by Clarence, her hip bumping his iron thigh, and returned to her seat.

"I'm kinda blown away here. Christ, Vic. What happened?"

Vic brought his eyes to Maureen's. "The train. He was lyin' on the tracks, passed out, I guess. No one knew he was there till after the train hit him. Dennis probably never felt a thing. Didn't seem like he tried to get out of the way. Happened right down the end of the street."

"That doesn't make any sense," Maureen said. "From the end of this street, there's no station for five blocks either way. How could he climb the fence if he was ready to pass out?"

"That fence is torn to pieces. You wouldn't have to climb it." Vic rolled his thumb over his bottom lip, stared down into his drink. "The cops, they seem to think the accident maybe wasn't entirely accidental, on Dennis's part."

"Suicide?"

Vic nodded. "In so many words, yeah. The cop in charge said they see it pretty often, mostly in the other boroughs but it happens here, too."

"That's just . . . I don't know," Maureen said. "Wow."

"Dennis seem funny to you last night?" Vic asked. "Like off or something?"

Maureen looked down into her drink. If she was going to tell the truth about last night, now was the time. But what good would that do? Who'd believe her? She wouldn't believe the story if she hadn't seen it herself. Could she trust these people? Vic had comped the hall upstairs for the fund-raiser. He knew Sebastian. She thought of Sebastian's warning to keep quiet. He didn't need to hear she was talking. And what about Dennis? Maybe he *had* killed himself to keep his secret. What right did she have to expose him now?

A highlight reel of jokes, stories, arguments, and minor flirtations with Dennis played across Maureen's mind, calling tears to her eyes. She wanted to do the right thing. She owed Dennis that much. Were she a cop, she'd want to know about Dennis and Sebastian's shared secret. But she wasn't a cop; she was a waitress. A young woman working nights and living alone. She had to protect herself. Keeping her mouth shut was her best defense. If the cops called the death suspicious, that would change things and she'd talk. But until then it was best everyone's secrets got kept.

"He seemed like himself," she said. "Same as he ever was."

"That's what everyone who worked last night told me," Vic said. He was staring hard at her now, into her. "But you saw him last, after the show was over, so to speak." He waved his hand over the empty room. "When we're open, everybody's got their game face on. I thought—you know—you might've seen something different *after*."

Maureen felt waves of panic rise in her gut. *After the show was over.* What did Vic know? Was he being obscure for Clarence's sake? Or Tanya's? Was he telling her it was okay to talk, no matter what Sebastian had told her? Or am I hearing everything wrong, she thought, because I've got a dirty conscience? She needed to remember when she had punched out, or if she had punched out.

Did Vic have proof that she was the last person to see Dennis?

Vic used security cameras for the registers and the safe in the office. No cameras monitored the public side of the bar, a deference Vic granted the minor mobsters frequenting his place. Vic probably never even watched the tapes; that would've been Dennis's job. And no way Dennis would've left the cameras running last night, not the bar cameras. Not if he was turning tricks in the barroom; that was guaranteed.

But the office camera might've caught her going into the office and coming out much later. Maureen recalled her sad attempt at masturbation. For chrissakes, how does one night slipping through my fingers manage to blow up my whole life? I gotta get my mind right. I gotta get the hell outta this basement.

"I don't know what to say," Maureen said. "Dennis seemed normal last night. I knew him, but it's not like we exchanged inner secrets or anything."

"For a while, at least," Vic said, "the cops are gonna stay involved. You might get a call. These things are complicated, apparently. Before they can officially say suicide, they have to be sure."

"Okay, whatever," Maureen said. "I'm available." No big deal, she told herself. You can't help Dennis. Make sure you help yourself. You can't always do the right thing. Sometimes you gotta do the smart thing.

Vic reached out and Maureen flinched, pulling back. He set his hand on the bar without touching her. "We're gonna be closed for the next couple days. It doesn't seem right, to go on like nothin' happened— 'cause it did. I know you got bills, I'm telling everyone, so if you need cash call me up and we'll work something out."

"Thanks, Vic, for the offer," Maureen said. "Whenever you need me back, I'll be here." Stuffing her cigarettes in her purse, Maureen got up from the stool, saying a prayer of gratitude that her legs held her. Now they had to get her to the bus stop. "Right now, I gotta go." She turned, willing herself to walk and not run for the door.

If I can help it, she thought, I am never coming back here again.

Heading up the stairs, Maureen suddenly felt guilty for leaving. As part of the staff, part of the crew, she felt a tug to stay with Vic, Clarence, and Tanya. Especially Tanya, who looked totally wrecked and could probably use some sisterly companionship. With Dennis dead, Maureen didn't know who else the girl had looking out for her. But the need to escape quickly beat Maureen's guilt into submission. You're flattering yourself, she thought. These people don't need you. You work with them, spend more time with them than anyone else in your life, but they're not your friends. Not even Tanya. You tried, both of you, but you never got there. Too many doubles, too many pills, too many parties.

When Maureen got to the door she put her shoulder to it and pushed her way outside, already feeling better to be standing on the sidewalk as the door closed behind her. She jogged for the corner as a train hurtled past the end of Dock Street.

Maureen let three buses come and go. Every time she felt calm enough to go home and lie down, or make something to eat, or pack up some clothes for the Laundromat, anything to help her feel normal—every time one of those things felt like a good idea, another train rattled down the tracks behind her, and the sound of the wheels on the rails shook her brain to pieces. Pieces like what was left of Dennis.

Dennis's death, everything about it, was too big, too fucked up. She was out of her mind to think she could go home like nothing had happened. Every dark car driving by reminded Maureen of Sebastian's black Crown Vic. If she had any say in the matter, she'd never set eyes on that man again. She hoped he won his stupid election. Get him off the island and up to Albany. Whatever weirdness Dennis had gotten into, with him or anyone else, had already come too close to touching her. She wasn't about to give anyone a second chance to put a hand on her.

After watching another bus drive away, Maureen dug into her purse for her cigarettes. Maybe she'd sit on the bench for a while. Without work, she had fuck-all else to do. She found the pack, but where was the lighter? Digging deeper, she found a sealed bank envelope. Without taking it out of her bag, she opened the flap. Her tip money from last night's shift. Dennis had slipped it in there while she was passed out, even cashing in her small bills, all those singles and fives, for big ones. The tears didn't just rise this time, they exploded from her eyes.

She started walking up Bay Street, her head down so no one could see her crying. She was terrified that if someone stopped her and asked her what was wrong, she'd tell them the whole story. Even the part about her fear that Dennis had died because of what she had seen, because of her mistakes. Was this what it felt like, she wondered, to kill someone? Was the man driving the train at that very same moment thinking the very same thing she was thinking? Was he thinking, like she was, that somebody died because the night was long and I was tired and I couldn't hit the brakes in time?

6

Maureen trudged the cold mile from the Narrows to Cargo with her chin tucked against her collarbone. The smoggy bustle of Bay Street traffic rattled by on her left, passing cars swirling paper napkins and potato-chip bags around her ankles. On her right, the humpbacked, bruise-colored bay stretched wide from the black pilings of the Staten Island piers to the feet of Manhattan's silver towers. As the sky darkened, she considered hailing a cab. A couple of drivers even slowed for her. But as the cabbies tapped their horns to catch her attention and leaned across their seats for a better look at her, Maureen grew suspicious. What were they gawking at, anyway? Her bulky peacoat distorted her shape and the upturned collar hid her face except for her eyes—two reasons why she loved that coat. Even after her teeth had started chattering, getting in a car with a stranger failed to sound like a good idea.

She couldn't count how many times she'd caught cabs home from work or the diner while drunk, high, and vulnerable. Yet she'd always made it home intact. She'd never had a problem. But that thought, instead of convincing her to accept a ride, only made her feel foolish and naïve, lucky to have avoided getting hurt. This did not seem the time to push her luck.

By the time she reached Cargo, full dark had settled. Well-lit, the place stood out against the stone-faced public buildings and weathered two-stories surrounding it. Yet again, the bar's owners, two painters, had redone the exterior. For the past several months, the boxy building had been taxicab yellow with black and white checkerboard trim. The new design featured giant tropical fish swimming on a Caribbean-blue background. Clever, Maureen thought.

The bar, its street side almost all window, did resemble an aquarium in reverse. A people tank is what it looked like. A giant cube of air sitting on the floor of a reef somewhere warm, surrounded by giant fish peering in at the small, strange creatures contained within. She expected the lemony angelfish to tap a fin on the glass, scattering the patrons inside under the tables and into the corners.

What a difference, she thought, reaching for the door, between the fake warm-water paradise depicted on the exterior of the bar and the frigid bay swelling up against the seawall right across the street. No pilings, no piers, no angelfish or purple coral there. Just the drop-off straight down into the dark.

Inside Cargo, a light crowd loitered, Saturday evening having not yet morphed into full-on Saturday night. Small groups of guys, pint glasses in hand, stood around at the bar. Their eyes settled on Maureen as she came in. She turned down her collar and pulled her hair out from under her coat, letting it fall down her back. If they're going to stare, may as well give them something to gawk at. But she kept her coat buttoned, self-conscious about being out in her battered and stained waitress black. Cargo was a lot brighter inside than the Narrows. Rough edges were hard to hide. From the corner of her eye, Maureen watched the blank male faces rotate back to a basketball game on the TVs behind the bar. She hadn't put on enough of a show.

She took a seat at the bar, four stools away from anyone, and ordered a Bass draft. As she drank, Maureen watched the two bartenders, one male and one female, with envy. Had she stayed at Cargo, she'd be bartending by now. Only women worked the floor but it was about fifty-fifty behind the bar, a pretty good ratio, actually. Vic had made her vague promises when he hired her. John had even called over and put in a good word. But Vic was old-fashioned, Tanya told her after a couple of months, and wanted only men behind the bar. The Narrows had never had a female bartender and never would. *Old-fashioned?* Maureen had said. *Sounds sexist to me and possibly illegal.* Tanya had only smiled at that. *So sue him*, she'd said, *and see what it gets you.*

Of course, Maureen had never confronted Vic, preferring instead the softer route of batting her eyelashes and cocking a hip at Dennis when bartending shifts opened up. She'd tried it only twice, ashamed of herself both times, giving up after realizing that she was neither the first nor the prettiest waitress to try that angle. Nor was she offering anything worthwhile, like her body, in exchange for the promotion. Not that Dennis was like that; he had never even hinted that getting on her back or on her knees would get her off the floor and behind the bar. She took several long swallows of her Bass. Dennis wasn't like anything now. All he was now was dead.

The female bartender, a petite pretty brunette a good five years younger and sporting fake tits three cup sizes bigger than Maureen's, grabbed up the pint glass and whisked it away for a refill. An impressive boob job, Maureen had to admit. The girl had stopped short of overdoing it, showing restraint many women didn't have. Maureen did think the girl's top stuck too tight to her shape. It was a wonder she could breathe. But then Maureen smiled to herself. Hypocrite. If you had that chest, you'd be wearing shirts just like hers—at least at work. Maureen peered down into her coat. Maybe she was better off on the floor; her legs and rear end were her moneymakers, not her chest. Her best features would be wasted behind the bar. And all things considered, she thought, she'd rather have the cash in hand than be wearing it around on her chest. When the bartender returned with her beer, she caught Maureen looking.

"Whadda think?" the bartender said, turning to give Maureen a profile. "Not bad, huh?"

"That's good work."

The bartender cupped her breasts from underneath, staring down at them. "They're still sore." She looked at Maureen, frowning. "Should I have gone bigger?"

"No, you got it just right," Maureen said. "A lot of thin girls like you, they overdo it. End up looking kind of—you know—obvious. And kinda freakish, to tell you the truth."

"Well, thanks," the bartender said. "I don't even ask the guys. They're useless. They always think bigger is better."

"They do," Maureen said. "And they always want us to think small is bigger than it really is."

The bartender laughed. "Amen to that. Maybe I'll try that with my boyfriend next time: 'It's okay, but can you go another size up?'" She laughed again, extending her hand. "I'm Tracy."

Maureen shook her hand. "Maureen. Nice to meet you. I used to work here." She leaned forward on her bar stool. "Is John working tonight?"

Tracy jerked her thumb over her shoulder. "He's in the back. I'll get him for you." She was gone before Maureen could protest.

During her walk to Cargo, Maureen had debated how to approach John, the closest thing she had to a friend right then. She remembered from working for him that he was fierce about his own privacy. He'd probably extend her the same courtesy and not ask too many questions. She needed to think out loud, to figure out what to expect next, if anything, from Sebastian, maybe from the cops, but she didn't want to give away any secrets. She wanted to stay out of the story as much as possible.

Tracy reappeared. "He'll be right out." She winked at Maureen. "And he said your drinks are on the house."

Maureen thanked her, immediately forgiving the dirty insinuation in Tracy's wink. That's the downside of being private, Maureen thought. People fill in the blanks however they want. After Tracy had walked away, Maureen slid a ten to the far side of the bar and settled in to wait, growing warm inside her coat. She felt small and hard to see, hunched over her glass and wrapped in her big coat, so she sat taller on her bar stool.

Moments later John emerged from the dark back hallway and into the light of the barroom, frowning at a clipboard, cigarette tucked behind his ear. The puzzled look on his face reminded Maureen of Vic's expression as he had studied her cigarette pack, but the resemblance to Vic ended there. John's fair Irish face had healthy color. His body was flat and hard where Vic's had gone soft. And while Vic sported a ponytail that grew grayer by the day, John had cut his hair so short that the blond close to his scalp was almost brown. And he wore glasses now, with thin copper frames that made him look as if he belonged at a lecture hall podium instead of in a bar. She thought of Jimmy the teacher. He and John were friends. Thank God, Jimmy had bailed early in the set last night, before Maureen had tipped totally over the edge.

Maureen smiled when John looked up from the clipboard. He was a handsome man. She pushed the tip of her tongue against her teeth. One of these days, I gotta get me one of those. A man like Molly had. Like Rose had. John looked, Maureen realized, more than handsome. Maureen saw a lot of good-looking men. Saw them every night. What John looked was happy. *That* was rare.

After thousands of nights reading people for a living, of judging what they really wanted—a better life—and seeing what they'd let themselves accept—a good time—Maureen had learned to spot the happy ones right away, those precious few who moved with ease and confidence, like well-fed lions on the plains and not like twitchy cats on a railing stalking a quick kill. Looking at John, Maureen felt something turn over in her stomach. Lust? The skin at her collarbone ignited; she touched her damp fingertips to it. No, not lust, one of the other six: envy.

John tucked the clipboard behind a register and from a cabinet under the bar grabbed a black leather coat. He came around to her side of the bar. "Hey, Maureen." She tilted her head and let him kiss her cheek. "How ya been?"

Suddenly she was choking on tears. John noticed. He slid his smoke from behind his ear. "Let's step outside."

Maureen bolted for the door.

Outside, the cold hit her hard, whisking the heat from her skin and the water from her eyes. This close to the harbor, the frigid air felt thick and smelled of salt. It felt good going down as she inhaled it through her nose. She strode across Bay Street and skipped up onto the wide brick sidewalk opposite Cargo. Keeping her back to the bar, she shoved her hands deep into the pockets of her peacoat and pressed her stomach hard against the metal railing that ran the length of the promenade, guarding the drop-off down to the water. Behind her, she heard John's boots on the pavement as he crossed the street, his pace relaxed and casual. She heard the ring of his Zippo as he paused on the sidewalk to light his smoke. With a long exhale, he settled in beside her at the railing.

They stood silent awhile, smoking beneath a thin, sickly maple tree, its bony branches clacking overhead in the cold breeze off the water. The maple was young, one of a matching underdeveloped dozen, Maureen saw, running along the winding promenade to the marble-columned Borough Hall at the end of Bay Street. Each tree had floodlights in its roots, pointed up at its branches. But, she noticed, at best only half the lights worked, throwing fractured, haphazard shadows up and down the promenade and over the Borough Hall steps like ink stains. The whole setup probably looked a lot better, pretty even, in the spring and summer, when there was color and life to balance out the vandalism. She couldn't remember ever noticing the trees before. Maybe they were new. Either way, the beautification project hadn't reached her end of Bay Street. She hoped the maples lived through the winter.

She turned and stared with John across the black water at the carnival lights of Manhattan to their left. Out there somewhere, lost at night against the sparkling backdrop of New Jersey, stood the Statue of Liberty. You could see her from the ferry, Maureen knew, even at night, but not from the island.

Maureen pulled her hands from her pockets and laid them on the cold metal rail. She studied the cracked skin and red knuckles of her fingers. She looked up at the stars through the tree's bare branches, crooked like black lightning against the night sky. Beside her, John's leather coat creaked at the elbows as he moved his cigarette to his lips. His coat was so worn out that the leather looked as if it might drop in pieces to the street if he moved too fast. What would John do if she went to pieces at his feet? His jacket, she thought, looks like I feel: faded, cracked, abused, loose at the seams. But the jacket worked, the leather held together, even if it groaned when pulled tight and tested. Maureen figured she could hold together, too. Her knuckles aching from the cold, she fished a cigarette from her purse again. She leaned close to John as he lit it for her. On his skin, he carried the scent, if not the warmth, of Cargo's overworked heater.

"I like the glasses," Maureen said.

"These?" He took his glasses off, tucked them inside his jacket. "New addition. I was standing at center bar one night and realized I couldn't read the score on any of the TVs. Plus filling out the schedules, the goddamn inventory sheets." He shrugged. "You can only fight it for so long."

Maureen looked down at her shoe tops, kicking the toe of one foot against the railing, making the metal hum. "You heard about Dennis."

"Fucking unbelievable. Had a couple of cops in for lunch talking about it."

"Bad news travels fast."

"Especially on Bay Street," John said. "We're a tiny colony on a small island." He raised his chin at Manhattan. "Not like over there."

"You heard how it happened?"

"Train got him." John blew out a long cloud of smoke that drifted away over the water. "Fucking idiot." He crossed himself. "God rest his soul. I always liked him. One of the few class acts left around here."

Maureen pinched her nose, willing the picture of Dennis on his knees from her mind. Pictures of him exploded on the tracks replaced it. Goddamn. Was that how she'd remember him? No. She wouldn't let that happen. The ugly pictures would fade. She'd just found out about his death. Things would change.

"You know where he was, right?" she asked. "On the tracks by the Narrows. Cops are calling it suicide. That's what Vic told me."

"It happens," John said. "Rough way to go, but he's not the first to try it that way and succeed. You see it in the papers. Though the cops told me most people do it at a station, jump in front as the train pulls in. Hell of a thing to do to everyone else just trying to get home for dinner, never mind the poor SOB driving the train."

"There's no station near the Narrows," Maureen said.

"He wanted privacy," John said, "or he didn't want someone getting hurt trying to stop him. Not everybody wants to be a public spectacle."

Maureen straightened as tall as she could. She took a deep breath. "I'm having a hard time with it."

"Who wouldn't?" John said. "I don't blame you. Death close to home is tough."

"It's more than that."

John's eyes narrowed. "You sleeping with him?"

"No," Maureen said. "God, why does it always come back to that? We're not all banging our brains out." She scratched at her scalp with both hands. "I kind of blame myself for what happened, maybe a little bit."

"How? Maureen, that's ridiculous."

"I worked with him last night."

John lobbed his cigarette high, sending it arcing into the water. "And so you could've stopped him? Should've seen something that gave away his plans? You should've done what, read his mind?"

"I didn't see anything," Maureen said. "I didn't."

"And that's no crime," John said. "I bet a lot of people are feeling exactly what you are right now, wondering how they let him get away from them. You can't blame yourself for this. It's not your fault. It's not anyone's fault. People keep secrets. Dennis had his, like the rest of us."

"I know, I know," Maureen said, turning away.

Of course John would say she wasn't to blame. Any reasonable person would tell her that. Any rational person who didn't know what she'd seen. Should she tell John about that? No. Why put this on him? There was no guarantee that what she'd seen had anything to do with Dennis's death. Besides, even with what he didn't know, John was right. What happened to Dennis, the train and everything he was involved in that came before it, wasn't her fault and it was none of her business.

"I shouldn't feel guilty, but I do," Maureen said. "It'll go away, I guess." And when would that happen? "But there's more to it. The cops. Vic said they'll do an investigation."

"Ah, I see," John said, glancing over at Cargo. "The police." He frowned at the bar as if it might bolt for the harbor and make a break for it if he wasn't careful. He watched the place like he'd watch a dog of questionable obedience let off the leash. "Maureen, what are you really worried about?"

"You think the cops will wanna talk to me? Since I saw Dennis last. Maybe. Probably."

"I'm not a cop," John said, "so I don't know." He looked at her. "You'll find out, though. If they want to talk to you, they'll come knocking. Trust me on that."

"If that happens," Maureen said, "what do I tell them?"

"The truth," John said. "What've you got to worry about? You weren't even around when he did it, were you?"

"No."

"Were you?"

"No, no. Of course not."

"Dennis didn't say anything to you," John said, "or anyone else that you know of about killing himself?"

"Like I said, I had no idea."

"Then what are you worried about?"

"Nothing, I guess," Maureen said. "Cops make me nervous."

"So you're using me for practice?" John lowered his eyes, studied the sidewalk. "You're hiding something and doing a poor job of it. And I'm no suspicious cop asking questions." He raised his eyes to her face. "If you want my help, you have to tell me what's really going on here."

Well, it's only fair, Maureen thought. If she wanted help figuring things out, she had to give up something. Did it have to be the truth? Maureen rocked back on her heels. The wind kept blowing her hair across her face, into her eyes. Maybe she could explain the situation in general, stay away from specifics.

"You've been in the business a long time," she said. "You know how it is after hours. It's late. Everyone's exhausted. There's booze around, maybe other stuff." She swept her hair from her face. "Things happen."

"What is it, then? Ecstasy? Coke? Don't tell me you went back to that shit. Don't even tell me you're dealing."

"It's not that," Maureen said. "It's Vic. It's the place I'm worried about." She took a deep breath. "There are things I know, about the bar, maybe about last night, that I don't wanna talk about." She paused. Had she gone too far? "For Vic's sake. I don't want to sell him out."

John nodded, thinking. "Don't worry. Vic's a smart man. And he's been in the business just short of forever. He knows what to keep under wraps. Tell the cops what you saw, which seems to be a whole lot of nothing. Anything Vic's got to hide is his problem, not yours. You got nothing to worry about."

"Right," Maureen said. "I got nothing to worry about. Other people's secrets are their problems." And mine are my own, she thought.

"Exactly," John said.

She looked up at John. Go figure. She'd given him nothing of substance in the conversation and in return had gotten nothing of value. And whose fault was that? I got nothing to worry about, she thought.

Right.

I'm only shaking because I'm cold.

7

Maureen anchored her end of the bar until closing time, alternating Bass and ice water in an effort to preserve her wits. Because of the registers and the bottle rack, she could see only the top of her head reflected in the bar mirror. Not having to sit there avoiding her own eyes made relaxing easier. She had to keep her cool if she wanted John to take her back on. She had to show she wasn't damaged goods. And she had to get herself home eventually; she couldn't move into Cargo. Being alone with everything had to happen.

She let John buy her dinner but insisted on paying for her drinks once she got through her third. She didn't want anyone, especially John, suspecting her of running a sympathy tab. Tracy stayed prompt with the refills no matter how busy she got but largely left Maureen alone with her thoughts, which was greatly appreciated. The young Jedi had a good sense of how to read her customers. Maureen was impressed. That was one spot behind the bar that wouldn't come open anytime soon.

Midnight passed before any of the guys tried sending Maureen a drink. As was her standard practice, she refused it. Tracy delivered the denial, handling the transaction with such disarming tact that no feelings got hurt. Either Tracy had admirable ego-preservation skills, Maureen thought, or the guy—pudgy, the thinning white-blond hair over his scalp set off by his pink Polo shirt—hadn't really wanted to buy her a drink at all and had used the offer as an excuse to talk up Tracy. No doubt Mr. Pink Polo had picked up on Tracy paying Maureen special attention. He'd probably built a whole set of fantasies around it.

Maureen didn't keep score of the quality and quantity of drink offers she got when she went out, but she was cognizant of the hour at which this particular one had arrived. Coming this late, the offer, had it really been for her, told Maureen that Mr. Pink Polo, sad sack that he was, viewed her as a second- or maybe even third-tier consideration. A hot resentment boiled up inside her. She wanted to walk over there and smack the guy's face. For a moment, she regretted not parting the fool and his money for the cheap price of a flirty smile and some small talk—two things that were practically reflex.

She glanced down the bar again and watched him tell Tracy a story, his head down so his eyes couldn't fixate on Tracy's chest. Give him a break, she thought. He's a regular guy out for a good time, trying to make headway with a pretty girl. Where's the sin? Mr. Pink and the rest of his shy but reliable herd paid Maureen's rent and bills with unerring consistency. Without Mr. Pink she'd be out of a job. She didn't want his drink, but she didn't have to be such a bitch about it.

Maureen lowered her eyes to the bar, her own words from earlier biting at her brain: *Bitter. You're a bitter old woman.* She sipped her beer and wondered if seven cats would be enough. And did it have to be cats? She hated cats.

After last call, Maureen headed out to the courtyard. She huddled under a heat lamp, chain-smoking cigarettes. She waited out there for over half an hour, staying out of the way of the cleanup and trying to raise enough nerve to ask John for a ride home. She wasn't blasted, but as she rehearsed the question, the many possible ways John could misunderstand her intentions got tangled in her mind. Such a simple, even logical, request. They lived in the same apartment building. She'd been drinking all night, and John knew she didn't have a car, knew she was stuck taking the bus or a cab. He had manners; he probably expected the question.

Of course, he also had Molly to think about.

Maureen found the idea that John might think she wanted to fuck him petrifying. She liked John a lot, but letting a man think, even a good man, that he had something you wanted made for bad dynamics. Still, something primal tapped at the base of her skull and reminded her that John was the nearest and safest attractive man.

What's giving me trouble, Maureen decided, is that sweaty, sheet-wrapped oblivion, an utterly mindless fuck, is exactly what I need right now. What she had to do was tamp down the cavewoman porn movies in her head when she asked for a ride. Ride? God, should she even use that word? If the question came out too breathy, or if she laid the emphasis on the wrong word, like *ride*, the misunderstanding could happen. She'd insult him and humiliate herself. And was it really sex she wanted or just a warm distraction from the shock and the grief? She watched John move around the yard, turning off the heaters one by one. He came over to Maureen's last.

"Sorry, Maureen," he said. He looked tired, like maybe he could use some affection himself. Where was Molly anyway? "But I gotta lock these up inside or they get boosted overnight."

"So," Maureen said, "you wanna take me home?" She forced a smile. Walk away, Maureen, she thought. Walk away, leave the bar, cross the street, hop the railing, and throw yourself in the ocean.

But John spared her. If he'd heard anything illicit in the question, he wasn't showing it. "No problem. I'm not outta here for another hour or so, but if you don't mind waiting, I'll drive you."

Maureen nearly melted with relief. She couldn't tell if it was the avoided embarrassment or the assurance of a safe trip home that did it to her, and she didn't much care. She held the door open as John wheeled the heater into the bar.

Not long after their arrival back at the apartment building, Maureen stood, shaking, with her palm pressed against John's front door. She hadn't knocked. Through the music playing in the apartment, she could hear John moving around. No voices. No sign of Molly. Maybe she was already asleep, her body warming the bed ahead of John's arrival. Maureen heard the squeak of metal taps, the drone of rushing water beating the floor of John's shower. Now she'd have to wait. She sat on the floor, her back against the wall, her knees drawn up to her chest and wrapped in her arms. Her eyes swept up and down the hall, searching, watching.

Earlier, when they'd reached the stairwell landing for her floor, Maureen had pinned John in place with a sudden rush of insipid small talk. Simple questions about Molly, mostly, to guard against giving out the wrong impression. Polite as he tried to be, John soon grew impatient with the conversation. It was late. He was tired. Regardless, she'd babbled on and on like a drunk who couldn't accept that the night was over and the bar was closed and nobody had to pretend to care anymore. She was stalling, dreading being in her apartment alone. She knew it, John knew it, and she couldn't shut herself up.

For a few brief moments, Maureen had searched for a delicate way of inviting John to her place or getting invited up to his. But a drunk and depressed single girl couldn't invite a man over at four in the morning and not give the wrong idea. Her own eyes crossing from boredom, Maureen finally thanked John for the ride home, gave his hand a squeeze, and headed, alone, down the hall to her apartment.

She never made it inside.

She found her front door ajar when she got to it, throwing her heartbeat into hysterics. She knew, knew, knew she had locked it. Saw herself turning the key as she left for work. Someone else had opened that door. No doubt. She reached out for the doorknob, her fingers hovering over it as if feeling for radiant heat.

She didn't live in the best neighborhood. The building had been robbed before, but never her place. Had her turn finally arrived? But building creeps came up the fire escapes and in the windows. They didn't use the front door. Paul, maybe, the landlord's kid? He was the de facto handyman. He had keys to the apartments. Had he tipped a few on a Saturday night and overloaded on liquid courage? Hard to believe, she thought. Schoolyard teasing was one thing, staking out her apartment was another. No, it wasn't Paul.

She unzipped her bag and searched its insides for her switchblade. She found it, drew it out, and flicked it open, the *snick* loud in the hall. Her palms started sweating. Her heart was a big bird in a small cage. She listened hard for any sound from inside her place: breathing, shuffling feet, street noise that signaled an open window. She heard nothing. She stayed in the doorway. The other side of it—that was *her* space. Hers.

Standing there, she realized that the night after she'd pissed off that creep Sebastian, the same night her manager had died, her home had been broken into for the first time. Coincidence? Maureen peered into the sliver of darkness between the door and the jamb, thought about stepping inside the apartment and hitting the lights. If he was in there alone, she might be quick enough to take him, or at least escape. But if he wasn't alone, she wouldn't have a prayer. Her apartment could be empty. A simple explanation for her open door might exist. For the life of her, though, she couldn't imagine what that explanation could be.

Stepping softly, she backed away from the door and headed upstairs to John's apartment.

John answered Maureen's weak knocks wearing sweats and a Mötley Crüe T-shirt, one skeptical eyebrow arched high on his forehead. When she'd announced her name through the door, he hadn't said a word, waiting a long moment before unlocking it. He stepped into the doorway instead of backing up to let her in, a clear signal her visit was not welcome. She swallowed her embarrassment and willed herself to look him in the face.

"John, somebody broke into my apartment. My door was open."

"Goddamn." John stepped back into his living room, making room for her to enter. "Come in."

As the locks clicked into place behind her, Maureen felt her back muscles unwind. She followed John to the couch.

"Have a seat," he said.

Maureen sat dead center on the couch, hands in her lap, while John retrieved his cigarettes from the bedroom. She made herself small, trying to minimize contact not only with his furniture but even with the air in his apartment. She felt like a contaminant, like something tracked into the apartment on a shoe.

"Drink?" John asked, passing through the living room, smoke dangling from the corner of his mouth. She nodded.

John returned from the kitchen with a short whiskey for each of them, neat, both glasses in one hand, his cordless phone in the other. The police. He expected her to call the cops. Of course he did. Who wouldn't? He set her drink and the phone on the coffee table in front of her.

Maureen took her drink in both hands but left the phone where it was. The whiskey went down easier than she expected. John tossed his cigarettes on the coffee table, waving his hand for her to take one or pick up the phone. She took a cigarette. John leaned over the table to light it for her. She wished he would sit. Maybe not right next to her, but close.

"What'd they take?" he asked.

"I don't know. I didn't look. I didn't even go in. I just . . ." She looked away from him, into his bedroom. A maroon skirt lay draped over the bottom corner of his bed. She shouldn't be there. "I was scared. I just wanted to hide."

"You did the right thing. A single girl living alone? Somebody could've been waiting for you."

She turned back to him. Thanks, she thought. Thanks for reminding me what an easy target I am. Guilt bloomed in her chest and she slumped, elbows on her knees. Ease up. The guy was trying to help, to show some support.

John picked up the phone, offered it to her. "Call the cops. I'll wait up with you till they get here."

Maureen leaned back on the couch. "I don't wanna bother with the cops. They'll keep us waiting for two hours so they can fill out forms and tell me they'll get back to me." She swept her hair from her face. "I thought maybe you could come downstairs with me?" She stopped. And do what? Be my guard dog? Sad. Even to herself she sounded like a woman spooling out a pathetic come-on: *Please protect me, you big strong man*. She forced a weak laugh. "You know what? Never mind. It's practically dawn. Who's gonna wait around all night for me to get home?"

"You wanna take that chance? What if he comes back?" John narrowed his eyes at her. "Your gut said *split*. Why question it now?"

Maureen set her drink on the coffee table and stood. "Look, I shouldn't have even come up here. I got frightened for a minute. I panicked. Forget it. I'll go home and count my losses."

She meant to head for the door, but her feet wouldn't move. Brave came easy while safe in John's apartment. But even if she got herself out his door, she'd never get through her own. John tossed the phone on the couch.

"You're a wreck," he said. He stepped between her and his door. First he wouldn't let her in, now he wasn't letting her out. "You hang around the bar all night giving me the eye. Now you show up at my door spinning some crap about a break-in. This shit ain't your style. Spill."

No, she thought, it's not my style. Not at all.

"John," she said, "I think I'm in a lot of trouble."

8

Once she started talking, Maureen couldn't stop. She told John about the previous night and that afternoon, starting with surprising Sebastian and Dennis after hours and ending with her bailing in front of everyone at the Narrows. Except for the cocaine, she included every embarrassing detail. John listened, sitting on the arm of the couch. He smoked one cigarette after another, staring out the window across the room, sipping his drink between drags.

Finally getting the story out, Maureen felt the same airy relief that followed throwing up after a long battle with the spins, like her gut was clean and empty and not spilling over with hot soup. She also felt as if she'd made a terrible mess on someone else's floor, a mess she couldn't clean up on her own.

"So what do you want from me?" John asked.

Maureen wasn't sure how to answer that; she hadn't thought that far ahead. He had listened; that was a start. "I don't expect you to get involved, but I don't know what to do. Now that Dennis is dead, there's no proof that anything I told you really happened. Sebastian's already angry. I can't have him finding out I'm talking to the cops, but I can't help feeling I stepped in some bad shit when I walked out of that office and that maybe I'm still standing in it."

John walked across the living room toward the window. What if, Maureen worried, someone hid outside, watching her apartment? Would they see her place was dark and know she hadn't gone in? Could they see her through John's window? Maybe John thought the same thing and was heading over to the window to draw the shade. But instead of the window, John approached a framed photograph on the wall beside it. He stared into the picture for a long time. Long enough that Maureen feared he was waiting for her to leave or had forgotten she was even there.

"My father's college football team," John finally said.

"I heard about what happened to him," Maureen said, "when I came to work at Cargo."

"Yeah, everybody gets that story. I should put it in the training manual. At least then it would get told right."

"Did they ever catch who did it?"

"Depends on who you mean by *they*." He tapped the glass over the picture with his finger. "Listen, Maureen. I know a guy who might be able to help you." He turned to her. "But he's a cop, and you have to tell him the truth. No games. That's the best offer I can make."

"Do you trust him?" Maureen asked.

"Absolutely."

"Okay," she said, nodding. "I'll talk to him."

"I'll call him in a couple hours," John said. "When the real world wakes up." He walked into the bedroom.

Maureen listened as John rooted around in his closet. Was she dismissed for the night? Was he getting ready for bed? She stood, looked at the apartment door, sat back down, stood again. She'd almost worked up the nerve to ask him for instructions when John returned to the living room carrying towels, a blanket, and pillows. He set everything on the couch beside her.

"Take your coat off, for chrissakes," he said. He held out his hand. "Gimme your keys."

Maureen fished her keys from her coat pocket and handed them over. She peeled off her peacoat. Hands between her knees, she stared up at John, looking, she knew, like a goofy friggin' puppy.

"Take a hot shower," he said. "Try to relax. I left some of Molly's things on the bed for you to sleep in. Pick whatever you want." He held up her keys. "I'm not going in, but I'll lock up your place." Now he went to the window and pulled the shade over the muted blue glow bleeding into the black sky. "Spend the rest of the night here. The couch is lumpy, but it's the best I can offer."

"Thanks. Thanks a lot. I mean it." Maureen reached over and touched one of the pillows. The cool, smooth cotton made her so sleepy she didn't think she could get her shoes off, never mind shower and change. Her pride resurfaced, forcing her to protest against John's hospitality. "Maybe this is a bad idea. What's Molly gonna think? I don't want to get you in trouble. I'm a woman. Believe me, she'll know I spent the night."

"Don't worry about Molly," John said. "If she found out I sent you home alone after what you told me tonight, she'd strangle me in the street." He held out his hands to Maureen. She slipped hers into them and John pulled her to her feet. "Now hit the showers."

Mid-morning, standing on the front stoop of the apartment house, Maureen spat a mouthful of coffee down the front of her coat when a dark Crown Vic turned the corner. Drop the mug and run for it, she thought. Even in this neighborhood, someone will notice a woman in full, terrified flight, at least during the day. They might even do something about it. But as the car slid up to the curb Maureen's brain argued down her adrenaline, ticking off crucial details to hold her in place. The car was dark green, not black, and it was filthy, neglected. Sebastian's car had gleamed in the streetlights. Most important, Maureen could see the driver, who was a very large man but not Sebastian. Had to be John's cop.

Maureen smeared the spilled liquid into her coat and sipped from her mug as the driver hauled his bulk out of the car. Over a wide spread of belly, he clutched his long wool coat closed in one gloved fist, holding a paper coffee cup in the other. The few surviving wisps of white hair on the top of his head blew straight up in the wind. Along the sides, his hair was a blend of dull, dirty grays. Like a seagull's wings, Maureen thought. Like the heavy clouds rolling overhead. The man caught her eyes and grinned, his cheeks bunching beneath wet, sad eyes.

He was slow coming up the steps, as if his back or his knees protested the effort.

Maureen had sympathy pains. She knew those aches. But she couldn't help feeling disappointed. This broken-down old man was the white knight John had promised? She corrected herself. John hadn't promised a white knight; he'd promised a cop.

The cop extended his hand as he stepped onto the porch, his coat flapping open in the wind. "I'm Detective Nat Waters."

Maureen watched her hand disappear into his. "Maureen Coughlin. Nice to meet you. Thanks for coming."

"Don't thank me yet."

John pushed through the front door. He glanced at Maureen, extended his hand to Waters. "Sheriff. Surprised to be back around these parts?"

"Surprised it took this long, Junior," Waters said. "Knowin' you."

"Always one for the warm and fucking fuzzies, I see," John said, looking over Waters's shoulder at the car. "Where's your other half? Couldn't get him out of bed this early on a Sunday?"

"Purvis?" Waters asked. "Haven't you heard? He left the department, took a job at the borough president's office."

"You're shitting me."

"Purvis seems to think he's got a bright future in politics," Waters said. "I'm flying solo these days. Suits me better."

"Five years," John said. "Five years before he's making a perp walk on the evening news."

"I got three in the office pool," Waters said. "Let's go inside, out of the cold."

John pulled open the door, bowed to Waters and Maureen like a butler.

"Junior?" Maureen asked, passing through the doorway.

"Long story," John said. "Nobody calls me that anymore."

Maureen let the men precede her up the stairs, listening as they talked about John's sister, Julia, and her budding art career. Two of her paintings hung in Cargo. Haunted and abstract, the paintings gave Maureen the creeps—after hours, at least, when the shadows hit them right. The owners loved Julia's work, though. That's what happens, Maureen thought, when you let artists own a bar. Yeah, as opposed to who, Vic? The Narrows, it seemed to Maureen, collected plenty of its own creeps.

At the landing for Maureen's floor, John took his leave and headed upstairs to his own apartment, where Molly waited.

Molly had arrived early that morning, letting herself into John's place. Maureen had been awake for a while, but she'd stayed curled up on the couch, feeling too warm and heavy to move. When she'd heard the key in the door, though, she cursed herself for not heading home. John had told her not to worry, but as the door opened Maureen wanted to yank the blanket over her head and hide from Molly. She'd drawn her covers to her chin, watching John's girlfriend with wide and fearful eyes, as if Molly were a monster emerging from a closet.

Despite the late-November cold, Molly didn't wear a coat. A long, thick Aran sweater curled over the thighs of her tight brown cords. She pulled off her knit hat, stuffed her gloves inside it, and dropped the hat on the end table by the door along with her keys. Molly shook out her cascades of hair, deep, dark brown with shades of red. Like a Coke loaded with grenadine, Maureen thought, held up to the light.

Molly came right to the couch, settling on the arm at Maureen's feet. "I'm Molly. I think we met at Cargo once or twice. You probably don't remember me."

Maureen did remember. She stared at Molly's shimmering hair, falling in waves over the shoulders of her sweater. That's what you get, Maureen thought, when you don't live in a world of grease and smoke and no daylight. "I remember. You're a teacher." She sat up on the couch, folding her legs underneath her, arms and legs still covered by the blanket. "Thanks, you know. For this. Rough night last night."

"Yup. Let me wake the lazy bastard up," Molly said. "And he'll make us some coffee, if he knows what's good for him." She stood up and picked invisible lint off her right thigh. "And you're welcome." She looked right at Maureen. "Just, you know, don't make a habit of it."

Now, the coffee gone cold, Molly and John together upstairs, Maureen followed Waters to her front door. Fear tickled the edges of her bones. She recalled her dread at Molly's arrival. Waters waited at Maureen's front door, his huge hands jammed in his pockets. Maureen looked at him, remembering her panic when his car came around the corner. She recalled Sebastian's quiet, menacing laugh. She frowned as she pulled her keys from her coat. Is this how I'm gonna go through life now? Afraid of everyone and everything?

9

Maureen let Waters lead her into her apartment. He didn't ask her to wait outside, nor did he cross the threshold with one hand on his gun and the other thrust out behind him, commanding her to stay back, lest there be danger, like cops did on TV. Waters didn't seem cautious, just tired and slightly put out to be going through the motions, like a guy on a dinner date he didn't want to have in the first place. If someone had been waiting on her return, Maureen thought, Waters didn't expect they'd stuck around. Who could blame him? Was she really worth the effort? Even to her, the apartment so haunted with threat and menace the night before now sat bland and empty in the daylight.

After clicking on the lights, Maureen shuffled along behind Waters, embarrassed at the state of her place and struggling to remember the last time anyone but her had seen it. She watched as his round gray head turned one way and then the other to survey the living room. The only sound was the detective's heavy breathing. She told herself he was assessing the situation, that he was detecting and not just searching for a clean place to sit. Watching Waters, Maureen thought of Sebastian.

The two men stood about the same height and were about the same age, though Sebastian took better care of himself physically, used a better tailor and a better hairdresser. Well, Sebastian had a tailor and a hairdresser and maybe a personal trainer. Waters had a dusty closet lit by a bare bulb, carried a fifty-cent comb in his back pocket, and thought trainers were for boxers, dogs, and circus animals. Both were large men. But while Sebastian had what Maureen figured for a longtime gym rat's build, too large in the shoulders and arms for his waist and legs, Waters carried his weight evenly if not without effort, like he was made of wet cement spread over a steel frame. His skin was nearly that color. He moved like a man who had been born into the husky section at Sears and had carried a large weight his entire life.

Waters, in fact, reminded Maureen of a big bear. Not a circus bear or one caged in a zoo, but like she imagined a grizzly might look, rumbling along in the wild: unhurried and graceless, asssured of its power and its place at the pinnacle of the food chain. Sure Waters was a cop, so he had a badge and a gun, but those things didn't give him his power. His height, his weight, that's what mattered. The back like a billboard, the arms and legs thick as water pipes, the hands the size of dinner plates. The sheer overwhelming, intimidating maleness of him.

What must it be like, Maureen wondered, to be that size? To be that strong? To know you can show your back to every dark stairwell, doorway, and alley. To have people stare at their shoes and not at your tits when you caught them looking. For people to step aside and not "accidentally" brush up against you when they passed in close quarters. What's it like to be *that big* instead of five-four, a hundred pounds, and female? For one week, for one day, I wanna be that size. A *guy* that size.

Waters lifted his left arm and pointed to Maureen's TV, turning to look at her over his shoulder. The screen had been kicked in, fractured in a thousand places like thin ice. She pinched the bridge of her nose, squeezing her eyes shut tight. Her new little flat-screen, less than a month old, dead where it sat. A treat for herself, for her very rare days off. She had paid extra for the built-in DVD player.

Her three movies, *Aliens* and the first two *Terminators*, had been stomped to pieces.

"That's new," Maureen said. "The damage. Wasn't like that when I left last night."

"Anything else? You see anything missing?"

Maureen hadn't really been looking, forgetting that while she had her own ideas about who had hit her apartment, Waters's natural assumption was a random burglary. Other than the TV, nothing appeared out of order. The cheap Georgia O'Keeffe print in the drugstore frame hung crooked as always over the couch. Her secondhand couch slumped against the wall to her right, unwashed black stockings that probably stank of sweat and smoke tossed over the back. On the coffee table, overflowing ashtrays and cocktail-sticky glasses sat atop stacked, unread paperbacks. Against the far wall, beside the kitchen doorway, the small cabinet bar stood untouched, her half-empty bottles of Jameson, Stoli, and Bacardi standing their ground between the broken lava lamp and the four dusty martini glasses, a housewarming gift from her mother.

What a dump, Maureen thought. I'm such a friggin' slob.

What must this guy be thinking? Where's the cats, probably. That bastard Sebastian. The flat-screen was the only thing of value in the whole apartment, so he'd gone right for it. To be cruel.

Waters turned to face her, hands stuffed in his pants pockets. To Maureen's surprise, he was grinning. "You work a lot."

Maureen blinked at him, surprised at the comment. "I do. I'm a waitress."

"Where's that?"

"The Narrows, over on Bay Street," Maureen said. "Ever been?"

"I know the name. Can't say I've had the pleasure." Waters sighed. "Your place looks a lot like mine."

Maureen laughed. "How's your wife feel about that?"

Waters raised his left hand, turned the back of it to her. "I'm not married. Was once. Long time ago."

Duh. The wrinkled, ill-fitting clothes, the bad hair and sad eyes. Had he taken a seat at one of her tables, she'd have read him easy. She was off her game. Widower, she figured, if she had to guess. Divorce, unless it was really recent, you had to dig for. Death lingered like a stray dog. "Sorry. I'm not much of a detective."

"I should go into the bedroom with you," Waters said. "For a quick look. But naturally you can go through your things yourself."

Maureen hesitated. Why bother? No one had come to steal from her. Sebastian had delivered his quick *fuck you* and that was that. But she didn't want to tell Waters about that. Besides, he had come out on a cold Sunday morning for her; the least she could do was go through the motions, give him a show. With the Narrows shut down, she had nothing better to do. She led Waters to the bedroom.

He waited in the doorway as Maureen made a cursory sweep of her closet, her jewelry box, the drawers of her dresser, running her hand under the bras and over her perfume vials, over the envelope of cash tips. She gave Waters a shrug as she went to the bed.

"Doing what you do," Waters said, "I'd imagine you've got cash around. Your neighbors know you're a waitress?"

"Maybe. I don't really talk to them." She glanced at the nightstand beside her bed, caught herself, and looked back at Waters. "Doesn't matter. The money's where it should be."

She hadn't gone through the nightstand, figured Waters had noticed the omission. She wondered what he made of it. He probably thinks that's where I keep my coke stash. Good for him, let him think what he wants. Tissues, loose change, half a dozen ancient condoms, and a vibrator with fresh batteries, that's what was in that drawer.

And there was no chance on God's green earth of Waters seeing any of it.

"We can check the kitchen," Maureen said, "but I don't think there's much point."

"What *is* the point, Maureen?" Waters asked. "Why did you want to see me? Junior told me about the break-in, reason enough to be cautious, but you didn't call the police last night, when we might've caught someone waiting on you or in the area, maybe hitting other places. Junior told me you'd rather not talk to us at all. We've done our little dance. What's this really about?"

When she sat on the bed, Maureen felt something under the covers, something like a deck of playing cards or a handful of business cards that had been scattered under the comforter. She looked at Waters, confused. Waters took a step into the room, frowning at her. Maureen stood and pulled back the covers. Strewn across the mattress were dozens of thin blue and yellow plastic cards, each a shade smaller than a credit card.

"MetroCards," Waters said.

He walked to the bed and picked one up. Maureen took it from him. She turned the card over in her hand, ran her thumb over the black strip across the front. She looked up at Waters. Fear twisted her stomach in its fist. She felt it tug at her knees. She was so scared, so angry she wanted to scream. Instead, she raised the card between her fingers to Waters's face.

"A MetroCard," Maureen repeated, "is the last thing you get before you catch the train." She flung the card over the bed. "Fuck."

"You work at the Narrows," Waters said. "Where that train accident happened last night." He reached for Maureen's shoulder. She jerked back her arm and cocked her fist. Waters didn't flinch or pull back his hand, holding his ground. "I'm sorry. Did you know him? The deceased?"

She backed away from Waters, out from under his hand, looking down at the cards on her bed. Her fist stayed locked tight at her hip. *Deceased.* The word floated around inside her head like a whisper. Maureen felt like her throat was closing. "I don't know anybody."

Waters's eyes softened. "This break-in wasn't a burglary, it's a threat. Who's trying to get your attention?"

"Nobody wants my attention." Maureen blew the hair off her forehead. "Who am I? I'm nobody." Straightening her shoulders, she made sure she looked Waters in the face. "I appreciate you coming out. But maybe you should go."

Waters turned and left the bedroom. He didn't leave the apartment. He settled himself on the couch, readying his notepad and pen. "I gotta justify my time here to the City of New York. Talk."

Maureen ignited her best flirty smile and stopped just short of batting her eyelashes. "This is obviously some bad prank. Come by the bar. I'll buy you a drink to make up for your wasted time."

Waters said nothing.

"It's just some weird thing with an ex-boyfriend," Maureen said. "Long story, kind of pathetic, I don't wanna waste your time. Or the city's time."

Waters didn't move, didn't write anything down. He just sat there looking at her, unimpressed and waiting, not unlike, she realized, the calico cat on her fire escape. Unfortunately, pouring beer on his head to chase him away was out of the question.

For a moment she considered trying one more time to tap-dance her way around the truth, fat lot of good it had done her so far. But looking at Waters she knew there was nothing she could sell him. He'd been a cop as long as she'd been alive. She had skills, but not like that.

"If I gotta find something here to bust you for," Waters said, "I can do that. I'll leave here with something."

So she would give him something. Maybe everything. Maureen knew she was about to step in it worse than she had the night before. Talking to this cop about Sebastian wasn't any different, wasn't any smarter, than pouring whiskey down her throat to counterbalance the coke she put up her nose. But like the booze and the coke, she was gonna do it anyway. What else could she do? She was stuck. You had to at least try.

"I need a drink for this."

"I got no problem with that," Waters said.

Maureen went into the kitchen for a glass and some ice. She noticed the bird feeder sitting on the counter. Be patient, little birds. It's for your own good. It'll go back up as soon as I get this other thing sorted out. Don't give up on me yet. She looked out the window for her birds and saw none. Not on the fire escape, not on the power lines running to her roof, not even in the bare trees behind her building. She took another moment to search for the cat but couldn't find him, either. She knew that didn't mean he wasn't around, maybe even right under her nose. If the birds were hiding, that cat was out there somewhere.

Standing at the bar with her back to Waters, Maureen fixed a screwdriver, a weak one with lots of OJ and ice. She didn't want the vodka taking a bite out of her, she only wanted enough to nip at her nerve and wake it up. She sipped her drink, the sharp, oily sting of the Stoli sliding through the acid tang of the OJ and pricking the back of her tongue. She resisted the urge to add more vodka.

She joined Waters on the couch, sitting on the opposite end, holding her drink between her knees. He didn't say anything, waiting for her to speak. Maureen lit a cigarette, then balanced it carefully on the edge of an overfull ashtray. She swallowed a mouthful of screwdriver, took a breath big enough to fuel the whole story, and started talking.

While she talked, Maureen kept a close eye on Waters's reactions to her story. He gave away nothing he thought or felt. He kept his eyes on the notepad propped on his knee, scribbling, nodding now and then to prove he was listening. Maureen was grateful he didn't interrupt with questions, though she knew they'd come eventually. She had the feeling that any pause in the story would wreck her nerve. If she stopped talking, she'd find a million lame reasons not to continue. She wanted to tell the truth like she tore a Band-Aid off a blister, in one quick, sudden motion.

Waters flipped his notebook closed. Maureen felt a rush of hope that he'd discovered a solution; that his notes mapped out a route back into the life, such as it was, that she'd had only yesterday. It was a foolish hope, but so big she nearly choked on it anyway. She knew she was setting herself up for disappointment. Typical. When, lately, had it been any other way? Especially when it came to what she expected from men.

"You ever see any evidence of a problem between Dennis and Sebastian?" Waters asked.

"Dennis acted like they'd never met, but Sebastian told me they knew each other." She shrugged. "As for me, I never saw Sebastian at the Narrows before this weekend."

"And you would remember?"

"It's my job," Maureen said, "to know when money walks through the door. I couldn't tell you where it's from, but Frank Sebastian's got money. You have to, right, to run for office?"

"I'd say so. Money of your own, other people's money. Did Dennis have money?"

"I doubt it. Seemed to me he was getting by on what he made at the Narrows, like the rest of us."

"Dennis have plans for the future? Ambitions?"

Maureen chuckled, looking down at her hands in her lap. "Funny you should ask. We talked about that, kind of, earlier in the night. The future. The lack thereof. Dennis called himself the same thing he called me: a lifer. One of those people who never, one way or another, get out of the bars, the nightlife."

Waters nodded slowly. "I'm familiar with the term." He looked up at Maureen. "So you've got no sense of a history there, between the two. Personal relationship? Business?"

"Dennis knew *about* him," Maureen said, "about the campaign and stuff. That was the whole reason Sebastian was at the Narrows. Maybe they knew each other, maybe they didn't." She frowned into her drink. "Work, the bar, it's like being onstage. You're acting all night. Dennis was in the business a long time; he had his act down cold. He could've hated Sebastian's guts, they could've been lovers for ten years, they could've known each other since they were six. No one would ever see it if Dennis didn't want them to."

"And if Dennis was depressed, or suicidal even," Waters said, "over something with Sebastian or over something else entirely, it's possible you could never have known."

"More than possible," Maureen said. "It's likely."

Waters rested his elbows on his knees, stared at the palms of his hands. "I would really like to know what Dennis was gonna tell you later. Obviously, he thought you could somehow help him out."

"He thought he could count on me."

"Or use you," Waters said. "Either way, Sebastian wouldn't want that conversation to happen. He might take steps beyond frightening you to make sure it didn't. I'd like to know what he did and where he went after he talked to you." Waters pulled a MetroCard from his shirt pocket, studied it. "Somebody wants you thinking hard about Dennis." He held up the card. "That's the reason for this."

Maureen sank deep into the couch, stared at her busted television. "You think Sebastian threw Dennis in front of that train?" She spread her hands. "I mean, just, forgetting everything else, that's no way to start a run for office."

"Cleaning out the skeleton closet? Makes sense to me." He looked down at his hands, then back at Maureen. "I have seen worse done, much worse, over less. Plenty of times. Trust me."

"Christ. You are depressing as hell."

"Comes with the job," Waters said. "Sebastian could be telling you you're next. Or maybe he's an opportunist using a legitimate suicide to scare you. There could be no connection whatsoever, though I really doubt that. Either way, you were smart to trust your instincts last night and not be home alone." He slipped the card into the back of his notepad, stuck the pad in his coat pocket. "I gotta ask you this, so don't take offense. You got any embarrassing secrets of your own Sebastian might be privy to? You got any reason to have it out for him? Better that I hear it from you."

"Am I the real opportunist here? That's what you're asking. Am I setting up Sebastian? Because he's the big shot. Because he's some slick up-and-coming politician and I'm just a dopey cocktail waitress. You know what? That's pretty friggin' insulting."

Waters stared at her, his expression blank. "So you're familiar with the scenario, then. You understand I'm not pulling the possibility that sometimes people try to take advantage of one another out of thin air."

"I'm the victim," Maureen said. "Sebastian doesn't need protection from me. But thanks for reminding me."

"That doesn't answer my original question."

"No, that hump doesn't know a thing about me." Maureen tucked a lock of hair behind her ear, looking away from Waters. "Nobody at that bar does." Her eyes landed on the liquor bottles, stayed there.

"Go ahead," Waters said. "I don't judge."

Maureen started to rise from the couch, thought better of it, and sat. Maybe she'd have another after Waters left, to settle down.

"I don't mean to offend," Waters said, "but you'd be surprised what women will do to get a man's privates in a vise."

"No surprises here," Maureen said. "I am a woman."

"Fair enough." He stood, glancing out the window as if studying the weather. "I'll get with the guys that caught the body and see if there was anything abnormal about the scene. They'll have grabbed up witnesses if there were any, talked to the motorman. They'll keep me in the loop."

"A dead guy on the train tracks isn't abnormal?"

"Unfortunately, no." Waters waited a beat before he spoke again, scratching at his forehead. "You know anyone else at the Narrows I can talk to about Dennis? Anyone he had a personal relationship with, maybe?"

Translation being, Maureen thought, Who was Dennis fucking?

She thought of Tanya, of her common-knowledge secret affair with Dennis. What had Dennis told Tanya between the sheets? If Sebastian really was cleaning up his messy secrets, Tanya needed a warning and maybe protection. Maureen looked up at the huge detective waiting patiently for an answer to his question. Tanya, with her handbag full of illegal prescription pills, would go to pieces at the sight of him, if she let a cop anywhere near her in the first place. Maureen knew she'd have to talk to Tanya first, explain the real danger and ease her into talking to

Waters. Maybe she'd set up some kind of "accidental" meeting between them. She could make it happen. Tanya trusted her.

"I can't think of anyone," Maureen said. "Dennis and I never talked personal stuff."

"Well, should anyone turn up," Waters said, "please point them in my direction."

"I will," Maureen said. "Listen, when you start asking around the Narrows about Dennis, you'll leave this conversation out of it, right? Vic, the owner, he knows Sebastian. I don't want it getting back to him that I've talked to anyone, especially the police."

"Dennis worked at the Narrows," Waters said, "and he died right next door. There's nothing suspicious about the police asking questions. Sebastian was at the bar. Dennis organized his event. Because they had contact last night, it makes perfect sense that we interview him. And that we interview you." He inflated his cheeks, tilted his head to one side, thinking. "Which could be moving him to lean on you. If he scares you enough, maybe you'll neglect to mention seeing him after hours."

"To keep his connection to Dennis covered up," Maureen said.

"You think like a detective, Maureen. I don't know if that's a good thing or a bad thing." He walked over to the shattered TV, straightened it on its stand. "Sebastian will want his secret kept. Be smart about who you talk to. I was a good start. And just to be safe, you got somewhere you can spend a few days?"

"You think he'll come back?"

"You wanna take that chance?"

"I don't believe this," Maureen said, furious. "I can't even stay in my own house. This is bullshit."

"I can't promise you it's safe here," Waters said. "He may have come in because you weren't here, but he may be disappointed and planning a return visit. There's no telling. Where can you go?"

A good question, Maureen thought. "For how long?"

"At least a couple of days."

Maureen could think of only one person who could put her up for that long. Her mom. God, that was the last thing she wanted to do. She almost preferred running into Sebastian to spending a few days with Mom. "I could go to my mother's."

"Do that," Waters said. He held out a business card. "You need anything, anything sets off your alarm bells, you call me, day or night. Anytime. I mean that. That card has the precinct number and my cell. I'll do everything I can, Maureen, but nobody can protect you better than you can. Be smart."

Maureen took the card, tucking it under her cell phone on the coffee table. She walked with Waters to the door. He stopped as Maureen opened it.

"Ask the knucklehead upstairs to keep his eyes and ears open while you're gone," Waters said, "and to call me if anything happens." He waved away his words with his hand. "Scratch that. I'll tell him myself."

Waters touched his knuckle to his forehead, as if tipping his hat, and ambled off down the hall. Maureen eased the door closed behind him and locked it. She ran her fingers through her hair. She was alone, she realized, all alone for the first time since she'd stumbled out of Dennis's office.

She walked into the kitchen, grabbing her cell and Waters's card off the coffee table on her way through the living room. She dumped the rest of her screwdriver down the drain and stood there, holding the glass in her hand, staring at the mess in the sink. Not a single dish. Not one pot or pan. Nothing but highball glasses, coffee mugs, and tarnished silverware she'd used to eat takeout right from the carton. Sad.

She hit the hot water, poured the last of her watered-down dish soap into a ratty sponge, and tossed the empty soap bottle in the trash. No need to get more if she wasn't going to be home for a while. Steam warming her cheeks, she started the washing with the last glass she'd used, then set to scrubbing everything else in the sink, twice, running the water hot enough to turn her hands bright red. How good it was gonna feel, she thought, to get in the shower and wash her whole body under water that hot. She'd step back out into the world feeling renewed. She'd be pulsing cardinal red, so clean her skin would squeak like immaculate glass.

When she finished the washing, wiping her throbbing hands on a dish towel, she studied the drying rack by the sink. When this ordeal at the Narrows was over, things would change. No more feeding the birds with more consistency and care than she fed herself. Once a week, she'd go shopping. Meat, vegetables, fruit. Fresh, not frozen. Not cooked and delivered by strangers. Real food-group shit. Grown-up food. She laid the dishrag over the sink to dry.

She found the phone book, tossed it on the kitchen table, and plopped down in a chair. She stared at the book's cover, riffled the pages with her thumb. Good luck finding a working locksmith on a Sunday. She swept the phone book off the table and onto the floor. What was she thinking, anyway? The landlord had to change the locks. And that asshole would make her pay for it. Maybe she could get Paul to do it. Or maybe that wasn't such a good idea; a favor that size would require serious flirting. Good luck getting Paul off her back after that. She didn't need to owe that guy another favor, this one bigger than the last. Like I need to be getting the landlord's attention anyway, she thought. If I can't go back to work soon, I'll never make the rent. No way I'm borrowing money from Vic, no matter what he says. And I'm definitely not asking my mother.

If I was Waters's size, Maureen thought, I could get the money, plenty of money, from Sebastian. If I was the size of a grizzly, I could threaten to paint Sebastian's secret all over town and get paid like crazy not to do it. I could beat the shit out of him just to make a point. But I'm not Waters. I'm a scared little girl who needs to call her mommy. Save the shower for after that, Maureen thought. So you can send that embarrassing conversation down the drain.

Wearing her threadbare terry-cloth robe, her wet hair wrapped in a towel, Maureen froze when someone knocked on her door. Relax, she told herself. She pulled the robe closed at the collar, tightened the belt. It's John, coming to check up. Or it's Waters. He's put the whole thing to bed already. Her visitor knocked again. Answer the door, Maureen. What're you afraid of? On her way to the door, she stopped in the kitchen and dug her knife out of her purse. She dropped the knife in the pocket of her robe.

At the door she took a deep breath, held it, and put her eye to the peephole. For chrissakes. She blew out her breath. It was Paul, the landlord's kid. When he raised his hand to knock again, Maureen yanked open her door.

"What?"

"Oh, hey, Maureen," Paul said. Automatically, he tried peeking down her robe but caught himself right away and directed his eyes over her shoulder. "How's the ceiling fan holding up? I see it hanging there."

"It's fine."

"It's not turning. Is it broke? I can fix it for you, no problem."

"It's not broken," Maureen said. "It's winter."

"About that," Paul said, now staring at her forehead, "now that you mention it, there's a switch on the fan, makes it turn backward. It'll blow the heat back toward the floor. 'Cause heat, you know, it rises." A pause. "Obviously."

Paul blushed, both cheeks turning tomato red. Maureen checked her neckline. She had nothing showing. What was he, twenty? Twenty-one? Too old to be blushing and giggly. Maureen felt kind of sorry for him and kind of disgusted at the same time. True, he'd had a crush on her since she'd moved in, and she was standing there in her bathrobe. But still, what was this, eighth grade? She knew the best thing for both of them was an end to the conversation.

"The ceiling fan is fine," she said. "Is that really what you're here for?"

"Well, no. I just noticed it when you opened the door."

"What can I do for you?" Maureen asked. "I gotta go to work." She wanted to be gracious, the guy really was harmless, but it was chilly in the hall and, harmless or not, there was no way she was asking Paul into her place.

"My dad asked me to talk to you," Paul said. "It's about last night."

"What about last night?"

"I had to come up here."

"Why?" Maureen got up on her toes and in Paul's face. "Who was here last night? Did you see someone? This is very, very important." She waited for Paul to ask why. He didn't. "My new TV got broken."

Paul leaned back, away from Maureen, keeping his feet rooted to his spot just the other side of her door. "My father sent me over here last night. To let those cops in."

Maureen thumped down onto her heels. "What cops?"

"The cops that broke your TV, I guess," Paul said. "Look, my dad called me last night, late, and told me I had to meet these two cops over here. That they had called him and told him they needed to get into your place. So he sent me here to let them in."

"And they had a warrant? You saw it, right? The warrant. They had badges, right?"

"I didn't see a warrant," Paul said. "I didn't see badges. They had guns; I saw those."

"Jesus Christ. You're sure they were cops?"

"Whadda you want from me?" Paul said. "It's my job to check? Listen, it was late, I was high as a motherfucker. I didn't feel in a position to be checking IDs. I didn't want those guys checking me out too close either, know what I mean? My dad said let the cops in, so I did. Listen, I'm not even supposed to be telling you this part."

"What did they look like?"

"Cops," Paul said. "Guns, like I said. Long coats. Shirts and ties."

"Was one of them an older guy, tall, silver hair?"

"They were older maybe, forties, maybe." Paul shook his head. "I'm not real good with ages. One had dark hair, the other was a redhead. Like you, only brighter."

"No big fat guy, either? Going bald?" Maureen asked.

"Like the cop that just left?" Paul asked. "No, that guy wasn't one of them."

"Wait a minute," Maureen said. "How'd you know that guy was a cop?"

"My dad saw him out the window." Paul cleared his throat. "He knows cops when he sees 'em, he says. So, yeah, about that. That's why Dad sent me over right now. I wasn't supposed to say anything over here other than my dad says you need to quit whatever's got cops coming and going from your place. Either that, or you're out on your . . . you're out of the apartment in one month."

Paul was a dim bulb, Maureen thought, but even he knew those guys weren't cops. He knew he'd been sent to Maureen's door that afternoon with half the truth, if that, which is why he'd let slip what he had. Not that he really cared about the whole story. Nor would I, Maureen thought, were our places reversed. Everyone has their own ass to cover, even if it still lives in Mommy and Daddy's house. Maureen closed her eyes and shook her head to clear it. What else could Paul be doing at her door, except following up on the message from last night? Had she gotten it? What was her reaction? He'd report back to his dad, who would report back to someone else. Three guesses who waited at the end of that game of telephone.

That had to be it. It had to be him.

Well, she thought, looking Paul up and down, may as well put the guy to good use while I've got him here and send him home with a message for that silver-haired bastard sending men with guns to my door.

"Thanks for the message, Paul," Maureen said. "Tell your father he's got nothing to worry about. Nothing at all. It was a big misunderstanding, and it's already all taken care of."

"Okay."

"Make sure you tell him I said no one has anything to worry about. No one."

"I got it."

"Thanks for coming over," Maureen said, reaching for the door. "Everything else we talked about, we'll keep between us."

When Paul was gone, Maureen pressed her forehead hard against her door, squeezing her eyes shut tight. Fuck me, she thought. Waters. He'd been seen, been ID'd as a cop. Hell, she'd admitted it to Paul. How long now till Sebastian knew she was talking to the cops? It had taken him less than a day to find her address and to lean on her landlord. If she had to, she could pass off Waters's visit as routine follow-up on Dennis. But on a Sunday morning, at her place? Not likely. She thought of Waters's advice to relocate. Maybe it was indeed time to pack a bag.

Maureen grabbed her phone off the coffee table. She had messages. When had the phone rung? She checked and saw she'd never turned the ringer back on after work. Another bad habit that has to end, she thought, is leaving that ringer off.

Yeah, you need to stop missing those calls from Brad Pitt.

One message was from Vic, checking up on her, asking if she'd heard from the cops about Dennis. Fantastic, someone else interested in her and the cops. The next call was from her mother, because it was Sunday. And the hits just kept on coming. Next came three calls from Tanya in quick succession, from earlier that morning. The first two were hang-ups. On the third, Tanya finally spoke, her voice hushed and hoarse.

"Maureen, I need to talk to you right away. It's about Dennis . . . and Frank Sebastian." A long pause. Maureen almost hung up. "Please, please call me. I need help. I need it bad."

10

That afternoon, Maureen walked into Cargo toting three days' worth of clothes and other essentials in a knapsack slung over her shoulder. She felt pretty much like she'd been run over by a truck. She had even nodded off for a minute in the cab, jumping awake with a yell that frightened the driver into nearly sideswiping a parked car. For the scare, Maureen added an extra five to the tip. Unimpressed, he sped off up Bay Street like he was glad to be rid of her.

Heading for the bar, Maureen saw Tracy. Standing behind the bar, her back to the room, she stood with a small clutch of customers watching the Sunday football game. The broadcast echoed through the mostly empty café. Maureen only knew Tracy's name and the story of her boob job but relaxed at the sight of a familiar face. Even the sound of the football game set Maureen more at ease. Nothing says *normal Sunday afternoon* like giant millionaires beating the hell out of one another for fun and profit.

John stood on the outside of the bar, at the far end. He leaned against the wall, arms crossed, his glasses hanging from the collar of his black sweater. He hadn't looked over when Maureen walked in the door. He was too absorbed in Molly, who was showing him a paper from the stack before her on the bar. She had a red pen in her teeth. Was she grading papers in a bar? Did teachers do that? John hadn't looked over when Maureen arrived but Molly had, a fast glance. So fast John probably hadn't even noticed. Molly looked 'cause she's a woman, Maureen thought. She can't not keep an eye on the door.

Surveying the room, Maureen spied Tanya tucked away in a dim corner, alone in a booth, half a cosmo before her. Maureen headed that way. Without even turning her head, sliding her eyes to the side, she snuck another look at the couple. Maybe it wasn't John that stung. Maybe it was Molly and what she had that Maureen didn't—someone at her side if she got in trouble. Not across the room, not in the apartment upstairs, but right next to her, practically inside her skin. Of course, women like Molly didn't stumble around dark bars with cocaine hangovers, barging in on 3 a.m. blow jobs. Get over it, Maureen. You did it to yourself. And maybe to Tanya, who was now out of her seat and hugging Maureen like she was a long-lost sister back from the dead.

When Tanya released her, settling back into her seat, Maureen let Tanya's hands slide down her arms and through her fingers. Poor Tanya. She smiled, bee-stung lips curling over perfect white teeth, her straight black hair falling in two perfect curtains on either side of her perfect face. She was, what, twenty-three? Twenty-four? Maureen realized she didn't know. Wasn't out of the question that Tanya was nineteen or thirty. The Life was funny and unfair in the way it added years to some people and took them away from others. Maureen thought of the way Paul had looked at her standing there in her bathrobe. One look at Tanya would melt that poor kid into a simmering pool of hormones, leave him seeping through the cracks in the street.

S-L-U-T, the other girls said. God, the other girls at the Narrows hated Tanya! Too young, too well built, too pretty. Working in bars, Maureen had learned fast that while a man couldn't be too handsome, a woman could be too beautiful, especially in the eyes of other women. It was cheap envy and Maureen held herself above it. Of course, it helped that the other girls weren't wild about Maureen, either, though they feared her in a way they never did Tanya. She knew they found her too bossy, too serious. Maybe a little too smart. Well, that was too bad. She had bills in the present and plans for the future. That wasn't her fault any more than it was Tanya's fault she was catastrophically gorgeous.

"Thanks for coming, Maureen," Tanya said, her big hazel eyes blank and vacant.

Maureen disguised her exasperated sigh with a fake yawn. Tanya was high. Was now really the time? Well, when *wasn't* the time for Tanya? "You're welcome, T. After what happened, we could all probably use a little help."

Tanya circled her fingertip around the rim of her martini glass. "Yeah. That." She looked out the window. "I talked to Vic. He said we're reopen-ing on Tuesday. We may as well try and get back to normal, he said."

"Vic say anything about a funeral?" Maureen asked. It was the first time she'd thought of it. Could you have a funeral with body parts? Did the family even claim those? She pictured severed arms and legs sliding around in a mostly empty casket. Gross. What was wrong with her?

"Vic said . . . Vic talked to the family," Tanya said, her eyes welling up. "They don't want anyone from the bar there. They blame us for what happened . . . for Dennis's lifestyle."

"Lifestyle? What lifestyle? He worked in a bar, he didn't belong to a cult." Maureen pulled a couple of napkins from the dispenser on the table. She reached across, patted a napkin at Tanya's tears. "What a bunch of assholes."

Tracy walked up to the table. "Everything okay?" She puffed out her bottom lip at Tanya. "You need something, sweetie?" Tanya shook her head. "Maureen?"

Well done, Maureen thought. Tracy remembered her name. And she'd had her eye on Tanya since before Maureen had arrived. She'd known from across the room that something wasn't right, and she'd been delicate about letting Maureen know it. John would do well to hang on to this one.

"We're all right," Maureen said. "Let me get another cosmo for Tanya. And let me have a Stoli and grapefruit. Maybe a basket of fries, too. I gotta eat something."

"I'm on it," Tracy said. She held Maureen's eyes for a long moment and headed back to the bar.

"The family," Tanya said, when Tracy was out of range, "told Vic that Dennis wouldn't have died if not for the drunks and drug addicts he worked with, that dragged him down. They actually said that. Can you believe it? I thought Vic was going to cry when he was telling me."

Maureen swallowed back the bile that rose in her throat. Like Dennis was a nine-year-old that the no-good neighborhood teens had corrupted with cigarettes and hits of cheap beer. He was a grown man who had made his own choices.

"Forget his family," Maureen said. "Where have they been? Where were they before this happened?"

Tracy returned with the drinks and food. "I'll run a tab at the bar."

Maureen took a few long gulps of her cocktail, thinking of her own mother constantly ragging on her to get a life. Had Dennis suffered the same abuse? It was indeed enough sometimes to make you want to stretch your neck across a train track.

"What about you?" Maureen asked, picking a lone hot French fry from the basket. "They at least gonna let you go to the services?"

Tanya, tears rolling again, shook her head. "They didn't know about me and Dennis. Nobody knew."

"Except for everybody."

Tanya grinned. It made Maureen feel good. "Except for that," Tanya said.

Maureen slid her drink aside and leaned across the table. "You mentioned Frank Sebastian on the phone. You said there was some connection between him and Dennis."

Tanya flipped open her cell and stared into it.

"T, it's important," Maureen said. "What does Sebastian have to do with you and Dennis?"

"Excuse me a second," Tanya said, neither making a call nor moving from her seat. "It's time." Maureen pushed the basket of fries across the table, but Tanya held up her hand. "I can't eat those. The grease, the fat. I'm not like you, lucky thing. I'll put on five pounds looking at them."

Tanya found an orange prescription bottle in her purse. She popped off the top with her thumb and shook out two pills. She considered them a moment, shook out a third, and downed all three with the remains of her first cosmo.

"I've been seeing a doctor, for anxiety," Tanya said. "This thing with Dennis hasn't helped." She stuffed the bottle deep into her handbag. "Oh, my bad, you want one? Helps take the edge off." Maureen nodded and Tanya reached into her bag.

"No," Maureen said, "I better not. I'm okay." She moved her drink back in front of her, wrapped both hands around it. "I'm not saying you're not okay."

Tanya reached across the table, set her hand on Maureen's wrist. "Don't worry. I get it." Tanya descended even further away behind her own eyes. Maureen swore she could see it happening, like watching someone sink beneath the surface of the sea. It was sad and frightening, and it meant she had to hurry if she wanted information. "Listen, does Sebastian know about you and Dennis? It's important. Did you and Dennis ever talk about Sebastian?"

Even through the bright gloss, Maureen saw Tanya's lips go pale as her mouth tightened into a thin line. Maureen still couldn't tell if Tanya had heard a word she'd said. "Dennis died because of me," Tanya said. "It's my fault."

That was news. "What're you talking about?"

"About a year ago," Tanya said, "right before you got there, Dennis left the Narrows to open his own place over close to the ferry, by the ballpark. Where they were gonna build all those condos. Microbrews and burgers." She looked around the bar. "I forget what he called it. It was kinda like this place. Anyways, the condos never got built and the bar went under in less than three months. Dennis had borrowed the start-up money, a lot of it, from Sebastian. Vic set it up; he and Sebastian go back." She rolled her shoulders. "Dennis had nothing to take to a bank. His family practically disowned him when he said he was gonna open a bar of his own. They wanted him in law school. They treated him like shit. Never even came in to see the place."

Tears came again.

"This thing with Sebastian, it was just supposed to be business, you know? Neighborhood business, one guy helping another guy out. But Sebastian got *pissed*. I don't know what his problem is; he's got lots of money."

She wiped her eyes with a napkin, taking care not to smudge her makeup.

"Sebastian found out about me and Dennis," Tanya said. "From Vic probably, though Dennis swore he hadn't told anyone." She tried to smile. "Who knows, right? You and everyone else at the Narrows figured it out. Prob'ly wasn't that hard for Vic." She lowered her forehead into her palm, letting her hair fall over her face. "Anyway, after that Sebastian got totally weird. He told Dennis to start making videos of the two of us, me and Dennis. Sexual videos. Sebastian was gonna do something with them, to make back the money, I guess. I don't know the details, but they were supposed to get Dennis off the hook for the cash."

"Jesus, Tanya, tell me you said no. Tell me you didn't do it."

Tanya nodded, covering her face. She peeked at Maureen through her fingers. "Just a few times. Dennis told me he'd doctor the video to hide our faces." She moved her hands to her cheeks. "We decided to get really fucking high and get it over with. I figured, fuck it, it's just sex. It's not like I loved Dennis or anything, but I didn't want to not help him when it seemed kind of easy. And let's face it, I'm a sucky waitress and the other girls hate me. Dennis should've fired me a long time ago. And I was having sex with him already, because I wanted to and not to keep my job if that's what you're thinking, okay? So what was the big deal?

Who would ever see it, really?" She paused. "Dennis was scared, Maureen. Sebastian said he'd make Vic fire him, that Vic owed him money, too, that he'd get other guys after Dennis, to do worse. To him and to me." Tanya flattened her hands on the tabletop and leaned forward, close to Maureen. "Dennis told me Sebastian knows people, all kinds of people, through his security company and from when he was a cop."

"Wait, wait," Maureen said. "Hold on a minute. Sebastian was a cop?"

"Like a million years ago, twenty or something. He was some big hero over in Brooklyn." Tanya took a big mouthful of cosmo. "Some fucking hero he is now, huh?"

Maureen stared across the table, willing any expression—confusion, pity, disgust—from her face. She resisted the urge to count up Tanya's mistakes, the drugs, the self-deception, the bad decisions that led her to fucking on film to pay debts she didn't owe. It wasn't like Maureen hadn't made her own mistakes and bad decisions, piling them one on top of another. She couldn't decide what she felt, what she had a right to feel. But Maureen did know one thing: were she in Tanya's place, she'd be swallowing pills six at a time, not three.

"I don't understand," Maureen said, "how this ends with Dennis on the tracks."

"Dennis told me," Tanya said, sniffling, "that he hadn't given the videos over to Sebastian yet. That he was working out something else. Something that didn't involve me."

"What was this other deal?" Maureen asked. Some kind of blackmail? Was that why Dennis saw Maureen catching him compromised the other night as a lucky break, one he'd been hoping for? Or even one he'd set up? Maybe those cameras behind the bar had been running after all. Had Sebastian found out? "Do you know what Dennis had planned?"

"I never knew," Tanya said. "Dennis told me not to worry about it."

"And the videos? What about them?"

Tanya blew out a long sigh. She seemed to be gathering herself back together, relieved, maybe, to be telling someone her secret. I know that feeling, Maureen thought. Either that or the drugs were kicking in.

"That's what Sebastian wanted to know," Tanya said, "when he called me last night."

"Oh, no."

"He talked like Dennis had never canceled their deal," Tanya said. "Which I don't understand, because Dennis had promised me he was working everything out."

Apparently not, Maureen thought, or he wouldn't be dead. "What did you tell Sebastian?"

"I told him we'd made the videos." Tanya looked down into her drink, shifted her eyes to her lap. "Except for some stuff I hadn't let Dennis do yet. I'm not, like, a prude or anything but some of the stuff?" Tanya seemed to shrink, to become suddenly tired and small. "Some of what Sebastian wanted sounded like it would've really . . . hurt. I think that's why Dennis decided to stop, to not hurt me or, you know, humiliate me. And him, I guess. Any more than we already had."

"But Sebastian wants them. Who's got them? You?"

"They're at Dennis's place, on the camera."

"I don't like where this is headed."

"I need you to come with me over there," Tanya said, "to find the camera. I can't go alone. Those other bitches at work, they hate me. They can't be trusted with a secret like this. But you can, Maureen. You're straight up and you always treated me right. We always got along, you and me. Like friends." Tanya reached out for Maureen's wrist again, grabbed it tight with both hands. "Sebastian said things to me. He told me he was gonna have his movies, even if he had to start from scratch and make them with me himself. He threatened me with things. Those guys that watch the parking lots by work, all up and down Bay Street, I don't know if you know this but they all work for him; that's Sebastian's security company. Some of them have driven me home from work. They know where I live.

"I don't want Sebastian to have those videos. Not for me, but for Dennis. Dennis went back on Sebastian for me. But I'm afraid of what Sebastian will do if I don't hand them over. It's shitty, I know, to give them up now. I should stand up for Dennis." She paused, staring at Maureen. "What do I do?"

Maureen opened her purse. Somewhere in there was Waters's card. She found it, pushed it across the table. Tanya kept her hands under the table but leaned forward to read the card. She looked up at Maureen. "Detective? You're talking to the cops?"

"They came to me," Maureen lied. "They look at things like Dennis's death, to make sure there's no foul play and stuff. It's standard procedure."

Tanya furrowed her brow. "No cops have called me."

Damn, Maureen thought. Maybe she's not as high as I thought. She faked a smile. "Alphabetical order. *M* comes before *T*." That seemed to satisfy Tanya. "You need to call Waters."

"I don't know," Tanya said. "If Sebastian finds out, it'll make things worse."

"You tell Waters that Sebastian threatened you with rape, for chrissakes, and Sebastian won't have the chance to do a damn thing."

"Nobody ever said anything about rape. Jesus, Maureen, Sebastian's famous. Besides, he was a cop. Waters is a cop. What makes you think Waters is gonna choose us over him?"

Maureen swallowed hard. Tanya had a point. She thought of the men Paul had let into her apartment. But Paul wasn't hard to fool. Suits and guns weren't proof those guys were cops. There was no proof they had anything to do with NYPD, past or present. They could've been from Sebastian's security service. That would make sense. Besides, she'd already spilled her guts to Waters; she'd already made her decision, right or wrong, to trust him.

"T, don't be stupid," Maureen said. "You said yourself Sebastian stopped being a cop a long time ago. Call Waters."

Tanya opened her phone. "I'll put his number in my cell, call him in the morning."

"Call him now. Please. For me." She took a deep breath. "You're not the only one having trouble with Sebastian."

Tanya stared back at her, struggling to compute Maureen's words, the drugs overriding the last of her lucid circuits. Maureen realized, too late, that she'd gone overboard, talking about cops and rape and Sebastian. Full of pills and guilt and fear, Tanya had started shutting down. "I can't talk to a cop tonight. Do you have any idea how fucking high I am right now?"

"Waters won't care," Maureen said.

"Do you know everything this cop cares about? You talk about him like you know him. Do you?"

"No, I don't. I met him this morning." She looked up at Tanya. "My place got broken into last night." She waited for Tanya to make the connection. She didn't. "He's helping me out."

Tanya raised her chin. "He probably wants to help you out of that sweater."

Maureen sighed. Pushing wasn't getting her anywhere. "Okay, promise me you'll call him in the morning."

"Oh my God," Tanya said. "What if he wants to search Dennis's place? What if he finds the videos? Jesus. Maureeen. Please come with me tomorrow. We'll just get the camera and go. Can't we do that first?"

Maureen raised her hands in surrender. "Okay, okay. I'll go. If you agree to talk to Waters, I will go with you to get the camera. Deal?"

"Deal."

"Call me in the morning and we'll go to Dennis's place. We'll get the camera first. We'll delete everything and leave it where it is. After that we'll call Waters and make plans to meet him. If you want, I'll go with you there, too."

"What do I tell Waters?" Tanya asked. "What about the videos?"

"Stick to Dennis's bad debts and Sebastian's trying to squeeze it out of you, that he's making threats." Maureen feigned a smile. "I think this cop is a soft touch. Make sure you cry at least once."

"That won't be hard." Tanya checked her cell again. "I gotta go. I gotta meet someone." She shrugged. "Told you I didn't want to be alone."

Maureen couldn't stop herself from rolling her eyes.

"It's not like that. Just some company. Junk food and Cartoon Network." Tanya gathered her jacket and purse, sliding toward the end of the bench. "You shouldn't be alone, either."

Maureen almost told her about spending the night at her mother's, but suddenly the idea felt embarrassing and ridiculous. Maybe she should go home. Do TV and junk food her own damn self. Then she thought of her TV. Well, junk food maybe. And vodka.

"Don't worry about me," Maureen said.

"I won't." Tanya was on her feet, her arms held out for a hug. "I betcha no one ever does."

Maureen rose from her seat.

Tanya's face was blank and cold, but her body vibrated in Maureen's embrace.

"So I'll see you Tuesday," Tanya said. "Back at work."

"Tomorrow," Maureen said. "Tomorrow morning."

"Right," Tanya said, backing away. "That's what I meant."

Maureen watched Tanya walk out of the bar, stop on the sidewalk, think about which way to go, and finally disappear from view. When she turned to the bar to signal Tracy for another drink, Maureen saw every face in the room staring at the empty space outside where Tanya had paused. Everyone except for John and Molly. They watched Maureen, their faces unreadable.

Maureen grabbed her smokes, her phone, and Waters's card and headed outside, turning the corner around the side of the building, where she wouldn't be seen.

11

Her back against the bright Caribbean-blue wall of the Cargo, her phone glowing in her hand, Maureen sucked down a smoke, shivering in the cold wind off the harbor. She thumbed Waters's cell number into her phone. She had to do her part. To do that, she had to trust someone, and that person was not Tanya. There was a good chance Tanya had forgotten their plans before she got three blocks away.

Phone at her ear, Maureen watched a city bus roll by, the blank faces turned toward her clear in the window, the riders looking right at her and seeing nothing.

"Nat Waters."

"Nat." Jesus. What's wrong with me? "I mean, Detective Waters. It's Maureen Coughlin."

A long yawn. "Everything okay?"

"It's all good," Maureen said. "I'm getting ready to head over to my mom's."

"Good."

A headache starting behind her eyes, Maureen lit another smoke. "I thought of someone you should talk to, another waitress. Her name is Tanya Coscinelli. I got her number."

"Gimme a second." Maureen heard the slamming of drawers and the shuffling of papers, some muffled swearing. "Awright, go ahead." Maureen recited the number. "How's Tanya holding up? I'm figuring she left you—what, five minutes ago?"

Maureen stepped quickly to the corner, looking up and down the street. Was Waters watching her? Had he been around all night? The thought made her feel better and creeped her out at the same time. She heard a gruff chuckle over the phone.

"I'm home, Maureen," Waters said. "Relax. I'm like you. I've been doing what I do and not much else for a long time. And let me tell you, covering your tracks with your co-workers doesn't help me any."

Feeling foolish, hoping no one inside the bar had seen her dash to the corner, Maureen stepped back into the shadows. "She called me after you left. I didn't know about her problems until a few minutes ago. I'm not hiding anything."

"Tell me what's worrying you," Waters said. "About Tanya."

"She's got problems of her own with Sebastian," Maureen said. "Tanya should tell you about it herself. You should meet up with her. I gave her your number, made her promise to call you in the morning."

"But?"

"But she's flighty. So maybe you can call her if she forgets to call you." She paused. "Just to be sure. We would've called you tonight but Tanya had to go meet someone."

"Did you explain to her that dealing with Sebastian might be more important than her social life?"

"I tried," Maureen said, "but I only work with the girl. I'm not her mother."

"Okay, if I don't hear from her by mid-morning, I'll call her." He paused. "I'd appreciate a call from you, too, in the morning."

"In case I remember anything else that might help?"

Another chuckle. "I wish there were fewer cop shows on TV. If you remember anything I'd love to hear it. Mostly, I want to know you're okay."

Maureen put her free hand to her warming cheek. Even her mother hadn't said that to her in a long time. "Okay."

"Good night, Maureen," Waters said. "Take care."

"There's something else," Maureen said. "Something Tanya mentioned."

"What's that?"

Maureen took a long drag on her cigarette, trying to figure why she was so nervous about asking a simple question. She didn't want to sound accusatory, but she wanted to know, needed to know the answer before things went any further. "Did you know that Sebastian used to be a cop?"

Now, it was Waters's turn to pause and think. "I did, though I can't see how that matters. It was over twenty years ago."

"Could he still know people on the force?" Maureen asked. "People that would do him favors?"

"I can't say," Waters answered. "I haven't been keeping tabs on him. It's possible he's got friends on the job. Lots of people on Staten Island have friends who are cops."

"Are you one of them? One of Sebastian's friends on the job?"

"What are you getting at?" Waters asked, his tone shifting. Maureen could tell that he was getting aggravated with the inquisition and knew she was holding back on him. "Tell me where you are. We should talk about this in person."

"Answer my question," Maureen said. She heard Waters draw a deep breath. He didn't like it much, she figured, the big bad police detective being interrogated by the little ol' waitress. Well, that was too damn bad. She had her own safety to worry about, so too bad for his fragile male ego.

"No," Waters finally said. "I can guarantee you Frank Sebastian and I are not friends. And if he's got friends who are cops, I don't know them. Anything else?"

He did it, Maureen thought, a bit shocked. He didn't hang up or pull an attitude on her. There was no *I'm the man, I'm the cop, I'm in charge here* bullshit. Instead, he had answered her question. She didn't give a rat's ass if he was nice about it. He wasn't a customer at one of her tables. As long as she could trust him she could forgive him a lack of manners. "Thank you. I'll call you tomorrow."

"Do that." Waters hung up.

Maureen closed her phone. She would definitely call Waters tomorrow, as soon as she and Tanya were done at Dennis's place. She'd lay everything out for him: her landlord, the message from Paul, the guys with guns. Maybe she could get Paul talking to Waters as well, find out for real who those guys were and who they worked for, the city or a more private employer. If we get enough information, she thought, between the two of us, Waters and me, maybe we can back Sebastian off some, off me, off Tanya.

She noticed her hands weren't shaking. She had no kind of shakes right then and felt pretty damn good about it. I know people, too, she thought, Mr. Silver-haired Hero-cop Politician Man. Better watch your back. Maureen leaned against the wall of the Cargo and took her time finishing her smoke.

All everyone had to do was make it through the night.

Out on Bay Street, another bus passed, this one heading in the opposite direction. Maureen swore she was seeing the other side of all the same faces.

When she went back inside the bar, nobody turned to look. John was nowhere to be seen. Probably in his office doing whatever managers did in there: nap, get high, skim the tips, screw up the next week's schedule. Maureen headed back to the booth she'd shared with Tanya. After a few moments, Molly met her there, gestured at the vacant bench.

"You mind?" Molly asked.

"Not at all," Maureen said, though she did. She'd really just come back inside to gather her things. She had a long bus ride across the island to her mother's.

"John told me," Molly said, sitting, "what Waters found in your apartment. Scary. You handling it okay?"

"It's disturbing," Maureen said, "but I'll be fine. The more I think about it, the more it seems like a dumb prank."

Molly rubbed her hands on her thighs, looking out the window, pretending to believe the lies Maureen told. Through her tight, long-sleeved white T-shirt, Maureen could see the rough lace of Molly's bra. She looked solid, tough. She made Maureen a little nervous. "Still, it's best to be careful," Molly said. She plucked a French fry from the basket, ate it. "Yuck. These are ice cold. Mind if I dump them?" She got up, basket in hand. "Split a burger with me?"

"Yeah, why not?" Maureen said. She needed something of substance. One French fry for every cocktail wasn't going to sustain her. And it wasn't like there was a home-cooked meal waiting for her at her mother's house.

"We'll get the works," Molly said. "Bacon, cheese, whatever they got to throw on it. I'll be right back."

Maureen watched as Molly walked to the bar, leaning over it to order from Tracy. Molly had a good-looking body, Maureen thought, even if she did carry something extra in her backside and thighs. Not that it seemed to bother John any, or Molly either, for that matter. She wouldn't be wearing pants that tight if it did, or ordering loaded cheeseburgers. Maureen rocked on her own sit-bones, lamenting the lack of flesh between them and the wooden bench. Those cords Molly's packed into would fall off me, she thought. She knew she should celebrate being thin, that most women, normal women, would prefer struggling to add on instead of fighting to take off.

Part of her, though, felt cast back to those high school days when every girl but her, the Mollys, the Tracys, and the Tanyas, day by day traded in their angles for curves. And Maureen knew full well what pert, perky Tracy saw from across the barroom, what healthy, curvy Molly saw sitting across the table: slumped shoulders; eyes big, blue, and terrified; deadly straight, cornflake-colored hair that frayed at the ends and fell flat on Maureen's shoulders. She twirled a dry lock around her finger. I'm a scarecrow, she thought. A winter scarecrow that bleeds hay every time she moves.

Molly returned to the booth with a condiment caddy and silverware. She set the table. "That girl," Molly said, sliding back into the booth, "the one who just left, she a friend of yours?"

"I suppose," Maureen said, knowing she was really saying *no* and feeling a twinge of guilt about it. "Her name is Tanya. We work together over at the Narrows. She's having some problems."

"I gathered that. What is she on?"

"Something for anxiety, or so she says. To be honest, who knows what she's popping. She's been high as long as I've known her. Never seen her eat anything but pills."

Shifting her eyes away from Molly's, embarrassed at her quick, decisive betrayal of Tanya, Maureen raised her glass to her lips to stop herself from talking. I'm picking sides, Maureen thought. I'm using Tanya's secrets to gain Molly's confidence. Why? Because she bought me a cheeseburger? Sellout. Maybe Sebastian had a point. Suddenly she couldn't keep her mouth shut about anything.

"I shouldn't tell tales out of school, I guess."

"I teach teenagers," Molly said. "High school. In any given class I have ten kids doped up on something: doctor's prescription, bought on the corner, or both. Half of them get it from their parents. They get that same glazed look, like the whole world is some television program and they're home on the couch watching it and they lost the remote."

"Tanya gets by," Maureen said. "She's young. And she's got her reasons." She stared down into her drink, swirling the melting ice around with her straw. She couldn't deny the fact that, telling secrets or not, it was a relief talking to someone who wasn't high or a cop. "Tanya was involved with Dennis, the manager from the Narrows who got killed by the train. She's having a really hard time with it. We all are. There are all these . . . repercussions."

"You should be having a hard time," Molly said. "It's okay. It is hard. We all grow up thinking dying is for old people, for sick people. That suicide is for star-crossed lovers and Roman senators. It's a shock, always, when we lose one of our own. It feels like it's the first time in history that it's ever happened. But it's not, and it won't be the last, either." Molly swept a thick curl from her face. It fell right back. "It's hard, Maureen, harder than people think, being one of the ones left behind. Believe me, I know. Give yourself some time. To sort everything out."

The conversation paused when Tracy arrived, and they both sat silent as Tracy set down their food. Maureen sat wondering what she was supposed to believe Molly about. She'd obviously lost someone important, and the bitterness over it lingered. Who had left her behind? Did John know? He had to. The loss, it wasn't something that Molly hid real well.

Before Maureen could ask any questions, Molly spoke. "I need your help with something, speaking of sorting things out."

"Shoot." Maureen picked at the new pile of steaming hot fries. Even after eleven years of a bar and diner diet, was there anything better than piping-hot fries? At least that never got old.

"I need you to explain to me," Molly said, swirling a trio of fries in a huge pool of ketchup, "where it is John fits into everything that's going on."

"I'm not sure he does," Maureen said. "I'm grateful for everything he's done." She watched as Molly cut the burger in half, jalapeños and mushrooms tumbling down the sides. Her mouth actually started watering. "I appreciate him putting me up, getting me in touch with Detective Waters. I mean, we hardly know each other and he really came through for me. I appreciate it, but I don't know how much more help from him I'm gonna need."

"John's good like that," Molly said. "He likes to help."

She set half the burger on an extra plate that she slid across the table.

Maureen attacked her food immediately. She'd had no idea how hungry she was until there was food in front of her. Warm blood trickled down her fingers to her wrists. Molly had ordered it medium rare, exactly how Maureen liked it. She thought right then she might be a little in love with John's girlfriend. Either that or she was just OD-ing on protein.

It wasn't until Maureen was down to her last couple of bites that she realized Molly wasn't eating. Instead, she gazed out the window, focused on something in the night sky outside that Maureen couldn't see. "What's on your mind, Molly?"

"These repercussions surrounding Dennis's death, what are they exactly?"

Maureen set down her burger and wiped her mouth with a paper napkin. She drained the last of her cocktail. "I'm not sure. I'm kind of still waiting to see for myself. There seems to be a lot of interest in it, is all. From people you wouldn't expect to be interested."

"You, this Tanya girl, Dennis. Death, cops, repercussions. All these things on my boyfriend's doorstep." She turned her full attention back to Maureen. "I'm not comfortable with it."

"Tanya was here for my help," Maureen said, "not John's. I'm not looking to involve him in her problems or anyone else's. The cops, they do what they do. You and I can't do a thing about that."

"But you have to admit that whatever's happening at the Narrows is no good, and you're right in the middle of it, and now you're bringing it in here."

Maureen sat back, stunned. "Thanks a lot, Molly. Just call me a fucking disease, why don't you?"

"Call it what you want," Molly said, "as long as you understand that I will keep John at a safe distance from anything that might get him hurt."

"As long as *you* understand," Maureen said, now feeling ambushed, "that while you're looking out for John, I gotta look out for myself, so no offense and your concerns are duly noted, but your boyfriend is your problem, not mine."

"My problem is not John," Molly said, nostrils flaring. "It's you hanging around under his wing like a foundling waif waiting to be rescued. No offense."

And here I sit, Maureen thought, seduced with a cheeseburger — shit, with *half* a cheeseburger. What the hell has happened to me? Molly had seized the given ground over the table, her arms crossed over her puffed-out chest, her chin tilted up, her shoulders set forward of her hips. Telltale signs of someone digging in for a fight. You know, Maureen thought, I don't know if I could take this broad. This one doesn't scratch and claw and pull hair; this one throws fists. Should've known. No way John dates a priss.

Maureen wanted to be angry, but what she felt was betrayed. She'd counted on Molly's being a woman to make her a natural ally. Surely she understood Maureen's situation. Strange men who might want to hurt her had invaded her house, her bedroom. Molly had certainly seemed to understand it yesterday morning. Then Maureen realized she'd forgotten a crucial point. Molly was a woman, sure, but she was a woman in love. There were limits to her patience with other females in her boyfriend's orbit. Her loyalty was to her mate and her nest; her teeth and claws came out for them only.

Goddamn. What would it be like, Maureen wondered, to love like that?

"You think any of this mess was my idea?" Maureen said, dropping her hands into her lap. "That I have any control over this? That I'm somehow *enjoying* this? I'm the *victim* here." She gripped the edge of the table, dug her nails into the wood. "All I had was my job and my apartment and now they're both ruined. I'm in this bar because I got nowhere else to go, Molly. I'm not like you. I have no boyfriend. I have no friends. There, I said it. You happy?"

Molly heaved out a heavy sigh. Like that, the hardness had gone out of her eyes, out of her posture. "I'm sorry. I'm not looking to throw you to the wolves or out in the street." She put up her hands. "I just — I didn't know you were so —"

"Hard up?"

"Alone."

"Thanks for the reminder," Maureen said. She pulled on her coat and grabbed her bag, sliding out of the booth. She dug some cash from her pocket and tossed it on the table. "Dinner is on me."

"Wait, Maureen," Molly said. "Please don't go. This wasn't supposed to be a fight."

Maureen slung her bag over shoulder. "Molly, fight's what I've got left."

After the long, cold bus ride, wishing she had a couple of Tanya's pills in her pocket, standing in a pool of yellow porch light on the concrete stoop, Maureen turned the key in her mother's front door. She wanted sleep. Sleep, sleep, and more sleep. On the bus, exhaustion had crushed her like an avalanche, leaving her eyelids fluttering, her forehead bouncing gently against the cold window. Pushing open the front door, her arms weighed a hundred pounds each and her back ached as if she'd worked a week of doubles.

Maureen dropped her bag to the floor in the foyer. Light shone from the kitchen up the stairs. Maureen blinked at it. If the light was on, her mom was up there. Her mom didn't call down to her. There was no *Is that you, honey?* Who didn't question someone walking through their front door after midnight? Amber Coughlin, that's who. Because she knew it could only be Maureen walking through the door. There was no husband, no boyfriend, and no other kids to do it.

She had hoped her mom would be asleep when she arrived. That way, she could crawl downstairs into the basement and pass out on the couch. But Maureen had heard the bored sigh and the gurgle of wine into a glass from where she stood. Her mom was letting her stay. The least she could do was say hello. Have a glass with her.

She hung her coat on the rack by the door and trudged up the stairs.

Her mom sat at the kitchen table, reading a furniture catalog that Maureen knew she'd kept at her elbow just to flip through when she showed up, because Amber wasn't waiting up, she happened to be awake. Her thin hair, the color of her name, was clipped in a tangle atop her head. White wine in a dirty glass stood at her other elbow.

Maureen got a glass from the cabinet. She held it up to the light and rubbed at the dishwasher spots with the sleeve of her sweater. She wondered if anything but wineglasses got run through that washer anymore — the washer her father had left unfixed, unfinished, and pulled to pieces when he decided to go ahead and disappear. In high school, she'd hatched the idea that he'd torn the machine apart on purpose, as some kind of final symbolic commentary on his marriage. By graduation, though, she'd decided that while this gesture was typical of people in books and plays, her father's talent for commentary had been limited to statements such as: *Would you please throw a goddamn strike already!* and *Chicken? Again?* Maureen eventually admitted to herself that she'd simply been searching for anything, even years after his departure, that might function as a good-bye.

Thinking of her father, Maureen realized she'd forgotten to check the staircase wall for his picture, the one her mother had left hanging for nearly twenty years. Every time she came back home, Maureen hoped her mom had finally taken it down. Every time Maureen was disappointed. It was a picture of her father alone, no Maureen, no Amber. Fitting, Maureen had always figured. It certainly seemed to match the way her dad saw the world. Maureen reached into the fridge for the bottle of wine. She poured a glass and pulled out the chair opposite her mother at the table. There were still three chairs.

"I thought you'd be over earlier," her mother said, studying the catalog. "Lucky for you I'm awake. Have some wine, while you're at it."

"Sorry. Thanks," Maureen said. Why did those two words always go together around her mother?

Amber looked up, her mouth pinched, dark circles of sleeplessness two decades old under her green eyes. "I think there's half a hero in the fridge." She didn't move to get up. "Italian. Help yourself." She looked down at her catalog.

"Maybe later," Maureen said, watching as her mother lifted a thin finger to her mouth, licked it, and flipped a page. "I ate before I came over."

"Wise," her mother said.

Amber wore a wrinkled, shapeless white dress shirt, the sleeves frayed at the buttonless cuffs. One of my father's, Maureen thought. Why does she do that? It can't possibly feel or smell anything like him anymore. There can't be anything left of him in that shirt. She couldn't recall the last time her mom had bought new clothes. She still wore her wedding ring, a thin dull band of gold that slipped on her finger when she moved her hand.

Ten years ago, on the anniversary of her father's departure, thinking she might help her mother finally start to close the door on her grief, nineteen-year-old Maureen had pooled a month's worth of tips from her first waitressing gig and bought her mom a pretty gold chain. With a chain, Amber could wear the ring around her neck and get it off her finger. Amber slapped her daughter's face and kept the chain. Maureen had never seen her wear it, and the ring stayed where her father had put it. Maureen had moved out of the house two weeks later.

Sometimes, like now, watching her mother turn the ring on her finger, Maureen felt she'd never earned back the cash she'd spent on that chain. She felt she'd never catch up; she'd never recover, no matter how hard she worked, what she'd given away a long time ago.

Her mom glanced up at her. "Tell me you're not pregnant."

"No," Maureen said. "I don't even have a boyfriend."

"Don't complain about it to me. Living like a vampire won't find you one, neither."

"I told you," Maureen said. "Landlord's fumigating the building."

Amber squinted. "That thing in your nose won't help, either. No matter what those magazines say."

"I like it. I think it's cute." Good Lord, how many times had they already had this conversation? Would having it face-to-face finally put it to bed? "I got it for me, not for boys."

Amber scrunched her lips. "Like that's a better reason. Pretty girl like you, punching holes in her nose. God gave you two, that's not enough? Like anyone in this family needs more holes in their head."

Family? Maureen wanted to ask, what family? It's just me and you, Mom, and this is the best we can do.

"If I get sick of it," Maureen said, "I can take it out. Hole'll disappear in no time."

"Makes you look like Rudolph," Amber said. Then she actually smiled. "In plenty of time for Christmas."

Amber gulped her wine. She watched her daughter over the top of her glass, waiting, Maureen knew, for her to say something. They both knew the wine, the multiple bottles Amber burned through every week, was Maureen's one fail-safe shot at her mother. When Maureen held her peace, Amber took another swallow.

Maureen touched the fake emerald in her nostril. It was sore and, she knew, red. She'd been so close, but then the coke had irritated it all over again. "Very funny, Miss Grinch. My nose will be its cute, perky, bejeweled self by Christmas, I'll have you know."

She finished her wine, got up for more. Her mother slid her own mostly empty glass to the table's edge for a refill. "You wear that thing to class?"

"Believe me," Maureen said, pouring them both more wine, "over at Richmond College I'm the tame one. No one will even notice."

"Then why even have it?"

Maureen slammed the fridge closed. "Jesus, Ma, enough already. It's just a goddamn nose ring." She leaned against the fridge, wineglass in her fingers, tapping her head against the freezer. Here it comes. I walked right into it. Nothing got her mom going like a good *goddamn*.

Amber raised a finger in the air. "Don't you dare swear at me in my own kitchen. Save the sailor mouth for your friends at the bar." She turned in her seat. "These places you work, these bars, they make you dirty. No matter what you do. Nothing good comes from them."

Maureen looked down at her mother, thinking of Sebastian. Ma, you have no idea, she wanted to say. But her mom did know what could happen in a bar. Maureen knew, too. Had learned before she ever delivered her first drink.

Amber turned away, reached for her glass. "Look what they did to your father."

William Coughlin. Though most often found behind a desk or atop a bar stool instead of at home, he kept the bills paid and the gas tanks and the cupboards full. Dad. Never missed a Patty's Day parade. Never missed Mass. Never missed parent-teacher night. Until the day he decided to miss the rest of his family's life. Dad. Gone to collect his Super Bowl winnings at Clancy's Pub twenty years ago and never heard from again. The only year he'd ever won. The first bet, he'd announced on his way out the door, that he'd won since scoring a date with Amber Fagan ten years earlier. On a Sunday. Dad. The trump card. But why not play it when it always worked? Cut Maureen's knees right out from under her. It had cut the heart out of Amber, too.

One month after William disappeared, a great big policeman informed Amber that the NYPD was closing the missing persons case. Along with William Coughlin and his car, a waitress from Clancy's had also disappeared that night, taking with her three suitcases and her husband's savings. The policeman handed Amber a photograph of the waitress and William standing on a beach somewhere, some tropical island, it looked like. The photo had arrived at the waitress's former place of employment with no note, no return address. While *missing* warranted a continuing search, the cop explained, plain old *gone* did not. Problem was, Maureen thought, the missing part had never stopped for Amber. She reached out her hand and set it on her mother's shoulder.

"It's not forever, Ma," Maureen said. "And I'm careful."

She felt her mother turn to stone under her hand. They were done talking for the night. They had moved miles away from each other while standing in the same room.

Maureen pulled her hand away. "Sheets and towels downstairs?" she asked. She swallowed the last of her wine, the sweet, cheap chardonnay on top of the vodka making her ill. She set her glass by the sink and headed for the stairs to retrieve her bag.

"Wait a minute," her mother said.

Maureen stopped on the top step, looked into the kitchen. Amber had her fingers splayed on the tabletop, staring through her yellow wine at the gold band on her finger. "It's cold down there. Heat's expensive these days. I made up your old room."

Maureen came back to the doorway. "Thanks, Mom. Thanks for letting me stay."

"You're welcome. Just don't expect me to do your laundry."

"I got it, Ma. I'm a big girl."

In her old room, Maureen drew the shade against the streetlights and the moon. She left the light off. She didn't need it. Even after ten years out of the house, she remembered every inch of her childhood space. Though she rarely came to visit and never stayed over, it wasn't like she never thought about it. Besides, her ladybug night-light, a rare gift from her father, glowed against the dusty floorboards. It seemed it was only weeks, maybe even days, after giving her the night-light that he had vanished. Had that been the good-bye? His idea, maybe, of something to watch over her?

As she undressed with a shiver, Maureen thought of her father's picture hanging in the lightless foyer he had stopped caring about long ago, watching over the front door no one ever opened but Amber. What was her mom trying to prove, leaving that picture up there? Was she trying to send her husband a message? Did Amber think if he watched her walk through that door enough times he'd remember how to do it and come home? Well, it wasn't that he'd forgotten, Maureen thought. He had chosen not to come home, had found a better offer. Was that Amber's message for her daughter? Never forget, him or what he did. And all the things he never did.

Naked, the sheets cold against her skin, Maureen pulled up the covers. The bed had felt a lot bigger and a lot warmer when she was a girl, just like the world and the people in it. Just like me, she thought. How'd that happen? That I got smaller as I got older? She could smell cigarette smoke in her hair, wine on her breath. An ambulance sped down a street not far away, a dog howling at the siren. Curled up tight in the blankets, inhaling the clean, empty scent of the sheets, Maureen watched the light from the kitchen glowing in a thin line under her bedroom door. It was still there when she fell asleep.

12

A little after nine the next morning, Maureen stepped into the cold sunshine sporting her high school track team sweats, one of her father's old wool caps pulled down tight on her head, and a long-forgotten pair of her mother's torn gloves on her hands. She knelt on the sidewalk in front of her mother's house to retie her running shoes, her breath a white cloud over her shoe tops, the cold stinging her cheeks. She had her smokes tucked in the fold of her cap. It was about a mile, she figured, from her mom's to Dennis's house.

She bent at the waist, reaching for her toes. Her hamstrings pulled her fingers up short on her shins. Her first run in weeks. No big deal. It was gonna hurt like hell. Starting over always did. She took a deep breath and hit the street at an easy pace, heading up Bovanizer Street toward Amboy Road. There she'd hook a left, then right onto Richmond Avenue and start uphill.

Maureen couldn't believe it, but Tanya had called. At 9 a.m. no less. Well, Tanya hadn't called technically; she'd sent a text. Dennis's address followed by the word *soon*. Lying in bed, reading the text, her limbs heavy as wet cement, Maureen had thought, Okay, then, let's go. She'd kicked off the covers and hit the floor for push-ups. She got in twenty before her shoulders and wrists started to ache. An improvement. A couple days off from work had done her good. Two days ago she had barely been able to force herself through ten. And now here she was, out running through her old neighborhood.

She hit the intersection of Amboy Road and Richmond Avenue at a good clip. She hung a right at the bank, passing the old Y as she crested the hill. Her aches and pains started falling away like old feathers, her legs rallying underneath her. Throughout her body, Maureen's muscles scrambled awake under the push and stretch and the oxygen and hot blood her pounding heart shot through her. She picked up the pace heading downhill, forcing her breath through her nose, fighting against letting her feet slap down heavily. She'd always had a light step, each foot only glancing the ground before it kicked up and out behind her again. A *light step and a long stride for a small woman*. That's what the track coach in high school had told her. Where had her step and her stride gone? I wore them out running laps, Maureen thought, back and forth from bar to table thousands of times in cheap black shoes. For years.

Her lungs started burning as she passed her old preschool. With a glance across the street, she saw it had a different name now, something that ended in Institute. She missed the rest of the building's new title. She was moving too fast. What had they called that place when she had gone there, fallen off the jungle gym and broken her wrist, and punched Timmy What'shisname for spitting on her? Suspended at five years old. She'd set a record and missed the trip to Turtleback Zoo.

The old name had been fun and simple: Playland or Kiddietime. Something suited for an amusement park or a toy store. She looked back, over her shoulder. Well, so much for that. Playtime was long over at the institute, it seemed. No jungle gym in the yard anymore. Monday morning and no sign of kids at all. The place looked like a miniature community college. It looked—well, institutional. Maureen coughed up something thick from deep in her lungs, held it on her tongue for a moment, and then spat it over her shoulder. She refocused on the road ahead of her. Keep it moving. Stay fast.

The traffic roared by just off her right hip, each car tailgating the one before it, creating a wind-tunnel pull like a passing train that threatened to suck her into the middle of the street. Every other car seemed the size of an ambulance. She had to pay attention. One stumble could land her in a wheelchair or worse. She could've moved onto the sidewalk, but the buckled concrete might send her flying. And moving over meant giving ground.

As she ran, Maureen passed one white duplex after another, the curtains drawn, the driveways and yards empty. No one was home. With the kids safe at the institute, their parents roamed free in the rolling bubbles of their enormous cars, pumping out a steady stream of exhaust for Maureen to inhale. She didn't pass a single person moving on foot. In a way, she had the streets to herself.

She coughed again, hard enough to stagger her stride. Up ahead, Richmond ended at the intersection with Hylan Boulevard, only six blocks away. Maybe she'd take a breather there. Go ahead, Maureen, she thought, have another cigarette. No break at the turn, she thought, keep it going. You don't know when you'll be able to run like this again.

Closing in on Hylan, she could see the Atlantic materialize through the tall bare trees across the boulevard. The trees, then the broad, shingled backs of the houses, and then between the branches and over the peaked rooftops the ocean appeared, like a second sky. Seeing the water down on the South Shore always surprised her. She'd reached the edge of the island. A pocket of sprawling waterfront houses down there, inspired by Hamptons and Jersey Shore pretensions, sitting fat and heavy on plank platforms and stilts. You know, in case a big hurricane came swirling up to Staten Island. The owners probably had their own separate institute for the kids, to make sure they didn't get dirtied up among the unwashed masses. Another world. Private streets and security patrols, like they weren't even part of the island, like money could turn the backside of Hylan

Boulevard into the Outer Banks or Hilton Head. But they did have their own beach, their own space. Piers and docks for their boats. That's what she'd heard. She'd never been down there herself. Probably never would be. Not without a tray in her hand.

She hung a left at the intersection, putting her right shoulder to the ocean, and kept running. Fewer cars on Hylan. The air tasted cleaner, a touch of sea salt stinging the back of her tongue as her breathing turned ragged. Everything is so jammed up around here, she thought. Everyone is packed in so tight it's hard to remember this used to be a beautiful island, a resort island, even. Out beyond the homes, the strip malls, the diners, and the barrooms, there remained on the island's edges secluded cattailed marshes stalked by gray-legged herons and ivory-feathered egrets, rocky shorelines surveyed from above by gliding osprey aloft on the drafts. At least on the parts of the coast that hadn't been plowed under for McMansions and their private piers.

Panting through her mouth, Maureen forced the air in and out through her teeth, refusing to let her jaw drop, or her arms, holding her fists high. She pumped her arms harder to make up for the weakening in her legs, their previous exuberance now fading fast. *This is when the work gets done,* her old coach had said. *When you're tired.*

I've been working, Maureen argued back, for ten straight years. When's the work over?

Underneath her cap, sweat broke out on her scalp. Stopping and tearing off the cap would feel so good. A few more blocks, she told herself. Make it like sex, like the shift's first cigarette. The longer you hold out, the better it feels when you give in. That was the myth, anyway. Believe it. Anything to keep going. She strained to read the street signs two, three blocks ahead, looking for Downey Street, giving herself a target. Keep going, she told herself, and eventually you'll feel great, even if it's only for a few moments. Her feet slapped the sidewalk now as if she ran in flippers. Her lungs couldn't hold a breath long enough to pull enough oxygen from it. A block short of Dennis's street, a killer stitch tore open in her side. All right, enough. This is exercise, not suicide. She sprinted to his corner.

Turning up Downey, Maureen forced herself to ease down on the throttle instead of slamming to a stop. No sense cramping and ending up flat on her back. She didn't need some dumb Samaritan calling her an ambulance. Hands on hips, chest heaving, she slowed to an easy walk for the next two blocks up Downey. Not bad, she thought. No one at the Narrows (except for maybe Clarence) could hit off a mile, more or less, right out of bed. Betcha Molly couldn't do it. John, either, no matter what kind of acrobatics they got up to in the sack. Waters would've had a heart attack after four blocks.

She pulled her smokes from her hat, tore it off. The cold wind in her hair felt wonderful. She closed her eyes, held her arms out at her sides. For a moment, she felt so light that a good gust might lift her right off the street. But after another half a block, the cold had crept in around the edges. She pulled her cap back on. She craved a cigarette but re-sisted. That's the problem with highs; they don't last.

Three-oh-two was the address she wanted. She checked the number on the house in front of her: 318. She reversed her direction; Dennis's place was back toward the corner. Maureen looked up and down the street. Where was Tanya, waiting in her car? Maureen didn't see it, and the few cars parked on the block sat empty.

She dragged her hand across her mouth, spat out a stray thread her glove left behind. Man, she was thirsty. Why hadn't she stopped sooner, picked up some water at one of the delis she had passed on Hylan? Could she raid Dennis's fridge or would that be too weird? She stopped at the end of the walk in front of Dennis's house. Where was Tanya? Goddamn, Maureen thought, that girl had better not pull a no-call-no-show on this. Wouldn't that be like her, though? And just like me to show up anyway.

Maureen was seriously considering heading back to her mom's when Tanya walked out the door of 302's side apartment.

"You went in already?" Maureen asked. "Am I that late?"

Tanya glided up the red brick walk. Her Pocahontas hair floated off her shoulders in the wind. She wore a heavy brown suede coat, brand-new and stylish, with a belt and a fur collar. The coat reached the top of her calf-length boots. Why does this girl, Maureen thought, always look like she's walking up a runway? Maureen tugged at her sweatpants, stuck with sweat to her thighs. And me? I look like a housewife who's been chasing the paper boy for bombing her hedges and teasing her dog. Well, fine then. Tanya couldn't have run that mile.

"I was freezing," Tanya said. She stopped on the other side of the gate. "You're not late. Did you run all the way here?"

Maureen sniffed in her snot. Her nose had started running. She couldn't decide what looked worse, wiping her nose on her glove or letting the fluid leak down her lip. She chose using the glove. Tanya didn't notice. She was distracted, disconnected. Well, like that's news. "It's not that far. I needed the exercise."

"They have gyms for that," Tanya said. "Warm, indoor gyms. Like Clarence's." She opened the gate, the frosted yellow grass of the dead lawn crackling under her boots as she stepped off the walk to let Maureen into the yard.

"So I've heard," Maureen said. She headed up the walk toward the house. She heard Tanya close the gate and hustle up behind her.

At the front door, Maureen stepped aside to let Tanya open it. Tanya settled her fingers on the brass doorknob, but didn't grip it, didn't turn it. Biting her bottom lip, she glanced at Maureen, looked back at the door. Maureen waited, tired, thirsty, and growing impatient. She was sorry Dennis was dead, she truly was, and she felt for Tanya, but enough with the drama. Couldn't she do anything for herself?

"I want you to know," Tanya said, looking up at the sky, "that I'm sorry about this. I wish there was another way."

"T, it's all right, let's just get it done. You can make it up to me at work, cover a shift for me. Is it kind of creepy in there?"

Tanya kept her gaze fixed overhead.

"We'll pretend he's just not home," Maureen said. She reached for the doorknob.

Tanya sucked in a wet breath through her nose. "Remember I said I was sorry."

From the other side of the door, Maureen felt the knob turn in her fingers. She jerked her hand away. The door opened. Sebastian stood not three feet from her, at the foot of a dark staircase.

"Enough already with the bullshit," he said. "Get in here."

Maureen stepped back from the doorway, out of his reach. "Fuck you." She glared at Tanya. "Fuck, Tanya. How could you? I tried to help you. I thought we were friends."

Tanya looked pale and horrified, her bottom lip trembling. "I'm sorry." Her eyes flitted from Maureen to Sebastian and back again. They finally settled on empty space. "I had to, Maureen. You don't understand."

"Upstairs," Sebastian said. He stepped aside to let Tanya into the apartment. She ran up the stairs. Sebastian glanced over his shoulder, then looked back at Maureen. "You too." When Maureen didn't react, he returned to the doorway. "We need to talk about you and the police. Come inside. Now. You're letting the fucking heat out."

Maureen backed up the walk, pointing her finger at him. "You take another step and I'll scream."

Sebastian stepped out the door. He closed it behind him and followed Maureen up the path, letting her keep a few steps' distance between them. He walked with one hand open on his chest, his other arm extended, as if inviting Maureen to dance. "I just wanna talk. Why is it you'll talk about us to everyone but me?"

Maureen wanted to look around, needing to pick a direction to run in. But she feared taking her eyes off Sebastian. If she let her guard down, he could close the few feet between them in seconds. "Go back in the house or I swear to Christ I'll scream bloody murder."

Sebastian glanced up and down the street. "You see anyone around to hear you? This is a family neighborhood. Work, school. People who live in the daytime, like normal Americans. The land of the living." He smiled, his nostrils flaring. "Anyways, you're not a screamer. I know people. I can tell."

"You are a fucking freak. Stay away from me."

"I'm a freak? Because I let Dennis suck my cock?" Sebastian frowned. "Really, Maureen, you're more enlightened than that. How do you know it wasn't his idea?"

"Tanya told me about Dennis and the money," Maureen said, "and how you were getting him and Tanya to pay you back. How about I call the *Advance*, the *Daily News*, and tell them what Tanya told me?"

Sebastian laughed. "Go ahead. You know what Tanya told you? Whatever she had to for you to show up here this morning. If she got overly dramatic or grotesque and she upset you, I apologize. Blame her. She always did want to be an actress." He smiled. "I made sure she was motivated to play her part." His smile, his humor suddenly disappeared. "Coming at it from another angle, what makes you think, for a second, that if those reporters do show up at her door, she's gonna say anything other than what I tell her to? Just like when I sent her looking for you."

"Maybe I invite them to *my* door," Maureen said, backing away. "Maybe I tell them what I saw at the Narrows."

"You'll get laughed at. Think, Maureen. Look at yourself, look at your life. What reporter is gonna believe you? Is even gonna risk talking to you? Especially without a single living witness to back you up." Sebastian stepped closer, his eyelids drooping lizardlike as his eyebrows drifted up his forehead. He spoke just above a whisper. "And what do you think, Maureen, the cops will find in your apartment should a single breath of that story ever surface? Dramatic and grotesque won't even be the start of it."

"The cops know about you," Maureen said. "They're plenty interested in what I know about Dennis and Tanya."

"Yeah, well, I know things, too." Sebastian stepped to her, looming over her now. "I know all about Detective Nat Waters, for instance. I've known him probably longer than you've been alive." Sebastian chuckled. "Waters didn't scare me back in the day and he doesn't now. You know what your problem is? You think you know who you're dealing with, and you don't. You think you're smart, and you're not. Next time you see Waters, ask him about me. Ask him about Brooklyn. Then come back to me and tell me which one of us you really want on your side."

Maureen had reached the end of the walk. Sebastian had her backed up against the front gate. Time to slip out to the sidewalk and hit the street running. Even if Sebastian chased her, he'd never catch her. She felt around behind her back for the gate latch, found it. But she couldn't raise it; it was stuck. She found something heavy with her hand. A padlock. She tugged. Locked. When they'd come through the gate before, Tanya had locked it behind them.

Maureen slid her eyes to the left and to the right. Both ways, Dennis's street was a ghost town, a low-rent suburban movie set. Out in the land of the living, Maureen realized, the middle of the day was no more alive than the middle of the night. The only sound she heard was Sebastian breathing. She brought her arms to her sides, clenching her fists. The eyes and the balls, she thought. Go for the eyes and the balls.

A car horn honked behind them. A car was coming up the street. Maureen's heart jumped. Finally, another human being. Sebastian ignored the sound. "Since we're suddenly pressed for time, let's simplify things. You like your apartment?"

"What?"

"Your apartment, do you like it? How about your job?"

The car honked again, the long angry note coming from right behind her.

Sebastian's eyes looked over Maureen's shoulder now. "Forget Brooklyn," he said. "Next time you see Waters, you tell him that, you and me, we worked everything out. Tell him whatever he needs to hear to crawl back into whatever rat hole he climbed out of." His eyes came back to Maureen's. "You do that and maybe I let you keep what little you have. Can you do that for me, like a good girl?"

Maureen turned when Sebastian took a step back, his hands in the air, his face lit up with a megawatt smile, warm and disarming. Maureen couldn't believe she was looking at the same man who had pinned her against the fence. Out in the street, a middle-aged man in a brown suit, a short, chubby version of Dennis, hurried around the front of a giant Chevy Tahoe, a ring of keys in his hand. An older brother, had to be. Tanya burst out the front door of the house, hustling up the walk, Dennis's video camera in her hand. She spotted the new arrival, stopped short, and tucked the camera behind her back.

"What're you people doing?" the man shouted. He unlocked the gate. "Who are you people?" He pulled up short as he recognized Sebastian. "I've seen you on TV. You're that politician, the state senator."

Maureen hurried away from Sebastian, through the open gate, and onto the sidewalk. Thank you, Dennis, she thought, for covering my ass one last time.

Sebastian dialed down the wattage in his smile, dropped his eyes in mock humility. "I certainly hope to be. You flatter me. The election hasn't been held yet."

Standing there on the sidewalk, Maureen felt as frightened by the bizarro charming Sebastian as she had by the menacing bully of a few minutes ago. The transformation had been as simple and as immediate as someone slipping off a pair of sunglasses.

"I knew Dennis," Sebastian said. "He helped me some with my campaign. I liked him, though I wasn't lucky enough to know him very well." He extended his hand. "You must be his brother. I am terribly sorry for your loss."

"Tony Lacoste, Dennis's older brother. I own this property." He gestured toward the Tahoe. "We were coming to close the place up, to sort through his things. Maybe find some photos for the memorial service."

"You'll contact my campaign," Sebastian said, "and let me know when that is?"

"Of course," Tony said. "We'd be honored to have you."

Maureen was ready to gag. So everyone from the Narrows, the people who worked with Dennis, talked to him, who saw him every day, they could go fuck themselves. But this lying snake, he was a guest of honor? She took a deep breath. Maybe she had it wrong. Clearly, Tony must've seen Sebastian threatening her. Maybe he'd called the cops. Maybe he was going along with Sebastian's bullshit to keep him calm, to keep him in place until the police arrived. She decided to remind Tony that she was there.

"Listen, Mr. Lacoste, I really need—"

But before Maureen could finish her sentence, Sebastian moved between her and Tony, blocking her from Tony's view. "Dennis's girlfriend here," he said, "needed to grab a few things she'd left behind. We didn't want to bother your family with it."

Maureen watched the questions cross Tony's face, the main one being where Sebastian fit into all this. A voice in the back of her head ordered Maureen to blurt out the truth, that they'd all been dragged there in Sebastian's effort to clean up his dirty business. Another part of her watched in fascination, curious to see what lies Sebastian would spin next. Maureen could tell that he'd seen the same questions in Tony's eyes that she had.

"The young lady," Sebastian began, tilting his head in Tanya's direction, "is one of my press people. She and Dennis met through my campaign, got together." Maureen caught Tanya's guilty eyes as she slipped the camera into her coat pocket. Tanya looked lonely and pathetic, like an angry kid thieving candy she didn't even want and waiting to get caught. But if Tony had even noticed Tanya leaving the house, and if he'd even heard Maureen's attempt to speak to him, he gave no sign. Tony's attention stayed fixed on Sebastian, the alpha male, the one who, though trespassing with possibly an eye toward kidnapping, had somehow managed to put himself in charge of the situation.

Maureen wanted to grab Tanya's hand and run for it. Then, once she and Tanya were alone, kick the living shit out of her. *I'll teach that stupid slut to pick the wrong side. Right after I save her ass.*

"We were in a staff meeting earlier," Sebastian said. "She asked for the morning off to come over here. I offered my company for support. Insisted, really." He held up his hand. "Tony, I owe you and your family an apology. I've invaded your privacy at a very difficult time. I just thought I could help."

For the first time since he'd arrived at his dead brother's house, sadness settled into Tony's face. "I'm sorry, I'm a bit shocked by everything. Dennis working with your campaign, a girlfriend. I never knew. He was getting himself together, I guess."

Tony glanced back at the car. Maureen figured the old people in the backseat had to be the parents. They gazed emotionless out their respective windows, pointedly not looking at Maureen or anyone else, their mouths moving as they talked to themselves or each other, looking like goldfish through the glass.

"I wish we would've known," Tony said.

Maybe if you'd ever called him, Maureen thought. Ever. Then she remembered that most of what Sebastian had said wasn't true. Good God, she thought, he's almost got me caught up in it. She couldn't settle whether telling Tony these lies about Dennis was cruel or kind. But the lies had nothing to do with Tony, or the Lacoste family, or Dennis. They were for no one's benefit but Sebastian's. Maureen watched as Tanya came up the walk, slipping her arm through Sebastian's when she reached him.

"Wow," Maureen said, causing Tony to notice her for the first time.

He turned to Sebastian. "Who's this?"

"I thought maybe you would know," Sebastian said. He turned to Maureen. "I'm sorry, miss. In all the confusion I didn't catch your name. Was there something we can help you with?"

Maureen looked from Sebastian to Tanya to Tony. Three blank faces stared back at her. "I, uh—forget it. I'm nobody."

Fuck 'em. She turned her back and headed down the street. When she got as far as the corner, she pulled her crumpled pack of cigarettes from her hat and lit one up.

From there she watched as Sebastian and Tanya climbed into a nondescript sedan that didn't suit either of them. No bodyguard, no hired muscle appeared. This really was private business. Sebastian didn't want anyone near him knowing where he was or who he was with. And if Tanya had made up all that shit about the loan and the sex tapes, Maureen wondered, why did she come out of the house with the camera? Method acting? Probably not. Tanya had set her up on Sebastian's orders, but Maureen believed Tanya had baited her trap with the truth.

After Sebastian and Tanya had driven away, Maureen, pacing in circles on the corner as she smoked, watched Tony help his fat, ugly wife out of the front of the SUV.

When they'd pulled up, hadn't these people—the two women, at least—seen Maureen was in trouble? They should've sensed something. Old, married, it didn't matter. You never forget the danger. Hadn't they seen her trapped in the yard, a giant man pressing against her, poised to bite off her head? Could it have been any more obvious? What they see is one thing, she thought; what they care about is another thing entirely. They'd lost a brother, lost their son. Dennis was theirs one day and gone the next. Maureen knew how that felt. Loss like that, sudden as a gunshot, left you blind. And cold.

After her father left, Maureen knew she looked at people, for months, maybe for years, only as objects in her way, things to be moved and manipulated and put aside when they ran empty, like so many liquor bottles on a shelf. Yeah, and she'd shoved everyone aside, even her own mother, on her way to what, exactly? To standing alone in the street, breathless, petrified, and invisible. Maybe—probably—she still didn't see people. Or she at least acted like she didn't, and what was the difference between the two?

Maureen walked back toward Dennis's house. She should say something to his family, something true. Something kind. That Dennis had been a decent man, and good to her. Dennis deserved it. His family did, too. But as Maureen approached the house, Mrs. Lacoste recoiled into her husband's arms as if Maureen had snakes for hair. Tony pulled out his wallet and snatched out a bill, holding it in Maureen's direction.

"Lemme guess," he said, "you just need bus fare, right? Or diapers for your baby? And you promise not to spend it on beer."

Maureen stopped in her tracks, staring at the dollar bill between Tony's fat little fingers. The kindness in her heart hit the street and shattered like a dropped glass on a barroom floor.

"I don't need to hear your bullshit story," Tony said. "Just take the money and quit botherin' us."

Maureen leaned forward and spat in the street at Tony's feet. Then she turned her back on Dennis's family and started running.

13

Back at her mom's, while Amber cooked breakfast, Maureen sneaked outside for a cigarette and a phone call to Waters. She got his voice mail. She asked him to call as soon as he could, but she offered no hint of her run-in with Sebastian. She was safe. No sense getting Waters excited. When she came back inside, the whole house smelled like bacon. Running home, Maureen had thought she might never eat again, the way her stomach was knotted after seeing Sebastian, but the scent and the sizzle of bacon and eggs had her mouth watering. Food first, she thought, heading up the stairs for the kitchen. Shower second. Who's around here that I gotta impress?

After she showered and dressed, Maureen joined her mother at the kitchen sink and helped wash the breakfast dishes, the sleeves of her gold peasant blouse pushed up to her elbows. The blouse and her jeans were high school leftovers found in her old dresser. Rooting around that dresser, she'd also discovered some cheap, frilly K-Mart underwear that she'd worn in high school. She'd called it lingerie and worn it under her school uniform, a private effort to feel grown-up and sexy. She never wore the lingerie on dates, only to school. She'd bought the frilly things for herself, not for boys. It was the best answer she had to the hips and breasts bursting out on what seemed to be every female body but hers.

At the sink, Maureen handled the rinsing, passing the dishes to her mother for inspection before they got loaded into the dishwasher. Amber occasionally handed back a dish, grumbling a demand for another pass under the hot water. Maureen wondered who had finished the repairs on the dishwasher. It felt like something she should know. She couldn't remember if she'd ever asked, but it was way too late to bring up now. Amber would say she didn't remember, whether she did or not. Too close to Dad to talk about. Nice work, Dad, Maureen thought. You left Mom so brokenhearted she can't even talk about the damn dishwasher. Sad.

It's long past time I cut Mom some slack, Maureen thought. She's a survivor. That counts for something—counts for a lot, in fact. She'd hung on to the only house she'd ever owned, had kept it clean and functioning, while at the same time putting herself through night school at Richmond. She'd parlayed a part-time accounting position at the Macy's in the mall into a full-time management position, one with benefits and a retirement plan. One could say she had a career. And she'd raised a daughter from eleven to nineteen on her own. And what had that daughter accomplished with far less on her plate? Not much. She had bills and she had birds—not even pet birds, but wild birds that she couldn't protect from the neighborhood felines.

Maureen handed over the last dish—two people didn't make much of a mess—and pushed her palms into the small of her back, stretching the kinks that ran along her spine. They were stubborn. She straightened maybe half of them out. She was starting to fear that the rest were permanent. Grimacing, she hooked her finger through a belt loop, hitching up her jeans. They hung looser on her hips than they had ten years ago. Wasn't the opposite supposed to happen? Shouldn't she be bigger? She knew she oughtta consider herself lucky.

Leaning against the sink, Maureen watched her mother wipe down the kitchen table, rubbing hard at a spot of egg yolk. Amber's bony elbows and shoulder blades pushed against her oversized T-shirt. That's me, Maureen thought. That's me wiping down a table at the Narrows, at Cargo, at the Haunted Café and the Bicycle Club. Back bent, elbows and shoulders churning, cleaning up again for and after someone else. She studied her hands, the fingertips wrinkled like the faces of old ladies, the backs red and raw. Ten years of bar work has put twenty years on my hands. If you put them side by side, she thought, could you tell my hands from my mother's? Maureen slipped her hands inside the waistband of her jeans, clutching her bony hips.

What has it done to the rest of me?

Waters hadn't called during breakfast. He was working, Maureen reminded herself. He was a city detective; her situation couldn't be the only thing, or even the most important thing, commanding his attention. But it was tough not to feel abandoned, tough not to wonder what had happened between Waters and Sebastian in Brooklyn. Of course, it wasn't out of the question that Sebastian was messing with her head; she'd watched him practically brainwash Tony Lacoste.

She grabbed a dish towel off the counter and dried her hands. She caught herself considering Sebastian's advice and, when she heard from Waters, calling the whole thing off. Then she recalled the look on Sebastian's face when he'd opened Dennis's door to find her standing there, delivered to his doorstep like a mail-order bride. She didn't know if her backing off the police would be enough for him anymore. It seemed to her that he wanted her at his fingertips more than he wanted her to go away.

To tell the truth, she didn't know what to do.

Maybe Sebastian had been right about one thing: she didn't know who she was dealing with. Maureen figured that if Sebastian knew plenty about Waters, as he claimed, maybe the opposite was true. Why not stick with the original plan? Lay out everything that had happened to Waters and see what he said about what to do next.

Groaning, Amber straightened, hitching up her jeans and pressing her hands into the small of her back. She wrapped the dishrag around one of her hands and sat at the kitchen table. "Do me a favor, get me a glass of water."

Maureen grabbed a glass from the cabinet. "Ice?"

"I don't need it too cold," Amber said. "Just let it run for a minute."

Maureen hit the tap and gave the glass a quick polish with her sleeve while she waited for the water to run cool.

"I got the craziest phone call," Amber said, "while you were in the shower."

"Did you win a trip to Costa Rica or a new car?"

"Don't I wish," Amber said. "You remember the Sebastians? From when you were little?"

The glass slipped from Maureen's fingers. When it hit the sink, it cracked from the bottom halfway up, but didn't break into pieces. "Shit." How could he possibly know where she was? Not only where she was but also, if he'd found her mother, *who* she was. Not good, not good at all. She turned to Amber, waiting to see if she was going to catch hell for the curse, the broken glass, or both. "Sorry."

Amber stayed tight-lipped and silent, staring at Maureen for a long moment before speaking. "Leave it by the sink. I'll wrap it in newspaper before I put it in the trash."

When Maureen picked up the glass, it went to pieces. She jerked her hand away and escaped with a small cut on the tip of her forefinger. She watched the pearl of blood form over the cut and then burst and seep into the wrinkles of her knuckles as she pressed her thumb hard against her finger. She heard her mother's chair scrape across the kitchen floor. Her mother appeared beside her at the sink, taking Maureen's injured hand in hers, studying it as if she'd never seen such a thing. Maureen tugged her hand away and stuck her finger under the running water.

"I hope you're better than this at the bar," Amber said, shaking her head, picking shards of glass from the sink with her fingertips. "Cost your boss more than you're worth in glassware and Band-Aids."

"Speaking of," Maureen said.

"In the bathroom, in the medicine cabinet. Where else?"

Where else, indeed, Maureen thought. Why'd I even ask? Probably the same box of Band-Aids as when I was ten years old. She hoped the cut wouldn't scar. She already had half a dozen tiny white marks on her hands. It really didn't take much to leave a lasting mark; a small slice could do it.

"I think there's some peroxide in there too," Amber said.

I'd bet anything, Maureen thought. "Ma, it's a tiny glass cut, it's not a dog bite. I'm not maimed."

"Well, then, quit crying about it to me like a bomb went off. But if you still feel you need major first aid, get to it. She's going to be here any minute."

Maureen turned off the tap. She held her injured hand against her shoulder. The cut had bled out plenty; time to settle it down and wrap it up. "And who's coming over?"

"Gloria Sebastian," Amber said, her voice breathy with exasperation. "Like I've been trying to tell you." Maureen half expected her to throw a *duh* on the end. "Don't you remember Frank and Gloria Sebastian from St. Stephen's?"

Maureen just gaped.

"Maybe not," Amber said. "You were really young and there were so many grown-ups around after Mass. We used to see them every Sunday, back before . . ."

Before Dad left, Maureen thought.

"Back when we still went," Amber said.

Gloria *Sebastian*, Maureen thought. You gotta be kidding me. "Is it her husband that's running for office?"

"Yeah, that's her. Him I can see you forgetting, but are you sure you don't remember Gloria? I think she taught you CCD one year. Maybe two. Third, fourth grade, maybe. She was close with the monsignor. I helped her with the Christmas Club. I used to see her all the time."

"I don't remember."

Amber set her hands on her hips. "That's so like you, Maureen. To forget the people that were nice to you. You need to treat people better. Now her husband's going to be someone important, someone who can maybe help you get financial aid for school, or get a real job someday, and you can't even be bothered to remember them."

The doorbell chimed. Maureen's throat went tight, and the blood rushed out of her face like it was desperate for somewhere to hide.

Amber glanced over her shoulder at the front door, then put out her hand. "Lemme see that cut again. You don't look so good all of a sudden."

"I'm fine. I'm not a huge fan of the sight of my own blood, that's all. Go ahead and get the door. I'm gonna get that Band-Aid. It'll just take a minute."

"Suit yourself." Amber shook her head, a bemused grin wrinkling the corners of her eyes. "I haven't heard from Gloria for years, and then she calls out of the blue, no warning. It's the strangest thing."

Amber went to the front door as Maureen headed for the bathroom.

Standing at the sink, Maureen splashed peroxide over her fingertip, grateful for the head-clearing sting. She opened the medicine cabinet and found the old box of Band-Aids. Over the chemical sizzle of the peroxide, she tracked the voices coming up the stairs and into the kitchen. Two women and a man. Of course he'd come too. Showing Maureen he could reach her mom was the whole point of Gloria's phone call, wasn't it? Maureen picked apart the Band-Aid's wrapper, doing her best to keep the sterile bandage clean. She fought back memories of hiding in the Narrows's bathroom, afraid to come out. Now here he was in her mother's own house.

She pressed her cut fingertip into the white pad, a stain of bright red blood creeping across it. She wrapped the rubber wings of the Band-Aid around her knuckle. She could hear Sebastian's voice echoing back to her through the house. What was it with men? Always pushing. You slap their hand away from your blouse, so they reach for the front of your jeans. How does that add up? Maureen bit her lip and took a deep breath. Messing with her landlord and her apartment was one thing. Messing with her mom was another thing entirely.

She held tight to the air inside her as she headed down the hall toward the kitchen. Frank Sebastian sat at her mother's small kitchen table in a dark suit, looking oddly gigantic, the coffee cup at his lips completing the image of a grown-up guest at a little girl's tea party. She knew it was illusion, but Sebastian seemed bigger, felt bigger, every time she saw him. His silver hair was perfect. His too-made-up dark-haired wife sat to his right. Amber sat at the head of the table, in the third chair.

Maureen noticed there was no seat for her at the table. She leaned back against the counter, the utensil drawer and its set of ancient steak knives at her right hip. She willed herself to think of Clint Eastwood, standing in the middle of Main Street in some Western town, his fingers wiggling over his holster. She made mental notes locating knives, scissors, vegetable peelers—any and all sharp objects she could think of.

Sebastian rose in his seat, bent at the waist like he might bump his head on the ceiling. "Please, Maureen. Come sit. Take my chair."

"I'm fine standing." The coffeepot gurgled behind her. Now that would hurt. Hot coffee in the face. Or the lap. That would cut him down to size.

Amber turned in her seat and gave Maureen a tight smile, a silent warning to mind her manners. "Maureen."

"I had a long run this morning," Maureen said. "If I sit, my legs'll tighten up and I'll get sore. I'd rather stand. Helps me stay loose. It's nothing personal."

Gloria chuckled. "You must be close to thirty by now. So little has changed. You're still a slip of a thing. I couldn't get you to sit in CCD, either." She sighed, shifting her eyes from Maureen to Amber. "It's good to see you again, both of you. Lord, you could be sisters."

Maureen wondered if that meant she looked old or that her mother looked young. Whichever way Gloria meant it, Maureen thought, at least mother and daughter looked human—unlike Gloria Sebastian, her skin pulled taut at the eyes, her lips puffy like lumpy pillows. And that ridiculous cleavage rising from her loud silk blouse. Boobs that big didn't float that high when you were twenty, never mind on the south side of fifty, which Mrs. Sebastian had to be. Maureen tried pulling up memories of Gloria from the after-school religion classes she'd endured at St. Stephen's. She got nowhere. Of course, who knew what Gloria had looked like twenty years ago? A slender blonde could be hiding under all that surgery, makeup, and hair dye, under all that money, and no one would ever know it.

"I thought the other night I knew you from somewhere," Sebastian said, folding his hands in his lap, looking at Maureen. "There was something so familiar about you. I couldn't stop thinking about it. It was killing me."

"I hate when that happens," Maureen said.

"She can be a thorn," Amber said with a smile. "Even on her best days."

"And then I remembered that we knew each other once," Sebastian said. "More or less. When you were a little girl I used to see you at church every Sunday. You, your mom, your dad. All together. Back then your hair was long, all the way down your back. And it was redder then, darker, red like a sunrise."

"I can't say I remember you," Maureen said. "I'm sorry."

"My hair was darker then, too," Sebastian said.

"It's no big deal. You know how it is with kids," Gloria said, talking to Maureen and then her husband. "Adults all look the same."

Sebastian glanced over at his wife as if he'd only then noticed she was next to him. He looked back at Maureen. "Well, I remember you. Clear as a bell." He glanced around the table. "You're more memorable than you think."

"I agree," Gloria said. "So smart. And not afraid to show it."

Amber straightened up tall in her seat, peeking into her guests' coffee cups. "Think you could warm us up, Maureen? While you're up?"

Maureen considered a comment about serving on her day off but swallowed it. She also let it slide that Amber's response to Gloria's compliments was to order another round of coffee from her smart and fearless waitress daughter. Maybe she didn't like Maureen being the center of attention in *her* kitchen. Whatever attitude her mom copped had to be forgiven, Maureen decided, and forgotten. She wanted to show solidarity in front of the Sebastians, him especially. He needed to see that there'd be no using her and her mother against each other. She grabbed the coffeepot and made the rounds at the table.

"So, Mom said it's been a dog's age since she's heard from you guys." She hovered with the coffeepot over Sebastian's cup until he nodded. "Why the sudden interest?"

"Well, I don't know if you've heard," Sebastian said, "but I started a new project for the parish some time ago, an outreach program between St. Stephen's and the battered women's shelter in Great Kills. Fundraising, connecting women in need with resources, that kind of thing." He reached into his wife's lap and patted her folded hands. "If you've followed the campaign at all, you know that troubled women are close to my heart."

Maureen turned her back to the room when she set the coffeepot back on the counter, to hide her face. Don't sell yourself short, she thought. Troubled boys are in there, too. "I've heard things to that effect."

"With the campaign heating up," Gloria said, "Frank asked that I get more involved, help round up some volunteers. Really get the thing off the ground."

"The more solid the program is when I get there," Sebastian said, "the more I can do for it from Albany."

"*If* you get there," Maureen said.

Gloria forced a breathy chuckle. "Oh, Maureen. Where's your faith?" Her eyes flitted from Amber to Maureen and back again. She felt the tension in the room, Maureen could tell, and it was confusing her. Gloria patted her husband's thigh. "Frank's so far ahead they shouldn't even bother with the vote. They should just send him upstate first thing tomorrow morning."

"Now there's an idea," Maureen said.

Sebastian turned to his wife. "People deserve their say, dear. You know how I feel about that." He turned to Maureen, raising his chin to look at her down his nose. "Besides, that would leave me with a lot of business to tie up in one night. It'd be irresponsible of me to leave loose ends all over Staten Island."

"The two of you," Gloria said, shaking her head. "Maureen, such fire. Listen to me, Frank Sebastian. If you've got a brain in your head, you'll reach out to this young woman from Albany. Put her to work."

Sebastian settled his weight in his chair, the frame creaking under his bulk. "I'm sure I can find just the place to put her."

"See that, Maureen?" Amber said. "Soon as you finish school."

"I confess, Am," Gloria said, "that it was Frank who first thought of calling you, after putting two and two together and remembering Maureen. But I did leap for the phone when he said your name. These women we're reaching out to, they really need help; a lot of them are single moms. A lot of them have other problems, like you did. They can relate to you." She looked down at the table. "I haven't been the greatest friend and I'm not afraid to be humbled about that in front of you and your daughter. I hope you can forgive me."

Amber drummed her fingers on her forearms. She looked around the room, anxious, it seemed to Maureen, for a safe place to rest her eyes, and cleared her throat a couple of times as if to start speaking. Finally, she reached across the table and patted Gloria's arm. "Of course I forgive you. What kind of Christian would I be if I didn't?"

When Gloria smiled, her apparent joy ignited the kitchen as if someone had lit a chandelier overhead. Maureen was stunned. She wondered for a moment if Gloria hadn't taught Frank a thing or two about working a room instead of the other way around. Maureen watched as, under Gloria's loving gaze, Amber's shoulders melted like a snowdrift under the sun. Ten years dropped off her face. Maureen felt she was watching Sebastian work Tony Lacoste all over again. She needed to break the spell.

"So what makes you such a great candidate, Mom, to liaison with a battered women's shelter?"

Amber held up her hand. She wouldn't look at her daughter, as if she knew exactly what Maureen was up to. "It's not what you think. Don't get upset."

"I'm not upset. I'm curious."

Amber turned, her face expressionless. "I was a psychology major in college. I did some volunteering."

"Bullshit."

"Maureen!"

"Ma, you went to school for accounting."

"Frank, Gloria, I'm sorry," Amber said, turning to her guests. "She's overworked, she's having problems with her apartment. She's short on sleep."

"She's standing right here," Maureen said, "and asking a simple question."

Sebastian took his wife's hand and stood. Maureen could see him straining to hold back a smile. No one else seemed to notice his effort. "Gloria, give Amber the envelope and let's get out of the Coughlin ladies' hair for the day."

Gloria pulled a manila envelope from a giant designer handbag. She slid it across the table. "It's a meeting schedule; we'll be getting together at St. Stephen's twice a month. And there's a phone list with the names and numbers of the other women in the group. I'll be having a little something over at the house for the whole group soon."

"You'll let me know?" Amber asked.

"You're first on the list," Gloria said. "I'd like for us to be close again. I never should have let that go."

Sebastian backed away from the table to let his wife come around in front of him. He waited, grinning at Maureen the entire time, as Gloria and Amber exchanged hugs and whispered farewells. When the two women broke their embrace, Sebastian took one of Amber's hands in one of his. He set his other hand on her shoulder.

"Just great to see you, Amber," he said. "Thanks for letting us intrude on your morning. And thanks for coming on board with Gloria's project. We're both very grateful, and I know those women you're going to help will be, too." He tipped an invisible hat to Maureen. "Maybe it doesn't mean anything coming from a boring out-of-touch old man like me, but I feel your pain. I know you're tired. I know it's hard to see your future. But never forget, ever, that it's people like you, women like you especially, that drive me. I promise you, I won't let you slip my mind this time." Sebastian settled his hand on the small of his wife's back. "Get some rest and don't be a stranger, if you need anything." He guided Gloria toward the stairs.

Maureen waited at the top of the stairs as Amber, after giving her daughter a long, dirty look, followed the Sebastians down to the front door. After Gloria stepped out, Sebastian turned. "Amber, I took the liberty of putting a 'Sebastian for Senate' lawn sign out front. I hope you don't mind."

"Not at all," Amber said. "Saves me the trouble of doing it myself."

The three of them exchanged one more quiet farewell; then Amber locked the door. She turned, hands on her hips. "What the hell is wrong with you?"

"You got an associate's in accounting," Maureen said. "Believe me, I know. You've told me a thousand times about your degree, about your heroic slog through night school. I can repeat it back to you if you like. What are you lying for? Especially to those two."

"Accounting came after your father left." Amber straightened his picture on the wall. "Before him, for your information, I was a psych major at Wagner. That's what I was when we met. I never finished but that doesn't mean I didn't study and didn't learn, like you and those books you pretend to read. So watch who you're calling a liar."

"So there's nothing to these 'other problems' you had that battered women could relate to."

Amber crossed her arms and leaned back against the door. "Listen, Gloria's putting on a show to help Frank get elected and she needs some help, not that he needs hers. She never could resist the urge to show off. Years ago it was jewelry and her daddy's car; now it's her new boobs and her big-shot husband. I promise you every woman she's recruiting for this outreach program is either divorced or widowed and probably broke.

"We used to know each other and she thinks I'm lonely and bored and easy to hit up for time, and she's right and so what? She's full of it and I know it and she knows I know it and we go through the motions anyway. It's what adults do, in case you hadn't noticed. It's how we have friends. You oughtta try it some time, get some of your own. Quit barreling into my life whenever you need something."

"You never answered me," Maureen said, sitting on the top step. "What does Gloria know about you and Dad that I don't?"

"Pffff, Gloria. She doesn't know half of what she thinks she does, that's what she knows. I never did like that woman very much. And we were never close, no matter what she says." Amber came halfway up the steps, sat a couple down from her daughter. "Anything I didn't tell you it's because it didn't matter."

"Ma."

"But if you're gonna pitch a fit about it." With both hands, Amber brushed her hair back from her temples. Maureen noticed that the ten years that had dropped off Amber's eyes under Gloria's smile had returned. They'd brought another five years back with them. Amber studied her fingernails as she spoke. "When you were six, your father and I went through a phase."

"Uh-oh."

"You asked," Amber said. "There was a girl up the block old enough to baby-sit. Your father and I hired her a few times—you were old enough for a sitter—and we went out. We tried having dates again, like before we were married." She forced a pained grin and turned it on Maureen. "These dates, they were mostly to bars around the neighborhood."

"I think I remember this."

"You might. So anyway, for example, one night we came home fighting. I wouldn't get out of the car. Your father pulled me by the arm too hard and I fell into the garbage cans out front. It made a real racket, left me with a sore shoulder. Here and there, for a while, a few things like that happened, silly things. Usually we ended up laughing about them. We both drank too much back then." She rubbed her hands on her thighs. "Rusty nails. God, I could drink those all night. Does anybody order those anymore?"

Maureen raised her hands. "Don't change the subject. Correct me if I'm wrong, but somewhere in there you just told me Dad used to get drunk and knock you around."

Amber stood, sliding her back up the wall. "You're wrong. Don't be like those damn know-it-alls at church like Gloria. Talking behind their hands, thinking they're so superior. For your information, yeah, sometimes those bumps and bruises came from falling into the garbage cans, but more often they were from—from other things." She took a deep breath, searching for the right words. "I'll just say those dates didn't always end in fights. If nothing else, for a while there I was having twice as much fun as those fake stuck-ups."

"Jesus, Mom, that's gross."

Amber didn't seem to hear. "Maybe I shouldn't have let those women think what they wanted. Maybe I should've stood up to them, Gloria especially." Maureen watched her mother's vision drift along the staircase wall to the photo of her vanished husband. "I should have, I admit it. I should've defended my husband, your father. Anyway, it's too late for any of that, but let me tell you one thing. Your father wasn't a wife beater. Don't let anyone tell you he was. Maybe he was capable of it, maybe he wasn't. But there's no way I would've stood for it."

"You really could've done that?" Maureen asked. "You really think you could've kicked him out? Or packed up and left, like he did?"

"Packed up and left?" Amber asked. "Never. I would've cut his throat in his sleep, buried him in the yard. Raised you in Mexico. Never mind rusty nails, we'd be drinking margaritas and having this conversation in Spanish. On a beach." She covered her eyes with her hands. "Christ, I need a nap."

Without another word, Amber went up the stairs and headed down the hall toward her bedroom. After Amber had closed the bedroom door, Maureen wished she'd reached a hand out as her mother had passed by, had touched Amber's shoulder or the back of her hand. She heard Amber lock the bedroom door. Maureen went down the stairs, grabbed her coat from the rack beside the front door, and went outside.

14

The cold hit her like a slap, watering her eyes and setting her cheeks stinging. God, it was cold. The first day of December. The weather would only get worse before it got better. She dug her smokes from her pocket, lit one with shaking hands, couldn't tell her cigarette smoke from her frozen breath. It was cruel and hateful, what Sebastian was doing, his reaching into Amber's life and using her loneliness against her. Maybe it was because her mom was involved, Maureen thought, but this move felt even more heartless than the way Sebastian had used Tanya. Maureen's conscience pricked at her. She knew her own neglect had helped make Amber so vulnerable. Something told her Sebastian knew it, too. He needed to be taken care of, and soon.

She flipped open her phone. No missed calls. No Waters. She tried his cell again. No answer. She found his card in her coat and called his number at the precinct.

On the third ring: "One-twenty, NYPD." A man, but not Waters. Younger. Chewing gum.

"I need to speak to Detective Nat Waters."

"This an emergency?"

"Maybe," Maureen said. "I don't know."

A pause. "You don't know. Can I have your name?"

"Can I speak to the detective?"

"He's not here. That's why I'm taking a message." Another pause. "Your name?"

How long could she wait for Waters to turn up? Would this guy give her Waters's home number? What kind of rumors would that start?

"You there, miss?"

"Maureen. Maureen Coughlin."

"Why didn't you say so?" The cop covered the phone, muting the swearing male voices in the background, including his. They know my name at the station, Maureen thought. That can't be a good thing. The cop came back on the line. "Ms. Coughlin? He left instructions that if you're in trouble you should come by the station and wait for him."

"What? Why?"

More muffled voices. "He didn't say. Do you have a car? If not, we'll be happy to send you an escort to the station."

"No, that won't be necessary. I'm not in trouble. He asked me to call him this morning, so that's what I'm doing. He's got the number."

"We'll get a message to him."

"Thanks." She hung up and slipped the phone into her coat pocket.

No, the cops coming to pick her up wouldn't work out. There'd be no explaining that to her mom. Besides, scared as she was, Maureen wasn't going to be babysat. She wasn't going to hang around the station like some dirty-faced runaway so a bunch of cops could gawk at her and whisper behind her back all day. It'd be like hanging around the boys' locker room. No, thanks.

Maureen looked up and down the block, lingering by the front door of her mother's house, checking for some sign of Sebastian. He wouldn't stick around himself; she didn't expect that. The candidate had a busy schedule. He was trying to get elected. Commitments, events, meetings required his attention. But he very well might have left an extra pair of eyes behind. He had the resources. She didn't see anyone suspicious, the block looked pretty much deserted, but Sebastian wouldn't put two guys in dark suits across the street in a dark car. He'd be more subtle. Maureen wondered who else on the block Gloria knew. Everyone?

Whether she was a sucker, a pawn, or a co-conspirator, Gloria wasn't to be trusted. She could be hunched over some other woman's kitchen table at that very moment, begging forgiveness for past neglect and mining for information about lonely old Amber Coughlin and her crazy daughter. Crazy Daughter needed to discourage this renewed friendship between Amber and Gloria. Doing that without revealing the real reasons for it would require some finesse. Finesse was not Crazy Daughter's strong suit.

Maureen walked to the curb for one more look up and down the block, sucking hard on the last drag of her cigarette before dumping the butt in the gutter and crushing it out. She headed back to the house. I've got to get out of here, is what I've got to do, Maureen thought, to protect my mother. He'll lose interest and so will Gloria if I get outta here, if Sebastian believes he can't reach me through her.

At the front door, she reached into her pocket for her keys. Not there. She'd left them in last night's jeans. She rang the doorbell. What was she gonna tell her mom? Nothing, that's what. I'll explain it all, Maureen thought, when it's over. I'll apologize for what happened with Gloria, be a better friend to her myself. She squeezed her eyes shut tight. I never should have come here in the first place, she thought. Take care of things yourself, like a grown woman should.

She rang the bell again, stomping her numbing feet on the stoop. C'mon, Mom.

The front door swung open. "You give up those nasty cigarettes," Amber said, "and things like this will stop happening to you."

"Ma, you don't know the half of it."

Maureen jogged up the stairs and headed for the kitchen. Frank Sebastian had a political campaign, a business, a home. He was a big shot, pretty friggin' famous, at least on Staten Island. Why was she sitting around letting him come after her? How hard could it be to drop in on him? And there it was, where it had always been, next to the fridge, third drawer down: the phone book. Which, looking at the cover, Maureen realized was three years old and useless. She dropped the phone book on the counter and went back to her room, where she grabbed her bag. She hadn't even unpacked. She looked around. God, last night her old room had seemed so small and lonely. She'd felt so pathetic being there. Now she wanted to lock the door and hide under the covers forever. Maureen saw the ladybug glowing against the floorboard. She pulled her foot back to kick it to pieces, but she stopped. Instead, she snatched it from the wall and stuck it in her coat pocket, the plastic shell warm in her fist.

Her mother stood in front of the door, her arms crossed, blocking Maureen's exit. She looked like Molly from the night before, if Molly was tiny and fragile. God, Maureen thought, Mom's barely my size. She does look scary, though.

"Where are you going?" Amber asked. "What's going on?"

"Ma, I gotta go."

"I don't know what it is, but I know you're up to something. Mothers can tell."

"The landlord called," Maureen said. "The building is habitable again."

"Oh, please," Amber said. "You didn't think I believed that crapola."

Maureen threw her bag over her shoulder. She raised up to her full five-four, eye to eye with Amber. "Please move, Ma."

"It's not right," Amber said. "I never hear from you, and then you treat my house like you're a crook and this is some convenient hideout. When are you coming back?"

"Don't worry about it, Ma."

"Then don't make me, Maureen," Amber said. "Don't think I didn't notice you didn't answer my question. That's never worked. Didn't for your father, doesn't for you."

Bringing up Dad isn't gonna work this time, either, Maureen thought. She took her mom by the shoulders and eased her to the side. She reached for the doorknob, stopped, turned, and grabbed Amber in a hug.

"It's all right, Ma. Don't worry. I got some things I gotta do, some errands to run. I'll call you later. I promise. I'm a big girl, remember?"

Amber stood aside, stepping under the dusty picture of William Coughlin. "Do me one favor, then."

Maureen opened the door and waited.

"Throw that dumb lawn sign in the trash," Amber said. "Gloria comes asking, I'll tell her it was stolen."

"You got it, Ma."

Outside, the empty street did nothing to settle the butterflies in Maureen's stomach. The cardboard campaign sign stuck in her mother's lawn bent over backward in the winter breeze. She strode to the end of the walk, looking around, shoulders set, head high, and yanked the red-white-and-blue sign from its wire frame. It was cheap and she tore it up easily, first in half and then into quarters. Walking up the driveway to the trash can, the pieces of the sign tucked under one arm, the wire stand in her other hand, she caught herself hoping someone was watching. So they could see she wasn't afraid.

She knew Amber stood staring at the front door, willing her daughter back into the house. Maureen could *feel* it. She also knew her mom was too proud to open the door and ask her to come back. But hiding out wasn't doing anyone any good. She couldn't wait around any longer for Waters. And she had to stop thinking of Sebastian as a specter and remember he was a human being. She had to think of him as a man, as a pushy customer at the bar, even. He had a weak point somewhere, a raw nerve she could tug. She just had to find it. She thought of Dr. Travis. One red hair had blown his shit to smithereens. She had a lot more than that on Sebastian. Someone in his world would react to it. She just had to find someone to listen to her. If not the press, maybe his wife?

She surveyed her mom's dead-end street. Homes as stunted and plain as the lifeless maples along the Bay Street promenade lined both sides of the block. Empty driveways spread wide in front of their two-car garages. All the houses had the same blank windows, dead lawns, flat concrete stoops, and fake gas-lamp porch lights. It's a wonder, Maureen thought, considering the many times she'd come home drunk in high school, that she hadn't rung the wrong doorbell at least once. Maybe she had. She had a brief image of her father making that mistake, of him walking through the wrong door, out of her life, and into another only a few yards away.

Maureen realized that Bovanizer Street, made up of small raised ranch homes wrapped in pale white, yellow, or blue vinyl siding, resembled the product of a kindergarten art project, one where each kid gets the same photocopied page from the coloring book and the whole class shares a single box of six broken crayons, the kind of project where students are rewarded for how closely their work mimics that of their neighbor. The washed-out sameness of everything, Maureen felt, caused the entire block, the whole neighborhood, really, to pulse with an emptiness that hurt her eyes, that she would've associated with standing in the desert or looking out over the black surface of the ocean at night. She smiled to herself. She felt marooned in a ghost town, or maybe adrift alone in a lifeboat. I grew up here, she thought. How is it possible I feel this alone?

Past the houses, the street ended at a battered guardrail split by a green post that hadn't worn a dead-end sign in Maureen's lifetime. Back through the charcoal-colored trees, on the other side of a chain-link fence topped with loops of barbed wire, ran the train tracks. Maureen figured if she really had to move without being seen, she could walk the tracks. That was one way to dodge Sebastian's watchful eyes, as long as she could dodge the oncoming trains. Shouldn't be hard. The tracks always started humming way ahead of the train. The tracks led from one end of the island to the other. She could pop back out into the world wherever she wanted and disappear just as quick. Like a phantom. Or, she thought, a hobo.

Ten miles. About ten miles along the rails from where she stood, Dennis's blood had stained the railroad ties. Walk the tracks. Yeah, right.

Raising her collar up against the weather, Maureen turned her back to the tracks. She jumped a crack in the sidewalk and headed for Amboy Road. She'd walk for a while, think of a plan. Follow Amboy to Richmond—those streets were full of traffic and people—and find a diner or a bar where she could get some sugar and some caffeine in her system. Someplace with a recent phone book. And after that a place with a computer. That was really what she needed, a computer. She'd been a college student three or four different times. She knew how to do research.

15

At the Golden Dove, Maureen sat at the counter, hunched over her third hot chocolate, letting the steam rise into her cheeks and forehead, her face sheltered on both sides by her hair. Her bag sat between her feet. She knew she should order something to eat, should pay rent on the counter space. But lunch was over and the counter had seats to spare. The waitress didn't seem to mind. If the place got busy again, maybe she'd order something to go. She wasn't sure where she'd take it, though. Maureen considered revealing that she was in the business, that she was a big tipper. But, being in the business, she also knew the verbal tip was death. She might want another hot chocolate.

While walking along Richmond Avenue on her way to the diner, passing under the Eltingville station as a train roared by overhead, Maureen had stumbled upon one of Sebastian's campaign offices. She hadn't even known it was there. A small storefront tucked in between a busy Chinese takeout and a dry cleaner's, its floor-to-ceiling windows were plastered with campaign posters. Maureen stood there, frozen for a moment under the gazes of three dozen silver-haired Sebastians. His strangely unlined faces, their seventy-two ash-gray eyes hovering over high pink cheekbones, smiled regally out at the neighborhood. All those faces gave Maureen the same skin-crawly feeling she got as a kid watching ants swarm over a lollipop melted on the sidewalk.

She stepped to the storefront glass, peeking around the posters for a look inside the office. No one was in there. A couple of long folding tables like the ones in the catering hall at work sat surrounded by folding chairs. More posters and yard signs sat stacked around the room. She tried the door and found it locked. Shading her eyes, she peeked in again. Dark and dusty, empty in the middle of a weekday, the office didn't look like anyplace the man himself had actually been. It looked left over from a long-ago election or one coming up, she thought, that everyone knew was a foregone conclusion.

She walked away from the building feeling the stares of the posters boring holes in her back, the faces following her with their eyes like portraits hung on the walls of a haunted house. She'd kept a quick pace all the way to the Dove, fighting the urge to look back over her shoulder.

At the diner counter, sliding her mug aside, she reread the list of names and numbers she'd copied out of the Golden Dove's phone book onto a napkin. Security companies. Four of them, any one of which could be Sebastian's. He was vain, but not enough to put his name on his business. Looking through the listings, Maureen had realized she didn't know him well enough to make a reasonable guess at which one might be his. Could be North Shore, could be South Shore, could be both or neither. She hadn't been surprised to find his home number unlisted. The campaign offices weren't in the book.

She folded the napkin and slipped it into her coat pocket. She wished she'd taken a look at that envelope Gloria had given her mom. That might have something useful in it. Could she get her hands on it if she went back there? Her resources, Maureen decided, were too primitive. Too bad she wasn't a cop. Files, records, friends to do her favors. She could really do some damage then, though the cops had been a fat lot of help so far.

Maybe she had panicked at her mother's house and confused the feeling with bravery. Talking to the cops had knocked her even more off balance. Could be that going after Sebastian wasn't her best option. What about blowback, repercussions? He might hit at her through her mom, or through someone else, though she couldn't figure who that someone else could be. Her other option was continuing to run. That was always what she chose, running. Plenty of boys and bosses out there could attest to it. Her first, most powerful instinct. Maybe it was genetic and she was just her father's daughter.

Maureen felt in her pocket for her phone. She'd told the cops she wasn't in trouble. Could she call back with a different story and expect them to listen? Who else could she call? John? Maybe not. Molly had a point. Maureen had no right dragging John into her troubles. What was he gonna do anyway, beat up Sebastian? Give Maureen a plane ticket? Hey, John, you hardly know me and your girl doesn't like me, but I couldn't lay off the coke the other night and now I got big problems. Can you help a sister out? Yeah, that would work. Maureen ground her palms into her eyes, setting off shooting stars.

Stop. Relax and think. Show some spine and call the cops back.

Somebody big and heavy walked in and sat on the neighboring stool. Maureen's gut went so tight that her toes curled inside her boots. She gripped her phone in her fist. She kept her eyes locked on the brown sludge at the bottom of her mug. Don't scream, not yet. The man beside her breathed heavily though his nose. Maureen could smell it, the maleness of him: a locker room, a stuffy closet, an old car with the windows rolled up. She held her breath. Not Sebastian. He didn't smell like that. The big man shifted in his seat, a hair farther into Maureen's space.

"You're a hard woman to keep track of," he said.

Maureen slid her eyes sideways, looked at Waters through her hair. "You seem to manage it okay."

"You don't make it easy. Answering your phone would help."

Maureen opened her phone, confused. When had she turned it off? She pressed the power button. The phone wasn't off; the battery was dead. Good thing she had a list of phone numbers in her pocket. C'mon, Maureen, she thought, help yourself out here.

"It's cold out," Waters said. "You're on foot. I got to your mom's not long after you left." Waters shrugged. "Detective. Kinda my job."

"My dad used to take us here," Maureen said, setting the useless phone on the counter. "He loved the waffles."

"Your mom told me that." A small smile. "Those waffles are good." He patted his gut. "Especially at three in the morning, piled high with ice cream." He nodded as the waitress set his coffee on the counter. "This place is a favorite of mine, too."

Maureen waited for Waters to ask what she had called about, to ask why she had left her mom's house. Instead, he sat there sipping his coffee as if they were two old friends gearing up for a long, lazy afternoon of checkers in the park. Then she realized why Waters wasn't asking questions; he already knew the answers. "I take it my mom mentioned our special guest over at the house this morning."

"She's worried about you," Waters said.

"What else is new?"

"You blame her? You show up late at night trailing a politician who's got a cop trailing him. That's enough to worry anyone."

"What'd you tell her?"

"More of the truth than you did, apparently," Waters said. "That there was an incident at the bar, a death after a campaign dinner for Sebastian. That I wanted to talk to you about it, among other people from the Narrows." He paused, as if waiting for Maureen to fill in the space. "Other people such as your friend Tanya."

Straightening in her seat, Maureen licked her lips. "Yeah, about that." She took a deep breath. "My mom's house was the second time I saw Frank Sebastian this morning."

Waters's head rotated slowly in Maureen's direction, his coffee mug frozen halfway to his mouth. He had tensed at her statement, like a watchdog stilled by a sound in the distance. He was trying to hide it.

"I saw him at Dennis's place," Maureen said, "when I met Tanya there."

"Interesting." Waters wiped his big hand down his face, trying to erase, Maureen could tell, the anger from it. He took a long moment deciding which fact to address first.

"Start at the beginning," he said, "or the middle, or start at the end and go backward. Just do me a favor and try to point out the truth on your way past it."

"Tanya said she had to get some things," Maureen said, "that she'd left behind at the apartment. She'd been involved with Dennis. She told me last night she was afraid to go alone, so I agreed to go with her. We made a deal. It was how I got her to agree to talk to you."

"Which hasn't happened," Waters said. "So much for your deal."

"I tried calling you all morning and couldn't get an answer."

"But I got your messages," Waters said. "She hasn't called me. I would know." He leaned closer to Maureen. "Would you know why she hasn't called?"

"She's with Sebastian. She set me up. He was waiting for me at Dennis's place." She swallowed hard. "He tried to force me inside the apartment."

"What happened?"

"I wouldn't go in, obviously," Maureen said, "so he came out after me. But then Dennis's brother showed up and Sebastian backed down." She noticed Waters hadn't taken out his notepad. "Shouldn't you be writing this down? Isn't this important?"

"I'm not gonna forget a thing. Trust me."

"Sebastian says he knows you," Maureen said. "He didn't seem very afraid of you—or any other cop."

"He doesn't know me as well as he thinks," Waters said. He knocked back the rest of his coffee.

"You told me," Maureen said, "that you guys didn't know each other at all."

"That's not true. I never said I didn't know him. I do, or I did, a long time ago, before he left the job. What I told you is that he and I are not friends. And that's true. We're not."

"Were you?"

Waters hesitated. "Hard to say. We worked together, briefly. We never socialized much. I promise you, Maureen, that you are safe with me. Whatever connection he and I had was broken a long time ago. For good."

"Because of what happened in Brooklyn?"

"He told you about Brooklyn. Wow." Waters wrinkled his nose, looked away from her, considering, Maureen could tell, how much more to say on the subject. He looked into her face for a long moment and decided they'd already said enough. "I need you to tell me what you and Tanya talked about last night."

Maureen dropped her eyes to the counter. She couldn't believe it; she'd done exactly what Sebastian had told her. Why? What was she thinking? It was pretty obvious that he didn't have her best interests at heart. There was no question, judging from Waters's reaction, that something big had gone down in Brooklyn. What that was, Maureen was dying to know. At least, according to Tanya, Sebastian had left the department a hero. Had Waters been the story's villain? Of course, Tanya wasn't exactly a reliable source of anything but grief.

"So we're not gonna talk about Brooklyn," Maureen said. "I should just believe whatever Sebastian told me?"

"This is some kind of quid pro quo? Because I'm the one helping *you* here. I don't really see what you have to offer."

"I'd feel better if we could put it to rest." She smiled. "Just point at the truth when you pass it."

"It's not half as interesting as you think," Waters said. "He and I worked vice together in North Brooklyn. The precinct was restructured, and our squad got busted up. He took early retirement; I moved to homicide and over to the island. Case closed."

Maureen waited for him to say something about the pun. He didn't. Waters's sense of humor wasn't the first thing you noticed about him. Or the second. Or the third. She wondered if he had always been that way. So serious.

"Can we get back to the matter at hand?" Waters asked. "Namely, what Sebastian and Tanya were doing at Dennis's house?"

"Dennis owed Sebastian money," Maureen said. "He and Tanya were working off the debt on film, if you catch my meaning. The camera was at Dennis's place. Tanya told me she wanted to get the camera and erase the videos before Sebastian got them. That's why I met her there."

"You believe her? About the movies?"

"Sebastian told me her story was bullshit," Maureen said, "and Tanya was getting me there any way she could. But she took the camera. I watched her pocket it. I don't know if he saw her take it or not."

"I wish I had known about Tanya from the beginning. Especially if she was involved with Dennis."

"I know, I know," Maureen said. "But she's a pill freak and paranoid about cops. She's humiliated by this thing she was doing with Dennis. I thought she'd never talk to you without me easing her into it. I tried getting her to call you, I really did. She has your number. I tried to get her on our side." Maureen shook her head. "I don't know why she chooses Sebastian over you."

"Because he scares her," Waters said. "That gives him power over her. And they have a history. He's the devil she knows. As far as she's concerned, he's a permanent fixture in her life. He can reach her anytime, anywhere. On the other hand, I'm someone from the outside, an unknown who will ask a few questions and leave her to Sebastian's retribution. She doesn't believe anyone can protect her. You. Me. Anyone."

"I know the feeling," Maureen said.

"What did I tell you back at your apartment?"

"That no one can protect me better than I can."

"Right. Keeping secrets from the people trying to help you isn't the way to protect yourself. A secret is what started this mess."

"Like you don't have any," Maureen said. "Mr. Flatbush Vice."

"Listen to me very closely," Waters said. "I didn't get your calls this morning because I was underground, literally. At the medical examiner's office in Brooklyn, down in the morgue." Waters set his mug down on the counter, turned it in place. "Maureen, the results came back on Dennis's autopsy."

"And?"

"Dennis was already dead when the train hit him. Somebody killed him, strangled him, and left his body on the tracks, hoping the train would cover up their dirty work."

"You're sure about this?" Maureen asked. "My God."

"I'm positive. A body prone on the tracks can come through more intact than you might think. I saw Dennis's eyes myself." Waters tapped a fingertip high on his cheek. "Certain blood vessels in the eyes will burst during strangulation. Dennis had the red lights in his eyes. It's a sure thing. He even had bruises on his throat. Dennis's death is a homicide. I took over the case this morning."

Maureen's hands flew to her mouth. "Sebastian fucking killed him. Or had him killed."

"Sebastian's someone I'd very much like to talk to. And I intend to do that." Waters put his hand on Maureen's shoulder. "But you are my number one priority. We have to keep a close eye on you."

A sudden thought struck her wide-eyed. "Holy shit!" She lowered her voice to a whisper when heads turned around the diner. "I'm a witness, aren't I? In a murder case."

"Yes, you are," Waters said. "Tanya, too. At least according to you, Sebastian was extorting money from her homicide victim lover."

"You know, I couldn't figure that slick son of a bitch," Maureen said, sitting up straight, wider awake than she'd felt in days. "The night I catch him with Dennis, he's desperate for me not to talk, and then we're on Dennis's front lawn after Dennis is dead and he's telling me no one will listen to me, no matter what I say or who I say it to." She looked at Waters. "The whole time, silly me, I'm talking about the blow job and I'm thinking he is, too. But it's not the sex, it's not the papers he's worried about, it's you people, the cops. Because he knew outside the apartment that Dennis had been murdered. Because he did it."

"That's the direction that I'm leaning," Waters said.

Maureen blinked at him. "But I'm *not* a suspect, though, right? I *was* one of the last people to see Dennis alive."

"No, you're not a suspect." He waved the waitress over to refill his coffee. "We're waiting for toxicology. Dennis may have been impaired when he was killed, but the marks on his neck show someone with stronger, bigger hands than yours strangled him."

"What a psycho," Maureen said. "I mean, you figure Sebastian's a creep, he's running for office, but this is seriously fucked up. At least now I can get back to my life. When are you gonna arrest him?"

"Not anytime soon. I have proof that Dennis was murdered. But right now I don't have anything that says who did it."

Maureen grabbed the lapels of her coat. "Me. I say who did it. I say *he* did it. Everything I told you isn't evidence? It's obvious."

"It's circumstantial," Waters said, "is what it is. It's hearsay. You know what that means, right?"

"I know what it means," Maureen said. "It means the word of a waitress ain't shit against the word of a pillar of the goddamn community."

"If it's any consolation," Waters said, "it has more to do with who he is than who you are."

"Or aren't."

"I believe you," Waters said, "about everything. And what you know, what you saw is important. But this is different than you telling me some guy is selling dope on your corner. Sebastian's the lead dog in the state senate race. My union is behind him. The mayor has his eye on him. It sucks, but that matters a lot. I can't drag Sebastian into the precinct on a murder beef without Christ coming off the cross and pointing His finger at him. He's protected. You have to understand that. Tanya's not the only one in this city that won't cross him. For your sake or for mine."

"So that's it, then," Maureen said. "I'm out of luck 'cause I walked out of the wrong room at the wrong time. He's got the mayor at his back and I'm living out of my knapsack with a target on *my* back. Out-fucking-standing."

Maureen opened her wallet, took out a bill. She tucked a ten under her mug. Would the change make a decent tip for three hot chocolates? Cash was getting tight. She added a couple of wrinkled ones. Sebastian may have choked off my income, she thought, he may have me running scared, but I'll be damned if he turns me into a shitty tipper.

"Nobody's throwing you overboard," Waters said. "I just have to be subtle. His people know I need some time with him. They know I need to talk to him about Dennis from the other night. He knows it, too. Remember, he was a cop. Law and order is the cornerstone of his campaign. He knows I can lean on him through the press. Believe me, it's gonna be in tomorrow's paper that Dennis was murdered. Sebastian doesn't need rumors floating around that he's stonewalling the cops on the investigation.

"He and I, we're gonna be in a room together." Waters stood. "And that'll be a start." He made Maureen think of a bear again, swaying onto its hind legs. "You lie low and let me work. No more secret missions." His car keys jingled in his hand. "I'll give you a ride back to your mom's."

Her mom. Shit. Maureen was half-glad her phone had died. Otherwise her mom would be lighting it up. "I'm not so sure I want to go back there right now."

"I think you should talk to her."

"She's gonna want to help, and I want to keep her out of it."

Waters frowned at the keys in his hand, disappointed. About what, her attitude toward Amber? Why did he care? And why did Waters's disappointment make her feel guilty? Like she needed his approval.

"Where to, then?" Waters asked. "I need to get moving. I got a long day ahead of me."

Maureen considered refusing the ride altogether, afraid that whatever destination she selected, Waters would take her back to Amber's house anyway. But her transportation alternatives, either another bus with a broken heater or another creepy cabbie, didn't appeal. "Actually, can you drop me at Cargo? I need to talk to John about a job. I got bills to pay. I don't feel safe at the Narrows anymore. I won't be going back there."

"I think that's wise," Waters said. He swept his arm, letting her move first for the door.

Crossing through the diner, Maureen watched Waters's reflection in the windows. Not once did he try to check out her ass. Or maybe he was really good at it. Either way, she was impressed.

On the steps outside, Maureen stopped to light a cigarette. "So, I don't know what it's worth anymore, since we've moved on to murder, but I got descriptions of the guys that broke into my apartment." She hung her smoke in the corner of her mouth, raised the collar on her coat. "The landlord's kid, he came over and let them in, if you can believe that."

Waters took a cigarette when Maureen offered, bent into her cupped hands for a light. "It's against my health regimen, but what the hell." He blew out smoke and patted his belly. "And why is this kid letting people in your apartment? I assume you asked him that."

"Someone called his daddy." Maureen led them down the stairs. They passed a young mother trailing two obese kids the opposite way, her nose in the air at their nicotine fumes. "They told him the cops needed in to my place."

"In relation to what?"

"We didn't get that far," Maureen said. "I don't think anyone but me is asking questions. But now his daddy's threatening to throw me out because cops keep turning up at my place."

"Did these guys turn out to be actual cops?"

"They had guns," Maureen said. "Long coats and suits and ties."

Waters, head down, nodded. "I had a feeling. Sebastian's guys, I'd bet anything."

"Rent-a-cops playing dress-up?"

"I doubt it," Waters said. "He's got a separate crew, ex-cops mostly, who do personal security. They guard celebrities, judges, politicians. Him. These aren't the guys falling asleep in the driver's seat in the mall parking lot, these are professionals. I'm sure they're who leaned on your landlord. It was probably one of them driving the car outside the Narrows the other night."

Maureen settled her hand on her stomach. She saw in her mind pairs of faceless men circling Staten Island in their dark cars, sharks orbiting a shipwreck, their lifeless eyes searchlights waiting to land on her. "I think I'm getting a headache. I never thought I'd say this to a man, but can't you lie to me a little bit?"

"I need you listening to me," Waters said, "when I ask you for the truth, when I tell you what to do. Understand?"

Maureen lit a second cigarette off the embers of her first.

Waters studied his own half-smoked cigarette. "It's always such a letdown after the first couple drags. That's why I never really got back to it."

"It's not that much worse for you than waffles and ice cream."

Waters's eyes got sad. He glanced over his shoulder at the diner, then back at her. "For what it's worth, I'm sorry about your dad. It was a shitty thing he did, to you and your mom."

"That was a long time ago," Maureen said. "Ages, it feels like sometimes. I guess my mom told you about that."

"I was the one who told *her*," Waters said, "when the search was called off. I didn't put your name on it till I stopped by her place earlier looking for you."

Maureen stared at him, his big round face awash in the past. "That's some memory you got."

"I remember you, too," Waters said, "from that night. Standing on the stairs. Even then, just a little girl, I think you thought I was coming for you. Your hair was darker then, and all the way down your back. Your mother chased you upstairs, right before she went to pieces." He squinted into the embers of his cigarette as if peering into a tiny crystal ball. "There are some things, some faces, that no matter how hard you try you can never forget."

In the parking lot behind the Golden Dove, Maureen shivered at the passenger-side door while Waters tossed files, old newspapers, and foam coffee cups into the backseat, his arms churning as if he were bailing out a sinking rowboat. The man didn't have company much, especially if he didn't unlock the door first thing. Maybe hanging around this guy will make me into a detective, Maureen thought. I'm already thinking like one, for all the good it's doing me.

As they drove down Richmond Avenue, Waters made idle chatter about the weather and the traffic. Soon, they swung onto the on-ramp for the expressway, heading north through the center of the island. As they sped past the old dump, Maureen pulled her legs underneath her. Waters had the windows cracked but the heater cranked. In her warm cloud, Maureen's eyelids grew heavy. She felt safer than she had since stumbling out of Dennis's office. Maybe she could ride around with the detective forever, curled up in the backseat. She'd promise not to make a sound. She slipped her hand into her coat pocket and wrapped her fingers around the cold ladybug.

Waters glanced across the car at her. "I saw you skip that drawer in your room. There are things you don't want me to know about you, and that's fine. I'm a cop. Everybody feels that way about me. My feelings don't get hurt. But is there anything else involving Sebastian that you might've seen? Maybe something you saw or heard in the past? Someone else the both of you know?"

"I don't know the first thing about that guy," Maureen said. "I never met Sebastian before the other night, unless you count when I was, like, eight years old. Tanya's the only person I know who might know details, and she's out of reach. Her or Vic. The night of the fund-raiser, Dennis told me Vic and Sebastian knew each other." She glanced across the car at Waters, trying to get a read on his reactions. "Maybe you know Vic, too, from back in the day. If there was vice happening, Vic was probably involved. As for me, looks like you're stuck with the worst witness ever. I never even knew that Sebastian, Dennis, Vic, and Tanya all knew each other."

"How long have you known Vic? How long have you worked at the Narrows?"

"Too long."

"Seriously, how long?"

"Just over a year," Maureen said. "So you're wondering how I could know nothing about a place where I spend most of my time."

"Pretty much."

"So many people pass through that place," Maureen said. "There's not a lot that sticks." She rose up in her seat. "I'm just a waitress. I don't ask questions beyond *What're you havin'?* I don't poke my nose in other people's lives. I go to work, put my head down, hustle my ass, and try to get home before sunrise without getting mugged or raped." She turned her head to the window and blew out a long breath at her reflection. "Maybe it's not much of a life but it's exhausting." She rubbed her eyes hard, like a little girl up way past her bedtime. "Cut me some slack, Detective. I'm just a waitress. And I'm tired."

Waters dropped Maureen across the street from Cargo. After promising to go in right after her cigarette, she waved from the sidewalk as Waters drove away, the fear she'd hoped to leave in the car dripping like cold water from rib to rib.

Maureen slung her bag over her shoulder and took a seat on a bench facing the water. She could stay there for the whole afternoon, she thought. Sit and smoke, watching the ferryboats rumble to and fro between the island and the city, southern Manhattan drifting in and out of focus through the fog hanging over the bay. But the metal bench was ice cold and had chilled Maureen through her jeans in less than half a cigarette. She got up and walked to the railing guarding the drop-off down to the water. A few feet below her boots, the cold blue harbor swelled and fell like a breathing animal, bumping plastic bottles and paper cups against the rocks. Out on the water, Maureen watched a cloud of gulls circle a chugging, huffing ferry, the birds skating at the edge of the ferry's black smoke, darting and diving for scraps on the observation deck.

Above her head, the wind off the sea tossed more gulls about like the abandoned gray and white pages of an exploded newspaper. When she threw her cigarette butt into the harbor, a gull dropped from the draft in pursuit. It hovered above the drifting filter, beating its sharp-angled wings and staring into the water with beady black eyes. Leaving the butt to soak and sink, the gull croaked its disappointment and rose back into the air. "Sorry, kid," she told the bird. "That's all I got."

Maureen looked over her shoulder at Cargo, the wind whipping her hair against her face. She wasn't going in there, not yet. The St. George library was only a few blocks away. The library had computers. Computers she could use to look stuff up. Learn some things about hero cops in Brooklyn.

Maureen wrinkled her nose when she caught a whiff of something foul off the harbor. No, not from the water, she realized, from the street behind her. She turned as a homeless guy ambled up to her, stinking of body odor and cheap wine, mumbling some story about needing a dollar for bus fare to the shelter.

"The shelter's two blocks from here," Maureen said.

"Full. Gimme three dollars," the guy said, "so's I can take the bus to the other one."

"What other one?"

"Whadda you care?" The guy glared at her, one eye closed, mouth turned down. "Fuck you, lady. I better not catch you on my bench later, 'less you want hell to pay." He straightened his busted-up Yankees cap and walked away.

Maureen looked again at Cargo, thinking of heading back into the bar, hat in hand, groveling for shelter of her own. If it gets a few degrees warmer out here, she thought, watching the bum walk away, spitting at passing cars as he went, you may have to fight me for this bench.

16

"Miss, excuse me, miss."

Maureen popped awake, drool wetting the back of her hands, the right side of her face hot, mashed, and crooked. She sat up, blinking into the face of a white-haired man peering down at her through bifocals perched on the tip of his nose. He had sculpted, snow-white eyebrows. A matching mustache twitched in the middle of his pink face. My God, Maureen thought, it finally happened. I fell down the hole and the White Rabbit has come for me. The alarm on his pocket watch rang and rang. He had his hand on her shoulder. The daylight through the windows was fading. How long had she been there?

"Cell phones must be turned off in the library," White Rabbit said. He pulled his hand away. "Sleeping is also prohibited."

Maureen patted her pockets, searching for her phone, mumbling an apology. By the time she found her phone, attached to the charger that she'd plugged into a wall socket, the ringing had stopped. She packed up the charger in her bag, along with her printout evidence from the library computer. She frowned at the phone. Not Waters calling, but a familiar number. No name with it. Who was it?

"Miss?" The White Rabbit held a crumpled five-dollar bill in his hand. "Do you need some help?"

Maureen looked at the money, then up at the pink face trying in vain to form a warm smile. You're gonna need help, she thought, pulling that five outta your ass after I stuff it up there. Inside, she laughed at herself. I should be nice to him. Maybe he can get me that magic cookie that makes me bigger. Or maybe he's Morpheus and he can put me back to sleep. Her phone rang again. Time to go. She jumped up from her seat, grabbed her bag, and darted for the door, leaving the White Rabbit holding whatever else he had to offer.

Out on the steps, she looked at the ringing phone. Same number. It clicked this time. Tanya. Maureen squeezed the phone in her hand. She didn't care what Waters said about fear and devils, that bitch had some nerve calling now. But maybe Tanya had slipped away from Sebastian, Maureen thought, and come to her senses. Maybe that's why she was calling. She answered.

"T? Where are you?"

"Hello, Maureen." Sebastian on Tanya's phone. "You know, I see you in your mother. You are definitely her girl, where the apple falls and such."

The words hit like a gut punch. "You stay away from her, you motherfucker, I swear to Christ I'll—"

Laughter cut her off. "You'll what?" He paused, as if expecting an answer. "What are *you* gonna do, spill hot coffee on me? I saw you eyeing that pot this morning. You act like it's hard to tell what you're thinking." He chuckled. "How long has she worked at Macy's?"

"Fuck you."

"You kiss your mother with that mouth? Were you a public school girl? Remind me to do something about that when I get to Albany. But seriously, what kind of daughter are you? Letting your mother drive around in a twenty-year-old K-car. It's unsafe. Have you no sense of loyalty? It stalls at traffic lights. Could be dangerous." His quiet laugh. "So what's got more miles on it? The car or you?"

"What have you done with Tanya?"

"Speaking of miles. You know, Maureen, we all wish we lived in a safer world. Alas, even here on Staten Island sometimes we swim in deeper, more dangerous waters than we'd like. It's one of the reasons I'm running for office. Public safety. It's important."

"What are you saying?"

"I'm saying that I know, for instance, that it's already dark by the time your mother gets out of work. Lots of things can happen to a middle-aged lady in an empty parking lot at night. I was a cop. You don't want to know what I've seen, what people are capable of doing to each other with their bare hands. You're a woman of the world; I don't think I have to spell out the sordid possibilities. The risks involved.

"If you wanted, as a favor, I could have a couple of my men meet her on her way to her car. I could have them follow her home. Maybe I'll do that anyway, for the sake of my own conscience. That's called leadership. You want me to show you and your mother some leadership?"

"I think what you're talking about," Maureen said, "is called felony menacing."

"So call a cop," Sebastian said. "Listen to me, Maureen. Stop thinking that we're the only two people involved here. That's a mistake. You need to remember that the things you do, they ripple out into the world and other people feel their effects. Other people have a stake. So think about which horse you're putting your hard-earned money on. Ask yourself the important questions. Can Waters protect your mother? Can he protect you? How hard is he really trying?"

"Let me ask you a question," Maureen said. "Which cheek?"

"Excuse me?"

"Before you quit the NYPD," Maureen said, "a low-rent pimp put two bullets in your ass. Two bullets. Which cheek, left or right? Or one each?"

A long moment's dead air. Had she hit the right nerve?

"I retired from the job," Sebastian said, "covered in medals. Covered in honor. And I took those bullets so some fifteen-year-old whore didn't have to. Ask that mealymouth ratfucker Waters telling bullshit stories where he was when the shit went down. How's *his* career turned out? How many night shifts have *you* got left in those skinny legs of yours? As for me, those two bullets are punching my ticket to Albany."

She'd hit something sore: a deep bruise, a loose nerve. The transformation, the sudden devolution from glib politician back to Brooklyn vice cop startled her even through the phone. Sebastian talked about swimming in deep, dark waters. Maureen pictured a creature from the blackest depths of the ocean, one of those big-mouthed fish with teeth like scissor blades, an ugly thing that, when raised from the darkness and held up to the light, can't hide its twisted innards.

"He tried to fuck you yet?" Sebastian asked. "Because he will, I guarantee it."

"You have no idea what you're talking about. And you're a sick man. Damaged goods."

"All of a sudden I'm talkin' to Little Miss Innocent," Sebastian said. "Don't even think you know him better than I do. I worked the streets with him in the hours after even skanky little coke whores like you went home. Take my advice and fuck your cop. You can't string Waters along forever. He's less of a man than me, but he's a man. When he puts his grubby hands on you, you better put out. 'Cause when you don't, he'll be history, and then, unless you smarten up, I'm gonna be reaching out to you for real, from so many different directions you won't know which way to point that dirty mouth of yours. I'm looking forward to it. It's gonna hurt you."

Maureen blinked up at the sky, breathing hard. No way, no way in hell was this sicko gonna make her cry, angry tears or any other kind. "You stay away from my mother or we'll see who gets hurt. We both know what I know and what I saw. I'm not proud. I'll shut up. I can live with a draw. But my mother stubs a toe and I go to Waters and I file every gross, disgusting charge I can think of against you and then I'm on the phone to every reporter in New York City. You'll spend every last day and every last dollar of your fucking campaign defending yourself against every sordid, nauseating allegation I can think of. And I got an active imagination."

"Waters putting these ideas in your head?" Sebastian asked. "Telling you that you can get away with a stunt like that? How's it feel to be used? You think he gives two shits about you? All you are to him is bait. So he can hang my head on his wall like he's been trying to do for years. You're a worm, wriggling on the end of a hook. Stale green cheese in a short skirt. *I* matter to him, not you. Ask him about it, I dare you. Or put that active imagination to good use. Honestly, I'm really starting to not give a fuck anymore. I'm getting real tired of you."

He hung up. And that was when she saw him.

Across the street, getting up from the bench in the bus shelter. A long black coat over his suit, his short silver hair hidden under a wool cap, wraparound shades masking his face. The bastard, he'd sat there for the whole conversation, watching her, playing her, reading her. He raised his hand. He held something in it. What was he showing her? Tanya's phone? Stupidly, as if entranced, Maureen raised her arm and waved back. A cab pulled to the curb in front of him, blocking most of him from view. He looked right at her over the roof of the cab before he got in. It was Sebastian, wasn't it?

Maureen, her heart twitching in her throat, dialed Waters's number, hoping he wasn't too far away. Hoping he had a reasonable explanation for the old newspaper articles she'd found about a vice squad in Brooklyn. She needed two hands and three tries to get the right digits entered.

At the curb outside the library, Waters leaned against the hood of his car, arms crossed. Maureen toed the sidewalk with her boot, hiding her face from the people walking by. What did they take her for, she wondered, as she stood there wilting in front of this obvious cop? Was she a prostitute? A runaway? If she were a guy, she'd be a thug. These strangers wouldn't stare right at her if she were a guy. They'd be too afraid. Sebastian's words, his questions, beat their wings against the walls of her skull.

"So you're sure," Waters said, "that your mom hasn't talked to Gloria since this morning."

"I called her while I was waiting for you. That's what she said, nothing since this morning at the house."

"So what he's got," Waters said, "is your job application from the Narrows. Think about it. Who's listed as your emergency contact?"

"My mom."

"Right. Her name, home phone number, work number. Listen, I don't think he's got a small army out surveilling and stalking your mother. He's in some back office at campaign headquarters or in the backseat of his limo messing with your head between interviews. You told me yourself that Sebastian and Vic go back. He leaned on Vic for info and got the application. End of story."

"You're sure? This is my mom we're talking about."

"Think about it," Waters said. "What'd he say to you? That the two of you look alike. He saw that this morning. He's known that for twenty-odd years. She works at the Macy's in the mall. Phone number's on the app. Not exactly a deep dark secret. Anything more than that?"

"No."

"So what does what he said really prove?"

"Not a whole lot," Maureen said. "But I'm telling you that really might've been him, right across the street."

Waters shook his head. "Not unless that cab took him back in time. When you called me, I was at the precinct watching him on television while he started a quality-of-life speech outside the old Black Garter Saloon, which means he was calling you from the other end of the island. No cab is getting him from here to the South Shore in the ninety seconds it took you to call me." Waters leaned closer to Maureen. "If you want, we can run over to Macy's right now. I'll even wait in the car while you go check on her." He waited for an answer. "I'm serious."

"No. My problems are not her problems," Maureen said. "What are we gonna do about Tanya?"

"I'm looking but I'm not optimistic, especially if he's calling from her phone."

"This is the part," Maureen said, "where you tell me he screwed himself by calling on her phone, right? Now you can bust him."

"Hand me your phone." Maureen gave it over. Waters thumbed through her calls until he landed on the one from Sebastian. "What do you see there?"

"Tanya's number."

"No, you don't," Waters said. "You see a phone number with no name that you say is Tanya's. Even if I could get a subpoena for her account information and prove that's her number, your grandkids will be reading about Sebastian in their history books by then. And I promise you that phone is without a doubt no longer physically in existence, never mind on his person."

"We need to find Tanya," Maureen said. "If she's with him, it's not by choice."

"Tanya might say different." With effort, Waters shifted his weight off his car and onto his feet. "No matter what the truth is, we can't count on her to tell it."

"What about my mom? Can we get her into witness protection or something?"

"Not for this," Waters said. "She's not the witness, first of all. And I can't do it without bringing his name into things, and I can't do *that* with what little I've got against him."

"Because what little you got," Maureen said, "is me. That's the real problem, isn't it? My word against his. This is bullshit. I'd have more credibility if I were a criminal. If I were some mafia hit man that killed a dozen people"—she raised her finger at Waters—"or if I were Frank Sebastian, you people would be falling all over yourselves to protect me and my family. But because I'm some normal person I can't get the time of day."

"I know," Waters said. "I'm sorry. It sucks. If it makes you feel any better, nobody listens to me much, either."

"Thanks. It doesn't," Maureen said. "Now what?"

"Let's get you home."

"Back to my mom's? No way."

"Listen, I'm not trying to play family therapist here," Waters said, "but you two are gonna have to work things out, at least for a couple of days. She's worried sick and your apartment's not safe. Where else you got?"

"Every place I go," Maureen said, "he turns up. He'll leave her alone if I'm not there. If he shows up at her house my mom can't protect me. I know it and you know it. All I'm doing there is putting her in danger."

Waters scratched at his gray stubble, worked his jaw, thinking. Maureen recalled Sunday evening, when she'd called him from outside Cargo and asked whether he'd known that Sebastian had been a cop. He hadn't liked her questioning his authority then, either. But she was getting to him this time, winning him over. Either that or she was wearing him down. Same result.

"Sebastian's not out to get your mom," Waters said.

"He got Dennis."

"Dennis was different," Waters said, "and you know it. I feel for the guy and I'm not saying he deserved what happened to him, but he was hardly innocent. He did business with Sebastian. Knew secrets about him, owed him money. Your mom is just . . . your mom. She lives in the daylight, out where Sebastian's got to smile for the cameras. He knows that as well as we do. He's just trying to get inside your head. Don't let him."

"I've got this bird feeder back at my apartment," Maureen said, studying her hands, curling her fingers into claws. "The birds come from everywhere when I put it out. And so does the neighbor's cat. Like clockwork. I can't get rid of him. But when there's no birds in the yard? No cat. Can't find him anywhere. I go running home and Sebastian sends one of his special geeks after me. Who knows what happens to my mother?" She shook her head. "No birds in my mother's yard. Hear me? I don't care. He doesn't get near her again." Maureen pulled open the passenger door of the car. "Get in."

"Seems you got it all figured out," Waters said. "Can I put my retirement papers in?"

"I want you to stand there," Maureen said, "and tell me—no, *promise* me—that I'm wrong."

Waters just stared at her over the roof of the car.

At Cargo, Waters held open the door for Maureen. As they walked into the bar, he held his arm outstretched in the air behind her back. John, behind the bar pouring a pitcher of beer, looked in their direction, then back down at his work, with no visible reaction. In the booth closest to the door, two guys in suits sat talking and finishing a late lunch. They went quiet and stared as Maureen and Waters crossed the barroom. Maureen gave them a quick glance, trying to return their stares, then dropped her eyes to the floor.

"Detective," she whispered, "those two guys sitting by the window. In the booth."

"Nothing to worry about."

"Are you sure?"

"They checked you out, head to toe," Waters said. "If they were waiting for you, they'd never have looked. One would get up about now and make a phone call outside."

Maureen risked another peek. The men had returned to their food and their quiet conversation. Neither of them moved or looked her way again. She pinched the bridge of her nose, fighting to steady her rapid breathing. This is bullshit, she thought. This no way to go through life.

The rest of the place was empty, except for Molly, who stood at the bar's far corner, unpacking papers from her schoolbag and organizing them on the bar. When she saw Maureen and Waters, she froze, papers in hand. Maureen couldn't read her face. She didn't know whether to wave hello or turn around and leave.

Waters leaned down and spoke softly. "Gimme a minute alone with the boss."

"Sure thing," Maureen said. "Take your time."

Waters raised his arm to get John's attention. He pointed at the pool table, then headed that way. John set the pitcher at the waitress station for pickup before ducking under the bar to meet Waters. Maureen found herself left alone in the middle of the barroom, stuck with no easy choices. She could defy Molly in the plain sight of an empty table, or she could give ground and loiter outside in the cold smoking cigarettes, or she could show some nerve and walk right over to her. She chewed her cheek for a moment. Well, what the hell.

As Maureen headed Molly's way, Molly never looked up from her papers.

"I wouldn't be here," Maureen said, taking a seat, leaving a bar stool between them, "if it wasn't for Waters."

"It's a free country."

Molly lowered her head over her club soda, sucking hard on her straw, dimpling her cheeks. Her focus stayed locked on her boyfriend and Waters, the two men in deep conversation, the green expanse of the pool table wide open between them. Bone-colored sunlight poured in on the men through the bar's wide, thick windows, setting aglow the dust motes hovering in a loose cloud over the felt. John, his back to the room, looked out the window at the passing traffic, tossing the eight ball up and down with his right hand. Waters, his hands spread on the rail of the pool table, leaned forward, explaining something. My valiant NYPD protector, Maureen thought, reduced to soliciting favors from the local bartender.

She knew she should be grateful for Waters's help and for John's willingness to at least listen, and she was, but grateful or not, her confidence in Waters was ebbing.

"I don't even know that they're talking about," Maureen said, swiveling her bar stool back and forth. "If I knew, I'd tell you. I swear."

"Call me crazy," Molly said, stabbing her straw at the ice in her drink, chasing the lime around the bottom of her glass, "but I bet they're talking about you. Just a wild guess."

Maureen restrained a sigh. Grinding her back teeth, she forced herself to look away from Molly and not punch her off her bar stool. This is fucking pointless, she thought. Waters, his bloodhound cheeks sagging, his wrinkled sleeves rolled up, his thick arms folded across his chest, stood listening to John, who still wouldn't look at him. Everyone's miserable, Maureen thought, and I'm the reason. Beside her, Molly was a block of ice. Maureen could feel the chill coming off her from three feet away. The exit to the courtyard was right behind them. John never locked the courtyard gate until after dark. Be easy to slip outside and vanish into the streets. That'd probably be best for everyone. She should disappear. The ferry was only a short walk away. She could ride over to lower Manhattan and walk around the battery, maybe up into the Village. And then do what? Maybe a change of scenery would show her something, inspire some solution she could navigate on her own. At least she'd be on her own.

She stood, pulling the strap of her knapsack tight against her shoulder.

"Don't go," Molly said. She reached out, setting her hand on Maureen's forearm.

Maureen stared at Molly's hand. She didn't return to her seat or take her bag off her shoulder. "I don't make a habit of hanging around where I'm not wanted." With her free hand, she brushed her hair off her temples. "I have other places I can go."

"Obviously, somebody wants you here," Molly said.

"It's obviously not you."

"Well, I'm not in charge here." Molly looked down, intent on brushing crumbs or some other tiny detritus Maureen couldn't see from the folds of her skirt. She stopped when she caught Maureen watching. Molly took a deep breath. "I never said I didn't want you here. Not specifically. I just . . ." Molly looked up at the ceiling and glanced again at Waters and John before turning back to Maureen. "It's like this. What's happening to you is unfair, Maureen. I know that. I can see it. I'm not cold-hearted.

And I feel for you, I do. But the truth is I don't want any part of it. I don't want someone like Sebastian anywhere near me or anyone I care about." She paused. "That doesn't make me a bad person."

"You're not the only one," Maureen said. She took her bag off her shoulder and hung it on the back of her bar stool. She slipped her fingers into her back pockets, cocked out her right hip.

"I know I'm not," Molly said. "We don't know each other that well, at all really, but we should stick together anyway, try to behave like decent people." She lifted her chin at Waters and John; Waters was headed their way. "We should try to not be afraid all the time. It can't be *that* hard."

Waters tried to smile as he approached, but it didn't stick. He couldn't hold it and Maureen failed to return it. Molly was right that she and Maureen didn't know each other, and neither did Maureen and John, for that matter. Not really. Her ex-boss, his girlfriend, and an overworked cop, Maureen thought. These were the people she had to count on. Did she even have the right? If things got worse, would they stick around? Waters, especially.

She liked him, she really did. She trusted him, for the most part, which was as much as she trusted anyone. But he hadn't accomplished much since getting involved with her, alternating as he did between chauffeur and babysitter. Even those duties were starting to wear on him. She wasn't a real case. She was some kind of pro bono side project he had taken on for reasons she didn't really know and hadn't really tried to figure out. There was no crime against her on file, no reports, no bagged evidence in a locker, no photographs or paperwork. And it sucked to admit it, but Sebastian at twenty years retired held more sway in the NYPD than Waters. She could tell, watching his slow, stiff walk that Waters's back was acting up. Was it time to think about letting him go? It might be merciful, for both their sakes. As he got closer, Maureen half-expected she'd hear his joints squeaking like the Tin Man's.

Waters put his hand on Maureen's shoulder, leaned down to look into her face. "You should know," he said, "that you've been plenty strong through this whole ordeal."

"For a girl."

"For anyone. I got a lot of respect for you. I know it's terrifying. You've been a good soldier." He straightened, taking in both women with his eyes, lingering on them. "Keep your eyes on the door. Sebastian can't afford anything public, but you never know."

He shook Maureen's hand. She thought her whole arm might disappear into his palm. She fought the urge to grab hold of Waters's hand and make him swear not to leave, or to go home and forget about her and Sebastian altogether, not for her protection but for his. She said nothing.

"I'll be in touch," Waters said. He turned away and headed for the door.

Maureen watched as John squeezed past Tracy, brushing up against her in the narrow space behind the bar. "I know there's no avoiding it," Molly said, "but I hate it when he does that."

"Hey," John said. He slipped his glasses off, clutching them in his hand.

"What's the story?" Molly asked.

"Maureen needs a place to stay for tonight."

"Here we go," Molly said.

"Sebastian's already sent people looking for me at my place," Maureen said, "so I can't go home. I went to my mom's. He came to her house this morning."

Molly held up her hand. "Wait a minute."

"We all had coffee in the kitchen together," Maureen said. "It was pretty horrifying. He knows where she works."

Molly spoke deliberately, as if talking to a lip reader, her hand still in the air. "Sebastian came after your mother."

"I can't go back there," Maureen said. "I can't have him looking for me at her house anymore."

"You're that afraid of him," Molly said.

"Yes," Maureen said, surprised at how easily the admission popped out. "Yes, I am."

"We need to force Sebastian to sit on his hands and wait out the night," John said. Acting casual, he pulled wineglasses one at a time off the shelf over his shoulder, polishing each one with a bar towel and setting it on the bar. "Waters needs a chance to play catch-up, to find a way to back him off."

Molly dipped her finger in her club soda and traced that fingertip around the rim of the wineglass in front of her, creating a faint musical note. Pressing the base of the glass with her fingers, she pushed it across the bar to John. "I'm getting a headache," she said to no one in particular. She looked up at John. "Can I get a Jack and water, please?"

John made Molly her drink. He set it carefully in the center of a fresh cocktail napkin. "Being in the same building as Maureen," he said, "my place is out. Sebastian's watching, for sure. She can't stay with me. Obviously."

"Maureen stays with me," Molly said.

Maureen's head snapped around. "Wait. What?"

"'Scuse me?" John asked. "No, Mol. I don't think so. That's not where I was going with this."

An uncomfortable silence half-settled before Molly struck it down. "Maureen stays with me. I mean it." She looked at John. "Where better? This guy has no idea who I am; never seen me, never heard of me. I live in a quiet neighborhood. My neighbors know me. Nobody we don't know would last five minutes sneaking around my block." She took a deep breath and let it out slowly through her nose. "I don't have any reason to be afraid of him. I don't."

"Molly, thank you," Maureen said, "but I can't. I just can't."

"Why not?" Molly asked.

At the question, Maureen turned to John, who watched her with his eyebrows perched high on his forehead, wineglass in one hand, bar towel in the other. She knew he wasn't waiting for the answer to Molly's question, but for the answer to the same question Maureen was asking herself—where were her people? Where were her friends?

The skin at the base of Maureen's throat burned. She could feel the blood blooming underneath it. Not with envy or lust this time but with shame. Was that one of the seven? Didn't seem like it should be, but she was guilty of it at least as often as she was the others. She stared at John. Her answer to him was simple. She hoped he wouldn't make her say it out loud. She didn't have any friends, not real ones. She couldn't afford them. The effort or the time they took. It was the price she paid to make her money and defend her space.

Years ago, she'd taught herself never to forget that everyone in her late-night world wanted something from her: a drink or two, a name and a number, a subtle stroke or an obvious grope, forgiveness for spilling or spewing or stepping out of line, a hit of blow or a blow job in the backseat. They wanted to be seen and heard through the lights and above the noise any way they could, no matter how crude or desperate they acted. In the morning, they could always blame the booze and the hour or blame her. Hadn't she done it to them, leading them into temptation by bringing them what they'd asked and paid for? Everyone in her life, Maureen knew, was a buyer or a seller, usually both, all the time. That fact was the cornerstone on which she'd built her survival. Hers was not a world where a girl could let her guard down. For anyone. Ever. Not if she didn't want to be left stripped bare as a stolen car.

Sure, she *knew* tons of people. She knew them by first or last name but not both, knew how much money they made, knew how well or how poorly they tipped. She knew people well enough to do shots or key bumps of coke with them, to babble politics and religion and sex with them in buzzed conversation. But people she could trust? She knew two, if she counted Waters. And she was looking right at the other one and he knew it. Wasn't the fact that she kept coming back to him enough? Was he really gonna make her crawl?

John had mercy, finally looking away from her, his attention drawn to a couple coming in the front door of the bar. He watched them sit, watched the waitress end her cell phone call and head their way, menus in hand. John's mouth moved, working over words, searching for the right ones.

Molly plucked the cocktail straw from her drink, laid it beside the glass. She swirled the ice cubes, sucked the whiskey off her finger. She performed the entire act without looking John in the face. "Don't even tell me, my love, that you don't want to leave her with a girl, that she'd be safer with a man in the house. You wouldn't think that."

John wiped at the corners of his mouth. He wouldn't look at either of them. Busted, Maureen thought. Molly had guessed exactly what he'd been thinking. Maureen felt like she was spying, watching them from outside their bedroom window. She'd seen it before, the way a real couple could shut out the rest of the room, conduct entire silent conversations with their eyes and hands as if they were an ancient tribe of two. She'd seen it before, anyway, even if she'd never lived it.

John looked at Maureen, his eyes sad. "I can't. I can't go along with this. It's not safe. I'm sorry, Maureen. You understand, right?"

Maureen felt the humiliation bubbling up in her again. She was a bomb in a cartoon that's juggled from person to person, the fuse burning down with every toss. Nobody wanted her to get hurt, but nobody wanted to get their fingers blown off, either. How could she argue? Look at what had happened to Dennis. John was protecting Molly. He loved her. She was more important to him than Maureen. That was how it should be.

Maureen knew she needed her own answers. She pushed her fingertips hard into her eyes as if the pressure would force the right images to appear. Vic wasn't an option. At least according to Waters, he'd already sold her out once. Paul lived right next door to her apartment. Too close. Besides, the way she'd treated him, he'd hand her over to Sebastian for new spark plugs and a six of Pabst. Could she find Clarence, stay with him and his wife? Would Sebastian think of that? And where did Clarence's loyalties lie? Clarence, who saw Sebastian at the gym, every morning at the break of day.

"Trust me, John," Molly said. "We'll be fine. We'll survive till you come protect us after work."

Maureen could tell John knew that Dennis had been murdered, that Waters had told him over by the pool table. But John hadn't decided how much to tell Molly about that and now she was pushing him into a choice. It wasn't right, Maureen decided. These two didn't belong in the middle of her mess, any more than her mother did. She wanted Molly's shelter, she really did. But she didn't deserve it.

"Listen, Molly," Maureen said. "Dennis didn't kill himself. He was murdered before the train hit him. The train was a cover-up. Waters thinks Sebastian is responsible. And now Tanya's missing; we think he's in on that, too. That's what we're dealing with here."

Molly stared hard at John, anger roiling her eyes. "You knew these things. You were gonna tell me when?"

John didn't answer. Molly breathed deep, rocking the bar stool on its back legs. Maureen waited as the couple held each other's eyes, neither one willing to back down. She realized why John had tried keeping the truth about Dennis's death a secret. Knowing about the murder would only make Molly more afraid, which would only make her more defiant, more willing to get involved. A warm affection for Molly swelled up in Maureen. The list of people I can trust, she thought, has grown to three.

Molly turned to her. "What happened to Dennis won't happen to you. You need a safe place to stay. I've got one. End of argument." She looked up at John. "That goes for you, too. Case closed."

"Then you stay till closing time, both of you," John said. "The three of us go home together. It's already after dark."

"We're leaving now," Molly said. She turned to Maureen. "Dinner, a hot shower. Sound good?"

Maureen nodded, embarrassed and uncomfortable with feeling forced to choose a side.

Wordlessly, lifting each clean wineglass by the stem, John lined them up on their shelf. As he slid the last one into place, a delivery truck rumbled by outside, vibrating the glasses and setting them ringing like wind chimes. He said nothing about Molly's demands. To the untrained eye he was pouting. But Maureen could see tightness under his eyes and along his jaw that showed he was straining to suppress his concerns about Molly's decision, shelving everything he wanted to say in protest for later or for never. It wasn't a decision; it was a process, one that took a little time.

She and Molly waited.

"I'll call Jimmy and Rose," Molly said finally, trying to sound soothing. "They'll come over and hang out with us until you get off. I'll tell them it's important." She waited for John to say something. He didn't. "You know they'll come."

John pulled his crumpled pack of cigarettes from his front pocket. He fished out two broken ones, tossed them in the trash behind the bar. "Fucking soft packs. What is wrong with me?" He found an intact smoke and put it to his lips. "Let me get my coat. I'll drive you home."

17

In front of Molly's house, as Maureen and John leaned on the hood of the car finishing off their cigarettes, a dirty white hatchback eased up the block and parked nose to nose with John's car. Maureen shaded her eyes from the glare of the headlights, turning her face into her shoulder and looking up at John for his reaction. He squinted into the lights until they went dark, dragging on his smoke. He didn't seem concerned about the new arrival, so Maureen decided she didn't need to be, either. The door of the hatchback creaked like an old oven door and the driver climbed out.

As the figure approached, Maureen hoped the shadows of the street-lights hid the misery on her face. Jimmy McGrath. God, how embarrassing. The married high school teacher she had a crush on was now one of her babysitters.

"That filthy white piece of shit refuses to die," John said, crushing out his cigarette in the street.

"My wife told her mother the very same thing the other night." Jimmy glanced over his shoulder. "Oh, you mean the car and not me. You're hilarious, Sanders."

Boys, Maureen thought. Go figure.

Standing about six foot, well built, with his black hair cut short above his pale, blue-eyed Irish face, Jimmy looked much more like a TV cop or a Hollywood firefighter than a real-life teacher. She could picture Jimmy at Waters's side, clad in the same long wool coat, the badge on his belt glowing red and blue in the crime-scene emergency lights. Was he cop enough to fool anyone Sebastian sent sniffing around? He might be. Maureen wondered if Jimmy's looks helped in the classroom. She'd tell him what he wanted to hear, no problem, either in detention or under interrogation. She noticed Jimmy's wife wasn't with him.

Strip search, Officer? Why, sure.

Jesus, she was losing it. Maybe it was best that she was being locked down for the night.

"Good to see you, Maureen," Jimmy said. "Out in the world, as it were. Wish the circumstances were better."

"Me, too," Maureen said. "Thanks for coming."

Jimmy slipped his hands in his pants pockets, rocking back on his heels. "Nothing to it. Rose is buried with some presentation for work. Football's only on Sundays. What the hell else was I gonna do, grade papers? No, thanks." He turned to John, chuckling. "You're getting smarter, lad, having Molly call for a favor like this instead of you. Female solidarity goes a long way in the McGrath household."

John leaned close to Maureen. "So does getting Jimmy's annoying ass out of the house when his wife has work to do." He checked his watch. "Speaking of work, I gotta get back. They tear the place up like drunken puppies if I'm not there."

"Go," Jimmy said. "We got it from here."

"Thanks for this, Jimmy," John said. "I owe you one." He slid his arm across Maureen's shoulders. "He comes off like a clown, but don't be fooled, I'd trust him with my life." He gave Maureen a hard squeeze and then climbed into his car, started it up, and drove off.

Maureen crossed her arms, her eyes locked on her toes, feeling very much like she'd just lost, or was it won, a round of spin the bottle. Jimmy stood close enough for her to inhale his aftershave. The sharp scent tightened her throat. She coughed. She knew her breath stank of booze and cigarettes. She didn't want to talk, but she did anyway.

"Listen, like I said, I'm really grateful for this. You don't even know me."

"John was best man at my wedding," Jimmy said. "I've known him and Molly since we were teenagers. If you're in with them, you're in with me, too." He set his hand on her shoulder and pulled open the gate with the other. "Now, inside with you. It's cold out here."

Maureen walked through the gate but stopped when Jimmy didn't follow. "What about you?"

"I'll be in now and again, but mostly I'll be out here. The car looks like junk but the heater works great; I'll charge John for the gas. They can't get through the door if they can't get through the gate, can they?" Jimmy opened the gate wider. "Go ahead, Maureen. You look exhausted."

Maureen headed up the walk. Safe and looked out for, that was how John and Molly and Jimmy wanted her to feel. She made a mental note to work hard to act that way, even if she had to fake it. She couldn't deny, though, as Molly came to the door to meet her on the walk, that staying here was a relief.

"You doing all right?" Molly asked, taking Maureen's bag.

"Hanging in. Gimme one second. I gotta call my mom and check in."

"Take your time," Molly said. She went back inside.

Maureen paced on the walk, the phone to her ear, waiting for her mom to answer. No way I should be here, she thought, while my mother sits home alone. She chewed her thumbnail. Have I ever thought that, even once, in the years since I left? Maybe I should move back home for a while. It would certainly help my wallet—and my mother, whether she admits it or not.

Amber answered. "So this is what it takes for you to call your mother."

Or maybe I'll keep my apartment, Maureen thought, and we'll go from there. "Hey, Ma. Everything okay?"

Molly leaned out the front door, mouthing a question: *Wine?* Maureen nodded, making the sign of the cross in Molly's direction.

"Fine. The same," Amber said. "No sign of that creep. I got my eye out for him, though." A pause for a sip of wine. "How about you, honey? You okay? You need anything?"

Maureen stared at her phone as if she'd never before heard the voice on the other end. "I'm okay. I'm staying with friends. Waters said it would be best."

"I know," Amber said. "He stopped by not long ago to check up on me, said he'd come by again later. He's a nice man. You can tell he used to be handsome."

"He is," Maureen said. "Nice, I mean. He's trying his best to look out for me."

Molly reached a glass out the front door. Maureen took it, waiting to drink until she was off the phone.

"Detective Waters is doing a better job of watching over us," Amber said, "than some other men I could mention, but won't."

Like that man whose ring you wear? The woman is never gonna make sense, Maureen thought, so let her be.

"I'm not far," Maureen said. "I'm over in Annadale."

"Don't tell me," Amber said. "If I don't know I can't tell that SOB if he comes looking."

"Ma, don't say things like that," Maureen said. "Did Waters put that idea in your head?"

"He didn't have to. I know how these things work. I watch TV."

Maureen spent a moment trying to figure out if her mother was serious. She decided that she didn't want to know. "This will be over soon. Don't worry about me."

"Look up at the sky," Amber said. She waited. "You looking?"

Maureen tilted her head back. May as well play along. "I'm looking, Ma."

"What do you see?"

"A few stars, mostly clouds. I think an airplane."

"You see any pigs flying around up there?"

Maureen chuckled. "No."

"When you do," Amber said, "call me back. That's when I'll stop worrying about you. You're my daughter, for chrissakes." She hung up.

Maureen looked up again at the sky. Was her mother losing it, she wondered, or finally coming back down to earth? How did you tell the difference?

For dinner, Molly reheated pot roast and potatoes left over from Sunday dinner at her folks'. *I promised you home-cooked,* she had said. *I didn't make any promises about whose home or who cooked it.* Maureen savored every bite, told Molly this would be the first thing she would learn to cook when she got back in her apartment, and that she'd cook it for her and John as soon as she mastered it. Molly promised that when that happened she'd bring dessert.

After they loaded the dishwasher, Maureen left Molly at the dining room table, hunched over her last few papers, Miles Davis soft on the stereo. She walked to Molly's living room window, pulled a curtain aside, and looked out at the front yard. The white pickets of the fence leaned like drunks in line for the men's room. The rocky yard dipped and rolled. Scraggly crab grass sprouted at random. The slate walkway looked beaten to pieces by a gang of hammer-wielding eight-year-olds. Not exactly the picture-perfect American Dream.

But Molly does live in a house of her own, Maureen thought, aching with envy, not an apartment owned by someone else. Molly lives in a house with a fence and a porch light and locks that no one but she can change or open. A house with rooms painted colors she chose, where she walks up her busted path to get her own mail and take the trash to the curb, and wave to neighbors who know and look out for her.

"I'm glad you came at night," Molly said, joining Maureen at the window. "That's when the yard looks the best."

"John doesn't mend fences?"

Molly laughed. "What a loaded question to ask an English major about her temperamental boyfriend."

"Then I won't ask if he gardens."

"That mess out there will keep," Molly said. "We'll knock it out after the school year, when I have the time."

"Is there a reason Jimmy McGrath is sitting out there in his car," Maureen said, "and not in here with us?" Reflected in the window, her face looked formless, as if made of wax. She squinted, thinking she could see the thumbprints of her maker in her cheeks. Please God, she thought, don't let that really be me. "Is he staying away from me?"

Molly frowned. "Why would you think that?"

"Just wondering," Maureen said. "I don't know what I'm saying." She set her wine on the windowsill and studied her hands. "I feel sometimes like Sebastian is some filthy disease I'm carrying and no one wants to catch it from me."

"Right. And that's why you've got a small army looking out for you. That's why I'm letting you stay in my house."

Maureen leaned her forehead against the cold glass. "I didn't mean it like that, Molly. I'm not ungrateful." She closed her eyes. "I'm tired. Not just in my body but deep down, deeper than my bones. I'm exhausted in my soul."

She waited, eyes closed, listening to Molly's breathing. Is this when I get kicked out? When everyone says *fuck it* and gets back about their own business? Somewhere in the house, the central heat kicked on. Wouldn't that be nice to have? Maureen thought. Heat, warmth on command.

She straightened, grabbed her wine, drained what was left of it. "Look, Molly—"

"I know how you feel," Molly said. "It's awful, like it takes everything you have in you to keep breathing. Things get bad, and then they get worse." She wrapped her arms around herself. "It's cold by the window. Let's sit."

They moved to the couch. Nestling into one of its corners, Maureen searched for something harmless to talk about. On the fireplace mantel sat pictures in drugstore frames. Molly in front of a classroom, Molly and John, Molly and a very handsome man that wasn't John, arms around each other, laughing, obviously very happy together. Maureen wondered how John felt about that photo. Well, she thought, it was Molly's house. Maybe that picture kept John honest, reminded him that while he may be the One, he wasn't the only one ever. "You and John have been together," Maureen said, "what, two years?"

"About that," Molly said. "This time around."

"Think you'll get married?"

"Marry him?" Molly said, grinning. "Then I'd have to live with him."

"The place is small for two," Maureen said, not entirely convinced that Molly was kidding. "That's for sure."

"John's a funny man," Molly said. "He's real impulsive in some ways. In other things, he's real deliberate. With us, he's deliberate. This place is small, but we could do two if we had to. And right now, this place is our only option. I'm not giving up owning my own house to rent an apartment." She crossed her legs on the couch. "Soon, we'll buy a place. We're both saving. I'd never get enough from this place alone. All things in due time. There's no rush."

At this point in the conversation, Maureen knew decorum dictated that she offer up some lighthearted sisterly criticism of John's bullshit stalling. She should warn Molly about John's genetic male fear of commitment and about the universal female trait of indulging it because *this* man was different, because *this* relationship was unique. The same lies every woman told herself and her mother and her sisters and her friends while waiting for the man she loved to evolve into a man she could marry. But Maureen came up empty in both the wisecrack and the criticism department. She wasn't sure why. Maybe she was blank because Molly spoke so matter-of-factly, without irony or defensiveness. Or maybe she wanted to believe in Molly and John—and Jimmy and Rose, for that matter—for her own sake. So she could believe that couples who made plans and promises and stuck together did, in fact, exist.

"It's not all John," Molly said. "I'd have a hard time letting go of this place; it was my brother's. His widow sold it to me cheap before she took the kids to Jersey. She was in a hurry. That picture you were staring at, the one that's not John. That's me and my brother Eddie, the summer before he died."

"What happened?"

"He was a cop. He was killed on nine-eleven."

Maureen couldn't resist looking back at the photo on the mantel. God, the family resemblance was so obvious, why hadn't she seen it right away? At Cargo, John hung photos of Trade Center dead behind the bar: former regulars, guys from the firehouse around the corner. Was Eddie in one of those photos? Surely John would know better than to put it up. Unless Molly wanted it there. Maureen couldn't recall seeing Eddie; the faces had faded in her memory. So many faces, she thought, come and gone, learned and forgotten, read and put back on the shelf. Who could remember them all? "I'm so sorry, Molly. That's awful."

"But not exactly rare around here. One reason my sister-in-law moved was to get off a block that's half widows. Anyway, it was a long time ago."

"Not for everyone."

"No," Molly said. "I guess not." She looked at Maureen over her wine. "Anyway, that was my time with a broken soul." She tried to smile. "It's not fatal, if you don't let it be. John helped. Still helps." She sighed, as if setting down a heavy weight. "How about you? Any siblings?"

"Only child. Just me and Mom. My father took off when I was eleven." She took a big swallow of wine. "My block was half single moms. Divorce was big in Eltingville."

"Not just there."

"Your folks?"

"Forty years together this summer," Molly said, nodding over at the mantel. "And going strong. Gives me hope."

"I hope your sister-in-law meets someone else someday," Maureen said. Immediately and massively regretting what she'd said, she stared down at her wine, her embarrassment so acute that it caused her physical pain. She could feel Molly's eyes on her. "Growing old alone hasn't worn well on my mom."

Would you please shut up, Maureen, she thought. Shame about your dead brother, Molly. Hope the widow doesn't dry up and blow away over it, though. Jesus. This is why I don't talk to people. This is what I get for attempting a woman-to-woman conversation about men and plans and family—three subjects about which I know nothing. Maybe Molly had the number for the animal shelter.

God, I don't wanna be a crazy cat lady. I fucking hate cats.

"That's nice of you to say," Molly said, "about my sister-in-law. I think the same thing. Eddie's life was enough of a loss, Denise shouldn't die over it, too.

"They were saving for a bigger place when he died." Molly put her hand on Maureen's knee. "Wanna hear something ridiculous? I think sometimes that's why I don't want John moving in. Another young couple saving for a bigger place. Something about repeating that creeps me out." Molly set her wine on the floor, rubbed her face with her hands. "God, I'm not usually this morbid."

"It's not morbid," Maureen said. "Everyone has things that are hard to let go of."

She thought of her father's picture hanging in the hall of her mother's house, of Amber's wine-sodden vigils, of her wedding ring. She thought about running from that house, from her mom, at nineteen years old, abandoning her mom as her father had. Yeah, it was different, in a way. As the daughter, Maureen was supposed to grow up and move out. But the move hadn't been a strike for maturity and independence. It was flight. She had run away. And even now, ten years later, she could hear the voice running through her head, the tone and the attitude true for sure, if not the exact words, as she packed while her mother was at work: *I am so done with you. See ya never.* Had her father heard the same voice as he walked out the door? Maybe all he had wanted was to get away. Escape was what his daughter had wanted, what she always seemed to want.

"Believe me," Maureen said, "I understand the urge to make a new start. To have something of your own, even if you don't know what it is you want." She lifted her glass to her mouth but didn't drink. Her throat was dry, but she'd lost her thirst. "And I know how hard it is to get that new start going."

Not long after, Molly collected the glasses and brought Maureen sheets, blankets, and a pillow. While Maureen took a shower, Molly slipped a pair of boxers and a T-shirt into the bathroom. Drying off, Maureen thought twice about the boxers, might be a bit weird if they were John's, but once she was dressed she felt pretty good wearing someone else's clothes. It was foolish, she knew, but it felt like putting on a disguise.

She could live with being someone else for a while.

When Maureen returned to the living room, Molly was on the couch, wearing pajama bottoms and an old oversized Mets jersey. I don't know about the boxers I'm wearing, Maureen thought, but that jersey is John's for sure. She stopped short. The gun, on the other hand. The one in Molly's lap. No idea where that came from.

"I suppose I should have warned you first," Molly said. "It's nothing to be afraid of. Have you ever used a gun?"

Maureen shook her head.

"I have to tell you," Molly said, "I'm surprised by that."

"About as surprised as I am," Maureen said, "that you have one."

Molly smiled. "Because of my overly shy and demure nature?"

"I thought we were going for safety in numbers?"

"Thirty-eight is a number. It's a semi-auto, so there are a few tricks to it. Come sit by me, and I'll show you how to use it."

Sitting close, Maureen learned how to release the safety and cock the hammer on the .38. She held it in her hand, pointed it. Using two hands she closed one eye and sighted the lamp across the room, the weight of the gun tugging at the muscles in her wrists and forearms. Though she hadn't the nerve to touch the trigger, she ran her fingertip along the smooth chrome of the trigger guard, the compact barrel. She liked the solid weight of the gun in her hand, the cool metallic smell, the way it gleamed in the lamplight.

Molly's white picket fence was a wreck, Maureen thought, but the woman took care of her gun.

Maureen recalled an old boyfriend who had owned a motorcycle, a Honda Shadow, that he adored. The .38 smelled like that motorcycle. Maureen never missed the boy, but sometimes she missed his bike. Wrapping her hand around the gun handle felt like gripping the throttle of the idling Honda. The boy had never let her ride on her own. He'd let her start the machine, but after that he insisted Maureen play passenger. She complained but never really pushed him, always secretly afraid that once she had control, she'd lose it and disaster would follow.

Maureen almost protested, almost confessed that she doubted she could pull the trigger, even if someone came crashing through the front door. She knew her first, most powerful instinct would be to run. But then, looking at Molly, she realized she was the last line of defense. She'd be the only thing standing between the intruders and Molly, and maybe John asleep upstairs. Standing her ground wasn't just about her safety. Other people had a stake. Like poor Jimmy. Bad news for him if someone made it into the house.

Maureen pictured herself kicking open the front door, gunning down a horde of faceless assailants pinning Jimmy to the hood of his car. Yeah, right. Calm down, girlfriend. More likely she'd be blazing away and spraying bullets through half the living rooms on the block, taking out Jimmy, the neighbor's dog, and the streetlights. God forbid she ever had to shoot, she'd be lucky to remember to keep her eyes open.

"Maybe we should give the gun to Jimmy," Maureen said. "He's out there alone."

"Jimmy can handle himself. And he's going home when John gets here. The gun is for you." Molly pressed her palms together, steepling her fingers. "Look, I thought it'd be a comfort, like a night-light or a guard dog. I wasn't trying to scare you. I'm really not expecting an assault team to hit the house in the middle of the night. It's more for the next few days than tonight. I get the feeling there's only so much sitting around and waiting you can tolerate."

Maureen looked down at the gun in her lap.

"If you'd rather not have it," Molly said. "I can take it back."

"I'll get used to it," Maureen said. She leaned down and slid the gun under the couch, where it lay hidden but easy to reach if she wanted it. She'd leave it there for the night and see how she felt about it in the morning, in the cold light of day.

Molly got up from the couch. "I only ask one favor."

"Anything."

"Please don't shoot my man when he comes home from work."

"I'll ask questions first," Maureen said, "and shoot second."

"Good enough," Molly said. "Good night. I'll try not to wake you when I leave for work in the morning. Stay as long as you like after I'm gone."

She turned off the lights and headed for the stairs.

"Hey, Mol," Maureen said.

Molly stopped on the third step. Moonlight through the living room window paled her cheeks, settled in her eyes like chips of ice. To Maureen, she looked like a ghost.

"Thanks. For letting me stay, for the wine, for talking. For everything."

"You're welcome," Molly said. "If you leave the house tomorrow, take the gun with you."

Hours after Molly had gone to bed, Maureen lay awake facedown on the couch. Only a few minutes ago, John had come home.

She'd traced his sounds from the Galaxie pulling up and parking out front, to his boots on the slate, to his key in the front door. As he'd crossed through the living room and headed upstairs, Maureen had kept her breathing deep and steady, her eyes shut tight, doing her best impersonation of being asleep. She felt a strange relief when she heard John close Molly's bedroom door. Weird, she thought. All this running around and here I am again, asleep one floor beneath Molly and John. The more things change . . .

Except for the occasional creak of the bed, someone rolling over in sleep and nothing more, the house was silent. In fact, the whole block was quiet enough to keep Maureen wide awake.

Molly's street wasn't like Maureen's block, where buses rumbled and hissed on her corner throughout the night, where ships passing into the harbor sounded their horns, where yard dogs howled at sirens and cars rolled by with the bass pumping at grille-rattling volume. And where, some nights, Maureen heard the *pop-pop-pop* of gunfire in the streets. It was funny, Maureen thought, how gunfire sounded without warning: no screams, no profane threats or warnings like on TV. A bus, then nothing, then a tanker, then *pop-pop-pop*. Sometimes followed by sirens a few minutes later, sometimes not.

Maureen wished Molly hadn't given her the gun. She wished Molly hadn't reminded them why Maureen was there, crushing the warm sleepover feeling that Maureen had been stoking in her imagination. And now Molly's upstairs with a warm body beside her, she thought, and I'm waiting down here with a loaner .38. Waiting for what, morning? Sebastian's evil minions? A call from Waters that he's solved my problems and I don't need a babysitter anymore? Ridiculous.

Maureen sat up. She rubbed the hem of her borrowed boxers between her fingertips. She looked down at her own clothes, folded in a pile on the floor. She reached under the couch and found the gun. She held it in both hands, savoring the pistol's weight. What Molly said was true; there was only so much idling Maureen could tolerate, but did toting a gun around really give her more freedom? She looked up at the ceiling. Or was Molly trying to put ideas in her head? Maybe there was something specific Maureen was supposed to do with that gun. Maybe the gun was the signal that she needed to take matters, literally, into her own hands.

On a rack by the front door hung the keys to John's Galaxie and Molly's Accord. Maureen knew she'd have to take the Accord. The Galaxie was a classic, and therefore conspicuous as well as noisy. Molly had given her the .38. Surely she wouldn't mind Maureen borrowing the Honda. Unless, of course, I'm totally wrong about everything, Maureen thought. She chewed her bottom lip, staring out at the cold night through the black square of Molly's living room window.

On the other hand, even if she was wrong about Molly's intentions, a trip to the Narrows looking for Vic wouldn't take that long. She'd be back before Molly was awake, never mind ready to leave for work. What had her father always told her, when she'd cautioned him against tossing popcorn to the monkeys at the zoo?

Forgiveness is always easier gained than permission.

She got dressed. She got as far as the front door, Molly's car keys in her hand, the gun in her coat pocket.

After a few long minutes in the doorway, she hung the keys back on the rack and returned to the couch, slipping the gun back into its cave. Too many people had taken risks for her. She'd made too many promises. She could sit still for one night. Constant motion hadn't accomplished a whole lot so far. And what if she was wrong and Molly found her out and never forgave her for taking—no, stealing—the car? What if she felt betrayed?

Climbing back under the blankets, still dressed, clutching the ladybug to her chest, Maureen's father's words came back to her again, but this time he wasn't speaking to a worshipful and naïve ten-year-old. That was the problem with remembering her father. He stayed the same and she got older. Because forgiveness was easier gained in theory, she told him, that didn't mean getting it was guaranteed.

I want to hang on to Molly, Maureen told her father. I'm not like you. I want to stick around. At least until dawn.

18

Just after first light the next morning, Maureen parked Molly's car on Forest Avenue. Turning off the ignition, she pocketed the keys and reached across the car, setting her hand on the lumpy brown paper bag in the passenger seat. It was warm beneath her palm. This stop would take five minutes, less even, not even enough time for the bagels she'd promised Molly to get cold. She rotated in the driver's seat, searching the street for meter maids. If she did get a ticket, she'd pay it off, hopefully without Molly ever knowing. Or maybe she'd get Waters to fix it for her. She shook off a chill; already it was cold inside the car. If she thought about her mother, if she kept Amber's face in her mind, what she'd come to do would be easy. She reached into her bag for her knife and slipped it into her coat pocket. She'd left the gun at Molly's. Too final, she'd decided, at least for this negotiation. A gun left no wiggle room. She wanted them both walking away from this. She hid her handbag under the driver's seat before stepping out of the car.

Clarence's gym sat centered in a run-down cluster of storefronts facing Forest. The off-hours entrance was around back, facing the chained-off parking lot. Maureen headed down the cracked concrete steps leading to the lot, her fingertips sliding along the cold metal handrails on either side. She held her head high, her eyes flashing in every direction. She was counting on her arrival being surprise enough to protect her. Well, that and the threat of Clarence. Maureen had once seen him carry a drunk up the Narrows steps with one hand, use him to shove the door open, and then launch him arcing over a parked Volkswagen. The drunk cleared the car by two feet and landed facedown in the middle of Dock Street. Even Sebastian was smart enough not to mess around in Clarence's place, not when Clarence might walk into it at any minute.

Maureen waved her membership card over the electronic eye by the door. With a faint beep the tiny lightbulb changed from red to green, like the warning lamp at a railroad crossing. The lock clicked open. Maureen reached for the door.

Inside the gym, her face flushed in the thick, warm air. Dull fluorescents flickered in rows along the ceiling. Deserted and silent, the gym was a depressing place, actually. Maureen wrinkled her nose, a familiar tang tickling her nostrils. Sweat. Heavy and male. The place smelled not unlike the zoo, she thought. Not quite the monkey house, but not too far removed from the elephants. Strange that she hadn't made that connection when she'd been in here signing up. Maybe the guttural grunting coming from around a corner at the back of the gym sparked the idea.

More groans sparked another, even less pleasant idea.

No way, Maureen thought, recalling Sebastian's pre-orgasmic groans from the Narrows, no way I've walked in on this shit again. Considering the time of day, it was nearly the same hour in the gym as it had been in the bar. Did the man ever sleep?

After another groan, Maureen heard the broken-church-bell clang of heavy metal plates slamming against one another, the sound of a barbell dropped home into its rack. Relieved, she slipped her hand in her coat

pocket, crossing the gym floor in quick, light steps. The hard rubber floor-
ing didn't give under her boots. She didn't weigh enough. She turned the
corner to the back room.

Sebastian, who hadn't noticed her arrival, lay flat on his back on the
weight bench, shirtless and shoeless in suit pants, pressing a barbell so
heavy with plates on each end that it bowed in his hands with each rep-
etition. As each rep peaked, Sebastian ejected a loud breath like a sur-
facing whale. White hair ran like a trail of snow from his belt buckle to
his chest, where it bloomed into a cloud of smoke. He had enormous
boxy muscles, as if he'd been built out of bricks and cinder blocks. While
Maureen watched him, Sebastian just kept breathing, lifting and lowering the barbell in a steady, relaxed rhythm, like a machine.

Maureen slid the knife out of her pocket. The weight bench next to
Sebastian's was empty. She flicked open the blade, moving toward the
empty bench.

"I see you," Sebastian said as she moved beside him. "Kind of early
for you, isn't it? On your way home from another stellar night at the office?" He didn't look at her. He pushed the barbell into the air above his
forehead. He may have noticed her approach, but by not really paying
attention to her, he'd missed the knife.

Maureen lowered the blade, settling the point on Sebastian's left
cheek, two inches below his eye. The eye quivered in its socket, refusing
to roll in her direction. Maureen sat on the empty bench, holding the
knife in place. "Seeing me gets a lot harder unless everything stays right
where it is."

Sebastian grinned and his eyes sparkled, with humor or hatred Maureen couldn't tell, but his nostrils flared bloodless and white with the
effort of holding the weight in the air. Supporting it without relief was
starting to tax him. "Agreed."

"You know what I'm here for."

"This is the part," Sebastian said, "where you tell me to leave you and
your mother alone or you'll take my eye out or something nasty like that.
And then I agree. And then I say I've met my match. And then I go out

and do whatever I want anyway. You're wasting my time here. I have a schedule. And a car coming. And I have two more sets after this one."

Maureen put pressure on the knife and broke the skin, a tiny puncture at the tip of the blade. Sebastian tried not to, but he flinched. A small bead of blood formed on his cheek. Then it slipped down his face, breaking and spreading into his sweat like a tiny red oil slick. Sebastian swallowed hard. Maureen watched his white-whiskered Adam's apple rise and fall. The slightest tremor ran down his arms. He was supporting close to three times her weight. There was no telling how many times he'd already lifted it. Maureen would never let on that she'd noticed, but Sebastian's physical strength was massive and terrifying.

"How can you possibly think that this little stunt will help you?" he said. "What tragic hormonal misfire makes you think that?"

Maureen squatted on her haunches, closer to him, turning the knife slightly from side to side, coaxing the thinnest rivulet of Sebastian's blood down the blade. The movement hid the shaking that had crept down her arm and into her hand. Fear shakes? Maybe, but adrenaline, too, no denying it.

"You do whatever you want," she said, "because you're so big no one can stop you. I get that. And I'm nobody, nothing, invisible. The dull background music to everyone else's exciting life. Fine. You know what that means? That no one's paying any attention to me. I'm as free and mobile as you are. So here I am, one flick of the wrist away from making you the most famous one-eyed politician in New York. My old Shakespeare professor would call that ironic. I call it something worth remembering."

She stood, wiping the knife blade on her jeans. She walked to the head of the bench that Sebastian lay on. Standing there, she looked down into his upside-down face. Thick veins bulged at his temples. Maureen spread her feet wide and reached out, wrapping her hands around the barbell, catching it before Sebastian could settle it in the rack. She leaned forward, putting her weight on the barbell, pushing it down. Her hair fell into her face. Sebastian's arms quivered. He pushed back. Maureen resisted. Their eyes locked. The barbell didn't move. She watched his massive chest rise and fall, laboring now. Blood continued running down his cheek. He tried not to show it, but her strength surprised him.

"Sometimes size doesn't matter, see?" Maureen said.

"Maureen?" She looked up at Clarence coming around the corner, arriving for the day. His gym bag hung from one huge hand. He held a cup of coffee in the other. His jaw hung loose in disbelief. "What are you doing?"

Maureen kept her weight on the barbell, her pulse heavy in the backs of her hands. "Mr. Sebastian was finishing a set. He needed a spotter. I was here. Lucky for him." She looked down into Sebastian's face. "Almost didn't make that last one. Got it under control?" She released the barbell and backed away from the bench, flexing her fingers.

Sebastian settled the barbell in the rack. His eyes stayed fixed on the ceiling. He lay prone on the bench for a few breaths, rolling and rubbing his wrists. "There's a special place for people like you, Maureen. It's dark there. And it's cold." The bench creaked under his weight as he sat up and turned to face her. "But don't worry, you have friends there. Waiting."

"Frank?" Clarence asked. "You know your cheek is bleeding?"

Sebastian glanced at Maureen and then looked back at Clarence. Maureen knew it was time to motor, but she had to stay put for Sebastian's answer. What would he admit to?

"Shaving cut," Sebastian said, touching his cheek. He rubbed the blood between his forefinger and thumb. "First time in a while I've been this careless." He held his finger up for Maureen to see. "Doesn't take much, does it, Maureen? One little slip."

"If you say so," Maureen said, trying and failing to force a smart-ass grin. "How should I know?" She hated it, but Sebastian's preternatural calm unnerved her. Now it was time to bail. She got a few steps toward the door before she heard Clarence's bag hit the floor and his heavy steps coming up behind her.

"Maureen," he whispered, overloud. "I need to talk to you."

Without breaking stride, Maureen spun to face Clarence, raising her hands in supplication and shaking her head. She had nothing to say and she wasn't about to stick around for a scolding. She'd explain everything later, or maybe never.

"It's important," Clarence said. He waved her back to him but had stopped pursuing her. "I mean it. This shit is serious."

Maureen dropped her shoulder into the door and shoved it open with both hands, bursting out into the cold daylight. In the wind, her hair exploded in every direction. At least she'd tried, she thought, taking the steps two at a time on her way back to the car. At least she'd gone down to the gym and done *something*.

Drawn first blood, she thought. That's what she'd done.

19

Back at Molly's, she parked behind Waters's Crown Vic. His presence was a bad sign. Nobody shows up at seven bearing good news. It had taken forty minutes to drive from the gym to Molly's place. Enough time for Clarence to call Waters. They had exchanged numbers over Dennis's death. She needed to walk in tight-lipped but with her head up. No feeling guilty or foolish or embarrassed over standing up for herself; she wouldn't let Waters or Clarence or anyone else do *that* to her. But she wasn't into making any big confessions, either. If Waters had questions about where she'd been, the bag of bagels under her arm would be all the answer she had to give.

Maureen paused a moment at Molly's gate, studying the house in daylight: the peaked slate-shingled roof and the brick chimney, the white shutters. This house, Maureen thought, belongs under a Christmas tree, with an electric Lionel locomotive chugging past the front door. Less than a month till Christmas. She could picture John on a stepladder, hanging strings of tiny white lights from rusty nails in the eaves. She could see Molly in the tiny kitchen making Irish coffees. She could see them together as old people, pictures of the grandkids on the mantel and glowing in the firelight. A gray-haired Jimmy and a white-haired Rose would be there, too, sitting on the couch, telling stories about the good ol' days.

And where am I gonna be? Maureen wondered.

Lost in the weeds again, working another dark room where the colored lights over the bar burn year-round. And when I get too old for that, when my ass sags and my knees give out, I'll be waddling along a short track behind a diner counter, pouring hot cocoa refills and handing out broken candy canes with the takeout change. Deck the friggin' halls.

Approaching Molly's front door, Maureen saw the black door of the Narrows in her mind. Was that where she really belonged? In *there*, that vault, with *those* people? No. Couldn't be. She wasn't a lifer, like Dennis had said. But then again she certainly didn't belong in Molly's house, did she? She couldn't see Molly wielding a switchblade at the neighborhood gym. So which of the two doors was really the rabbit hole? Which one led into the real world? No White Rabbit was coming to show her the way.

Before Maureen could knock, Molly opened the door, her Aran sweater hanging loose over her pajamas. Her face was tense and pale. Her hair was wild. Not the picture of a woman getting ready for work. Molly took the brown bag from Maureen's arms.

"Sorry they're cold," Maureen said.

"I guess you saw that Waters is here."

"I did." Maureen stepped into the hall, slipping off her coat. "Where is he?"

"In the dining room. John's asleep. Hopefully, he'll stay that way."

"Why is that?" John asked from the stairs, squinting like a one-eyed pirate. "What's going on? What the fuck time is it?"

"Waters is here," Molly said.

John swayed on his feet like an old wino woken up in a doorway, straining to recall both where *here* was and who this Waters person could be. There seemed to be some question about Maureen, too. Please God,

Maureen thought, don't let that be what I look like first thing in the morning. Molly must really love this guy.

"Coffee'll be ready in a minute," Molly said.

She led Maureen into the dining room, where Waters sat at the table, his own paper cup of diner coffee in front of him. He looked worse than any of them, as if he hadn't slept in days, far beyond the help of that small, pathetic coffee cup. He gave Maureen his best empty, professional smile. "Good morning."

"Is it?" Maureen asked.

Waters's smile died. "No, not really."

"Don't even."

"Your mom is fine. This isn't about her."

"You cop people fucking love waking me up," John said, shuffling through the dining room and into the kitchen. "Figured you'd have learned from the last time."

"I'm not here for you," Waters said.

"Pour three," Molly called into the kitchen. She set the bag of bagels on the table. No one reached for them.

"Everyone drinks black?" John said from the kitchen. Not waiting for an answer: "Good."

"Milk and sugar are in here already," Molly said. She turned to Maureen. "You see why I hoped he wouldn't wake up."

"Is he always like this?" Maureen asked.

"Nah," Molly said. "He's being nice this morning because we have company. I'm not kidding. Think about that before you rush out and bring one home."

John brought coffee to Maureen and Molly. He stood over Waters. "Well? Whadda you want?"

Waters held up his cup. "Yeah, I'll take a refill."

"I live to serve," John said, but he took the cup into the kitchen and topped off Waters's coffee.

"Now go outside and smoke a cigarette," Molly said.

"Mol," John said, setting Waters's coffee on the table. "This is serious. Waters is here."

Molly pointed over John's shoulder into the kitchen, at the side door. "Out. Go. We'll survive without you for five minutes. We need you human."

John took a deep breath, held it for a minute, exhaled. He stepped into an old pair of sneakers by the front door, cast one last forlorn look at the dining room, and went outside.

Over his shoulder, Waters watched John go out. "Not fully house-broken?"

"He does the best he can," Molly said.

Waters gestured at the other chairs. "Sit. Please."

Molly sat at the head of the table, Maureen across from Waters.

"I talked to your mother earlier," Waters said, "before she went to work. And then I followed her there. She's worried, naturally, but she's fine. Nothing happened at the house overnight."

"We getting any closer," Maureen asked, "to getting me out of this?"

"I need to ask you some questions," Waters said, digging his notebook out of his overcoat. He patted his pockets in search of a pen. He was acting like he hadn't heard Maureen ask him something.

She cast a quick glance at Molly, who, chin resting in her palm, watched her kitchen door and very intentionally showed her back to the table. Maybe Waters had told her about the gym and Molly was pissed Maureen had taken the risk. But did he even know about that? Or was it Waters that Molly wouldn't look at? Regardless, she was listening. She was paying close attention, focused, not distracted like Waters. Molly squeezed her coffee mug so hard Maureen thought it might burst.

"What?" Maureen asked, watching Molly. "What's going on?"

Waters flipped open his notepad. He tapped his knuckles on the table to get her attention. "Maureen, have you ever heard of the Black Garter Saloon?"

Maureen snapped back to Waters. This was certainly not the question she expected. And that knocking on the table, what was that about? "I know it by reputation. It's a low-class strip joint. Down the south end of the island by the Arthur Kill, where all the old boats are." Waters scribbled on his pad as she talked. "Everyone in service knows it, it's kind of the end of the line in the business, the last stop." Maureen straightened in her chair, trying to see what Waters was writing. "It's a real dive. Not my kind of place."

"What about your friend Tanya?" Waters asked. "You think she knows anything about it?"

Maureen looked again to Molly, still giving the table a stony profile, then back at Waters. "Not that I know of. She never mentioned it to me." She growled at herself. She should've been at the house when Waters arrived. "Why? Have you heard from her? Did you find her?"

"So Tanya never worked there," Waters said. "Or hung out there, even? Did she know anyone who did either of those things?"

"I don't know," Maureen said. "I don't think so. A couple of days ago, I would've said no way. But now, after that situation with her and Dennis?" Molly got up from the table in a huff. Maureen watched her storm into the kitchen. "But stripping? I don't see the point. And from what I heard, you can't even get decent drugs at the Garter." Molly leaned out the side door and called to John. "The Garter wouldn't make any sense for Tanya. All she has to do is walk into the room to get what she wants."

Letting the storm door slam closed, Molly came back to the dining room. John stayed outside. Waters ignored her.

"Tell me what you know," Maureen said. "Please."

Waters flipped through a few pages in his book. Maureen wanted to leap across the table, snatch up that book, and shred it in his face. Waters wouldn't look at her. "Do you have anything to do with the place? Have you ever? Do you know anyone who does or did?"

"No, to both," Maureen said. "Or all four, or whatever. I wouldn't have anything to do with anyone mixed up in that hole."

"Tell me about Clarence," Waters said, eyes on his notes, like he knew not looking at Maureen made her crazy. Even at work, customers ordering without doing her the simple courtesy of meeting her eyes left her wishing for talons on the ends of her fingers.

"Do you know him well?" Waters asked. "Very well, even?"

"What's that supposed to mean? Why won't you look at me?"

"Like if I asked, what's Clarence to you: friend, co-worker, acquaintance, more, less, something else entirely? What would your answer be?"

When Waters finally lifted his eyes to hers, Maureen just blinked back at him, unbalanced by the shifting subjects and the aggressive questioning. Since she'd sat at the table, his whole demeanor had changed; he was a different person. Maureen was reminded of Sebastian's performance outside Dennis's apartment, his effortless shifting of faces. That was not Nat Waters the benevolent protector sitting across the table from her. She was talking to Detective Waters, the cool, indifferent investigator. Was he gonna cuff her to the table now, start offering her sodas and cigarettes? This was a side of him she should've been anticipating, been ready to confront. He'd caught her with her guard down, like Sebastian had surprised her outside the Narrows the night all of this shit had started. After all she'd been through, how had she let that happen? That time or this one.

Maureen bit down on the tip of her tongue, thinking. Clarence. Tanya. The Black Garter. Which were the real questions? Where was he trying to lead her? To the gym? Maybe. Probably. Was it important in some way that she admit what she'd done before he accused her? There was probably no news about Tanya, Maureen decided. Waters was using the subject to soften her up. But if the gym was not what he wanted to discuss, she didn't want to lead him there. Growing up under fierce and frequent questioning from her mother, who would've made a hell of a cop herself, Maureen had fallen victim to that approach too often. So she'd avoid admitting anything about earlier that morning for as long as she could.

She offered Waters what she hoped was a guileless shrug. He wasn't the only one with a job that taught him to play a part. She could play dumb as skillfully as Waters could act the tough guy. "I know Clarence about as well as I know anyone at the Narrows, I guess. Not very well. Sorry."

Waters tossed his notepad on the table and then his pen, which rolled off the side. Nobody moved to pick it up. "Of course that's your answer. Why'd I even ask?"

Part of the act, Maureen wondered, or genuine frustration? She raised her shoulders. "What? What the fuck did I do? Am I in some kind of trouble?" A rueful grin curled one corner of her mouth. "You know, more trouble than I'm in already."

Waters didn't smile back. "You tell me."

Maureen felt icy water trickling down her spine and pooling in her gut. She licked her lips. Shit. She'd left Clarence and a pissed-off Sebastian alone together. Sound familiar? She crossed her arms and legs, settled her eyes on a corner of the ceiling. Stay calm, Maureen told herself. Someone, maybe Molly or maybe her brother, had painted over a shapeless water stain. There was, or had been, a leak in the roof. Clarence hadn't seen anything incriminating, Maureen thought. He did no business with Sebastian, as far as she knew. But like she had just admitted about Tanya, the past few days had proved she didn't know shit about the people in her orbit, people she saw daily. So, truthfully, who knew what the hell Sebastian and Clarence got up to? Maureen took some comfort that, at least physically, Clarence was no Dennis. He could handle himself. No one was getting his hands around that throat, not without a small army or a serious weapon. Both of which were only a phone call away for Sebastian.

John stood behind Molly's chair. "What'd I miss?"

"The Black Garter, John," Molly said. "You know it? The detective here is struggling."

"The Garter?" John said. "There's not a guy my age on the island that doesn't know it. Place is infamous. It's over by the water, near the old Atlantic train station. Middle of nowhere." He sipped his coffee. "Christ, I can't believe I ever went in there in anything less than a HAZMAT suit. Ugliest strippers I ever saw."

"And you've seen your share?" Waters asked.

"Of strippers or ugly?" John asked. He looked around the room. He set his hand on Molly's shoulder. "Oh, come on now. Don't act all surprised."

Nobody laughed. Maureen studied the others. Surely this early morning powwow hadn't been convened to discuss shit-hole saloons and ugly strippers. John, she decided, was in the dark like her. Uncomfortable with being left out, he was fumbling for information, trying to tease it out of a reluctant audience with bad jokes and bartender charm. But Molly and Waters, they knew something. Hiding it was making Molly hostile. She was so angry, or was it scared, that she vibrated with the fight to control herself. Waters was aggravating and insulting, Maureen thought, but looking at Molly made her afraid.

"What're you asking me for, anyway?" John said. "That place has been a cop hangout since the day the doors opened."

"Really? 'Cause I asked around the precinct," Waters said. He offered an exaggerated, sarcastic shrug. A gesture not very different, Maureen noted, from the one she'd just made. "Not much of a response."

"Ask harder," John said. "Cops live in there. At least they did back in the day when I was hanging around. They were out of uniform, of course." He smirked. "Must've been undercover." John slurped his coffee again, staring at Waters over the rim of the mug. He had the devil in his eyes. Waters had irked him in some way, the jokes, the dismissive shrug, maybe the early hour or the invasion of Molly's space. "I'm surprised you had to ask about it."

"Meaning what?"

"You've been in there."

"Never," Waters said. "Of course not."

"Sure you have. And not for an arrest."

"Are you saying you saw me?" Waters asked. "Because I don't think that's possible."

"I wouldn't go that far," John said. "I can barely remember being there myself, but still, you know, not even some years ago?" John looked everyone over. "C'mon, we're all friends here. Like I said, there's not a man on the island who doesn't—"

"I'm not your age," Waters said. "And I say I've never been in there. Are *you* gonna say that I'm a liar?"

"Of course not," John said, hiding his mouth with his coffee mug. Antagonizing Waters, Maureen decided, was John's way of sticking up for Molly. "Fair enough. I stand corrected. You've never been. I was just try-ing to, you know, lighten the mood. Since we're all opening up here."

Waters, his face now blotchy with red, stared John down. Maureen looked back and forth between the two men. Why the lie? she won-dered. Waters was lying about the Garter, either about his fellow cops or about going himself. He was lying about something. She was sure of it. John knew it, too. She'd waited on cops who had tried late at night to talk her into a trip over there. She'd heard others tell stories about the place. Maureen racked her brain for some connection between Tanya, Clarence, and the Garter, but she came up empty.

"I want to know," Maureen said, "what happened to Clarence."

"Did Clarence ever talk to you about the Black Garter?" Waters asked.

"I told you," Maureen said. "I don't know anything about that place." She was losing her patience. "Or Clarence, for that matter." Maureen took a long swallow of coffee. She cleared her throat. "If you need to know about Clarence so bad, go see him at the gym. I can tell you where it is. He's there every day. Those things I know. Anything else, go detect."

"I was there yesterday," Waters said. "I talked to him early this morn-ing. I've talked to Clarence a lot over the past two days."

"Then what're you killing me with questions for?" Maureen asked, her voice rising. "Christ." Fine, the truth was out, Maureen had taken matters into her own hands. Big deal. Let Waters slap the cuffs on her for assault, or battery, or whatever you called what she'd done at the gym. She'd call it self-defense.

Waters took a deep breath. "Maureen, we think Tanya's dead. That's what I talked to Clarence about this morning." He checked his watch. "I talked to him in his driveway about two hours ago."

Maureen slapped both hands over her mouth. Oh, no. Oh, God, no. *This shit is serious*, Clarence had said. And she'd thought he meant her confronting Sebastian in his place. "What makes you say you *think?*"

"Last night we found a woman," Waters said, "a body, floating in the harbor. Offshore from Cargo, washed up against the rocks right across the street, a location that means something to you, Maureen. Homeless guy gave us the location after a patrol picked him up breaking into cars. She was naked, so no ID was found but she fits the description. Fits it really well, I'm afraid."

"But you don't know for sure," Maureen said. She felt light-headed. Her breathing was fast and shallow. Was this what fainting felt like?

"We don't," Waters said. "Not absolutely." He opened his pad again. "Listen, I'm sorry I came at you so hard. I had to see what you knew before I hit you with this. Now, I'm gonna share some things with you. About relationships between Clarence and Vic. And Sebastian. I need to know if you can shed any light on these things at all. Can you do that? I need to make connections so I can figure out what happened to Tanya."

"If it's her," Maureen said.

Why was she even playing this game? She knew right down into her marrow that Tanya was dead. There weren't other girls that looked like that. Girls that looked like Molly, maybe a few floated around. And Maureen saw herself everywhere. But Tanya, she was one of a kind.

"Right," Waters said. "If it's her."

"I'll listen," Maureen said. She wanted to curl up under the table and stay there forever. "Other than that, I'm not making any promises."

Waters folded his hands on the table. "Clarence told me that he went to Vic in the spring for some extra work. Vic sent him over to the Garter, where Vic's friend Frank Sebastian has been in charge of security as long as anyone can remember. Cops or not, the Garter needs professionals, apparently. Clarence lasted about a month; he hated the place. Stop me when this rings any bells." He waited. "He said some of the girls looked young. And rough. Very young. Very rough." He looked over at John. "Worse than just ugly."

"News to me," Maureen said. "All of it."

She couldn't look at Waters. She picked a spot on the dining room table and stared at it.

"Clarence saw Sebastian there that month he worked the door," Waters said. "Saw him several times, heard from other employees that Sebastian had a special interest in the dancing girls. Clarence says he didn't see any specific activity, but he did notice that every girl in the place jumped when he snapped his fingers, and none of them would look him in the eye. Ever. This was back before Sebastian got tapped for the campaign. Not long before, in fact, Mr. Carmine Valario, the guy he's now looking to replace in the state senate, got busted with that dead underage stripper in Queens."

"Whoa, whoa," John said. "Hang on. Bells, I got bells. Mol, Maureen, you don't remember this?"

"I'm not talking to you," Waters said. "You've already overshared."

Maureen glanced at Molly, then back at John. "Remember what?"

"The girl." John snapped his fingers, over and over again, squeezing his eyes shut tight. "Christ, what was her name?"

"She was underage," Molly said. "High school. Her name wasn't released."

"I know, I know," John said, "but it went around the bars. It was something plain, simple. I can't believe I can't remember it."

"It wasn't long, anyway," Waters said, "before everyone stopped talking about her."

"Who?" Maureen asked. "Who are you talking about?"

"The girl Valario got caught with out in Queens," John said. "She was from the island, Prince's Bay, I think. It was such a big story. For a while, anyway. Like something out of a Scorsese movie. She cut her throat in the night. Valario woke up covered in her blood, screaming." He paused, lifted a finger at Waters. "She worked at the Black Garter. That's where Valario supposedly met her. Sebastian would've been working there then, too. He would've known her."

"Can you guys do the math," Waters said, "or should I spell it out for you?"

Maureen felt a flush in her cheeks, a thin sweat emerging along her hairline as if she'd broken out in a fever. So what was happening to her wasn't an aberration after all. It was, in fact, part of a pattern. A simple two-step sequence: use people up and then kill them. "So Dennis wasn't Sebastian's first victim."

Waters took a long time to deliver what Maureen thought was an obvious answer. "No. No he wasn't." There was a catch in his voice. He sat silent for a while, staring at the backs of his big hands. "Sebastian takes an interest in whoever looks useful to him. He probably never cared about Valario's senate seat until he saw a chance to take it from him. He's a predator. Like most predators, he prefers easier prey. Valario, his mistress, Dennis, all compromised or weakened in some way. Places like the Garter, even the Narrows, they're target-rich. You guys know this. They're filled with people who need things: money, protection, drugs. That need is like blood in the water."

"I see where you're going with this," John said. "But it's weak. No matter what the rumors are about what happens at the Garter, you can't hurt him with that place, even if you tie him to it. He was providing security, checking up on his men. A referral he got from Vic. That security business, it's like a free fucking pass, an excuse to be anywhere, the worse the environment, the better. If anything, that place plays as *inspiration* for his decision to run for office."

"It's perfect," Maureen said, "is what it is." She turned to Waters. "You stake the place out and grab him next time he shows up. No, no, even better. The night he shows up, you raid the place. Catch him with one of his 'special interests' and bust him with his pants around his ankles."

Waters shook his head. "He's smarter than that. He does his dirty work somewhere else. I promise you he doesn't even buy them drinks and hold their hand at the Garter."

"Somebody knows where he takes them," Maureen said, pushing up from the table. "I guarantee it. We just have to find the right person to ask. Or we stake out the Garter and follow him."

Maureen knew it was bullshit as she said it. Sebastian would never be that sloppy. He didn't leave witnesses. Except for her.

Waters raised his hand. "Enough with the *we* talk. There is no *we* when it comes to this." He checked his watch, his mouth in a tight frown. "However . . ." He let the space linger, raising Maureen's hopes. "Maureen, I do need your help with something." He opened his pad again, reached down with a groan, and picked up his pen off the floor. "Do you know anything about Tanya's family? We need a positive ID so we can be sure. Right now, she's just a Jane Doe."

"Leave Maureen out of this," Molly said. "It's not her job. It's yours. It's bad enough you use my house as an interrogation room."

"You know how to reach Vic?" Waters asked Maureen, ignoring Molly. "All Clarence had was a phone number, but there's no answer. There's no answer at the Narrows, either, the phone or the door."

"I got nothing," Maureen said. This time she wasn't playing dumb. "Vic lives on the North Shore, I think. But I couldn't tell you what street or even what neighborhood." She took a deep breath. "I'll do it. I'll do the ID."

Waters didn't say no.

"Oh, Maureen," Molly said. "Maybe that's a bad idea."

"No. I'll do it."

She pictured Tanya, naked under a sheet, alone in the cold dark vault at the morgue. No matter what underhanded shit she had tried, Tanya didn't deserve to be abandoned. Not like that. Not like trash washing up against the rocks. No one did. Tanya had been intimidated, taken advantage of. Had someone, anyone, Maureen included, really looked out for her, Tanya's life might have been different. It might not be over. But no one had protected her. Everyone had assumed that because of her beauty Tanya belonged to someone somewhere. Nobody left diamonds and gold and hundred-dollar bills and beautiful women lying around unclaimed. Except that they did. And then Sebastian had come along and snatched her off the street like a stray.

"Right now," Maureen said. "Take me to her right now."

"Don't do it, Nat," John said. "Do the job yourself and find her family."

"We've been looking," Waters said, "and we've gotten nowhere. If we're going to use her—" He stopped, raising his hand. "If Tanya's death, if it is her, is going to be part of a case against Sebastian, we need to keep moving. We only have so much time." He rose to his feet. "I'm only going to ask you once more, Maureen. Are you sure?"

"Yes," Maureen said. "I'm positive. Take me to her right now."

"At least let John and me go with you," Molly said.

"No," Maureen said. "You've got lives of your own. You're already gonna be late for work."

"This is a bad idea," John said.

"It's not," Maureen said. She pointed at John. "You go back to bed. Molly, you go to work. I'll be fine." She tried to smile at Waters. "It's not like I'll be alone."

"You will be after," John said.

"I'll look out for her," Waters said.

"John, she's a grown woman," Molly said. She let out a long breath. "Maureen can make her own decisions, whether we like them or not. Let it be."

John turned to Waters. "She comes right back here."

Maureen knocked on the table. "She'll do whatever she thinks is best. Can we go, Detective? I'd like to get this done."

"Lock up behind us." Waters gathered up his notebook and headed out of the room, down the hall, and into the front yard.

"At least let me make you a bagel," Molly said. "To take with you."

"Thanks, but no," Maureen said. "I might be best on an empty stomach."

Pulling on her coat, Maureen felt John and Molly watching her. Out in the yard, Waters walked to the fence, hand on his gun inside his coat, and checked the block. He turned back to the house and waved her out. She didn't move. He wasn't like this, Maureen thought, when he had first come to her apartment. From inside his coat, Waters retrieved his cell phone. Calling the morgue. Telling them to prepare the body. Maureen chewed her bottom lip, steeling herself for what lay ahead at the morgue and beyond. Molly came up beside her, pressed spare house keys into her hand.

"When you get back," Molly said, "make yourself at home. Whatever you need. I'll be home by four. John'll be napping before work. Don't worry about waking him up."

Maureen wrapped Molly in a hug. "Thanks so much. For everything." Her knees went weak as Molly's palm rubbed warm circles on her back.

"No problem," Molly said. "This will all be over soon."

The last thing Maureen wanted to do was leave that embrace and that house. But Waters waited outside. And Tanya waited, too, not at a friend's house and not in someone's arms but alone. Maureen slipped out of Molly's embrace and headed out the door. Waters stood at the end of the walk, holding open the gate. Maureen couldn't read his face.

As Waters pulled the Crown Vic away from the curb, Maureen reached into her coat pocket for the ladybug night-light. She came up empty. She'd left it on the couch at Molly's. Now she had nothing. She wanted Waters to take her back to Molly's house but couldn't bring herself to ask. He'd want to know why. I gotta stop running around with a detective, Maureen thought. He asks too many questions. She'd tell him nothing about her trip to the gym, she decided, not a word. The encounter had revealed nothing about Tanya, nothing that Waters would find useful, and he would stroke out in fury if he knew Maureen had put herself within arms' reach of Sebastian, no matter who had been holding the knife.

She made a fist in her pocket. Get a grip on yourself. That bug is a cheap piece of plastic. It's nothing. You lived without it for years. She took out her cigarettes. She lit up without asking permission.

"I'm not doing this for you," Maureen said, the car settling to a stop at a red light. The traffic signal rocked side-to-side in the winter wind. "I'm doing it for Tanya."

Waters's eyes flicked across the car and then settled back on the intersection. "I appreciate it all the same."

Maureen studied her face in the side-view mirror. She looked thinner in the cheeks, hollowed out. She looked like her mother. She took a long drag of her smoke. She couldn't remember her childhood room without the rose-colored glow of that night-light. She'd never slept without it, even as a teenager, not until she'd moved out and left it behind, until she had started her life of not sleeping until sunrise. And now here I am, she thought, older, wiser, and more afraid of the dark than ever. Stop thinking about it. It's a plastic bug. She was a big girl now, a grown woman.

"It wasn't fair," Maureen said, "the way you ambushed me at Molly's with all those questions. Like I was a criminal or something."

"You've held out on me before," Waters said. "About Tanya, especially." He glanced at her across the car. "You're holding out on me now. About what, I don't know, but you're sitting on something."

Maureen felt Waters's lie about the Black Garter land on the tip of her tongue. But considering the fact that she was indeed hiding something he'd want to know about, she decided to swallow her accusation and her hypocrisy. Disappointment bloomed in her chest, thick and heavy. She hated feeling that large and obvious lies had emerged between them like weeds creeping up through a crack in the sidewalk. She was at a loss for what to do, an increasingly familiar feeling these days. "I still say it wasn't fair."

She watched Waters fight a grin. A silent chuckle rippled his belly. His lips twitched but didn't curl. He couldn't keep the light out of his eyes. "What could possibly be funny right now?" Maureen asked.

"You're young," Waters said, "but you're not naïve." He raised his fist to his mouth to cover a yawn. "So stop acting like it."

He looked at her across the car. The humor in his eyes flared and then died, like a flawed match where the flame ignites but doesn't take.

Why did that seem to keep happening? Why did the life leave his eyes when he turned them on her? Like she was a reminder of something sad he was trying to forget. Maureen felt her throat go dry.

"Don't even pretend," Waters said, "that *fair* has anything to do with our situation. What we're going to see at the morgue isn't *fair*, no matter who it is we pulled out of the water or how she got there. Just go ahead and cut *fair* out of your vocabulary."

Maureen said nothing, turning away from Waters. She dropped her smoke out the window and watched it bounce off the pavement, tumbling across the white lines rolling out behind her. She watched the dead vegetation lining the road rush by, its ugly dandruff of branch-caught trash exposed in the morning light. She thought of Sebastian. Inches. She'd been only inches from him. Close enough to smell his sweat. She thought again of her lost night-light. At least now she had good reason to fear the dark. Now her monsters were real.

20

Riding in the elevator down to the morgue, Maureen felt haunted by the Narrows, by the long nights she had spent there that she had wasted underground. And by how Tanya's short life had led from one vault to another with scant daylight in between. Maureen pressed her back harder against the metal of the elevator wall. She crossed her arms, chewed a fingernail. Between Waters's bulk and the orderly next to them, precious little room remained for her and even less air.

The orderly, hook-nosed and pale, his long brown hair tied back in a ponytail, bobbed his head to a pulsing heavy metal song leaking from his iPod earbuds. At his waist, he carried a metal bin covered with a towel. The bin's possible contents fascinated and repulsed Maureen. Something inside her desperately wanted to peek under the towel, but she was afraid to get too close. Asking would be too weird. The orderly held the bin as if it contained nothing more than cold lasagna.

It's funny, Maureen thought, the difference distance makes. A swirling, crashing orgy of sound played in the orderly's head and he obviously dug it. To Maureen's ears, though, his music was tinny static, an unpleasant distraction. He had to know where she was headed. Waters, as if his appearance didn't scream *cop* loud enough, wore his gold detective's shield on a chain around his neck. That meant Maureen was making an ID. So that someone, maybe this guy even, had a name to write on the toe tag. Had the orderly seen Tanya? How many beautiful girls had he seen on a slab? Did they stand out among the other dead? Did the living? The expression on the orderly's face gave nothing away; he could've been waiting for a bus or on line at the bank. What kind of distance did this guy get from death? Or was it life to which he grew numb while working in a morgue? Was her life, Maureen wondered, or Tanya's life, or the stories in the paper about the girl from Prince's Bay, were they all just tinny static to him?

The elevator settled to a stop with the ding of an invisible bell and the orderly looked over at her. He smiled, winked, raised the bin a few inches. "A foot," he said.

The doors opened and he walked out, turning right down the hall. The explosion started deep in her belly. Maureen covered her mouth with both hands. It was no use. Loud snorts of laughter burst through her fingers. She couldn't stop them. Tears filled her eyes. She coughed. She worried for a fleeting moment that she might be sick. The orderly glanced back once at her over his shoulder. Maureen could've sworn she saw a smirk on his face. She couldn't stop coughing, painful bursts from deep in her lungs. Her nose was running; she wiped it on her sleeve. Dennis had been taken to the morgue in bits and pieces. He'd probably been loaded out of the body bag and into cold metal bins like the one the orderly carried. Christ, what was wrong with her? She blinked away the water in her eyes, tried to bring her brain back to the task at hand. She felt a thousand pounds lighter than she had getting on the elevator, either from relief, she figured, or severe oxygen deprivation.

Waters waited in the hall, his huge arm holding back the elevator doors. His face was the picture of patience. Was there anything, any reaction to death, or to the pressure of being alive and near it that he hadn't seen a thousand times? She knew he'd never ask what she'd found so hilarious.

"It's not too late," Waters said. "We can go back upstairs and I'll take you right back to Molly's."

"Sorry. I don't know what happened." Maureen peeled her back off the wall. "I'm good; just let's not linger."

Waters led her down the long, narrow hall, his shoes clicking on the tile. The fluorescents reflecting off the institutional-green wall tiles cast everything—the floor, the air, her hands—in an olive glow. Maureen wiped at her eyes with the backs of her wrists, sniffling as she walked. The hall smelled like a restaurant walk-in: cool recycled air gone stale from never-changing temperature, a trace of bleach from a recent mopping. No windows, Maureen noticed. Of course, she thought, they were underground. No windows at the Narrows, either. Who wanted a view of the dirt and rock that buried them?

They stopped at an unoccupied desk where Waters, after checking his watch, signed his name on a clipboard. He handed it to Maureen. She looked up and down the hall. Where was everybody? Well, the dead, at least their bodies, weren't real needy, were they? The doctors down here didn't worry about their patients sneaking out for beer and a ciga-rette. Nobody was gonna bail without paying the tab; paying it once and for all had put them here. She signed her name under Waters's, leaving her one name removed and a few inky inches short of the *Jane Doe* scribbled in sloppy doctors' scrawl.

With a big hand Waters waved her across the hall, where he stood at a metal door with a small window of thick plastic. Follow Waters's lead, she thought. Do everything he says and you'll get through this.

Maureen walked up to him, standing close, her eyes locked on his face. A sickly pallor had settled into his skin. Unshaven, his stubble was white. Waters looked like an ill old man who needed a shower, a salad, and a week's worth of sleep. Is that what I look like? Maureen wondered. Like I'm sick? Like I'm wasting away? Like I belong down here in the dirt and the dark?

"You're doing great," Waters said, putting his hands on her shoulders. "It's already almost over. The hardest part is getting here. This'll take less than ten minutes. We're going into a viewing room. It'll be the one body we're here to look at, and she'll be covered. Only the face will be showing."

Maureen nodded.

"Okay then," Waters said. "She wasn't in the water that long, so she'll look"—he paused, struggling for words—"mostly normal. You should know right away if you recognize her."

"So she drowned."

"It looks that way," Waters said, "but she'll go through the same procedure as Dennis and then we'll know for sure—that she drowned, at least—if not how she got in the water. You ready?"

"No." How did someone get ready for this? "But I'll do it anyway."

Waters rang a doorbell and an unseen attendant buzzed them through. They entered an anteroom. A couple of cheap plastic chairs and what looked like an old school desk, it even had names scratched in it, sat against the wall. On the desk a pitcher of water, a stack of paper cups, and a mostly empty box of tissues. Beside the opposite door in the far wall was a viewing window. Waters walked to the window. He turned back to Maureen. "We can do it from here, if that's easier."

"I want to go in." She did; she wanted to rush in and grab up that girl, whoever she was, and carry her out of this horrible place, out into the natural light and the real air. She wanted to hold her hand and brush her hair from her face, promise her she wasn't alone.

Waters rapped his thick knuckle on the glass and the door opened. The white-coated attendant stepped back to let them in and then stood, silent and motionless, beside the gurney holding the sheet-shrouded form. He watched Waters. Waters watched Maureen. Maureen stared back at him, blinking away the spots before her eyes. Unlike the anteroom or the hall, the viewing room glowed bright as a makeup mirror. Maureen narrowed one eye. She shook off a chill, shook it off harder when it regrouped at the base of her spine and sprang up her back again. Somewhere nearby, very close, maybe just the other side of the metal door across the room, lay many more of the dead. Through the soles of her boots, running up the bones of her legs, Maureen felt the vibrations of the massive cooling unit keeping all the corpses chilled.

"It's not too late to call it off," Waters said. "No one will think any less of you."

"Do it," Maureen said.

Waters nodded and the attendant pulled back the sheet, folding it gently over the dead girl's collarbone. Maureen stepped to the gurney. Tanya. Absolutely and positively her. Tears flooded Maureen's eyes, blurring her vision, but she had already seen what she needed to. Waters spoke from close behind her.

"Maureen, do you know this woman?"

"I do," Maureen said. She took a deep breath. "Her name is Tanya Coscinelli."

"How do you know her?" Waters asked.

"We worked together at the Narrows." Maureen wiped her eyes with her wrists. "I saw her four, sometimes five nights a week, for over a year. I saw her yesterday. Alive."

Maureen tilted her head back and blinked up at the bright overhead lamps. She looked back down at Tanya. It was mind-boggling. Amazing. Under the surgery-bright lights, Tanya's every flaw should've lain obvious and exposed, but Maureen couldn't find a single one. Even after drifting in the frigid harbor, even lifeless and laid out on a stretcher, her face brushed in blue and gray and violet, Tanya remained one of the most beautiful women Maureen had ever seen. Whole lot of good it had done her.

She fought the urge to touch Tanya's cheek. Tanya, the dead girl, looked hard and unbreakable. Maureen, the live one, felt as if she might crack and shatter from the inside out. She touched her fingertips to her own cool, smooth cheek. Letting other people get their feelers and their fingers into the cracks, into the fissures and the fault lines on the inside, Maureen thought, that's what brings you down in the end. Never forget that.

How close had she come, really, she wondered, to being the one on the gurney, her own face like stone, her devastated mother standing over her, saying, *Yes, that's my little girl, Maureen Evelyn Coughlin.*

"Can you tell us anything else?" the attendant asked. He laid the sheet over Tanya's face. The act, though necessary, struck Maureen as cruel, as if Tanya were being erased, dust-covered for storage like an old piece of useless furniture. Maureen wanted to punch him. "Her age?" he asked. "Her next of kin?"

"No," Maureen said, choking on sobs. "No, I can't. I can't."

"Take a minute," Waters said. "Catch your breath. You'll remember."

"It's not that I don't remember," Maureen said. Her tears fell on the shrouded body before her. "I never knew a single fucking meaningful thing about her."

She felt Waters's hand on her back. "It's okay, Maureen. It's okay." And to the attendant, "We're done here."

"No it's not," Maureen said. "It's not okay at all." She looked up at Waters. "And we are not done. Not by a long shot."

Later, reaching across the diner table, Maureen poked her fork into a soft mass of strawberry ice cream melting away atop a stack of waffles. Neither she nor Waters had eaten more than a few bites. I ought to be starving, she thought, but nothing at that moment seemed less attractive than eating. Her stomach was filled with concrete, with harbor water. She tossed her fork on the table, splattering Waters's tie with pink dots.

"Sorry."

Waters rubbed at the spots with a napkin. "Not the first time that's happened. Forget it." He cut one last slice of waffle and ice cream with his fork, ate it, and slid the plate to the table's edge. "Maybe not my best idea, this meal."

Maureen tilted her mug and looked down into the dregs of her hot cocoa. She pushed the mug aside. "It was a sweet idea. Thanks for trying."

She edged down the bench, away from the spreading pool of sunlight beaming through the window beside her. Outside, the first sunny day the island had seen in weeks spilled over the street. Maureen wanted no part of it.

Cars, buses, and delivery trucks, every one filthy, the hard sun glinting off their windows, jammed Victory Boulevard. People in heavy coats and sunglasses, coffee in gloved hands, newspapers tucked under their arms, rushed by the diner, moving twice as fast as the traffic. Morning people. She'd heard they existed. Schoolgirls in uniform, arrogant seniors blowing off first period, Maureen figured, clustered at the corner bus stop, their bodies in constant restless motion like a fluttering band of nervous birds on a wire. They wore their plaid skirts hiked up to the hems of their puffy coats despite the cold. Watching them, Maureen tried not to think about the dead girl found in Valario's bloody bed. Which school, which skirt, had she worn?

Once upon a time, a million years ago, Maureen had taken the city bus to high school in one of those skirts, had stood huddled on a street corner with the other kids, her skirt rolled up high on her skinny legs. Some days there were twenty of them at that bus stop: chattering, griping, flirting. The girls preening, the boys strutting. Pretty much the same kids every school day for four years. Maureen realized she couldn't say what had happened to any of those kids. She might be able to wrestle five names from her memory. *What the hell have I been doing for the past eleven years?* That girl who had died in Queens, Maureen wondered, what had Waters said her name was? The waitress came over and refilled Waters's coffee cup. HELEN, her name tag said.

Maureen studied Helen's face, the caked-on makeup around her eyes, her red, sticky lips set in a hard and phony grin. Only her body was at the table. Her mind was elsewhere, if not far. The next table, the register, the dish room. Behind the waitress's eyes, Maureen could see the turning wheels, the listing and prioritizing of the next fifty things Helen had to do before her own next cup of coffee. *I've been working,* Maureen thought. *That's what I've been doing. One shift, a decade plus one year long.*

When Helen met her eyes, Maureen looked down at the table, guilty over seeing not only her past in Helen's face but a future that scared her.

"When they were really young," Waters said, "I took my sons out to the aquarium on Coney Island. To see the belugas, the white whales. They looked into that tank the same way you looked out that window."

"And how's that?" Maureen asked.

"Like they couldn't believe what they were seeing."

"Morning isn't new to me," Maureen said. "But I usually see it as the end of the night, not the beginning of the day."

"I know the feeling," Waters said.

"You always work the night shift?"

"For a long time now."

"You like it?"

Waters pushed out his bottom lip, shrugged. "Mostly. There's more action at night, I guess. I don't know. As long as I can remember it's been more like one long shift with naps and meals mixed in."

"I get the same feeling sometimes," Maureen said, "though I don't know how many more nights I have in me. I've been spinning my wheels forever. And my car is upside-down. At least you're accomplishing something."

"I have my doubts about that," Waters said. "But I've never been able to sit around watching TV while men like Sebastian run free doing what they do. And there's always one like him on the loose. At least one. No one's found out yet how to shut down the machine that makes them."

"When this is over," Maureen said, "you should take a few days off, take your boys to the aquarium again. I bet they'd like that."

Waters tugged at the crooked knot of his tie, rubbed his thumb at the ice cream spots. "I don't think so."

"Then take 'em to the zoo. That was my father's thing, the Staten Island zoo. Twice a month, whenever the place was open." She felt her face warming with memory, or maybe from the sunshine through the window. "You know those peacocks they let walk around? They were my favorite. I was always asking Dad if I could ride one."

"I don't think the boys and I will be going to the zoo, either."

"And why not?" Maureen asked. "I bet you think your kids are too old for that stuff, but believe me, they're not."

"Because this trouble that you're in will end for you, and you'll go back to your life. But the work never ends for me."

"Your sons should be more important to you than your work."

"That's exactly what my wife used to say."

"Maybe she was right."

"Okay," Waters said, leaning over the table. "How about I take to-day off?"

Maureen pulled her legs underneath her, sitting on her knees and leaning forward until she was almost nose to nose with Waters. "Do it. I dare you. I've made it this far. I can make it one more day."

"That's all Tanya was trying to do," Waters said. "Make it one more day."

Maureen unwound her legs and threw her arms over the back of the bench, looking away from Waters. "Ouch. Is it illegal to say *fuck you* to a cop?"

"I'm sorry," Waters said. "That was uncalled for. The truth is, I haven't seen my sons in thirty years. When my wife left, she took the boys with her. I've never heard word one from any of them. I'm sure my wife told them I was dead, or a monster, if she told them about me at all. They were probably too young to remember I even existed." He raised his cof-fee cup, talked into it. "Better that way. That's what I tell myself."

Maureen knew she couldn't add up the time she'd devoted to her father's imaginary life. Was her situation better or worse, she wondered, than inventing lives for kids you never knew? You'd think it was a luxury playing God on behalf of the ones you loved. But even when her imag-inings were at their most generous, their most merciful, even when she'd convinced herself she understood why he left, in her dreams her father got sick, got hurt, got old, and died, again and again, from accidents or disease. She was sure Waters had played out a thousand lives each for his sons: some good, some bad, none of them real.

"For the record," Maureen said, "your ex is a bitch."

Waters held up his hand. "She did what she thought was best."

"Best?" Maureen asked. "It wasn't best for anyone but her, leaving you without your kids, leaving those boys without a father."

"I'm sure they had a father. It just wasn't me."

"Tell me you looked for them."

"I did. For a long time."

"And then you gave up?"

"Some people who don't want to be found have good reasons. Reasons that should be accepted."

"But you never went out looking for someone else," Maureen said. "Never tried starting over. Another wife. Another family."

"I never consciously ruled it out," Waters said. "And I certainly never set out to make myself a martyr, but, no, I guess I never tried real hard to start over. I missed my kids. I still think about them, try to imagine them. But after a while the job takes over. I met some women, had some fun, but nothing stuck. I fell into a rhythm with the job that I've never stepped out of, and I can't say I regret it. It is what it is. The sadness lingers, from what I lost. I got a bum shoulder from playing football, it hurts when it snows, but otherwise it's fine; the pain is like that. But I can't say I'm unhappy, or that—aside from those first few months after they left—I ever was. I don't know what that says about me, but there it is."

Maureen stared at him for a long time. "And you believe this shit you tell yourself?"

"Most days," Waters said, flashing a quick grin. He looked away from her, raising his arm, waving for the bill. "I gotta get moving. I got work to do."

Maureen stretched out her legs under the table, shrinking inside her coat. "So what do we tell ourselves about Tanya?"

"I'm stuck with the truth on that one." He paused as the waitress swept by and dropped the bill. "I was too slow to save her."

Waters slipped his hands into the pockets of his overcoat, his gaze floating over the diner. "I hate saying this, but Tanya's no ordinary victim. Her death gets me a lot more weight to throw around. It'll unlock more manpower, more resources. And you became a lot more important, Maureen, when Tanya died. You're a big-time witness in two homicide cases, now."

"Hooray for me," Maureen said. "I'm finally somebody."

Waters had a point about Tanya; she knew that. Once Tanya's gorgeous face hit the next day's papers, if not that evening's news, the public outrage would put serious pressure on the cops. Dead drug dealers, dead hookers and addicts, dead poor people? That was life in the big city, a back-page story. But Tanya would be front-page news. They'd move a ton of papers selling poor drug-addled Tanya as a murdered all-American girl, a serious American tragedy. Forget the front page, Tanya was satellite-ready national news. The TV would run a heartbreaker of a high school yearbook shot. The whole NYPD would be foaming at the mouth hunting her killer, seething for their chance to reap Tanya's vengeance.

And it wasn't lost on Maureen that if Tanya's homicide brought down Sebastian, Tanya might end up saving Maureen's life, more than enough payback for the original betrayal. But Waters's comment stirred up one thought that Maureen couldn't deny. Tanya was worth more to both Waters and Sebastian dead than alive. No, not true, Maureen thought. There was one crucial, absolute difference. If he could have, Waters would've kept Tanya among the living. Sebastian was the problem. She had to remember that.

"What happened to Tanya," Maureen said, "is not your fault."

"Nice of you to say," Waters said. He didn't sound convinced. He lifted his rump, reaching for his wallet. Maureen snatched the bill off the table. She dug some cash from her bag, held out her arm.

Helen grabbed the bill and the cash and stared at Maureen as if there was a mistake. She snapped her gum. "Change?"

"I don't believe in it," Maureen said. "That's all you."

21

Maureen followed Waters out the door and into the blinding, pain-ful sunlight. She stuck close to him; he was like a rock in the middle of a river; pedestrians flowed around him on both sides. With the traffic bunched as thick as the people, the air hung heavy and rank from ex-haust. The schoolgirls were gone. At the intersection, the lead car hesi-tated a split second at the green light. Four other drivers leaned on their horns. The bleating sliced jagged-edged through Maureen's brain.

She followed Waters around the back of the diner to the parking lot. The building muffled the street noise and Maureen's headache eased. When she got back to Molly's, she intended to sleep through the rest of the morning and maybe the afternoon, too.

Waters stopped at his car but didn't unlock the doors. He leaned against the trunk, crossing his arms. Maureen mimicked Waters's stance against the car. Maybe we look like partners, she thought. She imagined a gold badge of her own hanging around her neck. She could live with being taken for a cop. It'd be a step up from what she felt she usually got, especially these past few days. And if she had that shield, she'd be going on the hunt instead of back into hiding.

"I think you should avoid Cargo for the time being," Waters said.

Maureen hung her head. Jesus, couldn't she feel good for five minutes? "You said Cargo was safe."

"What happened to Tanya means Cargo is compromised," Waters said. "We were supposed to find her at that drop-off. As a threat to you, like breaking into your place and leaving the MetroCards, only worse. Sebastian could've easily put her where we'd never have found her. He knows you've been hiding out at Cargo. He might have someone on the inside. Any ideas?"

Maureen rubbed her arms. Tracy from Cargo came to mind. A younger Tanya in training, maybe? Had Sebastian found a way to get his claws into her? Maureen had trouble seeing it. Tracy had spine and smarts that Tanya had never possessed. Someone else? Sebastian's sexual appetite was unisex. A guy? A dishwasher or bar back? Every joint in the world had at least one crazy crackhead dude on the roster. Who was it at Cargo? Half the staff had probably turned over since she'd quit. Be that as it may, she couldn't imagine anyone fooling John.

"I can't see it," Maureen said. "John runs a tight ship, doesn't miss a trick. He's the one to ask."

"I'll do that."

"Say that's true about Tanya being a warning," Maureen said. "Why put her in the water? Why not leave her . . . somewhere else in the area?"

"The water washes away evidence. He can tell us he did it and cover his tracks at the same time. Sebastian's a lot of things, but he's not stupid."

"He had her under his thumb. Tanya did everything he said."

"Scared as she was," Waters said, "killing her was the only absolute guarantee she doesn't ever talk. He's probably started looking at you the same way. You scare him, Maureen. A lot."

"What, me? Nobody is afraid of me. You gotta be kidding."

"You're the last one left who knows about him and Dennis. You saw him with Dennis, and then Dennis is dead. You saw him with Tanya the day she died. On top of that, from that first night forward everything he's told you to do, you've defied him. How often do you think that happens to a man like him? You think he handles that well?"

"Jesus. I'm sorry I asked."

"I wouldn't tell you the truth," Waters said, stepping closer to her, "if I didn't think you could take it. Bullshit gets us nowhere. We have to trust each other."

He reached out for her shoulder. She flinched, pulling away. Was this it? she thought. The moment Sebastian had promised? The time when Waters put his hands on her? She turned away, watching Waters through loose strands of her hair, ashamed of letting Sebastian's sickness into her brain for even a moment. Waters stepped back, lowering his arm. Maureen watched his huge hand drift to his side. He curled it briefly into a fist before opening it again. The gray insides of his knuckles were dry and cracked, the palm pink in the center. She looked up at him, moving her hair from her face.

"You're a good soldier," Waters said. "I won't let anything happen to you."

This was a good person, Maureen thought, a good man. They existed; she knew they did. She wanted to believe. She thought of Waters's lost sons, how tiny their hands must've been in his. A good soldier. The words, coming from a man she hardly knew, moved her more than they should have. She could be a soldier, a warrior who stood her own ground. She took a deep breath, puffing out her chest. She wanted to believe, she really did. But there was one thing she needed to know.

"You all right?" Waters asked. "You having heartburn or something?"

"Why did you lie to John?" Maureen asked. "About the Black Garter."

"Excuse me?"

"I know you're a detective," Maureen said, "but I've been watching men lie — to each other, to women, to themselves, for a long time. Back at Molly's, you acted like you knew nothing about the place. Why?"

Waters shoved his hands into his overcoat pockets. "It's not important."

"Then why lie?"

"It's not important. To you or your case."

"Let's hear it," Maureen said.

"Suddenly you don't trust me?"

"And whose fault is that?" Maureen said. "You've been good to me so far, don't blow it now." Waters squinted at something in the sky over Maureen's head and behind her. She turned to look, but couldn't find what he was watching. She tucked loose strands of hair behind her ears, letting Waters see her face. "Listen, if we've hit a point you don't wanna go past, I understand. But maybe I need to know that."

Waters sniffed hard, then let loose a long sigh—the sound of a man confident he was making a mistake. Maureen had heard it before. Hands jammed deep in his coat pockets, Waters spoke while focused on that invisible object over her shoulder. "Back when I was working on the vice squad with Sebastian, after a big night—a big arrest, say—the Garter was where we went afterward to wind down. The place was outside Brooklyn and virtually twenty-four hours back then, especially for cops."

Big deal, Maureen thought. News flash: cowboy cops hit the late-night titty bars, film at eleven. Not enough, she thought, for Waters to lie about in a room full of people. Something else was up. "The owner must've loved you guys."

"He did, actually," Waters said. "He loved the fact that ten cops might walk through the door at any moment, as long as it was us. Helped keep sort of a lid on other things. Kept other, maybe less tolerant cops from getting too interested in the place. We looked the other way on a few things. The owner did, too."

Maureen sucked in her cheeks, her eyes narrowing. She felt a lightness opening inside her, a slow-growing surprise, as if she were filling with helium. She closed her coat over her chest. "Detective, are you trying to tell me you were a crooked cop?"

Waters rubbed his fingers into his chin. His eyes remained evasive. "At least you had the decency to use the past tense."

"Like you mentioned so kindly before," Maureen said, "I'm not naïve, so let's not act like it. I'm not exactly walking on gilded splinters over here. I know that. I try not to judge. And I don't tell other people's secrets—most of the time. But I think I have a right to know how lamed up you are, really, when it comes to helping me."

Waters waited a long time to respond. Maureen thought for a moment he might get in the car and drive away, pull the car right out from under her and leave her standing there in a cloud of white exhaust in the cold parking lot. Might that be best?

"*Crooked* is a powerful word," Waters finally said, "when it comes to cops. Once you get it on you, it doesn't come off. People put the barrel in their mouth over it. It's a word to be careful with. I'm not proud of some of the things that we—that I—did back then. I don't like thinking back on those times if I can help it. But *crooked* is not a word I'd use for what I did, for what I was."

Leaning against the car, Maureen raised one foot against the bumper, wedging her boot heel between the bumper's edge and the trunk. She believed, if not in Waters's innocence, then at least in his lack of complete crookedness.

Which, at the end of the day, wasn't much to believe in, was it?

Looking away from Waters, Maureen watched a dishwasher bounce trash cans down the diner's back stairs. He stopped to light a cigarette then dragged the cans toward the Dumpster, the dirty strings of his apron pulled taut against his lower back, the hard muscles in his arms bulging at the cuffs of his filthy white T-shirt. He puffed smoke over his head like a locomotive. Twin trickles of brown liquid leaked behind the cans, running over the asphalt like dirty rivers winding across the face of a map. She was torn. She didn't see much point in ditching Waters, but she didn't see many reasons to stick with him, other than that they'd gotten this far. Which was where, exactly? She realized her legs were aching. She was so fucking tired. Tired of being afraid, of thinking, of waiting. She was so sick of giving up and running away.

"Sebastian's gonna call you again," Waters said, "and try to reel you in. We need to talk about what you're going to do when that happens."

"I got no problem with that. We'll set our own trap this time."

"No," Waters said. "I'm not using you as bait. No way. As soon as you know it's him, you hang up and call me with the number."

"Like he'd be dumb enough to use a number you could track."

"Let me worry about that."

"You gonna talk some sense into him?" Maureen asked. "Frighten him with your shiny new resources?"

"Maureen."

"No, I'm sick of this shit. Now I can't even answer my phone? This prick has ruined my life. He *kills* people. I wanna *do something*. And you? You keep stopping me. Why is that?"

"How about staying alive?" Waters said. "Is that *doing something* enough for you?"

"No. Duck-and-run is not enough. Surviving is not enough."

"I'm gonna get him," Waters said. "I can get a couple other detectives on the case. I got friends, too. We work backward from Tanya's death. I'll guide things where they need to go. I'll get him, I promise you."

"When?"

"Soon."

"Not good enough."

"It's gonna have to be."

Maureen set her feet. She squared her shoulders. She knew what was coming. Bigger and stronger, Waters would use that advantage to get what he wanted. He'd try to back her down. Try to make her give in, to make her calm down and be reasonable. She'd heard it before. Her boy-friends, her bosses, they always did it and she always caved in.

Not this time. Not to Waters, not to Sebastian.

"I'm gonna answer when he calls," Maureen said. "And I'm gonna arrange a meeting, and then *you* better hope you get him first."

Waters sucked in a deep breath, nostrils flaring. Maureen could feel his temper rising. Too bad.

"Don't even try to tell me," she said, "I'm not *allowed*."

Waters rose off the car trunk and walked a few steps away, struggling for control of his temper. Maureen watched him roll his head from side to side, stretching his neck, trying to stay calm, trying to hold, Maureen could tell, something back. He turned. "You don't get it, do you? You cannot fuck with this guy."

"So I've heard," Maureen said. "He's a major player. He's got juice. I fucking get it. And here I still am. Seriously, half the time you sound more like you're protecting him than me."

"If Sebastian gets you before you get him, or before I get him, you know what's gonna happen. We've both seen it. You wanna go back to the morgue, get a better look at what you're gambling with? You wanna be carried around in little tins like the one that cracked you up in the elevator?" Waters strode back to her. Maureen thought he might run her over. He stopped when they were toe-to-toe, looming over her, this time bringing the full weight of his size to bear. "You know what your problem is, Maureen? You're not as smart as you think you are. You think you know what you're dealing with, but you don't."

Maureen trembled, bile kicking up her throat. Fighting back, holding her ground, was harder than she thought. She turned her head and spat onto the pavement. She looked up at Waters. "So educate me."

Waters backed away, staring at Maureen for a long time, thinking. She could see the secrets pulsing behind his eyes. She wanted to back off. She couldn't. "What don't I know that's so fucking important?"

"You only know half the truth," Waters said. "About everything."

"Then stop bullshitting me and tell me all of it," Maureen said, "or leave me alone." She'd gotten to Sebastian once, she thought, without any help, without guns and badges. "Or leave me alone permanent. I mean it."

"You think you know why Sebastian left the NYPD."

She could get to him again, hurt him much worse than a scratch on the cheek. "He got shot. Twice."

"But what you don't know," Waters said, "is that I shot him."

Maureen steadied herself against the car. The helium balloon inside her had popped. "What?" She blinked at Waters, maybe more shocked at this revelation than she'd been walking out of the office at the Narrows, and she was desperate to hide her surprise. She crossed and uncrossed her arms, settling her hands on her hips. She frowned in false skepticism. "But that doesn't make any sense. You guys were partners."

"I worked in his squad," Waters said. "Not as partners. He was my superior."

Maureen caught herself laughing. "That makes it better?" These things Waters was saying made no sense to her. But what possible reason could he have for lying, for telling her he'd shot Sebastian if he hadn't? Was this some bizarre effort to impress her, to make up for losing Tanya? She concentrated on leveling out her breath, trying to get her head together. "It said in the papers that some pimp shot him. Every article I found had that same story."

"Because that was the story he and I cooked up while we were waiting for the ambulance." Waters smoothed his tie with the flat of his hand. He tilted his head sharply to one side. Maureen heard the compressed vertebrae crack like dry sticks. She wasn't happy that he had a reasonable explanation ready every time she argued with him. Waters let out a long sigh. "There was no one else around at the time to contradict us."

Why did that sound to her like a threat? Couldn't be. She was spooked out by Waters's temper, by the news of the shooting on the back of the trip to the morgue. Waters was looking out for her. That was the reason he was around. Maureen dropped her foot off the bumper. She moved away, arcing around him like a cat wise to the limit of a dog's leash. "On the crooked scale," she said, "where do you rank shooting another cop? And then conspiring with him and covering it up? Christ Almighty."

"See, there it is again. You think you know things."

"I know what you told me just now," Maureen said. "That's what I know. Don't talk like I'm making things up." She recalled Sebastian's admonishments about Waters from outside Dennis's house, from the phone outside the library. "This whole thing really is about Sebastian for you, isn't it? I'm just the excuse, the random connection. He was right. Sick as he is, he was right about you."

"Don't be ridiculous," Waters said, his voice loud enough to turn a few heads yards away on the sidewalk. Red blotches colored his throat. "You think I need you to find him? He's hardly been hiding out since his retirement. If I wanted him, I could've had him." Waters, breathing slow and deep, leaned hard on his palms on the trunk of his car, his weight enough to dip the Crown Vic's back end, his elbows locked as if something were inside the trunk and fighting to get out. But Waters's face wasn't that of a fighter's or a kidnapper's or a bully's. He looked sad and defeated and for a moment, to Maureen, like a suspect waiting for a pat-down. A suspect with a knife in his pocket and a gram in his shoe who was wondering why it took so long for him to end up pawing the trunk of a cop car.

"I shot Sebastian," Waters said, his voice low enough that Maureen had to lean in to hear, "to save a girl's life. It wasn't about him or me. It was about her."

Maureen moved closer to him. Arms crossed, she leaned her hip on the quarter panel of the car, a foot or two beyond Waters's reach. She straightened her back and dug her nails into the thick wool of her coat sleeves. She wasn't running away this time. No scampering off to the bus stop or the bathroom like she'd done at the Narrows. "Who was she?"

"You need to understand the circumstances," Waters said, cringing at his own words. Maureen could tell what he was thinking from the embarrassment rippling across his face: *Excuses, excuses. Could I sound any more like a two-bit criminal?*

"You may as well tell it," Maureen said. "Maybe I'll believe you. And maybe I *won't* go blabbing what I've heard so far all over creation. I want to know who this girl was."

Waters frowned at his knuckles, like he was fascinated at their turning white under the pressure of his weight. "Like the other guys, I had informants. Kids, most of them. Junkies, prostitutes, low-level dealers."

He turned to Maureen, looking right into her face now, challenging her, she felt, with the intimated direction of his story. "They were younger than you by ten years, at least," he said. "And older than you by a hundred."

"How sadly poetic," Maureen said. She held his stare, the folds of her coat sleeves tight in her fists. She could feel her pulse throb in her fingers.

"Anyways," Waters said, watching his reflection in the dirty back window of his car, "one night one of these informants calls me, this skinny black-haired white kid, he'd blown a basketball scholarship on dope. He had this stupid nickname, some kind of clown, like Beppo or Bozo. He needs to see me, he says. It's some kind of emergency." He frowned again at the trunk of the car. "It was always an emergency with them, some fire they needed a ten or a twenty to put out. But I went. You never know. That's the reason you have people on the streets in the first place, right? Stuff comes up at odd hours. It was legwork I didn't have to do."

Who are you trying to convince? Maureen wanted to ask, but the question that came out was, "You remember him?" She caught herself racking her memory for this basketball player that she could never have known. "You can remember that one informant from twenty years ago? Down to his nickname?"

Waters raised his huge shoulders. "You want me to forget about you? I've tried to remember them all, the snitches, the vics, especially. I feel like I've done a good job, but I know there are some people I've forgotten. Law of averages, right? I guess maybe I remember him because he was part of that night." Waters spoke as if he was at the same time trying to concentrate on music playing far away. He raised one hand and wiped it across his chin. His fingers left streaks of dirt from the trunk on his face. He didn't seem to notice or care. "I get to the alley and the kid is nowhere to be found. I'm aggravated over it, but what am I gonna do? It's not like junkies are real reliable. It's part of the job. But then I hear noises from down in the alley. Like a scuffle, maybe someone crying out.

Fantastic, I figure, the kid has gone and gotten himself into trouble. Or even worse, he got found out and is getting his ass beat while I'm standing there. Whatever he's into, I feel halfway responsible; I gotta get him out of it." Under the influence of his memories, Maureen noticed, Waters looked like Tanya had that night at Cargo, sinking into the warm bath of her pills. She wondered if he'd ever told the story she was hearing now, truthful and intact, to anyone else. She wondered if he even remembered that she was there, listening.

"So I pull my weapon," Waters said, "and head into the alley. It's pitch black so I'm stuck following the sounds. There's this rhythm now, dull thuds, which I recognize, someone's getting hit all right, but then there's this weird ringing like little bells, like a toy tambourine.

"I hit my flashlight. In one of the corners between the brick wall and the fence, I see a guy, a big guy in a long black coat, hunched over. My light is making shadows and so this guy, he looks huge and shapeless like Dracula in one of those old movies. I move closer. I see he's wearing a ski mask, black gloves. I step to the side. That's when I see her."

Waters stopped talking and licked his cracked lips, his eyes flitting to Maureen's, then away again, landing on his reflection in the Crown Vic's back window. He was hoping, she could tell, that she'd let him off the hook for the story's end. She had no intention of doing so. Was it her that he hated talking to, Maureen wondered, or was it his own face in the window? Why didn't he just turn his back on it? After a few more long moments, Waters started again. "Some skinny little girl maybe the size of you if she's lucky is crumpled and squirming in front of him. He's holding her up by the hair. Her knees are bloody and scraping the ground. She's wearing nothing but these torn-up denim shorts and cowboy boots. All of this, it happens in seconds."

He paused, making one last effort, Maureen realized, to hold back the rest of the story, like he would somehow spare them both a measure of pain by leaving the ending suspended between them in the air. She'd given up on a happy ending to this story, had never really entertained any hope of one, but what hurt her at that moment was the impression she got that somehow Waters *hadn't* lost hope for that girl in the alley, not until this very moment with the two of them standing there, until reaching the end of this story that she had forced him to tell. Where, Maureen wondered, after all those years on the streets, had his armor gone?

Waters's breathing was shallow, rapid, and wet, his huge back rising and falling as he leaned on the car. Watching him, Maureen thought again of a bear. A big brown bear slumped and panting against a boulder, the shrill yelps of a boiling pack of hounds echoing in the distance.

"And this guy," Waters said, "he is just . . . brutalizing this poor girl. Those little bells I'm hearing? He's swinging on her so hard I can hear the change jingling in his pockets. Every time he hits her blood goes flying. He's so focused on what he's doing that he doesn't even react to the flashlight. He doesn't react when I identify myself and holler at him to stop, once, twice. And then everything happens all at once: his arm comes up, the girl goes limp, I can see it, and I squeeze off two rounds. He drops the girl, hits the deck hard. I charge him, pin him. I pull off the mask."

"And it's Sebastian," Maureen said.

"My boss," Waters said, "is staring up at me, and the look on his face is like a wild animal." Despite the cold of the parking lot, sweat slicked his temples. "Like he doesn't even recognize me. He's panting through his teeth and bleeding hard all over this dirty alley from the two bullets I put in his hip. I drop him, call in shots fired, officer down."

"Everything I read," Maureen said, "talked about Sebastian walking away from the department a hero."

"There was no pimp. I was off the clock, carrying a personal weapon, not my service revolver. I put that gun in the harbor along with the gloves and the ski mask. He and I made up our story and stuck to it. We'd gone to the alley together, we said, to meet one of his informants, that prostitute. He'd gone down the alley alone because she didn't know me, and he didn't want to spook her with an extra cop. I heard gunshots and when I got there Sebastian had been shot and the pimp who was beating her had gone over the fence and run for it. That was the story, as far as the rest of the world was concerned. It still is the story."

"The girl?" Maureen asked. "What about her? What happened to her?"

She waited, watching the lie materialize in Waters's face like a fish rising to the surface of its tank. Maureen thought she might go completely berserk if Waters told that lie. He must've felt the fury radiating off of her. Or maybe he decided on his own to stick with the truth. Either way, something inside him had tapped the glass. The lie vanished in a flash.

"She died," Waters said. "She was breathing when I got to the end of the alley. She was dead by the time the ambulance arrived."

Maureen felt she might go berserk anyway. "He beat that girl to death. Beat her. To death. And you let him get away with it." She pointed a quivering finger at Waters. Any empathy Maureen had allowed as he'd suffered through the story had died with the girl in the alley. "You let her die, smashed up in an alley like a bag of trash, while you covered up for the man who killed her. For twenty years. You're right, that's not crooked. That's evil."

"I shot him, Maureen."

"Only because you thought he was someone else. I cannot believe this."

"I caught up to my snitch a couple of nights later," Waters said. "He was never in that alley but he knew the girl, knew she was one of Sebastian's informants. Sebastian specialized in prostitutes, boys and girls. What we didn't know was what he did to keep them in line. Ambush them. Beat them. Rape them. Whatever his mood dictated. Anything to keep them afraid. The scene I walked in on? My snitch thought I'd turn Sebastian in when I saw what he was really like. He thought that I'd choose what was right over another cop. It was a trap for Sebastian, set up by people who thought they were smarter than him, and it backfired badly.

You understand now why you can't have anything to do with him? Why I'm not setting any traps with you as bait?"

"Who else knows about this?"

"Sebastian and me," Waters said, "and now you. Just us three. Now you know the worst about both of us."

"You gotta come forward with this," Maureen said. "Come out with it. No one will listen to me, I'm just a waitress, but you, you're a cop. A decorated detective with thirty years on the job. At the very least it'll *crush* his campaign."

Waters shook his head. "I'm a bitter old man with a vendetta. Any accusations I make will roll off of him and kill what career I got left."

"What are you talking about? Don't be a fucking coward. Not again. You owe that girl."

"After Sebastian was shot," Waters said, "I got command of the squad. Rumors got around, probably started by him, that I'd tailed him to that alley, popped him to get his position. Or for other reasons. This was the early nineties. The Russians were moving into Brooklyn. There were whispers on the street that they'd been using Sebastian to squeeze the Italians. That he was taking orders and money. That it was the Italian mob that plugged him in that alleyway. That they paid me to do it. IAB sniffed around some. It's no secret when Internal Affairs comes looking for you. Everyone knows. Every cop on that vice squad had secrets that coulda got us tossed, got some of us jail time even. I didn't last two months in charge of that squad. Nobody trusted me. The squad got busted up, I transferred outta vice and outta Brooklyn." He spread his hands. "And here I am. And don't tell me what I owe. I did the best I could, Maureen. I got him off the street, off the force."

"And covered your own ass in the process," Maureen said. "You let him scurry off and find a new place to hide, like a rat down a sewer. You let him—you *watched him*—walk free and get rich and famous. Don't play hero with me. You let him kill that girl last summer. You let him kill Dennis. And now Tanya."

"You think I saw this coming back then? When you walked out of

Dennis's office, did you see the future? No, you didn't. Handling the present took everything you had. I didn't kill Dennis or Tanya or anyone else any more than you did. Sebastian did it. He's responsible. Only him.

"Back then I was young. I was in love with the department. On my way up. The only cop in New York City on a faster track than me was Sebastian. He was like the goddamn Wyatt Earp of North Brooklyn. I idolized him. Little old ladies from the neighborhood brought trays of eggplant parm to the precinct for him. We thought he was the cop we all wanted to be.

"That night in the alley, after the shooting, I had to decide things too fast. I was terrified. I couldn't think. I made the wrong choices. I couldn't bring him down without ruining all of us. We were good cops. We were trying to get the right results. We thought we knew who the bad guys were. The truth about Sebastian would've hurt the whole police department if it got out citywide. I had to protect him in order to protect other people who deserved it, even if he didn't. The guys from that squad, we've done a lot of good over the years in this city."

"You guys did more good," Maureen said, "than a handful of terrorized young strippers and hookers would've done, right? How do you live with yourself after what happened to that girl from the Black Garter?"

"Let's see you scratch out another forty years in this fucking city, Maureen. See if you have any fingers left to point after that."

She shook her head, bringing her hair in front of her face. "I won't do it, Waters. I'm my own person with my own life; I won't be your penance project."

"I don't need you for that, thanks. I lost my wife, my sons, because I couldn't stay at home and be a husband and a father. I've paid my tab. You can withhold your forgiveness from me, Maureen. It won't break my heart. All I care about is keeping you alive."

"That dead girl in Queens," Maureen said. "What was her name?"

Waters was pacing now, excited. He threw his hands in the air, moving around to the driver's side of the car. "What's it to you? Get in the car, already."

"Tell me her name."

"You don't remember it? It went around the bars. Or did you not even care enough to notice her when it happened? Or maybe you had a few shots, sucked up a few lines, and laughed about her?"

"Tell me her name," Maureen said, "or you'll never see me again."

"Fine." Waters raised his hands defensively then settled them on the roof of the car. He squinted into the sky for a long moment. This is it, Maureen thought. He remembers fucking Beppo from twenty years ago but he doesn't remember the dead girl's name from last summer. I knew it. I am so done.

"Danielle," Waters said. "Danielle Price. Black hair, blue eyes. She was fifteen. She had a little brother named Bruce. He was eight. At her funeral he put his favorite stuffed animal, a little blue mouse, in her casket." He raised an eyebrow at Maureen. "Had enough yet, or should I keep going? Maybe you don't remember her, but I do. Get in the car. We're done here."

22

Sitting in a plastic patio chair at the round red weather-beaten picnic table in her mother's backyard, Maureen took the mug of coffee from her mother in both hands. Amber, using her bare hand, swept the dirt and dead bugs from another chair and dragged it next to Maureen's. She wiped her hand on her jeans and sat, letting their knees touch.

At Molly's place, along with her clothes and the ladybug, Maureen had packed Molly's gun. At that moment it was in her bag, in her old bedroom. Having that gun, Maureen felt transformed from protected into protector, a role she'd never had the chance to play, outside of benefactor to her yard birds. She felt good, maybe dangerous, even if she was the only one who knew about the gun, even if she was afraid to carry it around Amber or tell her she had it.

Leaving the diner parking lot, another argument had flared up concerning Maureen's next stop. Waters wanted her hidden at Molly's. Maureen needed to be with her mother. Maureen knew lying was easiest, letting Waters take her to Molly's and then just doing what she wanted.

But that move felt much too high school and not the way a brave person went about her business. So when Waters insisted, Maureen resorted to the simple truth: unless Waters cuffed her to a drainpipe, Maureen would be headed to her mother's house anyway, ten minutes after he left Molly's. Waters relented and took her there.

Slumping in her patio chair, Maureen blew on her coffee and slurped some up, desperate for the caffeine and sugar to kick in and clear her head. She needed to be sharp, vigilant, as if Sebastian and his minions might come scaling over the fence at any moment like the bad guys in that dumb Christmas movie. No, it wouldn't be like that. There wouldn't be anything comic about it, and she had more at stake than putting her eye out. She was grateful Waters had promised that by nightfall he'd have cops in a car stationed at the house. On an afternoon in early December, darkness was only a couple of hours away.

Maureen had slept well past the morning, heading straight to bed and missing the conversation between Waters and her mother about witness protection. Probably a classic. One for the ages. It had been a long time since a cop had brought Maureen home to her mother. And then it had been for something meaningless, like shoplifting or maybe drinking in the park. This was the first time they'd be hanging around to keep an eye on her. She hated admitting it to herself, but cops outside the house made her feel even better than the gun did.

"I haven't sat out here in years," Amber said. "It's not too cold in the sun." She stroked her daughter's hair, her eyes drifting over the dead lawn, the stained concrete of the small patio. A dented plastic kiddie pool leaned against a neglected shed, the padlock brown with rust. "Couldn't face the mess, I guess. I had enough to take care of inside, even after you left."

Maureen leaned her head into her mother's hand and stared at the kiddie pool. Black eyeliner tears of dirty rain streaked the laughing green turtles and dancing red starfish. Her father had promised her the real thing, a big blue aboveground pool with a ladder and an electric filter and room to float around on a raft without touching the sides. One like the neighbors had. Well, he'd promised a lot of things. Had he known when he'd made those promises that he had no intention of keeping them? Sure would've made them easier to make. Had his bullshit promises started at the altar, Maureen wondered, the day he put the ring on her mother's finger? Or before that. One thing she'd do, she decided, before she left her mother's, was drag that wasted kiddie pool to the curb and send it off to the dump.

She pulled on her woolen watch cap and turned to her mom. "I'm sorry about this trouble, Mom. Thanks for letting me stay."

"None of this is your fault," Amber said. "Not Dennis and not Tanya. I'm sure Detective Waters told you that."

"He told me a few things," Maureen said. "You ever been to the Coney Island Aquarium to see the belugas?"

"What? No. What are you talking about?"

"Nothing," Maureen said. "Never mind."

"You should listen to that man. He knows what he's doing."

"Did he tell you," Maureen asked, "that he's the cop who delivered the news about Dad?"

"No, he didn't. Why would he?" Amber pushed up out of her chair. She hadn't touched her coffee. "These questions. Are you feeling okay?" Her face drawn, she looked ready for her wine. "Why'd you have to bring that up?"

Amber walked away from the table and across the yard, over toward the chain-link fence. Along the length of it, towering, aged rosebushes grew gnarled and tangled. She reached out and touched a branch, testing an old thorn with her fingertip. "Seems they won't give out, no matter how badly I neglect them."

"Why'd you never remarry?" Maureen asked. "From what I can remember, you never even dated."

Amber shot her a look. "You got nowhere else to go, so suddenly you're interested in your mother?"

"Ma, I had to go look at Tanya's dead body," Maureen said, "'cause there wasn't one other person on this island that could do it. And then I had to tell Waters I didn't know anything about her other than her name and what she looked like. I couldn't tell him a single thing to help him find either her family or her killer."

Amber crossed her arms and cocked out her left hip, her mouth turned down at the corners. That's me, Maureen thought. That's me when I get sick of a customer's bullshit. She swallowed a big mouthful of coffee and pulled her hands into the sleeves of her sweater.

As a girl, Maureen had nagged her mom to hang a hummingbird feeder in the rosebushes. Amber had refused, telling Maureen time and again that hummingbirds didn't live on Staten Island, that the feeder was a waste of time, that the sweet syrup it dispensed only attracted ugly things like the insects that already were too plentiful in the yard: flies, wasps, and the Japanese beetles that feasted on her roses. But Maureen hadn't surrendered the idea for weeks, her imagination fixated on a parade of buzzing, glimmering jewels, a flock of pocket-sized airborne peacocks flitting around the garden. She wanted to cup one of the tiny birds in her hands, to feel the vibrating engine of its wings pulsing like a heart against the soft skin of her palms. Sometimes, she imagined the hummingbirds as miniature chubby old men in fancy suits with dark jackets and satin vests of every color, drinking and gossiping and laughing.

Looking over her mother's yard, Maureen thought now of her fire-escape bird feeder, of the dull procession of starlings and sparrows that formed its most consistent clientele. Those plain birds reminded her not of jewels or peacocks but of bar patrons bunched together over drinks and drafts, their ears attuned to every sound, their nervous yellow eyes glancing over their shoulders for the next threat to their precious perch.

"I got a life full of strangers," Maureen said, "people I see all the time and know nothing about. I met Waters three days ago and I know more about his life than I know about yours. Why is that?" She dug her fists into her armpits. "I don't wanna be strangers, Ma. Not now. Not anymore."

"I didn't date because I had you," Amber said. "I had to work, go to school, take care of the house. Send you to private school. By myself." She rubbed her arms, turning away from Maureen and into her memories. She was trying, Maureen could tell, to tell the truth for once and not play for pity. "And you were a handful. Not that I'm blaming you. I could've gone out, I guess, if I wanted to. It never seemed that important. Where was I gonna meet someone, anyway? Everyone at Richmond College was ten years younger than me. So I should go to some bar and chase some other poor woman's husband? No, thanks. Bars were never good for me." She wrinkled her nose. "Next thing you know, I'm fifty years old and that's that. I know this is not the thing to tell your young single daughter, but I don't feel like I missed a whole lot."

"What about now? Your life isn't over, Mom. You know you're still cute."

Amber plucked dead leaves from her rosebushes. She dropped the leaves from her thin fingers to the lawn without watching them fall. *He loves me*, Maureen thought, watching. *He loves me not.* Amber didn't seem to be keeping count, so Maureen didn't, either.

"You get to be my age," Amber said, "and looks are what matter the least. I've got nothing to offer. I've got nothing to say, even to you most of the time, like you just told me. It's okay; it's the truth." She walked away from the roses and back to the table. In a huff, she snatched up her mug and tossed her coffee out on the lawn. "Can't even make decent coffee." She held out her hand to take away Maureen's. "And Detective Waters isn't my type."

"Do you even know what your type is anymore?" Maureen clutched her mug to her chest, the ceramic warm against her heart and the palms of her hands. "And my coffee is perfectly fine. Better than the shit I get at work."

"Young lady," Amber scolded. "Always with the sailor mouth."

"We're not in the kitchen. And I wasn't trying to set you up."

"I'm gonna go inside," Amber said, "and order a pizza. We're losing the sun. Come in whenever you're ready." She looked around the yard. "And yes, you were trying to set me up and I appreciate it. Where were you ten, fifteen years ago?"

"Busy, I guess."

"Yeah," Amber said. "Me, too."

Maureen stayed alone in the yard until the last of the sunlight faded and left her shivering in the shade, listening to the clack and rattle of the dried rosebushes shaking in the wind. Aches groaning in her back and knees, she was slow to get up when her mother called her in for dinner.

After two slices of pizza and half a glass of wine, Maureen was ready to fall facedown in her plate, exhaustion wrecking her again. She let her mom walk her to her room and help her off with her shoes. Curled up on the edge of the bed, fighting to keep her eyes open, Maureen watched for her mother's reaction when she asked her to plug in the night-light. But Amber didn't say a thing, betrayed no emotion. She grabbed the ladybug off the dresser and bent to plug it into the outlet. Once it was lit, she did stand over it for a moment, arms crossed, left hip cocked out, and stare into the rose-red glow. Maureen closed her eyes. As she drifted off, the neighbor's dog barked. The scent of her mother—baby shampoo and Palmolive dish soap—settled over her. Amber's warm lips on her cheek. Then nothing.

At half past two in the morning, wrapped in an old blanket, Maureen sat cross-legged on the living room couch, her arms folded over the back of it, her chin resting on her forearms. Her phone, set to vibrate, sat on the window ledge. She looked out the picture window and down to the street, watching the unmarked cop car parked under a streetlight. The shadows of two men darkened the front seat of the dark blue sedan. Maureen hadn't even thought to check for them before passing out, but sometime after sundown, it seemed, the reinforcements had arrived as promised. Waters had been true to his word.

Maureen reached out and touched her fingers to the pane of cool glass between her and the night, thinking of the zoo, of the many trips there with her father. Had he really taken her as often as she remembered? Or had she instead strung one memory over a number of days simply to make more of them, like cashing in a tattered beer-soaked five-dollar bill for five crisp singles, the latter worth nothing more than the former, even though they felt better in your hands. Couldn't be, she decided. She remembered too many distinguishing details: his peacoat rough on her cheek, his aftershave stinging in her nose as he carried her through the entrance in the fall, his thick bare arms covered in dark hair and hanging from his T-shirt in the summer as they held hands. They had gone, over and over again. Why? Had she asked that many times? Loved it that much? Or was Amber the reason? Had Maureen and her dad needed to get away from her badly enough to use the zoo as an excuse until both of them found a way to leave for good?

Maybe the woman he'd run away with, the anonymous waitress, had been there, hiding in the distance and waiting to steal a kiss while Maureen tossed popcorn to the monkeys. Was that the reason for the zoo, secret meetings in the guise of a father-daughter outing? No, the other woman hadn't been there. Maureen couldn't remember her father, at least at the zoo, ever leaving her side for a moment. How hard would it be, though, for two wily adults to fool a little girl? But no matter how she framed it, and she'd tried before, over the years, Maureen couldn't buy into that scenario. She wished she could. Remembering him would hurt less if another woman had been lurking around. Because then Maureen wouldn't have had to wrestle the contradiction of her father acting so often like he loved his daughter, only one day to vanish into thin air. If her father had used her for cover, she could straight-up hate him. Maybe living with that wouldn't be easier, but it would be a lot less complicated.

Maureen let loose a sigh, fogging the window. She had told Waters that the peacocks had been her favorite part of the zoo, and that was true. Shimmering and strutting free over the grounds, their arrogant sapphire heads held high, the blue birds appeared like royalty to her. When her father had explained that only the boy peacocks wore fancy plumage and that the girl birds were the dull brown hens hiding in the trees, Maureen flat-out refused to believe him. Girls always dressed up, especially with boys around. Everyone knew that. Didn't she have blue ribbons in her hair, right then, especially for him? Her father said the strangest things sometimes. He had never shared her interest in the birds anyway. He never stood on one leg with her in imitation of the flamingos, never chattered with her to the parakeets. He never once shared her awe at the golden-eyed owl, never ached like she did for just one glance from those huge, serious, burning eyes.

The reptile house. The snakes. That was what her father liked best.

He could stare forever, it seemed, his restless fingers jingling the change in his pockets, at the motionless snakes in their glass boxes. She hated the dark and smelly reptile house. The snakes didn't scare her, they bored her silly. They never moved. Ever. You couldn't tell if they were even alive. Unless you looked real close at their eyes, you couldn't tell they were any different from the cheap imitations on sale in the gift shop. Whether wound in a tight coil or draped in lazy loops over a bare branch, those damn snakes never moved an inch. What the hell had her father been looking at? The same snakes in the same glass boxes, every time.

Now, eighteen years later, draped over the back of the couch, her legs coiled beneath her as she gazed out the window, Maureen knew what her father had seen in those glass boxes. He'd seen himself, and the similarity didn't end with living in a box. She knew that, like her father, had one of those pythons or boas conjured the energy to make a break for it, he would've left his mate and offspring behind as he slithered away under the door. Maureen figured both she and her mother should've spent more time looking into her father's eyes. Maybe one of them would've spotted him for the fake he was.

Glancing over her shoulder, watching and listening for her mother, Maureen yawned, wondering if she should go back to bed. It might be nice to fall asleep quietly for once, she thought, and enjoy a slow, soft descent, instead of passing out as if falling off a cliff. She settled her chin on her arms and resumed watching the cop car. No. No more sleep.

An hour earlier, she'd shot awake in her bed, gasping for breath, frightened awake by her phone buzzing like a wasp on her nightstand. It took her a full minute to remember where she was, and why. Catching her breath, phone clutched to her chest, she lay still for a while, listening to the dead silence of her mother's house. Her own apartment was never quiet, a pipe, a door, a floorboard always pinging or groaning or creaking, as if the building were uncomfortable on its cramped square of land. The house on Bovanizer Street, however, had settled into its bones long ago.

When her senses had returned, she'd checked the call. Unknown number. Ghost digits on the screen. A simple text message waited, a command from Sebastian: DON'T IGNORE ME.

Maureen dressed in pajama bottoms and one of her mother's old sweatshirts. In the bathroom, she brushed her teeth hard, scrubbing away the taste of wine and cigarettes in her mouth. She avoided the mirror, focusing on the water rushing from the tap and swirling down the drain. Headed for the living room, she realized she felt more alert and rested than she had in days.

Now, after an hour of riding her spinning thoughts, she was weary again. She picked up her phone off the windowsill. Should she call Waters? And what good would calling him do? Waters was NYPD, not FBI or CIA. He wasn't sitting at a computer running taps and accessing phone records. He wasn't triangulating cell towers with satellite data or some shit like that. Maureen half hoped that Waters had given up on her, that instead of stalking the streets, he was home in bed. He certainly needed the rest. She watched her bodyguards. I'd make a good cop, she thought. I'm smart. I like long hours. I'm not afraid of the night shift. I can smell bullshit before it turns the corner. I have no life to come between me and my work.

She pulled up her sleeves and flexed her fingers into and out of fists, watching the muscles of her hands and wrists and forearms tense and release. Sure I only weigh a hundred pounds or so, she thought, but it's a tough, hard hundred. The academy would add weight, put on more muscle. Her size might come in handy. The uniform wouldn't stop men big and small alike from underestimating her, from making the mistake of letting their guard down. She pulled her arms back into her sleeves and narrowed her eyes. Let his guard down one more time, that's what we need Sebastian to do. Even if he is much bigger than I am, Maureen thought, he's no better, no braver, and he's got a lot more to lose. And he knows it. Waters was right; Sebastian feared her.

Even as a vice cop he had been a coward, preying on the frightened and the compromised. Despite his current status, despite his future prospects, Sebastian hadn't changed since those days in Brooklyn. He'd only gotten better at using masks, at hiding his true nature.

Maureen tilted her head at her own reflection in the window, making fists again inside her sleeves. She thought of Dennis and Tanya, the break-in, Danielle Price. She thought of her mother asleep in her room, of John and Molly asleep in their bed. She thought of Molly's gun. How much motivation did she need? She picked up the phone, called the unknown number. Sebastian answered on the first ring. He'd been waiting, the phone by his side. He wanted an end as badly as she did.

"Hello, Maureen," he said. "You're up late."

"I have a lot on my mind."

"That makes two of us," Sebastian said. "You know what I've been thinking about? I've been wondering how many dead girls it's gonna take before you get the fucking point. You got some kind of mental dyslexia? Everything I tell you, you do the opposite. A fucking ballbreaker, that's what you are."

And you are a fucking animal, Maureen thought. But she didn't say it. She needed to keep him on the line, to learn what she could. "You're talking about Tanya, aren't you? You did that. You killed her."

"Me? I'm the one who fed her pills all those years?" Sebastian asked. "I'm the one who tried talking her into betraying the people she trusted?

That was me? Tanya always was half outta her mind, but if anyone pushed her the rest of the way, I'm guessing it was you, don't you think?"

Maureen looked out at the cops. She should be out in the street, having this conversation on speakerphone. The cops outside, they'd be Waters's handpicked guys. They would know who she was dealing with and why. They'd be on her side. She got up from the couch.

"Such a beautiful girl," Sebastian said. "Such a waste. And Dennis. One of the nicest guys I ever met, if a touch naïve, and look what happened to him. You're like a little redheaded angel of death. How do you live with yourself?"

Sebastian danced around killing Tanya and Dennis, but she could get him to give up something. She headed down the stairs. She had to keep him talking and get outside so the cops could listen as he did it. She reached for the doorknob.

"There are men outside your house in a car," Sebastian said. "You think they're cops." Maureen froze, her hand halfway to the doorknob. "And maybe you're right. Maybe they are." Maureen pressed her hand, then her forehead, against the cold front door. "But maybe they work for me and I put them there. Or maybe they are real live cops and they work for me anyway. You just never know with me. It's part of my charm."

Maureen leaned her shoulder against the door. Motherfucker. In her ear, she could hear the scratching of Sebastian's fingers working his goatee, the sound an insect inside her head.

"You can't fight everyone and everything forever," he said. "You just can't."

Maureen moved her hand back to the doorknob. Forget your fear and think. Don't play his head games. She pulled the door open. She looked at the houses on her block. Not a single light. Everyone's shades and curtains were drawn. Amber's beat-up old K-car sat in the driveway not ten feet away. Should she make a run for it in the car? Would the guys across the street, whoever they worked for, chase her? If they did, where would she lead them? When she'd seen the car out front upon waking, she'd assumed they were Waters's men but she didn't know for sure. Her eyes flew again over her street, from car to car, house to house. Driveways, stoops, porches, garages, windows, rooftops. So many shadows, so many dark places, large and small, for someone to hide, for someone to drag her away, one hand over her mouth, the other around her throat.

"Stop looking," Sebastian said. "Stop looking for that line I won't cross. It doesn't exist."

Across the street, one of the men had noticed her at the door and was getting out of the car. Sebastian could be bluffing. He could be playing on her fear. She was so sick of being afraid. He had to know that. So was he trying to goad her into a mistake? To force her out the door, make her so angry that she walked right into his arms? Maureen stared at the man. He wore a long dark coat over a suit. He stood beside his car, his hand atop the open door. She tried to read his face. Blank. Expressionless. Cop or criminal or both? She couldn't tell. She bit her front teeth into her tongue. She couldn't do it, couldn't take the gamble.

Maureen raised her hand and waved. She forced her mouth into her best thanks-for-the-dollar-tip smile. The man waved back and eased into his car, watching Maureen over his shoulder. She closed the front door.

"Go to a front window," Sebastian said. "I've got something I want you to see."

Maureen pounded back up the stairs. She crossed the living room, stepped up onto the couch. Was he watching her, watching the house? One way to find out. With her free hand, she pressed her middle finger to the window, hissing through her teeth. "Can you see this, mother-fucker?"

Sebastian laughed. "I'm not even in the state, but I'm sure whatever you're doing is very impressive. Now, pay attention to the street. I'm tied up tonight, but when I call in the morning, you better answer." Before she could respond, he hung up.

Maureen dropped to her knees on the couch, her eyes scanning the windows, rooftops, and cars of her block, slower this time. Was he somewhere close? She stared down at the car. He could be right there in the backseat. Or he could be in another state like he'd said. She had no way of knowing. He talked like he was looking in the window, but he'd really said nothing specific, about her or about the house. Could've been co-incidence that he'd caught her at the front door. And it was no great leap to figure that Maureen and Amber had been placed under protective cus-tody, unless of course Sebastian knew the men outside because he had sent them. Here I am, right back, Maureen thought, to thinking exactly like he wants me to. How did I get so paranoid and so predictable?

God, I was easy. I barely even put up a fight.

All she'd wanted last Friday night was to make some extra cash to pay her bills. She was a good woman trying to do good things. Out in the street, the mystery man in the driver's seat waved up at her. She lifted her hand in reply. What's the sign language, she wondered, for *we're all totally fucked?*

Then the headlights came on, followed by the siren lights in the dash and the rear window, and the car rolled away from the curb. Cops after all. Maureen's jaw dropped. What the fuck? She ran down the stairs and through the front door, jogging out into the middle of the street. She stared in disbelief, the wind whipping through her thin cotton pajama bottoms, her hands and her bare feet stinging in the cold. The car sped up the street and made a hard right turn onto Amboy Road at the corner.

Maureen ran back inside and grabbed her phone, dialed Waters. Wait-ing out the rings, she could hear her mother stirring in the back bed-room. She reached Waters's voice mail, hung up, and tried again. She wasn't into waiting for a callback. The toilet flushed in her mother's bath-room. Maureen hoped nature's call was what had Amber awake and that she'd go back to bed. The detective's phone kept ringing. Finally: "Detec-tive Waters."

"Where the fuck are my cops going?" Maureen said, just above a whisper. She needed to keep this from her mom. "My cops are gone. They were *my* cops, right? Where are you?"

"Maureen?"

She could hear traffic in the background, voices. Waters was on the street somewhere, out of his car. She hoped he was close. "I just got off the phone with Sebastian."

"Wait, what? I can't hear you." A long pause. "Calm down. I'm sorry, hang on a minute." Muffled voices, the slam of a car door. He came back. "I'm at a crime scene. We had a shooting in your neighborhood, at the Gulf station. Your guys got called to it." He let loose a long sigh. "It's night watch, we're short-handed."

Maureen fought to stay calm. Panic was exactly what Sebastian wanted. No sign of her mom. She stared out the window at the empty parking space the cops had left.

"I'll send a patrol car over," Waters said. "Maybe I can scare up a second cruiser, take a look around the neighborhood. I'll be over myself as soon as I can. Sit tight."

"What's going on? Who are you talking to?"

Maureen turned to see her mother, housecoat clutched in one hand over her chest, standing in the doorway to the kitchen. There was a sharp edge in Amber's voice. Maureen couldn't tell if it was fear or aggravation. The living room was too dark for her to see her mother's face. Lock the doors and cross your fingers, Maureen thought. Fuck that. Let Waters babysit her mom. Maureen had to move.

"You sit tight," Maureen told Waters. "And keep your cruiser. I'm coming to see you."

She closed her phone without waiting for his answer, stashing it behind her back as if hiding it would make lying to her mother easier. "Mom, I need to go see Detective Waters. That was him on the phone. There's been a break in the case." Maureen winced at her own cop-speak cliché. She hoped her mom's faith in TV crime dramas held true. "Can I borrow the car?"

Amber waited to answer, making Maureen squirm. There has to be one time, Maureen thought, a single time when I told her the truth about where I was going in the middle of the night. Forget those other times, Mom. Remember that one time I was honest. Think of me. Don't think of Dad. "I'll be back in no time. I swear."

"The keys are by the door," Amber said. She switched the kitchen lights on and turned her back to her daughter. Maureen walked to the kitchen. She watched as Amber disassembled the coffeemaker, getting it ready to brew a fresh pot. "I'll be waiting up."

Maureen walked to her room. It was a struggle not to run. She had to get away before that patrol car arrived, but she had to keep her mom as calm as possible. Best not to tell Amber the cops were coming, again. She hurried into her street clothes: jeans and boots, a heavy black sweater, her father's watch cap and coat. Dressed, Maureen threw her bag over her shoulder. The weight of Molly's gun thumped against her back. She made a mental note to keep the bag out of Waters's sight. If he found her with a gun, he'd take it away. She went back into the kitchen.

"The look of you," Amber said, turning, holding the empty coffee-pot in one hand, "you'll be lucky the detective doesn't lock you up on sight."

"Make sure you lock the door behind me," Maureen said.

"Well, duh," Amber said, "it's the middle of the night. No smoking in my car. And bring it back with a full tank."

23

the red light, Maureen saw that the Gulf station crawled with police. Red and blue lights blazing, patrol cars had the station entrances blocked off. Cops, in uniform and out, stood huddled against the cold in small groups, talking. An ambulance, its back doors hanging open, spilled white light onto the black asphalt around it. A lone medic stood with her hands on her hips, her blue jacket open despite the cold, at the rear of the ambulance, watching the backs of the cops. She was the only female that Maureen could see on the scene. Nobody moved with any urgency. Maureen knew it didn't take a cop to figure out what the idleness meant. The shooting victim had died before anyone in a uniform had arrived.

Through the crowd, Maureen spotted Waters on the far side of the gas pumps, over by the garage doors. He stood under the bright glow of halogen lamps, at the edge of a box squared off by crime-scene tape. He pointed at something in the box, speaking to two younger detectives beside him. The traffic light turned green and Maureen pulled her mom's

K-car into the parking lot of a pizza place across the street from the gas station. Enter female number two, she thought, climbing out of the car. Crossing Richmond, her hand out to stop the nonexistent traffic, she wished she had a badge to clip on her belt. Maureen glanced at the medic, now standing with her arms crossed and looking down at her tapping foot. I have no intention, Maureen thought, of waiting around for someone to tell me what to do. Not anymore.

As she walked around the front of a patrol car and into the station parking lot, a uniform approached her. "Sorry, miss. Station is closed."

"I'm here to see Detective Waters," Maureen said.

She could hear the creaking leather as the cop grabbed his gun belt. He shifted his weight to one foot. Maureen leaned on the cop car, the hood warm against the backs of her thighs. As the young officer sized her up, she did the same to him. He was young and blond, blandly handsome and thin for a cop. His uniform hung at least a size too big on him. It looked fresh out of the box. He said nothing about her leaning on his car.

"The detective is working a crime scene," the cop said. "He's gonna be tied up for most of the night." He smiled, relaxed his gunfighter's stance. "Maybe you can leave me a phone number?"

As if to emphasize the young cop's point about the crime scene, the ambulance doors thumped closed. Maureen watched as Waters gave the doors two loud slaps. He stepped back as the ambulance rolled into motion, lights on, sirens quiet. Maureen waved, but Waters didn't return it. Can't see me, she thought, through the emergency lights. She looked back at the cop.

"He's expecting me," she said. "I'm a witness in another case of his." She felt like adding, *which means you're in the way, here, sonny*. It's almost like pulling rank, Maureen thought, and she enjoyed it. "It's confidential. You understand."

The cop narrowed his eyes, seeing her in a different way this time, turning Maureen's words, she knew, against her in his mind. Witness? Sure. Rat is more like it. Which kind will he pick? Maureen wondered. Junkie prostitute, reluctant drug mule, some car thief's bitchy girlfriend.

What did it matter? Let him think what he wanted. This skinny kid would never see her again. And he'd get his ass chewed something good if he talked the nasty shit he was thinking to Waters.

"You're not allowed onto the scene," the cop finally said, reclaiming some of his authority, "but I'll tell the detective you're here."

"I'd appreciate that."

Walking away, the young cop glanced back at Maureen, as if saying *See? I'm still more special than you*, then headed over to Waters, who had to stoop to hear him. With his hands, Waters shielded his eyes against the bright lights surrounding him. He peered across the lot at Maureen. She stepped away from the police car and started walking over to him. Waters gave her the halt sign, shaking his big head as he trudged her way. Maureen stopped. She lit two cigarettes as she waited. She offered one to Waters as he reached her.

"No, thanks," he said.

Embarrassed and hoping the young cop hadn't seen Waters's rejection, Maureen dropped the extra cigarette. She ground it out beneath her boot.

"You shouldn't be here," Waters said. "You're safest at home."

Maureen took a good look at her protector, absorbing his lined and sagging face. She'd never seen anyone, in all her years in the bars, looking more fried, more flat-out spent, than Waters did right then. She couldn't conceive of him as a newbie like that blond cop, his uniform fresh out of the box, his cheeks shining from a recent shave. If Waters had collapsed at her feet in a rumpled heap, Maureen wouldn't have been surprised. Despite their falling out, she wanted to stuff him into the K-car and drive him back to her mother's house, where he could sleep away the winter and wake up in the spring to one of Amber's huge, greasy breakfasts.

Seeing Waters this way, seeing the drain of the past days on him, Maureen realized that pursuing Sebastian and protecting her, while at the same time beating back the old, ugly ghosts that her case had resurrected, had grown into something Waters could no longer contain. A tar pit was opening under his feet. He was spread thin as a shadow. Stretch him until he breaks, Maureen thought. That's Sebastian's plan. He had to know what horrors Maureen's case dredged up for Waters. Then, with the big detective out of the picture, he could pounce.

Despite his bluster and his body count, Sebastian really was a coward.

"What did he say to you?" Waters asked, tilting his head, impatient.

It wasn't even worth going into, Maureen thought. She shouldn't have called Waters or come to the gas station. Things couldn't continue this way, her constantly dumping more weight on Waters's shoulders, him struggling to stay upright. He'd insist he could take it, and maybe he could, but Maureen was starting to feel like Sebastian's assistant in doling out punishment.

She had to take matters into her own hands. She had to break the cycle.

It didn't matter anymore whether what Sebastian had said was true, that Waters was keeping her around as bait, or whether what Waters himself had claimed was true, that others had bogged down his best efforts to protect her in bureaucracy, politics, and red tape. She'd made a terrible mistake, inserting herself between them, accidentally or not. Waters was doing the best he could for her, operating with the best of intentions. Maureen believed that. But the fact of the matter was that people hadn't stopped dying around him, hadn't stopped dying over what Maureen had seen. Things had only gotten worse since he'd come around.

As much as she wanted him to be her answer, and regardless of whatever he had been in his glory days, Detective Waters was now an old man battling windmills. She couldn't be part of the end of his days anymore. Not as anything more than a companion over a cup of coffee.

What had Waters told her back in her apartment the day they met? That no one else could protect her better than she could protect herself, not even him. What was true then was certainly true now. Someday, she'd tell Waters how grateful she was for all he'd tried to do, but right then and there, tonight, he had to go.

"Sebastian didn't say much of anything," Maureen said. "The same kind of mysterious shit he gave me outside the library. Forget I mentioned it." She'd play out this last meeting, go through the motions, and find out what she could that might be useful. After that, he was on his own. Waters said nothing, rubbing his fingertips into his eyes. Maureen wondered if he wasn't considering taking her advice. "Don't you ever sleep?"

"I got work to do." He pointed his thumb over his shoulder. "Now more than ever."

"You're gonna get stuck with this case? Aren't there any other detectives on this island?" She gestured at the multiple cars and the numerous cops surrounding them. "All these other cops, let them handle it. You can't solve every crime."

"There's plenty of other detectives," Waters said. "Every one with as much work as me if not more. Every one of these guys is as tired as I am. This homicide, like Dennis and Tanya, is staying with me."

"Because of me," Maureen said.

Waters agreed. "Sebastian is behind this. It's as shitty a fake robbery as I've ever seen. Worse than your apartment, maybe. Few fistfuls of candy bars missing, some shit knocked over. No money gone."

"Could be some amateur-hour thing," Maureen said. "You don't know for sure what happened yet. Some drunk, some junkie could've gone in thinking simple holdup and botched it."

Waters surveyed the crime scene, widening his eyes as if trying to let more light into his head. "Not in this neighborhood. Besides, most amateurs look right up into the security camera, like they can't help themselves, if they even remember it's there. You'd be surprised at how often that happens." He looked at Maureen, blinking. "Whoever did this got the attendant outside at gunpoint while dodging the cameras the entire time. He left us nothing but the body." He scratched at his stubble. "This guy was shot to get those cops off your doorstep. I'm convinced."

"He kills some poor, innocent gas station attendant to spook me? What the hell for?"

"He's showing you what he can do." Waters said. "And what we can't do, like stop him or catch him or prove anything. So it looks like he's stronger, like he's winning. He wants these bodies on your mind, on your conscience. He wants you to think you can stop the killing and make a sacrifice of yourself. Just like the others did."

"And if I do," Maureen said, "then what?"

"That girl I watched him beat to death in the alley," Waters said. "She and her junkie partner thought they could use her to stop Sebastian from hurting anyone else. It didn't work. They failed and got her killed. Twenty years later, Dennis got defiant and then got on his knees, and it wasn't enough to save him. Who knows what Danielle Price had to go through? Or Tanya?"

"Twenty years ago," Maureen said, "you should've aimed higher."

"I know what you're thinking," Waters said. "Don't go to him. Don't go after him. Go home to your mother and let me work. I can't have another body on my conscience."

24

Before reaching Bay Street, Maureen made a quick stop at an all-night deli for a fresh pack of smokes and a giant cup of day-old lukewarm coffee. She called her mom, told her Waters needed her, and they'd be at the diner. Maureen promised she was safe and she wasn't smoking in the car. Go back to bed, she told Amber, there's nothing to worry about. Maureen knew the ruse was doomed. As soon as he was done at the Gulf station, Waters would head for her mom's to make sure everyone was safe in their beds. He was gonna be pissed when he found Maureen was missing. Amber was gonna be livid when she found out Maureen was off on her own. But until that happened, why worry her mom?

Maureen parked at the back of the lot across the street from the Narrows, up against the fence and under the busted-out streetlights. Someone leaving the bar might spot the car if they were looking, but she'd be nothing more than a shadow behind the wheel. She killed the headlights. A train rolled past, vibrating the driver's seat, flashing its empty white windows and blowing trash through and over the chain-link fence. At the Narrows, the golden glow in the front door's beveled glass told her that the bar was open. Vic would be in there. He had nowhere else to go.

Low in her seat, Maureen lit a cigarette, cupping it in her hand to hide the glow. Considering the circumstances, she figured her mom would forgive her for stinking up the K-car. She needed her nerves, her focus. She couldn't be sitting there nic-fitting when the time came. Might slip or twitch and pull the trigger. It was bad enough that after only half a cup of coffee she had to pee so bad her teeth were floating.

She looked at the foam cup in one hand, the cigarette in the other, and then the Narrows. Would you look at me? Hundred-pound Maureen Coughlin on a stakeout. Shoulda stopped for Chinese. Was this how Waters did it? She shifted in her seat, trying and failing to comfort her aching bladder. One thing Detective Nat Waters didn't do that hundred-pound Maureen Coughlin was gonna have to do was squat and piss in a dark and dirty parking lot. It's not easy to feel tough while squatting with one elbow propped on the car's back bumper and your lily-white ass hung out in the cold, she thought. At least another train wasn't due for almost half an hour. May as well get it over with.

Back in the front seat, Maureen watched as staff and patrons stepped outside the Narrows for cigarettes. She remembered that she was supposed to work that night. Did the regulars miss her? she wondered. Did they ask why she wasn't there? Or was she already just another girl come and gone at the Narrows?

After three more trains, Maureen's patience was rewarded; Vic walked the last of the staff to the door and locked it behind them. No Clarence. After Waters's visit and Maureen's escapade at the gym, the big man had probably given the Narrows a big peace-out. His absence worked in Maureen's favor. No Clarence, no Maureen, no Tanya. Vic would be shitting himself. All to the good. The more isolated he felt, the more willing he might be to turn on Sebastian. Vic would take a few minutes for one more sweep of the place, then he'd leave. Maureen moved the gun from her bag to her coat pocket. She wanted to give Vic every incentive to see things her way. She stepped out of the car.

Crossing the street, Maureen checked the block for other people. Not a soul. She pressed her back against the brick wall by the door. Elbow cocked, she held the pistol up against her shoulder, her head turned toward the door. She forced herself to breathe, her heart punching at her ribs. She tried willing her mind to be calm, her eyes fixed on the puddle of light on the sidewalk before the door. Sell it, Maureen, she thought. You have to sell it. Hard. Like you do with the customers. They don't have to *believe* you're gonna do them, they just need to think there's a chance, however small, that you might. Vic doesn't have to believe you'll shoot him. You only need him to believe you might.

She heard Vic's feet on the steps inside.

Maureen sucked in her breath, held it tight. Toughen up, she told herself. You're not a scared little girl. You can't afford it. People are depending on you. The light behind the door went out. The door opened, and Vic stepped through onto the sidewalk. Maureen stretched her arm, pressing the gun barrel into Vic's temple. He froze.

"Back inside," Maureen said, her voice cracking so bad she couldn't be sure Vic heard her. But he understood the gun. Maureen held it steady, kept the pressure on his temple. Vic dropped his keys and raised his hands.

"Go." This time she spoke with force. "Leave the keys. Back inside."

Vic did as he was told. Maureen followed him in, keeping the gun pointed at the back of his head. Vic couldn't see the threat, but she knew he could feel it. She could feel it too, the gun handle slick in her sweaty hand, her adrenaline surging, every muscle in her body tense and ready. So this is what it feels like, she thought, to be on the other side, to be the one giving the orders. She needed to take advantage.

She hit the lights. "Turn around."

"Jesus Christ Almighty," Vic said. "Not only a broad, but *you?*" He couldn't have looked more shocked if Maureen had been standing there naked. "What the fuck are you doing? First you no-call no-show for your shift and now this? Have you lost your mind?"

"Shut up."

"There's cameras everywhere," Vic said. "You know this. You *work* here. If you needed money I told you I'd *give* it to you."

"I worked here long enough to know those cameras are never on the room." Both hands on the gun, using both thumbs, she pulled the hammer back, like Molly had shown her. The lazy click of the hammer made her almost giddy with excitement. "Stop with your bullshit."

Vic had lost his color. He said nothing, reached a shaking hand behind him, felt for the brick wall. He leaned back. For a moment, Maureen feared he might pitch headfirst down the stairs. What would she do if she gave the poor bastard a heart attack? She recalled Sebastian's soulless cool under her knife at the gym. Vic and Sebastian may be friends, Maureen thought, but they are different animals.

"Don't even try to tell me," she said, "that you don't know why I'm really here. Where is he? And don't fuck with me. I don't wanna know about his house. I don't care about his campaign offices. I want the real him."

"I have no idea about that," Vic said. "I haven't heard from him since Dennis died. Same thing I told the cops. I don't know any better than you."

"Don't lie to me."

"Honest. I don't know."

"You think I won't do it? He's been to my house, my mother's house. If it's you or us, who you think I'm gonna choose?"

"Maureen, it's me, Vic. You know me. I'm harmless. Put the gun down and let's talk."

"I don't know you," Maureen said. "I don't know anybody. Don't tell me what the fuck to do. You notice anyone else missing tonight? Where's Tanya? Tell me that."

"Yeah, she didn't show for her shift. That's fucking news? That's a crisis?" Vic laughed. "Tanya's probably wherever Sebastian is."

"It's funny? It's funny what he made her do? What's wrong with you?"

Maureen tightened her grip on the pistol, furious at Vic's laughter. He doesn't know, she thought, that Tanya's dead. Clarence didn't tell him. When Maureen opened her mouth to say it, using the news for maximum impact leaped to her mind. Tanya's death is your ace in the hole, she thought. Hang on to it. Work up to it, like Waters had with Clarence.

"No, Maureen, what's wrong with *you?*" Vic peeled himself off the wall, his breathing calmer, his color returning. "Where'd you get the idea that Tanya's doing anything she didn't volunteer for?"

"From her," Maureen said.

"Somebody's been messing with your head. Tanya's been working for Sebastian since before you got here. They're a team."

"That's bullshit."

"Who do you think talked Dennis into borrowing his start-up money from Sebastian? She led that poor boy around by his dick, just like she was told." He shook his head. "I tried warning him."

Maureen didn't know why, maybe her arms were tired, but she lowered the gun. Vic was fucking with her. He had to be, didn't he? Don't think, she told herself. Act. But she couldn't decide what to do. Her control of the situation was slipping away. You're scared, she thought, and you're in way over your head.

Vic turned and walked down the stairs, hitting the lights for the main room on his way. Maureen didn't protest.

At the bar, Vic righted two stools. He patted one like a kindly grandpa getting ready for story time. "Come, sit. Let me buy you a drink. You need it."

Maureen came halfway down the stairs and stopped, the gun hanging at her side. She didn't need a drink. She didn't need some bullshit story. What she needed was to leave the Narrows having altered her circumstances. She watched Vic moving around behind the bar, pouring a Goose neat for himself and a Bushmills the same way for her. He took his time doing it, whistling some old soul tune. Gun or no gun, he'd already written her off as a threat. Maureen looked at the pistol in her hand. She couldn't blame him. She didn't feel very scary. But who knew a better way, Waters? If his way worked, what was she doing at the Narrows waving around a loaded .38? What was Sebastian doing, walking around not only free but prosperous and on his way to even more power?

Elbows on the bar, Vic grinned at her. "Sit. We'll work something out."

She moved down a few more stairs, then stopped, staring at Vic. Don't do it, she thought. Vic doesn't give a shit what Sebastian does, to you or anyone else.

"Maybe you should just go home," Vic said, waving a dismissive hand at her. He set her drink on the bar and sipped his vodka, swirling it in the glass. "I'll talk to Sebastian. I know he can get overbearing at times. Let ol' Vic take care of it for you. I know him. Come see me back here tomorrow night. Come work your shift."

"What's he got on you, Vic?" Maureen tucked the gun into the back of her jeans. "What do you owe him? You let him use and abuse Tanya, right under your nose. Now you're trying to give him me."

Vic, glass in hand, came out from behind the bar. "'Scuse me?"

"Must be something big, this debt," Maureen said. "He's got you lying, covering for him. With the cops. With me. I come in tomorrow, and you'll have him here waiting for me. What's he offering for that, for selling me out?"

"You're being paranoid, Maureen. You got me all wrong. And Tanya made her own choices." Vic sat on the stool he'd set down for Maureen. "You can't make me feel guilty about her." He patted his shirt pocket, looking for his cigarettes. He found the pack on the bar and lit a cigarette. Maureen noticed he wouldn't look at her.

She crossed the barroom in long, easy strides. The closer she got to him, the more Vic shrank into himself. "Dennis was murdered, Vic. Someone strangled him before they put him on the tracks. The cops are looking at Sebastian for it."

Vic tried, but he couldn't keep his eyes from the mirror behind the bar. "Nah, you're lying. Waters was here last night running the same shit on me." He talked more to his reflection behind the bar than to Maureen. "I know you're afraid of Sebastian and, like I said, I'll help with that, but you're talking crazy. It's bullshit. Waters is playing you. I know them both from back in the day, from when they worked together. He's had it out for Sebastian for years. Sebastian warned me about him, right away from when Dennis got killed.

"Waters shot Sebastian, for chrissakes, his own boss, another cop. Over some hooker or stripper or whatever. How're you gonna trust a man like that? Waters is the one you should be worried about. You know me, Maureen. Listen to reason."

"It was your place, wasn't it?" Maureen said. "In Brooklyn, the alley where Sebastian killed that girl. You were running the place. *That's* how you know Sebastian. What about the Black Garter? That your place, too?"

"I don't know what you're talking about."

"The hell you don't. This has been going on for years, hasn't it? His cash and your girls."

"It wasn't just girls," Vic said.

"That's a fucking relief."

"Oh, please," Vic said, "you talk like you've uncovered some big conspiracy, like this is some big secret plan we sat down and figured out. Like it's news or the end of the world. Yeah, I ran strip joints. Yeah, some were low-class joints full of low-class people. We all gotta start somewhere. Yeah, I had some girls working for me that knew some guys that did things that might interest a cop or two. Twenty years later, I still do. It's not exactly a real bizarre coincidence that some of the same girls that worked for me also snitched for Sebastian, he and I drawing from the same employee pool like we did. Believe me, except for the guys that got busted, nobody had a fucking problem."

Vic held out his hands, pleading as if the logic of his argument was carved into his palms.

"For fuck's sake, Maureen, you know how this business is. Things happen. I didn't keep tabs on how Sebastian did his job or on his social life after he quit. You treat me like I invented the fucking rules. I live under them same as you. I was the one that decided that people like power and need money? That shit is *ancient*. You know this."

"Tanya's dead," Maureen said. "Sebastian killed her, too. Because of things she knew about him and Dennis."

"Fuck you."

"No," Maureen said, "fuck *you*, Vic. I saw her. I went down to the morgue myself and saw Tanya dead on a slab."

"Enough," Vic said, raising his hands. Again, quieter: "Enough." His Adam's apple worked overtime, trying to swallow nonexistent spit. "Really?"

"Yes, Vic, she's really dead. I did the ID. He's killed someone else." Hearing the truth about Dennis had shaken him. The news about Tanya rocked him. Maureen knew she had to keep the pressure on, had to keep agitating. "How many do you think there have been, between that girl in the alley and Tanya? How many times have you helped him do it? Gimme a rough guess."

Vic was silent. He'd started to sway in his chair. Maureen worried again about giving him a heart attack. Too bad if he couldn't take it. She needed her answers; she needed to find Sebastian.

"Vic, Sebastian killed Dennis. He *killed* him and threw his body in front of a train. Left nothing but bits and pieces for his family. He killed Tanya. He's a murderer. He has been for years, and now he's after me."

"You got no proof of that," Vic said. "About Dennis. Or Tanya. Any of it. Nobody's never proved nothing. Even that girl in the alley. That was always just a rumor that there wasn't really a pimp there. He just had a bad reputation. People were out to get him. No cops, no lawyers have ever proved a thing. Now I'm supposed to believe *you*?"

Turning in his seat, he plucked a cocktail straw from a caddy behind the bar, stuck the straw in his mouth, his hands shaking so badly he nearly took out his eye. Maureen met his eyes in the bar mirror.

"Don't you turn your back on me," she said. "Or on Dennis. Or Tanya and Danielle. I won't allow it."

Vic turned to face her, twirling the straw between his molars. Waiting. Thinking. Not about her, Maureen thought, or about his murdered employees, or the others like Danielle Price that he surely knew Sebastian had put in the ground. Like he'd always done, Vic was shelving the truth so he could concentrate on saving his own ass.

Fine, Maureen thought, let's play it that way. "You think I haven't made friends of my own working here? Friends that do me favors?"

Vic turned her words around in his head, checking the angles. What regulars did she know better than him? Which customers came around only on nights she worked? Maureen decided to help him out. Staten Island crawled with cops. Vic knew they were everywhere. Like Waters had said, everyone on Staten Island knew a cop.

"Maybe I haven't made the right introductions," Maureen said. "Sometimes we get busy and my manners go out the window." She had the perfect face in her mind. Clean cut, but not too much. "I ever introduce you to Jimmy McGrath? 'Bout six foot, short black hair. He likes the corner tables in the back, where he can see the whole place laid out in front of him."

"The teacher?"

"Teacher, my ass," Maureen said. "Try New York State Police."

Knocking back the rest of his vodka, Vic rose from his seat. "No. No way. I've seen you put that shit up your nose. Seen you buy it, seen you sell it. Things ain't like they used to be. Maybe twenty years ago you woulda fit the profile, but now? No cop would use you for nothin'."

"You think anyone cares what some loser waitress does compared to the leading candidate for a state senate seat? The CI by my name on the paperwork stands for *confidential informant*, not *constant integrity*."

Vic drank down Maureen's whiskey, tossing the glass on the bar. It rolled off the bar and smashed in the sink. Vic took a step in her direction. She reached her hand behind her back. "Careful, Vic. Jimmy's taken me shooting. I'm pretty good."

"You wouldn't," Vic said. He laughed, but he stayed where he was. "It's not in you."

"You have no idea what I've got in me," Maureen said. "I knock over a couple of chairs, make one hysterical phone call, and presto, you're a rapist, Vic." She pulled the gun from her waistband, aimed it at Vic. "A gut-shot rapist bleeding out from the bullet in his soft pink belly. I'm a single girl who works late at night for cash. Why wouldn't I carry a gun? Thank God I did, with what you had in mind. What choice did I have against a man twice my size? I'm only a little girl. Maybe I call an ambulance for you." She cocked back the hammer on the pistol. "But maybe I panic, in my rush to get away, and don't."

Vic slid his hand through his hair, rubbing the back of his neck under his ponytail. He returned to his stool, rubbing his palms on his thighs. "I been in this business too long."

She lowered the gun. "Listen, help me out here. I don't care what you're into Sebastian for, but you help me and maybe I can help get him off your back."

Vic crossed his arms. "He and I are old friends. What makes you think I want to get rid of him?"

"Men like him don't have friends. You know that better than I do. You comped him a couple grand worth of food and bev and service the other night. Why? 'Cause you like how he's gonna vote on state education policy? It's not 'cause he's your friend."

"Because he mostly owns this place," Vic said, sagging. "His cash keeps us going." He stared up at the ceiling. Maureen watched his eyes drift around the room. "Yeah, we do good business, but not good enough. You know what this place costs? You see what's going on by the ferry: the ballpark, the new stores? You can't imagine the rent, and every six months the Russian pricks that own this place jack it up. They fuck me every chance they get. Everything I got is tied up in this place. It goes under, I go down with it. He owns me, Maureen."

Moving behind the bar, Maureen poured Vic another shot. She slid the glass into his hand. "Where's Sebastian get this cash?"

"I don't ask," Vic said. "He does good with the security."

"That doesn't mean you don't know. Why does he keep you afloat?"

"I don't ask that, either."

"C'mon, Vic."

Vic pulled another cigarette from the pack on the bar. "Girls like Tanya. That's what he gets outta this place. That's how it's always been. It only got worse when he wasn't a cop anymore. He keeps the cash coming; he takes his cut . . . however he wants. I don't ask and he don't tell."

"But everybody knows anyway."

"Everybody but you, apparently," Vic said. "Jesus, I can't believe Tanya's fucking dead."

Why can't you believe it? Maureen wondered. Because she was so pretty? You think that made her any safer than the rest of us? Shit, if she was ugly, she'd probably be alive.

Vic sucked hard on his smoke. He stared at the floor as he spoke. "C'mon, Maureen. You think she got those clothes, those fancy pills, working here? You broads don't make that kind of money. And she was the worst goddamn waitress I ever saw." Vic raised his eyes, grinning at Maureen, mirthless, showing his teeth like a cornered animal. Fear, Maureen realized, like it had made Tanya stupid at Cargo, was making Vic nasty. "These cops you know, do they have any idea how naïve you are?"

"It's my best asset," Maureen said. "Stupid people are always telling me things they shouldn't."

"Yeah, right. It's an act. Keep telling yourself that."

"An act? I'm the one with an act? For chrissakes, Vic, you're a fucking pimp."

"You girls make your own choices," Vic said. "You're adults. I just order the liquor, open the doors, and count the money."

"How many people has he destroyed?"

"I count the money," Vic said, "not how many of you birds flit in and outta here. I'm not your fucking mother hen."

"You pathetic piece of shit." Maureen wanted to spit in his face. "You think being broke, high, and half the size of Sebastian gives you fucking choices when someone like him comes knocking?" Maureen raised the gun. "Tell me where that cocksucker is. Right fucking now."

"You shoot me today," Vic said, "or Sebastian does worse to me later."

"Jesus Christ, Vic, what happened to you? What kind of man are you?"

"Life happened to me. Same as everyone else. So I learned how to survive. You could take some lessons from an old man like me."

"Those girls are somebody's daughter," Maureen said. "They're somebody's sister. Those girls are me."

"You think I haven't thought about that," Vic said, his glass at his mouth, "a thousand and one fucking times? Whadda you want from me? The man is a horror, okay? I admit it. But I can't stop him." He slurped at his vodka. "And you can't either. Bigger people than you have tried, from both sides of the law. For years." He set his glass down and surveyed the room. "And I don't see them around."

"So you do nothing about the people Sebastian destroys right in front of your eyes? Just ignore them, look the other way, that's the answer? Not for me. I'm not you."

"Some things are too big to fight," Vic said. "They have too many arms and heads, too many teeth. Sebastian is one of those things."

"So I lay down for him," Maureen said, "like you did? No way. I won't do it. I don't wanna learn that lesson."

Vic spread his hands. "Then run for it, Maureen. Blow town. I'm telling you this for your own good. Maybe I *am* done, maybe I made too many mistakes, but a young, pretty girl like you? You got a future. Anywhere you want."

"I'm not running away anymore. I'm too fucking tired." She recocked the hammer on the .38. "End of the line, Vic. Tell me where he is."

Maureen knew she was looking at a beaten man. The last of the fight had gone out of him. And it wasn't her information or her accusations or her gun that had wrecked him. He'd finally hit the point where he couldn't continue swallowing how he felt every minute of every day: sick, defeated, hollow, and unable to recall a time when he'd felt any different. Running her eyes over the brick walls of the Narrows, Maureen realized she knew that look on Vic's face, and not from the million and one hours she'd spent working the floor. Of all places, she knew it from the zoo.

As a kid, she'd seen that yellow-eyed death mask haunting the face of the Staten Island zoo's one lion. The one that hadn't even had the energy to pace his cage. The one that lay on his side in the corner, his matted mane rife with flies, just breathing, waiting for his heart to stop its pointless, mindless beating. *If I blew Vic away right now,* Maureen thought, *I'd be doing him a favor. And letting him off too easy.* The lion was a victim; Vic deserved his cage. She lowered the gun.

"What're you gonna do, Vic? I'm tired of waiting."

"Can I have another drink?" Without waiting for an answer, he got up and walked behind the bar. He ran his palms over the mahogany. "You shoulda seen this place a few years ago. It was somethin' else entirely." He poured himself another vodka. "So was I."

"Vic, I don't give a fuck."

Vic picked up a pen from beside the register and wrote something on a cocktail napkin. Reaching over the bar, he handed Maureen the note.

"Sunnydale Suites?" she said. "What is that?"

"A motel," Vic said. "Over in Jersey, on Route Thirty-five."

I got plans tonight, Sebastian had told her. *I'm not even in the state.* She stuffed the napkin in her pocket.

"It's the kinda place," Vic said, "that rents rooms by the hour and doesn't ask any questions. Mirrored ceilings, mirrored walls, leather sofas—"

"I get the picture."

Vic chuckled, lowering his eyes. "No," he said. "You don't."

"Well, then, maybe I oughtta see for myself. When does he go?"

"He's there tonight." Vic checked his watch. "Right now. It's a satellite operation of what he had going at the Black Garter. When he took the political nomination, he had to move some of his personal business off the island. He does it late nights now, over in Jersey."

"Does what exactly?"

"It's the kind of thing," Vic said, "that you have to see for yourself."

Maureen tried not to think about what a satellite operation meant in Sebastian's world. It didn't matter. She was going. "How do I know you're not calling Sebastian the minute I walk out the door?"

"'Cause I'm tired, too. Tired enough to give you a shot. I'm not a bad guy; I'm just exhausted."

Eyes to the floor, Vic stroked his ponytail, more a man watching his memories than the reality in front of him. He could be telling the truth, Maureen thought, or he could be hedging his bets. If Maureen succeeded in whatever she had planned, Vic got out from under Sebastian for good, his debt wiped clean. If she failed, Vic had a reward coming from dropping Maureen in Sebastian's lap. Either way the tired old man came out a winner, at least until the next rent check was due.

"I swear to God, Maureen," Vic said, "I'd heard the stories, even this summer, but I never thought he'd killed anyone. Not really."

Not anyone important is what you mean to say, Maureen thought. *Not anyone worth saving, worth paying attention to, or remembering.*

"What did you think would happen," Maureen said, "if no one stood up to him? That he'd see the error of his ways? That he'd change his stripes and grow out of being a complete fucking psycho? Jesus. And you call *me* naïve."

Vic threw back the rest of his vodka. "Who knows, Maureen? Maybe you're my chance at salvation."

"The fuck I am," Maureen said. "You're on your own, same as the rest of us."

She put the gun in her coat pocket and headed for the stairs, leaving Vic sitting at the bar, the bottle standing beside his glass.

Maureen turned once on the stairs to look back at Vic. He seemed to have no interest in the phone or in moving at all. He sat at the bar, one hand over the top of his glass, the other hand propping up his head. His cigarette burned unattended in the ashtray. On her way out the door, she stepped on Vic's keys. She picked them up and walked back into the bar.

"Vic," she called from the landing, holding up the keys, jingling them.

He didn't turn, didn't say anything. "Vic, it's late. You probably want to lock up."

He dismissed her with a wave of his hand. "Kill the lights on your way out."

Maureen stood on the top step, looking at the keys to the bar in her hand. "What was her name?"

"Who?"

"The girl he killed in Brooklyn in the alley, the one who worked for you. What was her name?"

Vic frowned into his empty glass, pretending to search for a name. "I dunno." He looked across the barroom at Maureen. "I'd tell you I forgot it, but I don't think I ever knew it to begin with."

Maureen set the keys on the top step and left Vic alone with his bottle and his thoughts. She left the lights on, unable to decide whether turning them out was too cruel or too merciful.

Walking across the parking lot, all the way back to the car, she kept one hand tight on the gun. Every shadow vibrated with threat. Only when she was back in the car with the doors locked, the engine running, the wheels turning, and the headlights slicing through the darkness, did Maureen realize she'd been holding her breath ever since she'd left the bar.

25

Maureen cruised the right lane of Route 35 through Sayreville, her brain going numb at the endless succession of traffic lights, mini-malls, strip clubs, diners, and gas stations, the same five hundred yards of highway repeated on an endless loop while an infinite chain of white lines disappeared under her wheels. Had she passed the motel? Should she double back? She shifted her rear end constantly in the driver's seat, trying to work some new blood into one side and then the other. She chain-smoked cigarettes, apologizing to Amber with every one. She hoped once the cops had Sebastian in cuffs that her mom would forgive her, for stinking up the car and for everything that had come first. Her back ached, and the warm air blowing out of the heater made her sleepy.

While on the Outerbridge Crossing on the way over to Jersey, she'd called information and gotten the number for Sunnydale Suites. The desk clerk, her voice parched from cigarettes, held silent for almost a full minute after Maureen had asked directions to the motel. Sunnydale was not a place many people sought out. It was like Staten Island, Maureen thought, like this bleak stretch of Jersey. Shit, except for the rampant sex, Sunnydale's a lot like my life.

It's not a place you plan to get to; it's a place you end up.

Finally, as Maureen hit the blinker for a gas station and another rotten coffee, Sunnydale's roadside sign appeared at the top of a hill. Good Lord, Maureen thought, they put a fucking *rainbow* on that sign. Under the rainbow, the neon letters *a-c-a-n* burned bright red. According to the sign, Maureen noticed, pulling into the parking lot, the Sunnydale Suites were *able available* as well. She didn't stop at the front desk to thank the clerk for her directions. She parked in the spot farthest away from the two-story row of rooms and killed the engine and headlights. Of the twenty rooms, lights shone in three of them.

Which room, if any, hid Sebastian? Find him, call the police, and get outta the way. That was the plan. Don't even get out of the car.

Scanning the parking lot, Maureen noticed a dark Crown Vic parked two rows in front of her. Had to be Sebastian's. Could be a coincidence, though, however unlikely. She couldn't call it in unless she was sure. Calling out the Jersey State Police only to put them on the wrong car would make things much worse, and get her in considerable trouble. The Staties did not mess around. In a way, Sebastian had done her a favor. The Jersey State Police wouldn't give a fuck who he used to be or what he was running for now. Bringing them in is like sending in the Marines. Man, I wish I was a Statie, she thought. I could kick ass from six ways to Sunday. Just once, I wanna be the cavalry. She reached into her pocket, fingered the phone.

Leaning over the steering wheel, Maureen tried reading the Crown Vic's license plate. Could she get the number and call it in to Waters? Get him to look it up and confirm they had the right car. Right. And then he'd flip out over where she was and what she was doing. She sighed, fogging the windshield. Forget Waters. She rubbed away the cloud with her coat sleeve. She licked her lips. She could follow Sebastian when he left the motel. And end up God-only-knows where, lost and far beyond the reach of any help. Not much of an idea.

She was so sick of waiting. If Sebastian was at the motel, she had to get him now. She had to do more than sneak up on his car. She had to peek in some windows. She reached her other hand into her other coat pocket and gripped the gun. Spying. Waiting. Hoping. Were these really the things she'd come out here for?

She took a deep breath and checked the bushes behind her in the rearview. So get out of the car, girl. Go get your man. She released her breath and reached for the door handle.

A shadow moved in the driver's seat of the Crown Vic. The dark of the lot hid the face. Maureen shrank in her seat, hiding from the Crown Vic's rearview, her heart beating so hard she could barely think. Had Vic ratted her out? Shit. Had she been seen pulling into the lot? Whoever sat in the Crown Vic expected her, expected someone, to leave the K-car. Was he watching, waiting for Maureen to make the first move?

In the Crown Vic, the figure drew a shadowy arm back to itself. A lighter flared and Sebastian's profile hovered over the flame. The lighter went out. Maureen watched the glowing coal of Sebastian's cigarette float across the front seat as he resettled his hand on the headrest beside him. If he'd seen her, would he let her sit there watching? He might, Maureen thought, to mess with her head. Had he known she'd go to Vic and that Vic would send her to the motel? Had Sebastian planned the whole thing?

Maureen rubbed her hand over the gun in her pocket. But what if he *didn't* know she was there? One shot and she'd be rid of him—she and a lot of other people. People who'd never had the chance she had now. People who would've killed him already. After all this time, who knew how many would've given anything to be where she sat right now?

Vic knows where I am, Maureen thought. He'd know I did it. But Vic was a toothless old lion sleeping under a tree, waiting for a woman to do his dirty work. He'd cover for her. Maybe. He had a lot to gain if Sebastian went away, and he certainly had enough to hide. He had sent her to the motel. Might make him an accessory. And the cops would look hard for Sebastian's killer. Retired or not, he'd been NYPD. What would

Waters do? You didn't need an experienced detective to add this one up: Sebastian gets shot the same night Maureen goes missing in her mother's car. It was a lot to ask, that Waters look the other way, no matter how he felt about Sebastian or Maureen. She drew the .38 from her pocket, set it in her lap, stared down at it: Molly's gun, going cold in her hand. She was in her mother's car.

Someone might see her driving away, might get a description or a plate number. Someone might see her ditch the gun. She couldn't drag innocent people down with her. She'd already caused enough trouble. But, but, there he was right there in front of her, his back turned. And she did have a gun. She stared hard at the back of Sebastian's head. If she just thought of her mother, the rest would be easy.

She jumped, almost yelling in fright, when a second head rose from the darkness into her view. The passenger settled into his seat, raised a hand to his face. He rolled down his window and spat into the darkness. With a short snap of his arm, Sebastian backhanded the man's face. Maureen heard the crack of the slap from where she sat. Sebastian yelled something Maureen couldn't make out, punctuating his message with a pointed finger. She didn't need to hear the words to figure out what had gone on in the car. She was looking at Dennis's replacement.

The other man got out of the car, waiting beside it as Sebastian reassembled himself. Maureen didn't know the new boy, from the Narrows or anywhere else. Some hustler? Some junkie Sebastian had picked up in the neighborhood? Didn't look like it. The guy looked sturdy. A slick haircut and a pricey leather jacket. Maureen's age, maybe a couple years older, he was no street kid; he was another poor slob deep in debt to the wrong man.

Maureen inched down in her seat, peering over the dash as Sebastian got out of the car. The men crossed the lot with their backs to her, walking at arm's length. She watched what room they entered. The light around the edges of the curtains didn't match the other rooms. Sebastian's room was whiter, brighter. Maureen pulled her phone from her pocket. Sebastian was right there. She even had his room number. Time to call. She hesitated. The state police would laugh her off the phone for calling in a blow job in the Sunnydale parking lot. But if she could find out what Sebastian was up to, see what was in that room, she could get enough to bring the cops, and then she could call Waters. She could tell him she had everything handled, under control. Go home, get some rest, I got this. It's done.

She dug her switchblade from her bag. She slipped the knife in her boot and hid the bag under the seat. Reaching up to turn off the dome light, she eased open the car door, making sure to leave it unlocked. If she needed to make a quick escape, no need to delay it. She'd be quiet. She'd be quick. Then she'd make the call.

Hands in her coat pockets, phone in one fist, gun in the other, Maureen walked the length of the fence running along the back of the parking lot, staying in the shadows, careful of kicking the old beer cans and broken liquor bottles. At the end of the fence, she jogged across the lot and pressed up against the wall three rooms down from Sebastian's. She spent a few breaths looking around. Nothing from the other rooms or the other cars. No reaction from the check-in desk. It seemed everyone at the Sunnydale Suites had activities under way that commanded their full attention. Maureen moved along the wall until she stood at the edge of Sebastian's window.

At her toes, a sliver of white light cut the surface of the sidewalk outside the window. Spotlights, Maureen thought. The kind used to light a room for a camera. No voices came from inside the room, only moans. One woman. Maureen tucked her hair into the high collar of her coat. She took a deep breath, held it, and pressed her back hard against the wall. With a slight lean, she peeked around the curtain and into the room. The bed sat close to the window. On her side of the glass, Maureen stood barely three feet from it. She had a bird's-eye view.

On the bed, under white-hot lights, a naked woman lay spread-eagled on her back, the black bedsheets bunched at her bony hips. Another woman knelt above her face, grinding her crotch down hard and moaning at the ceiling. Both women were blindfolded with long red scarves.

The kneeling woman crushed her own breasts together hard enough to stretch white the skin over her ribs. Maureen could count the runners of sweat leaking from her armpits and dripping over her ribs. Three knuckles on the hand Maureen could see swelled black and blue, freshly broken. The top woman's hips pushed and rocked and rotated, as if searching for the best, softest place to do damage to the face beneath her; she moved to punish.

The woman on her back, her wrists and ankles bound in leather straps tailing off the corners of the bed, writhed and fought for air. Where she was bound, her marble white skin glowed red and raw, as if she'd been resisting her torture for a long time. Maureen could see the black whisker-length hair on the woman's shins, the purple track marks dotting her fish-belly inner thighs. Her hips pumped in the air. Between her pointed hip bone and her dark pubic hair ran an elaborate calligraphic tattoo. One word.

Mercy.

Maureen panted through her teeth, forcing herself to continue looking. Forget the girls, Maureen thought. They're not what you came for. She looked away. No, don't turn away. She fought the urge to jump in the car and keep driving till she hit Ohio. No. Don't run away. Those girls are *exactly* what you're here for. She flashed on the cash and the coke and the pills and whatever else they hid in their dresser drawers. She didn't recognize either girl from the bar or anywhere else; the Narrows wasn't Sebastian's lone hunting ground. But Maureen felt she'd heard their voices. They were never her friends, but they were always right there, living on the other side of the glass Maureen held up between herself and the rest of the world. She thought of the young girl twenty years bloody and dead in the alley, wearing nothing but denim shorts, the thundercloud-colored marks of Sebastian's hands all over her. She thought of little Bruce Price's dead sister. Of Tanya.

Maureen peered back in the window. The arms and legs of the woman on her back started to jerk and flap as if she were trying to fly. That's when Maureen noticed the men. Each leather strap led to a fat-bellied man, each man naked except for a black rubber hood. Their eyes, all she could see of their faces, stared transfixed at the action on the bed. Jerking the straps, the men worked the woman on the bed like a sail in heavy wind. In his other fist, each man stroked an ugly half-hard cock. Were they actors? Paying customers? Maureen looked away again, shutting her eyes, sick to her stomach. She saw stars across her eyelids, as if she'd been struck. The moans went on, pain beyond the physical rippling now beneath the false pleasure. One more time, she commanded. One more look. Find Sebastian. Put him at the scene.

She struggled to see more of the room without giving herself away, without her reflection appearing on one of the mirrored walls. She couldn't see the camera or Sebastian. Then, leaning another inch, Maureen found him. Away from the bed, fully dressed and out of the camera's eye, Sebastian sat on the arm of a black leather sofa, speaking into a cell phone. He wore a campaign pin on his lapel. His companion from the car sat at the other end of the sofa, slumped over a mirror on his knee and sucking rails of coke up his nose.

Sebastian watched the bed, his face as blank as a man watching bowling in his underwear. He tucked the phone between his ear and his shoulder, scowled, and tapped the face of his wristwatch. He was supervising, Maureen realized. Like he did with his security firm, like Clarence had said he'd done at the Black Garter, like he'd done with his Brooklyn vice crew and his stable of teenage informants.

This was what Sebastian had been doing at the Garter, overseeing some kind of sick torture porn operation. Maureen thought again of Tanya. This motel room explained Sebastian's demands from her on Dennis's debt. Those things Tanya had said Sebastian wanted her and Dennis to do, those things that would hurt; Maureen realized she was seeing a similar script acted out on that bed. She knew she was seeing Sebastian's real face, the true depth of the abyss of his appetites. She wondered, and the thought shot her through with despair, if Tanya wasn't better off dead if this motel was where the devil she knew was taking her.

Bizarrely, Maureen thought of Dr. Travis, the black-clad Shakespeare professor from Richmond College. What the hell did he have to do with . . . ?

No, not him, that stupid poem he used to recite in bed; that was what she was thinking about, the poem with its seductive rock-star devil who loved power in Hell over service in Heaven. She'd always thought she knew that devil, appreciated his disdain for his all-powerful boss and his ass-kissing co-workers. She'd thought herself at times: *Man, if I could just get my own joint, I wouldn't have to put up with any of this shit.* But now, before her eyes on the other side of the glass, Maureen saw there were devils neither she, nor Travis, nor anyone she knew had ever imagined.

Maureen backed away from the window, her fingers steepled over her nose, cold tears running down her cheeks. Breathe. In and out. In and out. Breathe. Keep your head together, she told herself, and you can put a stop to this. Right now. Tonight.

She jogged back to the car, her hand over her mouth. Why hadn't she listened to Vic? Or her mother? How had she ended up *here*? Maureen made it to the back bumper of the K-car before she puked on the pavement.

Squatting, her hands on her knees, Maureen spat whatever she could gather from her mouth, sucking in deep, noisy pants of cold air through her nose. Get it together. Stop shivering. Stop sweating. *Get it together right now.* She couldn't stand it, the stink of her own fear. When her pulse finally backed down out of her ears, she stood, looking back at the hotel room. Fuck the consequences. Shoot that bastard.

Maureen watched the hotel room door, in case someone had heard her moving around, but no one appeared. They could be in there for hours, she thought, or they could be done any minute. She couldn't get caught hanging around the parking lot when the party broke up. But she wasn't leaving. That shit inside would not continue. Get Sebastian outside alone, she thought. That was the trick. Call him and tell him she was there. Blow his brains out the second he walked out the door. He'd never suspect her capable of such a thing. Never. In the panic after the shot, she'd get away.

Maureen spat at her feet one more time. The world went blurry around the edges. Her hand reached into her pocket, her fingers wrapped around the gun, her index finger tapping the trigger. Her legs started walking back toward the motel. Her eyes scanned the dark doorways for a hiding spot. Do it like that, out of the dark like a monster.

Call him. Kill him. Run.

Simple.

She pulled her cell from her pocket. It rang. Really fucking loud.

The screen lit up and the phone rang again, impossibly loud in the quiet parking lot. Maureen dropped it like it had bit her hand. The phone clattered on the pavement, sounding in her ears like a car crash. No. No way. It rang again. She looked up at the motel room. No way that motherfucker inside is reading my mind.

She dropped into a crouch and grabbed the phone, scuttling back to the car, falling on her ass at the front tire. The phone rang again. She flipped it open and pressed it to her ear, panting into the mouthpiece and staring at the hotel room door.

"Maureen? Where are you? What are you doing?"

Shit. Waters. "Where am I? I—uh, I'm in Jersey. Why?"

Jersey. Fuck. She'd just told Waters too much, blown her chance. No way she could do Sebastian now.

"Why are you not here?" Waters demanded. "With your mother, like you said you'd be."

Maureen's belly tightened and turned cold. Not with fear but with disappointment. She couldn't believe it, the crushing weight of it. This was what she'd been reduced to. This was the arc of her life. She'd gone from a little girl crying for her daddy to come home to a small woman weeping at a lost chance to commit murder.

"Maureen." Gentler this time.

She felt worse, a thousand times worse, than when that prick professor had left her hanging on the edge of an orgasm. Like that, but worse. At least back then she could sneak into the bathroom and finish the job. Not the same, not satisfaction, but a relief nonetheless. Tonight, there'd be no relief. Just more running, more hiding. Just more faking it.

"Maureen," Waters said, "tell me you're okay."

Maureen couldn't do anything but sputter into the phone, her brain blanking on any reasonable lie. She had no motivation to tell one. She didn't feel like faking it tonight. She supposed, though, she should say something.

"I found him. I'm looking at his motel room right now. What he's doing, it's fucking awful."

"Listen to me," Waters said. "You gotta get out of there. Immediately. I know about the gun, about your mom's car. I can figure out the rest."

"Detective, huh?" Maureen asked. "Then how come I found out what Sebastian's been doing before you did? How come I know where he is and you don't?"

A long pause. "If you do this, I cannot protect you. It'll be impossible."

"I'm out here *alone*. Doing *your* fucking job."

"I can't protect you from the consequences," Waters said. "You or your mother. You think she wants to see you through Plexiglas for the rest of her life? 'Cause that's where you'll be. It's murder this way. Think, Maureen. Of her, at least."

"That's not fair."

"It's the truth," Waters said. "Fair's got nothin' to do with it. Do you still have the car?"

"Yeah, so?"

"Get in it," Waters said. "And come home now."

"Why don't you come get him? I'm at Sunnydale Suites, on Route Thirty-Five. He's got girls here, doing things for him. And guys. Doing sick things. Why don't you come and stop him? You can't let him get away again."

A long pause. "You saw these things?"

"Yes. Sex, torture, drugs. I saw the whole thing. It's a nightmare."

"I'll send someone," Waters said. "I'll get the state police on it. But promise me you'll leave right now. I can't say when they'll get there."

"Don't you need me here? I can be a witness."

"You can be a witness," Waters said, "from someplace a lot safer than where you are now."

"I got a gun. I got a blade. He doesn't know I'm here."

"And Sebastian has how many guys with him?" Waters asked. "All of them with guns. Count on it. And they are definitely better shots than you. For chrissakes, Maureen, have you ever fired a gun in your life? Never mind *at* someone."

Maureen let her phone hand drop into her lap. She tapped her head on the car fender. Waters made sense. She'd done her job. She had Sebastian nailed. She was the wounded soldier in the foxhole, calling in air support. Nothing cowardly in that. It didn't matter who called the cops, as long as they came. She looked at the phone. The longer she dicked around, the longer it would be before help arrived. Waters wouldn't make that call until Maureen promised to come home. She put the phone back to her ear.

"Okay." She got up, pulled open the car door, and climbed in. "I'm in the car." She started the engine. "I'm on my way back now."

"Good," Waters said. "I'm gonna hang up and call the Jersey State Police. You did the right thing. We'll be here when you get back."

Maureen tossed the phone on the passenger seat and swung the car toward the road. From the parking lot exit, in her rearview, she saw Sebastian step from the hotel room. He looked her way, frowned at her taillights, and then bent his head over his lighter.

"Good riddance, motherfucker," Maureen said. "One day you'll know it was me that got you." She turned out onto 35 and drove away from the motel.

Sitting at the U-turn, waiting for the light to change, Maureen considered pulling onto the shoulder and waiting for the blue lights of the state police to come ripping through the night. How many cars would they bring, five? Six? It'd be something to see. She was sad to miss it. She could read about it in the papers, maybe watch it on the news—if she could get herself a new TV in time. Maybe she could watch it over at Molly's. They could drink champagne toasts, to the people they'd saved from Sebastian and to the people that they hadn't. Maureen felt her eyelids drooping. God, this was a long light. Should she run the red?

The bright headlights of a car coming up behind her bounced off the rearview and stung her eyes. She blinked up at the traffic light, half blinded, and saw it change from red to green. White light flooded her car. That prick behind her was coming on way too hard. He'd never stop in time; he'd have to swerve hard to cut around her. Unless he didn't. Maureen stomped on the gas, cutting the wheel. The K-car's tires screeched and spun in place. The car gained some forward momentum. Then she got hit. The impact was like a thunderclap.

Maureen shot forward, her chest and forehead slamming against the steering wheel. She bounced off the hard plastic, thrown back against the seat, the air punched out of her body. She'd gone blind in one eye. The other eye saw four traffic lights hanging above. Shouting voices in the street behind her. Male voices. The crash, the adrenaline surge, left her badly nauseated. She raised her hand to her cheek, felt the warm blood on her fingertips. A gash on her head, pouring blood into her eye. Out, she thought. Out of the car. The car door flew open when she leaned into it, and she tumbled into the street, the asphalt biting into her hands and knees. She could breathe, but every inhalation felt like being stabbed. Two hands grabbed her coat and pulled her to her feet.

Against her will, Maureen's head rolled back and her good eye saw nothing but black sky. More hands. In her coat pockets. She could feel her feet on the ground but couldn't feel her legs. Her head came forward and she focused on the blurry faces, the face in front of her: silver hair, gray eyes, the spark of a flash of smile. Sebastian.

Her scream came out as a gurgle.

She found her legs, kicked out. Sebastian laughed and threw Maureen hard against the car. She collapsed in a heap against it.

"This is what she had," the other man, Sebastian's boy from the parking lot, said.

He held out the gun. Maureen pawed the blood from her eye.

"Don't need it," Sebastian said. "And neither does she." He leaned over her. "Sorry about your mom's car."

Mom's car, Maureen thought. Fuck me. He'd seen her as she pulled out of the motel parking lot, and then he'd run her down. The other man tossed the gun into the weeds of the divider. Maureen bent her knees, drawing her feet underneath her. The blade, she thought. They haven't found it, haven't even looked for it.

"Put her in the fucking trunk, Rico," Sebastian said.

Rico had his hands on her before she could reach the knife. When he yanked her upright, Maureen's hand came away from her boot empty. She slapped his face. He punched her in the mouth. She blacked out, came back in an instant. The boy threw her over his shoulder. Maureen screamed and kicked and punched. The boy dumped her in the trunk of the Crown Vic. Maureen spat the blood from her mouth in his face. He backed away, wiping at the spit and swearing. When Maureen tried to sit up, Sebastian pressed a gun to her forehead, pushed her onto her back in the trunk. He said nothing, leaning into the gun until Maureen went still.

"You ever have one fight you like this?" the boy asked.

"Not for twenty years," Sebastian said. "That's what makes this one special. The fight in her."

He slammed the trunk closed.

26

Panic. Panic is the enemy here. That's what Maureen told herself as she bumped along in the trunk of the car. She needed to breathe as best she could despite the dampness that surrounded her, seemed to coat her lungs with mold. She needed to focus on where they were taking her and what she was going to do when she got there. Thoughts of her possible fate—of being thrown off a bridge or being burned alive along with the car, of being gang-raped by masked men—she forced away, out into the dark where they could swirl around her like ghosts but couldn't touch her. Pay attention, she thought. Stay here. Stay with now. When that trunk opens, you have to be ready. You can't lie there big-eyed and twitching like a fish in a bucket when the time comes.

After only a few moments in the trunk, Maureen realized they'd been traveling too long to be headed back to the motel. When the car picked up speed, moving in a straight line, she knew they'd left the local routes for the highway, though she couldn't tell in what direction they were headed. At one point, her heart jumped and she reached for the knife as the car slowed to a stop, but then it was moving again. She kept the knife in her fist. One by one, Maureen put the sounds around her together. The stop had been a tollbooth. A metallic hum underneath the wheels confirmed her hunch: a bridge, the Outerbridge Crossing, probably. The trip hadn't lasted long enough to reach another bridge. So Sebastian was taking her back to Staten Island. To the Narrows? To the tracks where Dennis had died? Maybe some abandoned pier, the same one where they had set Tanya afloat. Stop, Maureen thought. Pay attention. When you get out of this trunk, you need to know which direction to run.

Not long after crossing onto the island, they left the highway, the car slowing and stopping for signs and lights. No sense, Maureen thought, in attracting attention to the car. Not with a live girl in the trunk. Because they had left the highway so soon, Maureen knew they were staying on the South Shore, the quieter, less populated end of the island. The roads got longer, the stops less frequent. The sounds of other cars disappeared. As the Crown Vic bounced through one pothole after another, Maureen cradled her head as best she could in her arm.

They were headed to the industrial end of the island, not far from the Outerbridge, where paint and concrete and tile got made, where dump trucks and cement mixers pounded the roads to hell and the buses hardly ran, where the corpses of old tugboats and abandoned ferries tilted half sunk in the waters of the Arthur Kill, rotting for decades on end and forgotten. Sebastian and his boy were taking her to the part of the island where practically nobody lived or hung around at night after the whistle sounded and the workday ended. A part of the island where the cops hardly ever ventured—a forgotten corner of a forgotten borough. They would leave her there and forget her if she let them, dead and half sunk in the cattail marsh that ran the edge of the Arthur Kill. Food for sandworms and crabs and whatever else made its home in that dirty water.

Then it hit her: the Black Garter. The real Sebastian's real headquarters. That's where they were taking her. Which probably meant they wanted to keep her alive.

Just don't think, she told herself, about why.

The car turned a corner, leaving even the battered asphalt behind. Maureen listened to the crunch of gravel under the slowly turning tires. It wouldn't be long now. She did her best to get her cramped legs underneath her, to brace herself on one arm. She rolled her wrists and ankles, trying to work the feeling back into her limbs. With the way her heart was beating, how could any part of her be short on blood?

She flicked open the switchblade, put it in her teeth for a moment to wipe the blood and sweat off her palm. Panic is the enemy, she thought, not only for her but for her captors, too. All she needed was a moment of confusion. Enough time to get her feet on the ground. Once she got moving, no one would catch her.

The car slowed. It came to a stop. The first one reaching into the trunk would get the knife. In the eye, the hand, the belly, anywhere she could reach. Maureen heard the slam of one door, then the other. Neither man spoke. She heard their shoes on the gravel road as they came around the back of the car. Maureen took a deep breath, squeezed the knife as hard as she could in her fist. The key was in the lock.

The trunk lid opened and Maureen launched herself at the figure leaning in, stabbing straight ahead. Her hand split the arms reaching toward her. She didn't know who she'd hit, blood splashing her eyes before she could make out the face. But this time it wasn't her blood. She heard a gasp and a gurgle and saw her knuckles pressed hard against an Adam's apple. She saw her white fist wrapped tight around the black handle of the knife, buried to the hilt in a pale throat. She twisted the blade a quarter turn. The mouth at the top of the throat spat blood. She pushed against the weight of the man falling in her direction: not Sebastian, but the boy who had put her in the trunk. As he collapsed, he reached for his throat. Maureen pulled away the knife.

She tumbled out, landing flat on her back on top of the twitching boy, blood in her hair. Her eyes searched the sky for Sebastian. A dull fluorescent glow emanated from somewhere and provided enough light to ruin her vision after the time in the dark. Sebastian appeared, looming over her like a giant, reaching his long arms and his huge hands down for her. Maureen knew she'd never reach his throat or his heart before he grabbed her; she was too small.

She feinted for his face with the knife, then cut her stroke and plunged the blade into his leg, hoping for the knee, a tendon, an artery. Anything to cut him down to where she could finish him off. There'd be no second-guessing this time, no hesitation. Again, the blade penetrated to the hilt. But Sebastian didn't go down. He roared and ripped his leg away, the knife going with it as he staggered from the road to the edge of the cattails.

Maureen rolled off the boy and onto her hands and knees, stones scraping her palms. Dust flooded her nose and mouth, stung her eyes. Maybe another weapon lay in the trunk of the car. Forget that and get going, she thought. The time for hand-to-hand combat was over. She rose up into a track start and launched her right foot, then her left. Sebastian caught her by the hair.

He yanked her to him, grabbed her head in both hands, and threw her down in the road. Halfway to standing, Maureen's knees gave out and she went facedown in the rocks and dust. Blood thickened in one nostril, clogging it. She gagged, short of breath. Not now, she thought, not here. Don't give out now. She turned to see Sebastian lumbering toward her, one leg all but dead, her knife sticking out of its calf. With his good leg, he threw a kick into her gut. His bad leg wouldn't hold him and Sebastian collapsed.

Dry-heaving, her middle spasming with pain, Maureen tried crawling for the reeds. She could smell the brackish Arthur Kill in the distance: sea salt and rust and gasoline leaked from the tanks across the water. There had to be half an acre of marsh between her and the deeper water. If she could reach it, filthy or not, she could get lost in that half-acre. If she had to, she could hide all night in the weeds. But before she made the cattails, she crawled on top of Sebastian's shoes.

Maureen rolled over onto her back, panting, staring into his upside-down face.

"You are a piece of work," Sebastian said, heaving for breath. "I gotta be honest. I've about had it with you."

Maureen flipped onto her knees, lunging for Sebastian's calf. She got fistfuls of his torn pants. The knife was gone. Sebastian reached down and gripped Maureen's skull in both hands. He lifted her by her head and gathered her to him. Maureen could feel his ragged breath in her hair.

Sebastian held her tight, pinning her arms to her sides. He dragged her alongside him, the two of them limping down the road toward the lightless Black Garter Saloon. The old bar showed no signs of life. Maureen forced herself not to think about what might be waiting for her inside. She thought about fighting but knew she lacked the strength to do anything but collapse if she did manage to escape Sebastian's embrace. Maybe now, for these few moments, she had time to rest, to find whatever shreds of strength she had left. Maybe he'd have to let go of her at some point. Maybe to unlock the Garter's front door.

"All this effort, all this blood," Sebastian said, his voice hardly above a whisper. "For what? What did you accomplish? Nothing."

As Sebastian drew breath, Maureen heard a crackling wheeze in his chest. He wasn't lifting his bad leg as much as dragging it. He was wounded and bleeding hard. Keep bleeding, motherfucker. She looked around, letting Sebastian lead her. They went right by the dark hulk of the Garter. Not in there, then.

To the water, she figured, the slimy old Arthur Kill.

She could hear the tide now, washing into the reeds. In the distance she could see the cattails swaying. Then she saw, off to the left, a dark, raised platform silhouetted against the squat blue gas tanks on the Jersey side of the water. The bar had blocked her view of the other structure, but now she saw it clear in the glow of the incandescent lights from across the Arthur Kill. A train station. The old Atlantic station. The one that got only half torn down a couple of years ago, replaced by another, bigger station somewhere up or down the line. The trains didn't stop at

Atlantic station anymore. They ran right through it at full speed; on quiet nights you could hear them rattling along the island's spine for miles. That's where Sebastian was taking her. Not to the water but to the tracks.

Sebastian quickened his steps and then Maureen heard it. A train was coming. A ways off yet, but coming. Coming for her.

Without even trying, Maureen went limp in Sebastian's arms, her boots dragging. He stumbled, then collected her back to him, growling with the strain. Against every effort, Maureen started to cry. Tears blurred Sebastian's face and the stars sprinkled over his head in the night sky.

They got closer to the tracks. The train raced closer to them, its rattle now a rumble. Panic wasn't the enemy now. It was all Maureen had left. She pushed against Sebastian, kicked at him. She screamed, though there couldn't be anyone to hear her for miles. Sebastian laughed at first, squeezing her tighter to him, but as she kept fighting the laughter became a growl of frustration and pain. He clamped his hand over her face and she bit him. He threw her down, had his gun out and on her in an instant. From her elbows, Maureen stared up at him. He crouched, leaning forward, his free hand supporting his weight on the knee of his good leg.

"Holy Christmas," Sebastian said, gasping, "I am so gonna fucking kill you."

"Then do it," Maureen said. "It's the only way I'm going on those tracks."

Sebastian stood and straightened, stretching his back and cracking his neck as if he'd had a long morning mowing the front yard. "You know, there was a time I woulda taken you apart. Just pounded your skinny bird bones into powder with my own two hands." He smiled, baring his teeth. "Right after I bent you over a garbage can and fucked your insides into jelly." He turned away and spat into the reeds.

"The cops are all over Dennis's murder," Maureen said. "They know it was you. They'll get you for it, and for Tanya, and for me."

"These days, my back goes out." He tapped his gun against his right hip. "This here acts up in the cold from where your sugar daddy shot me. Doctor told me the other day I might have arthritis in my shoulders. I'm not the man I used to be, that's for sure. Not that I can't still kill a bitch when I need to."

Maureen scuttled away from him on her elbows and heels, never taking her eyes from his. If Sebastian had heard or if he cared about what she'd said, she couldn't tell. His eyes had gone glassy, become distant. "Now I got that other body up there by the car to deal with. I don't know if he'll fit in the trunk, I just don't know. Fucking mess, is what it is. I hate a fucking mess. I should make you help with that. I should."

Maureen backed up against the gravel embankment of the tracks. She was doing Sebastian's job for him, but there was nowhere else to go. Over her shoulder, the iron rails hummed like a giant tuning fork.

"Oughtta just burn everything," Sebastian said, talking to himself as much as he was to Maureen. He dragged the back of his hand under his runny nose. "Light the Garter up, too. Burn everything. Fuck it, right? I'm starting over." He took a deep breath, coughed, puffed out his chest. "State Senator Francis Jordan Sebastian. Senator Sebastian. Got a lovely fucking ring to it. I'll get used to it in no time."

Her hands behind her, Maureen scratched for purchase, trying to get to her feet without turning her back on Sebastian. She would not let him force her onto the tracks. Behind her back, something sharp cut her hand. She swallowed the pain and let her fingers explore. A broken bottle. A weapon. Thank the Lord for loitering teenagers.

She stopped retreating and let her fingers settle across the bottle's neck.

"At least the train'll take care of you," Sebastian said. "Driver won't even know he hit anything. Nothing left of you, like you never existed." He jammed the gun in his belt and reached for her. "Dennis, Rico, Tanya, you. The others. Eat or be eaten. It's the fate of the weak to feed the strong, Maureen." Grabbing her by the coat, Sebastian smiled. "This isn't news to you. You're tiny, Irish, and a woman. You never had a chance."

He lifted her upright, pulled her close to him, bracing himself to toss her on the tracks. Maureen clutched the broken bottle in her hand, hidden behind her back. She tightened her grip. She was right where she wanted to be, inside the reach of Sebastian's powerful arms.

She thrust the broken bottle from behind her hip and stabbed it into the side of Sebastian's neck. His eyes went wide with shock. Spittle sprayed Maureen's face. She yanked the bottle free, twisting it, leaving jagged shards of brown glass stuck in Sebastian's flesh. She stabbed again, aiming once more for the throat. Sebastian got a hand up, but not enough to fully deflect the strike. Maureen heard the tinkle of the breaking glass, felt tiny shards sting her cheeks, the bottle collapsing into pieces, most of them lodging in Sebastian's throat. Warm blood poured over her fingers like sugar syrup.

Sebastian staggered forward and tripped over the rail. Turning, falling, he reached out and grabbed Maureen by the coat, pulling her down on top of him on the tracks. They were nose to nose, close enough to kiss, Sebastian clinging tight to her coat, Maureen pressing her hands against him, straining uselessly to get free, to slide out of her heavy coat, her fingers slipping against his slick, blood-soaked chest. The train roared toward them and Maureen flashed onto a trip to the beach from years ago. With her mom and dad watching from the sand, a big wave caught her by surprise and knocked her under. She didn't know which way was up, could hear nothing but the roaring surf in her ears. She was drowning, her mouth flooded with water. Then her father, out of nowhere, had yanked her into the air. But now her father was gone.

The train's headlights hit them. The brakes screamed as the wheels clawed at the rails. Maybe the train, Maureen thought, when it hits, will feel like that wave. That wouldn't be so bad. Her world went white. Then she was airborne.

Weightless and blind, she soared, her breath left behind on the earth.

Maureen landed hard on her back, her feet higher than her head as she lay sprawled on the embankment. She watched in mindless shock as the huge, roaring train hurtled by over the tops of her toes. Then, in a rush of silver flashes and lighted windows, the train was past her, the brakes screeching and throwing sparks. She watched as it barreled away from her, swaying dangerously. The last car jumped the tracks and derailed, wiping out a hundred yards of chain-link fence. Finally, after a howl of angry metal, white and amber sparks shooting everywhere, the train came to rest, the last car teetering on the embankment, only a few feet short of pitching into the Arthur Kill.

Maureen lay on her back in the dirt and gravel, looking up at the stars and feeling completely, utterly numb. I can't be dead, she thought, I'm still on Staten Island.

Fear flooded her insides. If I'm not dead, maybe Sebastian isn't either.

Maureen rolled onto her hands and knees, searching in the darkness for a weapon, another bottle, a large rock, anything. She'd come up with nothing when she spotted him, a large man flat on his back a few feet away. Of course he wasn't dead. Sebastian needed to throw her off to get out of the way of the train himself. Men shouted from the direction of the train wreck. She heard sirens in the distance. Police, fire, ambulance. That was quick. The motorman must've warned someone about the impending crash.

Crawling along the embankment toward the dark form, Maureen saw one of its legs kicking out over and over. She looked ahead at the wreck, strangely quiet now, the train like a silver snake with a broken back. The emergency workers would find them soon. All those brave men would save her. And then those brave, dumb bastards would save Sebastian. That couldn't be allowed to happen. She crawled faster. She hadn't found a weapon. That's fine, Maureen thought.

I'll finish him barehanded.

I'll tear out his throat with my teeth.

When Maureen reached the man, she flung her body on top of his, wrapped her hands around his throat. But there was no blood under her fingers, no glass. She pushed up on her arms and looked down into the face below her. Sad, terrified eyes stared back at her. Waters. The man underneath her was Detective Waters. Maureen's hands leaped from his throat to her head. Waters had pulled her from the tracks. She could've kissed him, she was so happy to see him. But then Maureen noticed that Waters didn't seem to see her. The fear in his eyes was total, primal. His fingers clawed at his shirt, at his tie. His breathing made only ragged squeaks. The badge around his neck glinted up at her in the industrial lights from across the water.

Maureen flattened herself on top of Waters, trying to keep her weight off him and on her knees, her hands flying through his pockets. Nothing in his coat, nothing in his suit jacket. In his pants pocket she found his phone. She flipped it open and dialed 9-1-1.

"I'm on the tracks behind the train wreck," she told the dispatcher. "At the old Atlantic station. I'm with a cop. I think he's having a heart attack."

The dispatcher told her to hold the line. "Help is coming," Maureen told Waters. "Keep fighting. Help is coming."

Waters had stopped moving. His hands, his chest, his eyes, everything had gone still.

Setting the phone down beside his head, Maureen pinched Waters's nose closed. Then she leaned forward, covered his mouth with hers, and breathed.

27

Maureen swirled her thumb over the tips of her fingers, massaging the stain of cold and sticky blood. Her own blood. Cigarette lodged in the corner of her mouth, she huddled tighter against the brick wall outside the emergency room doors in a vain attempt to hide from the December wind. She'd abandoned her father's coat, without even meaning to do it, in the treatment room where the doctors had attended to her wounds. Soaked with blood—hers, Rico's, Sebastian's—the coat was gone when she'd returned from X-ray, thankfully concussionless. She had always been hardheaded.

She figured the coat had been shoved into a biohazard bag and locked away somewhere in the hospital, wherever it was they kept thoroughly bloody things. She'd have to remember to ask about getting it back before she left. Or not. The coat would be a bitch to clean, maybe even impossible. Probably best to leave it behind, she thought, and let it find its way to the incinerator. She looked down again at her fingertips, then up at the night sky.

Above the glow of the light poles illuminating the hospital parking lot, high above everything, hung a full moon skirted by clouds, blue and purple at their edges. Watching the clouds glide by through her cigarette smoke, Maureen touched her fingers to her tender, bruised cheek, where Rico had belted her before dumping her in the trunk what felt like a lifetime ago. The ice pack meant for her cheek now cooled the bottom of the nearby trash can. It was too cold outdoors to stand around with ice on her face.

Seagulls she couldn't see circled overhead, somewhere in the darkness between the parking lot lamps and the moon, laughing in that eerie way that gulls do. Maureen thought of how often she had heard invisible gulls at night; did the birds ever sleep? Pigeons, filthy, bobbing their heads like arguing waitresses, strutted in circles and pecked at empty prospects in the gutter. They scattered, cooing their complaints, when Maureen flicked her cigarette butt into their midst. But in moments they returned, back about their business as if they'd never been disturbed.

Maureen stuck her thumb in her mouth, sucked it clean, then touched her fingertips again to the bandage on her forehead, feeling more, but not much, fresh blood. Underneath the gauze throbbed the thirteen stitches the doctor had used to close the gash the steering wheel had torn open. She could feel the throb of each individual thread. She'd have to forget any plan to cut her bangs. Or maybe not. Maybe she'd show the world her scar. She thought of the ice pack—she might want a new one to take home—and thought of Rico, pretty much an ice pack himself, bagged and shelved as he was in the hospital's lightless underground cooler.

At least there'd been something left of Rico to bag.

Other than a healthy dent in the lead car of the crashed train, little evidence of Sebastian remained on the tracks. After Waters was rushed away, the other cops set up light towers and searched the tracks for scraps. Maureen sat on the back bumper of an ambulance as the EMTs washed the blood off her hands and bandaged her forehead. She watched the police officers work the tracks and answered a detective's questions about how she'd arrived where they found her. There were lots of questions, but no one had any answers about the health of Detective Waters.

Just as detectives called Maureen's story into question, a uniform finally found a bloody black leather shoe, the freshly shorn foot still in it. Several yards away they found a SEBASTIAN FOR SENATE campaign button, dead grass stuck in the dried blood that covered it. The foot and the button were bagged and tagged and sent along to the morgue in a coroner's van. Not long after, the police put their lights away and shut down their sirens, and the fire department moved in to wash whatever else was left of Frank Sebastian off the tracks and into the dirt.

Dragging on her cigarette outside the hospital, Maureen thought of the ponytailed orderly she and Waters had stood beside in the elevator on their way to see Tanya. He'd have another foot to put in a tray and scare the girls with. She squeezed her eyes shut tight and swallowed hard against the next image of the orderly that arose in her brain: bobbing his head to his awful music while he tied an ID tag to Waters's toe. Not gonna happen, Maureen told herself. He's not gonna die.

Waters had started breathing again in the back of the ambulance. She could swear she'd heard somebody say it. One of the numerous cops, she thought, who had surrounded her in the waiting room when she emerged from getting her stitches. But that had been hours ago. Everyone was still waiting on official word about his condition.

Maureen had spent those hours in the waiting room engulfed in a crowd of anxious cops. She recognized some of them, including the young kid from the Gulf station crime scene. But this time neither he nor any of the others gave her funny looks. No cynical eyes scanned her in an effort to assign a ready, cheap identity. She had one tag and one tag only. Every cop in the room pinned it on her like a medal with his eyes when he asked Maureen if she needed more coffee, or ice water, or a cigarette, or something to eat. When they looked at her, when they talked to her, the cops didn't see a criminal or a victim or a foundling waif or a damsel in distress. Who they saw was Maureen Coughlin, the woman who had started Detective Nathaniel Waters's heart after it had stopped dead in his chest.

Were it not for the reason she was at the hospital, Maureen would've reveled in the attention and respect. Like several of the cops in the room, she had chewed her nails down to the skin waiting for word of Waters's fate. All she wanted was to hear that Waters was okay and after that run home as fast as she could and hug her mother.

She had felt somewhat better, but not much, when John and Molly arrived at the hospital, Molly toting a change of clothes for her. Maureen washed up as best she could in the ladies' room and dressed in Molly's clothes. The gray and green flannel shirt pretty much fit but the pants, Molly's tight brown cords—well, they were baggy.

Not long after she emerged from changing, a handsome young lieutenant named Swain took Maureen aside and explained how Waters had found her at the tracks. It had not been a miracle, Swain said with an admiring grin, but simple detective work.

The trail had started with her mom's wrecked car being discovered by the Jersey State Police while on their way to the motel. One unit had peeled off from the parade and investigated. They found her bag under the passenger seat and in it her ID and Waters's card. The Staties called him, telling him they had recovered not only the bag at the wreck but a cell phone and a .38. His number had been the most recent call on the phone. The gun had not been fired. The driver of the car and the second vehicle in the accident were nowhere to be found.

It was Maureen who figured out the rest, explaining to Detective Swain the situation with Sebastian and guessing that what Clarence had told Waters about the Black Garter had led the detective there.

"It's what predators do," Maureen said. "They bring their prize catches back to their lairs."

Once arriving at the Garter, Maureen went on to explain, Waters must have followed the sounds of the struggle down to the tracks. There he had called for reinforcements, Swain added, and Maureen realized that the first sirens she'd heard after the wreck were on their way not to the accident but to rescue her.

Swain crossed his arms, bowing his head. He looked up at her, his blue eyes electric under dark brows. "It's a good thing," he said, "that you never stopped fighting."

Maureen nearly leaped out of her skin when the hospital door slammed open. She turned to see Swain leaning out, his eyes wide, his face pale. "Doc's comin' out."

Maureen hurried inside.

The fidgety cops, their eyes darting everywhere, formed a silent semicircle around a short, round, middle-aged woman in a long white coat. No one spoke. The news hadn't been delivered yet. Everyone, including the doctor, had been waiting for her. The doc gave her a nod and then turned to the cops.

"Massive coronary," the doctor said, "but he's stable and we're optimistic." The room exhaled as one. Maureen felt tears burning her eyes. The doctor turned to her. "The immediate CPR saved his life." The doctor smiled. "You must be stronger than you look, young lady. That's a big man in there."

"I am," Maureen said. "And Detective Waters has a heart like a wild lion."

28

A month later, three days after the start of the New Year, Maureen stood in the middle of her mother's kitchen, scared to move a finger. Amber had scrubbed everything to a shine. Maureen, having spent the afternoon carrying the last of her North Shore apartment into her mother's basement, dripped with sweat. Figures, the day she picks to move is the warmest January Sunday in twenty years. That's what John had said anyway, huffing and sweating as he and Molly loaded boxes into their cars for the trip over to Eltingville. Molly had quickly instructed Maureen to ignore the comment, adding that John wasn't happy unless he was miserable.

Maureen said nothing. Though she knew it wouldn't last, she was happy to get a break from the cold.

The coming Wednesday night she was taking the couple to dinner in Manhattan. The meal for three would seriously dent her leftover tips from the Narrows, and there wouldn't be more money coming anytime soon, at least until her student loans arrived, but she would take John and Molly somewhere classy anyway. She owed them that, and more, and she intended to pay up.

Dinner for three, Maureen thought. Why does that ring a bell?

Glancing down at the kitchen table, she noticed three places had been set. Oh, shit, that's right. Company for dinner. A few times in the past month the Coughlin women had hosted a guest for dinner, but Maureen still found company in her mother's house a tough concept to grasp.

Her mother, makeup freshly applied, new dress snug enough to flatter, turned the corner into the kitchen and headed for the stove.

"What the hell are you doing?" Amber asked. "He'll be here any minute."

Maureen gestured at the kitchen table, which had earlier been a mess of mail and bills. "What happened to my letter? Where is it?"

"Where it belongs," Amber said, stirring a simmering pot. "On the fridge."

"Aw, Ma," Maureen said, crossing the kitchen to the refrigerator door. She touched the sharp bottom corner of the letter, the one outlining what she'd need for the summer class at the NYPD academy. "He's gonna see it up there."

"He's a man. He won't notice a thing"—Amber smiled—"until I point it out."

"I wish you wouldn't do that," Maureen said. But she left the letter where it was.

"Yes, you do. And you should. He's very proud of you."

"And what about you?" Maureen asked. "Are you proud?"

"I'm worried," Amber said. "You're small for a police officer." She set down her spoon and turned to her daughter. "But yes, Maureen, I am very proud of you. Officer Coughlin, someday Detective Coughlin—they have a nice ring." A pause. "Now go get dressed."

Maureen lingered in the kitchen, letting her mother's rare compliments settle into her skin. "It smells awesome in here. What're we having?"

"Wheat pasta and baked salmon," Amber said, pulling open the oven and bending to check her fish. "I hope I haven't dried it out."

"Salmon? You never make me salmon," Maureen said, smiling as she spoke. "What was it the last time, lemon chicken? What happened to frozen pizza?"

Amber straightened, hands set firmly on her hips, the picture of matronly disapproval. "Nat has to watch his diet. He needs to lose weight for his heart." She shook her head. "You know this. A man cannot live a healthy life on waffles and ice cream. Poor old thing."

Amber blushed. Maureen smiled. For the first time in years, Amber had something bringing color to her cheeks other than wine: Detective Nat Waters, retired. Her mom's new boyfriend. The doorbell rang. Amber bolted for the door, not even bothering to demand that Maureen answer.

Maureen stayed in the kitchen, listening. Quiet pleasantries, the front door closing, a kiss, Amber hanging up Waters's coat. Another kiss. On the cheeks or the lips? Maureen wondered.

Amber appeared in the kitchen, a bouquet in her hand. Behind her stood Nat Waters, a few pounds lighter, his wrinkled dress shirt and his stained tie a thing of the past. When he smiled at Maureen, she noticed his eyes were clear and happy and that the black shadows that had hung beneath them, haunting them, had all but disappeared. "Hey, Maureen."

Amber held up the flowers. "Let me get something for these." She disappeared down the hall.

Waters walked into the kitchen, reaching into his pocket. "Your mother called me yesterday about your letter from the academy. I've got something for you. These days, its value is only sentimental." He held out something in his hand. "But I thought you'd like it anyway."

Maureen reached for her present. His badge. She felt tears rise in her eyes. "I don't know what to say."

"Sometimes I won, sometimes I lost," Waters said, "but I did a lot of good carrying that thing around. Maybe it'll help you do the same."

Maureen stared at the gold shield in her palm, brimming with gratitude for the gift and burning with desire for one of her own. One day, she knew in her heart that she would carry a shield out into the world.

Amber reappeared in the kitchen, setting the vase of flowers at the center of the table. She turned to Maureen. "Dinner's almost ready, young lady. Would you *please* go get dressed?"

"Right away," Maureen said, bowing. Clutching the badge in her fist, she headed off to her room.

Since moving back in with her mom, Maureen had slept in her childhood bedroom while she and Amber worked overtime, cleaning out the cluttered finished basement and turning it into a livable apartment.

The weeks following her abduction had been filled with nightmares. Many nights, Maureen lay in bed, staring at the ceiling, listening for even the faintest sound in the house and breaking into a cold sweat every time she heard a train roll by the end of Bovanizer Street. She never cried out when the nightmares came, never called for help, but she liked the security even on the cusp of thirty of having her mom asleep in the room next door. It would never happen until Maureen moved downstairs, but she looked forward to the time when Waters, which was all she could manage to call him, started spending the night. Amber's steady breathing and the creak of her bed as she rolled over in the night offered Maureen even more comfort than the ladybug night-light that she had returned to its place in the baseboard socket.

Maureen had made one trip to the Narrows, riding the bus across the island in the gray early afternoon of New Year's Eve. Wearing a thick NYPD sweatshirt, a Christmas gift from her mother, the hood pulled up, she stood across the street from the bar's black door. She smoked cigarettes and watched the banquet staff get ready for a holiday party in the upstairs hall. No one came to open the Narrows for the second biggest party night of the year. She knew no one would. The place had closed, probably for good.

The day after Sebastian died and Maureen didn't, cops doing follow-up found Vic dead, facedown on the bar, the blood from his self-inflicted neck wound a pungent, thickening pool on the dark mahogany, an empty vodka bottle shattered on the floor. It was hard to be too exact with such things, Swain told her, but Vic had probably died before Sebastian. He didn't even wait, Maureen had thought at the time, to see if I pulled it off. Standing across the street that afternoon, Maureen wondered if Vic had used the white-handled knife, the one behind the bar for cutting lemons and limes, the knife the staff always complained was too dull. Guess it wasn't. Not if you were motivated.

Now, standing in front of her mirror, buttoning up her silk blouse, the blue one she hoped not to stain at dinner, Maureen stared down at the badge resting on the corner of her dresser. Its gold face glowed in the last light of sunset streaming through her bedroom window. She walked over to the night-light, its rosy glow faint in the shadows along the floor, and bent over, reaching for it. The ladybug went dark when she pulled it from the wall. She straightened to her full height and then tossed it in the trash can beside her dresser.

A few things from her old room would make it downstairs to the apartment: her running trophies, her mirror, her dresser, her books, some of the old clothes from high school, at least the stuff that hadn't dated too much. But the ladybug night-light, that precious gift from her father that had for so long chased the monsters from a scared little girl's room, its time had ended.

ACKNOWLEDGMENTS

Thanks first and foremost, as always, to the loving and loyal McDonald, Lambeth, Loehfelm, and Murphy families.

Thanks also to Rick Barton, Joanna Leake, Joseph and Amanda Boyden, and everyone else at and around the University of New Orleans and the UNO Creative Writing Workshop, which manages to quietly produce talented and successful writers one after the other like there's nothing to it. It's more like joining a tribe than going to graduate school, which is as it should be. Others may be more famous, but none are better.

John Cooke, we miss you, pal. I'm still learning from you.

To Jarret Lofstead, Joe Longo, and everyone at Nolafugees.com and Nolafugees Press, thanks for your fierce devotion to the truth, to laughter, and to the idea that the two are not mutually exclusive. Soul is, indeed, bulletproof.

Thanks to Britton, Ted, Amy, Jamie, and everyone at the Garden District Book Shop. Thanks also to the staff and ownership of the Rue de la Course, CC's, and Mojo coffeehouses of Magazine Street. Keep it hot and black, y'all.

A big, fat WHO DAT to Justin and everyone at Handsome Willy's bar for game-day festivities, and especially for *that* mad game. We'll always have that special Sunday night in the Quarter.

A humble bow and deepest gratitude to my agent, Barney Karpfinger, for really pulling the rabbit out of that hat this time. Without his faith and hard work, and that of his staff, a lot of good things don't get the chance to happen. Let's keep it rolling. Much gratitude also to Sarah Crichton for always having the right answer and, maybe more important, the perfect questions. Thanks also to Dan Piepenbring, for knowing where it is, where it's going, and when it's supposed to get there.

Special thanks to the Gaslight Anthem, whose music was huge in finding and maintaining the tone for this book, and to Tori Amos for the same, and for the color of Maureen's hair.

Thanks to Rob of the NYPD for answering a lot of bizarre questions without a lot of context. Forgive the parts where I ignored the answers and made it up anyway. Forgive also, dear reader, my mangling of Staten Island geography for the sake of the story.

Finally, all my love to my stellar and talented wife, AC Lambeth, who every day makes of herself a light so that I may see the good in the world. Without her, all would be darkness.

A NOTE ABOUT THE AUTHOR

Bill Loehfelm was born in Brooklyn and grew up on Staten Island. In 1997, he moved to New Orleans. He is the author of the novels *Fresh Kills*, which won an Amazon Breakthrough Novel Award, and *Bloodroot*. Loehfelm lives in New Orleans's Garden District with his wife, the writer AC Lambeth.